Memory Guy

David Bathurst

www.publishnation.co.uk

PROLOGUE

Most walkers have sandwiches in their rucksack but I have to be different. I'm the one with the urn and the ashes.

I've left my car at the top of the road known as Firle Bostal and am setting out along the South Downs Way aiming for Firle Beacon. My load weighs a ton. I'm labouring and I can feel salty globules across my forehead. I'm still short of that imaginary line, the line beyond which it becomes acceptable to greet strangers and pass the time of day with them. All the time I remain on the near side of the imaginary line, people coming the other way either ignore my eye, or look askance at me as though they were questioning my right to be occupying any space on the planet at all. But then I cross the imaginary line, and no sooner have I crossed it than I receive a smile and a cordial greeting from a white-haired man coming the other way. He wears shorts and sandals and has red hairy legs. He clearly thinks my walk is a lot longer than it is, and he's asking me how far I've come and how far I've got to go. Soon after he's gone past, I see ahead of me a portly middle-aged woman in tight leggings and trainers. She's running but even my walking pace exceeds her speed. I can hear her wheezing while she's still twenty yards apart from me. As I pass her, she says hi and compliments me on my rate of progress.

I keep going and the number of walkers around me, considerable as I set out, continues to dwindle. I like to think I'm now established in what my mum, a passionate walker, would call walkers' terrain, as opposed to trippers' terrain. "There is a difference," she'd say. Then she'd go on to remark about how much the trippers were missing by not being walkers. As I continue to gain height, I feel surer than ever that she had it right. Below my feet is a rich emerald carpet, a carpet so smooth and gentle it might have been expecting a royal procession, while just above my head two cabbage white butterflies are dancing the fandango. The sun creeps over a bank of cloud. The Sussex coastline including Newhaven and Seaford is opening out to my right, while to the north-west I can see the summit of Mount Caburn and the Ouse valley, and to the north-east is a generous slice of the Low Weald of Sussex. There are so many landmarks to choose from as I gaze, but today, targeting the sights of the Low Weald and its surrounds, I pick out the Elizabethan manor house and adjoining church at Glynde, the wind turbines above Ringmer, and, closer still, the nineteenth century round castellated tower in the grounds of Firle Place. I permit myself a pause for breath. I find a tissue and wipe the muck from my forehead, and also take a couple of gulps from my plastic water bottle. Then off I go again.

I'm now just two hundred yards or so from the Beacon. The only person in my line of vision is a woman walking alone. She's coming towards me and as she approaches I see she's wearing a light green fleece top with the words Mountain Warehouse on it.

Immediately I see it I begin to shake and my knees turn to dishwater.

It's an identical garment to that which Lisa-Marie Williams took from Mountain Warehouse on a Monday afternoon last October.

And had she not taken it I'd never have met and grown to love the amazing, extraordinary man that was Memory Guy.

1

I can't sleep. I very rarely can when I'm on police station duty. Emma's never insisted on my kipping on the settee; she's a light sleeper and says if my phone goes she generally gets woken whether I'm next to her in bed or downstairs. But it's a fact that the phone noise is a lot less intrusive for her if I am in the lounge. Whenever I sense she's more tired than usual that's where I'll go, and, this last night, that's where I've been. It's now 6.30am and although it's still dark – it's late October but the clocks haven't gone back yet – I decide it's pointless just lying here any longer. There's an hour and a half or so that I can spare before breakfast and I decide to go for a run. It's just possible the phone will ring and I'll be wanted down at the nick straight away, but it's most unusual in my experience for that to happen at this particular time of the morning, and I decide to chance it. I scramble into my running gear, and forty minutes later I'm at the top end of the railway path, which follows a section of the now disused line linking Brighton with Devil's Dyke. If I had longer I'd carry on to the Dyke itself. But the views from where I've stopped are still good and the solitude is even better. Then a Lycra-clad cyclist approaches me and asks if I'm interested in a charity biathlon, running and cycling, along the South Downs Way next Saturday in aid of leukaemia research. I tell him to get on his bike. In every sense. He disappears and it's all mine again. Then after enjoying the serenity and the sense of ownership once more, I head back to Brighton and our semi in Preston Park, just to the north-west of the city centre. As I run I can almost hear the splash of the cold milk on my Jordans Country Crisp.

The Country Crisp doesn't disappoint. That isn't the problem. The problem is sitting opposite dipping her spoon into her Rice Krispies.

'Got to work late tonight,' she announces.

'Okay.'

'Can you get milk and bananas. We seem to be out of both.'

'I'll do it. On my way home.'

'Did you know you left the grill switch on last night? Could have set the house on fire?'

'Sorry.'

It's another of our OIS conversations as I call them. An update on her situation. A request for me to do something. Then a rollicking for something I did do but shouldn't have done, or vice versa. Just three responses required in that order. Okay. I'll do it. Sorry. At the end of that round, Matt Chalmers, you have scored three points, no passes. Thank you very much. Can we have the next contender please.

I'm not sure where the love, both the emotional and the physical, went, or when it went, or how it went. It was there once – well, we expressed our love for one another to each other enough times so I suppose it was there. But imperceptibly, subtly, slyly, it's managed to slip round the automatic barriers, evade the prying eyes of the security staff and drift away into nothingness. And yet we never seem to sit down and ask ourselves whether we're capable of summoning up a fresh supply. I think we're scared. Well, I am. I'm scared because it may mean our having to concede that it's impossible to source and we have to accept the reality either of lovelessness together or loneliness apart. We don't row. We never have. I don't think we ever will. We're not rowers. I think we quite like each other. We always have. I like to think we always will. But I'm scared that that isn't enough. These days I keep finding myself seeking reassurance that it is enough. Sometimes, while queuing at supermarket checkouts, I might take one of the magazines from the impulse purchase racks by the till. Then in between its covers I'll search for something, anything, whether it's by an expert or correspondent, acknowledging that a marriage along the lines of our own is eminently sustainable and healthy: an amicable coexistence where the physical side is essentially dormant. But for every one such expert or correspondent I find, there's another who's saying that if you're not giving your other half your all at least twice nightly, making allowances for that time of the month and that time of life, you're in a dysfunctional partnership that you need to get out of faster than you can say Relate.

I'm just about to leave the house when the phone goes. It's

the defence solicitor call centre, inviting me to accept responsibility for one Lisa-Marie Williams, adult female, arrested for theft and possession of class A and B drugs with intent to supply. I duly accept the case, as I'm bound to, then ring the police custody centre for further details and to tell them I'll be acting. The proper practice at that stage is to speak to the client direct to confirm I'm acting and ask if they've any issues or concerns I can assist with. As a rule, on speaking to a client at this stage, I can expect a torrent of anger at the unfairness of their detention, as though I were in some way to blame for it, and a demand to know how long they're going to be stuck there. My response is necessarily always the same: there's nothing I can do, not yet anyway, about the police's decision to detain you, and I can't tell you how long you're going to remain in said detention. It's never the most congenial of conversations, and I'm only too pleased to ascertain that Ms Williams neither has any wish nor is in any fit state to talk to me. I then ask the custody officer when they're likely to need me to come in to represent her for her police interview. 'We'll let you know,' is their wholly predictable response. If it hadn't been that reply it would have been one of the others. Be ready when it's ready. Will take as long as it takes. How long is a piece of string. After a while you're tempted to feed them the lines yourself. And since I know they'll also want to make a thorough search of her home, or wherever it is she's supposedly dealing from, I'll be lucky if I'm called in this side of the third Sunday after Epiphany.

Twenty minutes later I'm at my desk and I'm needing matchsticks to keep my eyes open. At least when I was on Ellman Rich's intellectual property (IP) side, I could choose when I wanted to work into the small hours, knowing the bosses would let me have the time in lieu once the pressure was off. No such luxury now I've espoused the dark side of the legal world. On my desk is the morning mail. There's never much of that these days – criminal clients seem just as happy as my IP clients to use email or text. Today however I've a white envelope with my work address handwritten on it and it's an invite from my uni alumni society to the Foundation Diamond Anniversary Ball, with the Lord Chief Justice as guest of honour. Kind of them to invite me and kinder still to let me know that they'll accept the £100 per person ticket cost in two instalments. The accompanying bumf explains that while the ticket cost may seem high, the profits from the evening will be donated to the uni's benevolent fund. The invite is soon airborne and seconds later, after the obligatory phone calls to loved ones, is making a crash landing in the round metal filing cabinet. No survivors.

I may not feel under any obligation to support the uni financially but I've always felt I owe some sort of a debt to my IP lecturer in my final year there. He not only got me a First in the subject, which in turn helped me to an Upper Second degree, but he taught me to be more passionate about IP than I could ever have thought possible. I'd decided after my first two years that I didn't want to make a career in the law but this guy changed my mind. I got through the boring stuff on the postgraduate Legal Practice course, and then had a two-year training contract with a firm in Hove, dividing my time largely between conveyancing, will-drafting and divorce proceedings, counting the hours until I could start properly to do what I knew I loved best. I'd chosen the Hove firm because they had an IP department but even after I'd finished my training I got little more than a sniff of IP and was forced to continue almost exclusively on the same diet...of conveyancing, will-drafting and divorce proceedings. The diet may have allowed me more calories than the F-Plan but the fare was infinitely less digestible. I was doing it for so long that clients whose divorces I'd handled at the start were coming to me when their next marriage went tits up. And the marriage after that. I was getting quite good at it by the end. Anyway, praise be, a vacancy came up in the IP section at Ellman Rich in central Brighton. During the twelve years I was in that section I loved it. Not just for the financial rewards, although those helped, but for the cerebral challenge each new case generated, and the satisfaction that came with each email that began "You did such a great job for us three years ago. So we're hoping that you can do the same for us again."

It was all going so well. Too well.

Back in January this year, I'm acting for a guy who's set up

6

his own company, manufacturing collapsible tables and picnic chairs that are light and compact enough to fit inside a rucksack. Brilliant concept. The client's given the furniture the brand name of Foldilox. Unbeknown to him, and most unfortunately for him, a company in London, which specialises in selling iced drinks at outdoor festivals, has chosen to give these drinks the brand name Coldilox. They've tried to stop my client using the name Foldilox. But my client likes the name and doesn't want to change it. Attempts at settlement have broken down. It's war. But just as I'm ready to march my troops into battle, Gordon in the criminal department goes off on long-term sick. Matt, you need to drop everything you're doing, cover for just a few months, we'll fast-track you through the accreditation process, don't worry, you'll be out in August, possibly earlier with good conduct. But Gordon has now been discharged on medical grounds, my sentence has been extended indefinitely, and my application for release on licence seems to have got lost in the post. As for Coldilox v Foldilox, where I knew I had a winning strategy, we have to get someone else to fight the battle for us and we get taken out by a sniper seconds after going over the top. Even the merest reminder of that fatal shot makes each day of confinement in my current prison wing seem twice as long as before. And what makes it worse is the peculiar work pressures that go with the criminal parish. We're not just dealing with the day-to-day but also taking our turn with police station duties both in and out of office hours, covering slots on the duty rota shared out between firms across the city and being on call for own clients, that is existing clients of the firm, whenever they're conveyed from their homes to spend time in the custody block's free bed and breakfast facility. The gloopy mess that our clients leave behind them has to be cleared up, somehow, and not just 9 to 5 Monday to Friday. It can be any hour, like it or not. And it's always when it's least convenient to be at the nick that I'm called upon to present myself at the custody centre's reception area with the floorcloth and disinfectant.

I hear the squeak of shoes on the carpet in the corridor and a moment later Danny heaves his seventeen stone into my office, clutching a single sheet of paper.

'Busy one last night was it, Matt?'

'Ish.'

'Should have been on last Saturday. Phone never stopped.' His voice, as always, reminiscent of a 1980's station announcer on a wet Monday at New Malden.

Please, Danny. I know you're head of the criminal department and you've had it tough all your life, and you've been doing this job fourteen years as you constantly remind me, but this morning I'm just not in the mood for the you-don't-know-you're-born routine. Still less the you-wait-till-you've-done-this-half-the-length-of-time-I-have act. Please remember it must be at least an hour since your sausage and egg McMuffin and it has to be time for skinny latte with extra chocolate shavings in that cracking little coffee shop you like so much. The one at least thirty minutes' walk away from my desk.

'Couldn't Judy or Martyn help?'

'Judy was away. And the partners have just taken me to task over Martyn's consultancy fees. More or less ordered me not to use Martyn unless I have to.'

He manoeuvres his body onto the chair beside me and looks around him. Great. The quiet chat. My latest transgression, whatever that may be, about to come back and sink its teeth into my accoutrements. 'The closing letter you sent Jade Marwell.' He plonks Exhibit A on the desk in front of me.

I run my eye down it. I'd got Jade Marwell an undeservedly good outcome on an assault matter last week. She'd sworn at the victim, thrown beer in her face, punched her at least half a dozen times, the punches causing her to fall to the floor, and then kicked her twice when she was on the ground. All this, not after closing time in some ghastly corner of town but in a crowded Toby Carvery on a Saturday lunchtime with what by all accounts had been the whole of Class 2 at Reading Road Infants present to witness it. She had previous for affray and offensive weapon and was looking at a prison sentence. Not just a few weeks. Months. At the very least she should have had a suspended sentence and even her getting off with that should have convinced her that all her Christmases had come at once. But somehow I'd got her a community order with unpaid work.

8

The letter confirmed the sentence, confirmed how lenient the sentence had been, explained our involvement would now cease, told her how she could access her file until it was destroyed in six years, and offered her my very best wishes for the future. I'd also wished her a safe and pleasant forthcoming trip with her partner to southern Thailand which would have been an inevitable casualty of an immediate prison sentence of any more than 21 days, and possibly any prison sentence at all depending on the strictness of Thai immigration laws. It so happened that a few years back I'd been with Emma to the same part of Thailand myself so at the end of the letter I'd gone on to mention to her a couple of sights she ought to visit while she was over there.

'I'm sorry, Danny, I don't get what's wrong with it.'

'There's nothing legally wrong with it,' says Danny. 'No, it's the last bit. The Thailand bit.'

'You didn't like that?'

He moves his chair closer and I can smell his aftershave. It's not a brand I'd have chosen for me. It's not a brand I'd have chosen for anyone who valued the company of a warthog, never mind other human beings. 'Matt, we're a criminal law firm.'

'I think that was my point.' I edge my chair away from his. 'I'm trying to be human. Show that we're human. Real people. Not just guzzlers of legal aid funds.'

'I see where you're coming from,' he says. 'But this is a business relationship and a business letter. It's not a Twitter message you've dreamt up in Tenerife airport.' He reaches out and touches me on my arm. 'Matt, you're doing a great job with us. I know you'd prefer to be back on the top floor. Doing what you do best. But trust me, you're a life-saver. I value you. Partners value you. You're good. Very good. Just...' He points to the letter. 'Just remember what we're here for. What we do. They may be happy with that kind of thing in the world of IP, probably what you're used to in the world of IP, but it's not okay in my world.' He pauses then breaks into his affected laugh, a laugh which reveals two lines of yellowing incisors. The laugh of one trying to be nice through the rollicking. A ray of sunshine through a biting northerly wind. I'd almost rather he just lost it completely and kicked me round the office and out of the window. I find myself doing what I always do when he breaks into his affected laugh. I flinch. I shrink back. And I'm sure if I could see my face in the mirror it would be going the colour of the Wimbledon Centre Court. 'Sorry, Matt. What am I like. Just listen to me, hey. The Danny Letwin Lecture of the day. I know I sound a bit pompous.' The affected laugh fades, right on cue from the director down in the stalls, and the shutters come down in front of his rotting gnashers. 'Just keep that bit of distance, all right. It's a legal practice. Where, on the criminal side at least, we keep our distance from clients and save the human stuff till after work. Okay.'

Now for the real punishment. The let's-be-adult-about-this, after-all-we're-all-in-this-together handshake. The damp wrinkled palm is heading in my direction and there's nothing I can do to stop it. There seems even more hair on the upper side than I remember from the last one. I wince as I feel the squeeze and hear the accompanying squelch. Thank goodness he slackens his grip, and releases his hand, and rounds off the physical chastisement with a final slap to the shoulder. Then he waddles out of the office and I'm once more a free man.

Or so I thought. Five minutes later there's an electronic bleep from my laptop and in my inbox is a re-send of Ellman Rich's client care and ethics policy and a covering email from delightful Danny drawing my attention to paragraph two thousand six hundred and ninety-seven sub-paragraph 1b which decrees that any inappropriate conduct towards clients is a disciplinary matter. Inappropriate conduct for the avoidance of doubt including conduct which is over-friendly, intrusive or invasive, and/or which involves taking an excessive and or unnecessary interest in a client's personal affairs, whether such conduct is wanted or unwanted.

My phone rings. It's the nick. Lisa-Marie Williams will be good to go at half twelve. Or, since I'm not sitting in the departure lounge at Parma, sorry Danny, that should be Ms Williams will be ready to be interviewed at twelve thirty o'clock British Summer Time. The officer explains that an appropriate adult has also been asked to attend because in the police's opinion the client has mental health issues. Great.

10

The city's police custody centre, where my prospective client is being held, is out in the suburbs of Brighton and isn't realistically walkable from the office or our house. Emma and I have one car between us and on days that we're both working, she uses it to commute to her work in Worthing, while I walk from home to our office in the city centre. She normally gets home early evening, meaning that if I have an out-of-hours police interview I'll be able to drive to the custody centre. But if I'm needed there in the daytime and Emma's at work, I have to get the bus. The buses are usually pretty reliable and so they are today: I find myself arriving at the custody centre ten minutes ahead of the appointed time. Fifteen minutes later DC Sarah Janman is with me in one of the consulting rooms giving me a document containing the pre-interview disclosure.

The document tells me that yesterday, Monday, 22nd October, in the late afternoon, the suspect, a 33-year-old female, was seen to pick up a light green fleece top in the Mountain Warehouse store in Queen's Road, Brighton, and walk out of the store without paying for it. The suspect was apprehended by two police officers a short while later and was found to have not only the fleece top in her possession but a bag that contained a significant quantity of heroin, a quantity the police say is inconsistent with purely personal use. She was arrested and while she was in custody a search was made of her home, the ground-floor flat at 88 Slimwood Parade in the eastern outskirts of the city. There the police found a total of five phones as well as a set of electronic scales, a large amount of a substance believed to be crack cocaine, a sizeable stash of cannabis, and some £300 in cash. She has a previous conviction, three years ago, for possession of amphetamines. DC Janman tells me that after interview she'll be released under investigation while the substances are analysed and the phones examined for text messages and phone numbers that might support evidence of dealing. The police will also want to take statements from neighbours about callers to the address in question, again in an attempt to provide supporting evidence of dealing from the client's property. I ask DC Janman, as I'm bound to do, if there's any information she's withholding, and she responds, as I know she will, that there might be, but she wants to hear what my client has to say first. I tell her I've no further questions and am ready to meet firstly the appropriate adult and then the client for pre-interview consultation. DC Janman says she'll facilitate that, and disappears. A few minutes later I'm at the bridge, the custody centre's reception area, introducing myself to Wendy Jacobs, the aforesaid appropriate adult. She's said she's spoken to the client and extracted the information she needs. Because she's not bound by professional privilege I don't want her to be present during my consultation with the client but I will ask her to join us as soon as the consultation's over and the interview is ready to start. I ask her to confirm she's aware of her role at the interview, namely to ensure the welfare of the client is safeguarded throughout the interview process. She says she is.

Then I return to the consulting room and await the arrival of said client.

I don't need to look out of the consulting room door to realise she's getting near. I can hear a woman's voice, or rather a woman's shouts. 'Just wanna get out. You said you'd ring my mum. I want my meds. Need my meds now.' I hear sobs and snivels. Then comes the squeal of the hinges as the consulting room door edges open, to reveal a uniformed female custody officer. She's accompanied by another female, early thirties at a guess, with straggly blonde hair, blue jogging top, grey jogging bottoms and pink trainers. Miss Williams, the custody officer announces. Then the custody officer disappears, leaving me alone with my new client.

She's shaking and her face is decorated with streaks of tears and runny eyebrow pencil and runnier eye shadow and smudged lipstick. I shake her hand and introduce myself but that's as far as I'm able to get. Before I've even established her full name, address or date of birth she's going into the merits of the evidence against her. She momentarily runs out of steam, enabling me to confirm her personal details, explain my function in the process and advise her of the confidentiality of our dealings and the consequent need for Wendy not to be present for our consultation, but hardly have I paused for breath than she's summing up the case for the defence, and without any further intervention from me the jury foreman is announcing a not guilty verdict. All of which would be easier to cope with if her legal and evidential arguments were coherent and comprehensible. But they're a jumble. No, they're more than a jumble: they're a tangled cooked-spaghetti-shaped mess with a Bolognese sauce of irrelevancies, half-remembered facts and speculation, and with each of her points come more tears, and sobs, and wails: plaintive wails, angry wails, South Wales, West Wales.

She'll be hopeless in police interview, no question. I manage to sift most of the hysteria out of the way and get the gist of her defence down on my laptop but I've already discovered more contradictions than were found across the entire duration of the Enlightenment. So I advise her to make, and provide to DC Janman, what's called a prepared statement. I explain we'll put down in writing the basis of her defence, and I'll then advise her to decline to answer any police questions other than to respond "no comment." If the issue arises in court we at least have the statement as evidence that she's not fabricated her version of events after her release from police custody.

We get there in the end but there must be a good hour between my opening a new Word file on my laptop, in readiness to draft something that stands a chance of being believed, and reading it back to her upon completion.

'"I accept that I removed a fleece top from Mountain Warehouse on the afternoon in question but was in a state of intoxication and was incapable of forming the necessary intent to steal. I have no need for a fleece top. In fact I have just given some away to a charity shop because I had too many. Regarding the drugs, I am not a drug dealer. I had some heroin on me but only for personal use. There may have been quite a bit but I am addicted to it and need it. The phones are all old ones. I keep losing my phones and only find them after I've bought new ones. There will be no evidence of dealing on those phones. I was unaware of the presence of the scales, cocaine and cannabis in my flat. I had a friend who was a dealer and he may have left them by mistake and without my knowledge. They were nothing to do with me. I deny being involved in dealing in

13

drugs myself. Regarding the cash, my mum had given me £300 from her savings account to pay a decorator who had been doing some work in my bathroom. He said he only took cash. I was intending to drop the money round to him the next day."

We then move from the consulting room to the interview room and we're joined by Wendy and DC Janman. Shortly afterwards the interview begins. Following the usual formalities, I read the prepared statement and undertake to email it to the officer without delay.

Of course it would be too straightforward for my client to answer "no comment" to the questions that follow. She stays silent in response to some of the questions. To others she begins a garbled explanation which then peters out into a wilderness of unintelligible monosyllables. And before long her strategy for responding to the interrogation is thumping the table in the interview room with her fist and demanding to know how much longer she's got to wait before she's getting out. Although she's not the easiest interviewee I've represented, she's not the craziest either; there does seem to be a thin streak of logic running through her arguments, and at no stage has Wendy expressed any concern about her fitness to continue to be interviewed. DC Janman's undoubtedly seen and heard it all a hundred times before: the same display of outraged innocence, and with it the same mannerisms, the same dramatic pauses, the same theatricals and the same histrionics. And judging by the persistence of her questioning it seems she's in no hurry to bring on the interval ice-cream or ensure the driveway outside has been cleared to accommodate the post-performance carriages. But at length the curtain does fall and DC Janman confirms Lisa-Marie will be released under investigation. She says she's sure I'd like a few minutes alone with my client and invites us to stay in the interview room while she and Wendy return to the bridge.

After she and Wendy have gone I slip into autopilot as I go through the usual post-interview rituals. I explain to Lisa-Marie what's going to happen, give her my business card, and tell her that I'll keep in touch with her. I also get her to sign a form which would enable us to apply for legal aid, that is, state funding of representation in court if it gets that far. By now my eyes are cricket balls and I'm just wanting out. I can feel my talking pace increasing from *andante* to *molto allegro*, bordering on *presto*, trusting that my businesslike delivery will forestall any further invective on her part. It seems to work. Nothing's coming back save a few nods and a barely stifled yawn.

Once I'm done, I get up and motion to her to do the same. At the door I offer my hand to her.

She takes it. And she doesn't seem to want to let go. 'You've got a nice soft hand,' she says. The anger has disappeared and there's a mellowness and smoothness in her voice for the first time since she was introduced to me what seems like half a century ago. 'I'm sorry I was like an animal in there.'

I should extricate my hand but I don't. 'You were upset,' I say. 'It happens. I've seen worse, believe me.'

'Not fair on you though, is it?'

I smile. 'It goes with the territory.'

'Tell you what,' she says. 'You're a good solicitor. Thanks for putting up with me.'

'It's what I do.'

'Tell you something else,' she says. 'You've got a nice smile as well.'

She's still clasping my hand.

*

Emma's cooked us a moussaka for tonight's dinner. I've never eaten any moussaka anywhere else on earth that's anywhere near as good. But I'd have been just as happy, if not happier, with processed cheese on toast if only we were talking. Properly talking.

'I want to watch something on Channel 4 at eight o'clock. If you want *Holby City* on you can watch it on your laptop. Or on catch-up.'

'Okay.'

Silence.

'We need a new bulb in the downstairs loo. Best get a pack of four, couple of others are flickering.'

'I'll do it. Tomorrow.'

15

Silence.

'And can you not keep leaving your shaving hairs in the sink. Not very nice when I want to wash my face in it.'

'Sorry.'

We were great for a long time. Trouble was, we tempted fate by calling ourselves The Unstoppables. Nothing could come between us, we agreed, and there was no end to our ability to satisfy each other. If ever we asked more of each other, we found it within ourselves to give it. We'd met twelve years ago on the commute to work in Brighton from Shoreham where we both happened to be living. Me, the IP guy, having only recently started at Ellman Rich, she, the retail manager with the shoulder-length ginger hair, the fresh blue eyes, the pinstripe business suit and high heels. It was late September and I was just about to turn 30; she was a year younger. We kind of matched, that is to say I too had – still have – reddish hair, albeit not in such generous quantities as her, and I too had blue eyes and pinstripe business suit. I didn't think high heels would do it for me though. Especially as at just over six feet I was comfortably taller than her even in my boring brogues. We'd sit, or more often be forced to stand, just chatting in the same train carriage each day, comparing notes on what we were to do that day, or what we might do that evening or that weekend. And before long we realised that whatever we wanted to do, we wanted to do it together.

I didn't want anything, or perhaps more potently, anyone in the way of our togetherness. And that was what I was convinced a child would have been: not an enhancement to the quality of my relationship with Emma, but a barrier. At school I was friendly with a girl called Terri. We've stayed in touch ever since. I remember one day at school she announced that her life ambition was to climb Mount Everest. And although she never made it to the very top of the world she succeeded in bagging, with her partner, the complete set of Scottish Munros, the 283 mountains in Scotland over 3000 feet high. She wrote a number of books and newspaper articles about their adventures. I've still got a couple of her books. They're compelling. Then she had Angus and Lola and Sammy and the things that gave both identity and uniqueness to the life of her and her partner were cancelled. Well, that was how I saw it. And that was how, on reflection, Emma came round to seeing it: to seeing motherhood as an end of living rather than a new phase of living. It took time for her to see it, longer for her to see it than for me. But while the path of our relationship moved along without the obstructions, child-shaped or otherwise, we began to find ourselves forgetting what we were walking along that particular path for. And I found myself wondering if we ought to be stopping in our tracks, checking the map and seeking out a path with more extensive views and more interesting sights. I was sure Emma was wondering the same. But we never discussed it. We'd just wandered on together. And as we've wandered on, we may have stayed together and done things together and occasionally laughed together. But the smooth reservoir of the physical aspect of our togetherness has been sucked almost dry, leaving a few feeble pools, acres of exposed concrete with banks of crumbling dry earth and desultory vegetation, and the announcement of standpipes in the street unless six months' worth of rain fall by Friday fortnight.

And as Emma and I face each other over our plates of moussaka I feel, as I've never felt before, the fear that we'll never see those downpours that will reinvigorate the physical in our landscape. As I look for a moment into her tired blue eyes, I'm guessing that she feels this fear as much as I do.

'I need to take the car into Swayne's tomorrow. They may have to keep it in overnight. I think you said you didn't need it, that's right, isn't it.'

'Okay.'

'Can you find out what time the buses go from there to my office? I can never make head or tail of their website.'

'I'll do it after dinner.'

Silence.

'And you will get rid of that pile of CD's and lump of chewing gum on the back seat won't you. Like yesterday.'

'Sorry.'

I swallow the last mouthful of moussaka and dinner's over.

*

Six days later, Monday the 29th, I'm in the office late afternoon and a call comes through from Lisa-Marie. She tells me she has the receipt for the payment of the £300 to the decorator. She also has the original estimate for the work, and her mother has the receipt for the withdrawal of the money from her account. She's asking if we can let DC Janman know all this. She says she also wants the chance to give a proper account of herself, which she didn't feel she'd had last time.

I tell her I can't promise anything. She's not automatically entitled to be re-interviewed. DC Janman could agree to take the documents but refuse a re-interview. Having said that, I learnt a while ago that if you don't ask in this business, you don't get. So I phone DC Janman and ask her.

A couple of phone calls later and a rematch is arranged. Five thirty tomorrow evening back at the custody centre. I'd have preferred later so I could have the car but DC Janman's got other commitments so five thirty it has to be.

*

I'm standing at the entrance to the custody centre. Wendy's already arrived and is in the building but I just know Lisa-Marie is going to be late. All my criminal clients are late. It seems to be an unwritten but rigorously observed rule that the moment you get into trouble with the law you move your watch back by fifteen minutes. I've tried to phone her but inevitably she's not picking up.

I gaze at my watch and sigh. It's now five forty and I tell myself she can have ten minutes and then I'm going. At five fifty-five I'm telling myself she can have five minutes and I'm definitely going. At six oh two I pull out my phone to advise DC Janman I'm going, and to attempt to agree with her a date and time when we might give it another try. I'm just about to dial when I see someone advancing towards me.

Lisa-Marie.

Her blonde hair is tinged with streaks of purple and turquoise and no longer straggles. It's frizzy, it's clean, it's fresh and it's vibrant. Her face is no longer tear-stained but smooth. Her lipstick is hardly subtle but it's not crassly overdone. She

18

wears a light blue denim jacket, a red polo-neck mohair jumper and jeans of darker denim thrust into shiny black knee-length lace-up boots. She's smiling broadly.

It's like the first time I saw Harriet.

Harriet. The one whose smile could light up New York and who had a crowd of potential boyfriends that could fill Grand Central Station. That Harriet.

I extend my hand to hers and she takes it. Then holds onto it. Still smiling.

'D'you like what I've got on?'

I gulp. 'I…er...' And I realise I'm not standing outside the custody centre at all. I'm sitting at the controls of an HGV in the fast lane of the M6 and my foot is pressed too hard on the accelerator pedal. I force my hand out of her grip.

'Wasn't sure about these boots,' she says, lifting her right foot and pointing it towards me. 'Took me ages to lace up. That's why I was late. Good aren't they though. Got them from Camden years ago. They all come with zips now. Cheating. Bloke once, he used to sit and watch me lace them.' She giggles. 'He said it turned him on. What do you think? Do you like them?'

I somehow find the brake pedal. 'Lisa-Marie, this isn't a fashion show. It's serious. You're in serious trouble. Class A drug dealing. You do get that, don't you.'

'Oh, yeah. Yeah, of course.' She smiles. 'I'm just glad it's you. Much nicer than my family law solicitor. He was crap anyway.'

'Flattery will get you everywhere.'

She brings her face forward. I can tell she wants to kiss me. I don't let her. I increase the pressure on the footbrake. I turn my head and I see instantly the brown of her cheeks turn a flustered pink. I daren't imagine the colour mine must be.

I secure entry to the custody centre and after the usual formalities we're shown into a consultation room so I can talk with my client before the re-interview. I let Lisa-Marie sit down first then take my seat at the opposite end of the table. She asks how I've been. I mutter the word okay then explain that this evening is another chance for her to tell the police her side of the story. I go through her prepared statement with her again and ask if there's anything in there that she wants to add to or change. She tells me she likes my hair and says no, nothing to add and no change. I ask to see the estimate for the work done in her flat, her mum's receipt for the £300, and the decorator's receipt for the same amount. She says she likes the colour of my shirt and then produces the requested documentation from her bag. The paperwork is crumpled and it stinks of weed. I may not smoke weed myself but I know what it smells like. Then having recovered from the shock to my nostrils I ask her if she's prepared to go into any more detail about the bloke who left the scales and the drugs in her flat. Even if she was, I somehow doubt he'll want to come forward as a witness, but stranger things have happened. She asks me what I'm having for my dinner. I tell her I've no idea and that I'm more interested in an answer to my question. Do you, I ask, want to tell me more about the man who left the stuff in your flat. She says she doesn't want to. I tell her I can understand that, but her unwillingness to co-operate in this regard isn't going to help her defence. I ask if she wants to add anything or if she has any questions. She asks me if I'm married. I tell her I'm not sure it's her business then get up and ring the buzzer on the wall to indicate we're ready to start the re-interview.

She asks me why I've gone and done that when the police would have given us as long as we wanted. And longer besides.

*

You can never quite tell with police interviewing officers. I've been in more than one interview where my client has been given the third degree, the officer rubbishing every other syllable of their explanation, and asking them what part of the expression "gossamer-thin tissue of lies" they aren't getting – then half an hour later the client is on their way rejoicing having been told there's to be no further action taken against them. And then there are those officers who listen carefully, sympathetically, nodding, smiling, on first-name terms, reassuring the client "we've all been there, I know," and who then proceed to throw not just the book at the hapless client, but the big-print 20-volume set of *War And Peace*. DC Janman lets

Lisa-Marie talk, and Lisa-Marie talks with coherence and confidence that during the previous interrogation had been registered as missing persons. Occasionally she slurs her words. From time to time she stumbles. I'm aware of a slight smell of alcohol on her breath. Even so, she has no difficulty in saying what she needs to say, and on the face of it, the officer seems almost too ready to lap it up, pausing to lick her milk-stained whiskers in the process, as though this additional material were the golden key to the mystery not of this particular crime but of the origins of life itself. Lisa-Marie might well be forgiven for thinking DC Janman's on her side and is simply, by her questioning, wanting confirmation of what she believes, namely that the client is innocent of any dealing. But I know, the officer knows, and I suspect Lisa-Marie herself knows, that there are still some significant gaps in the story, and nobody knows what's happened to the Polyfilla. The interview draws to a close. DC Janman switches off the recording equipment, thanks Lisa-Marie for the additional information, agrees to retain the documents we've produced, and tells her that as there are still outstanding enquiries to be made, it could be some while before a decision is taken as to how she's to be dealt with.

She asks for Lisa-Marie to confirm her mum's number, which she'd given on arrival in custody following arrest, and says that copies of the documents we've submitted will be waiting for us after my post-interview consultation. Fifteen minutes later, the copies now in my hand and the formalities of release now complete, Lisa-Marie and I are back outside the custody centre in the darkness.

'What are you doing now?' she asks.

'Going home,' I say. 'If that's any business of yours.'

'I only asked,' she says. 'Look. Is it because you're my lawyer?'

'Is what because I'm your lawyer?'

'You being like this. All stuffy, all pompous.'

'The word is professional,' I tell her. 'I have to be professional. That's what I'm here for. Not to be a mate. Not to be a buddy. Here to do a job. Defend you.'

'Okay,' she says. 'What if I'm like, I didn't want you. Sacked you. Told you I wanted another solicitor.'

'That's your privilege,' I say. 'You can instruct who you like.'

'Fine,' she says. 'You're sacked. Now d'you wanna be a mate?'

*

The Half Moon is just a couple of minutes away. Its proximity to the nick may have provided a convenient pit stop for me before or after a police interview, but it isn't a place I'd want to linger in for any length of time after downing the final dregs at the bottom of my pint glass. Still less is it an establishment where I'd feel comfortable about entertaining someone I still wished to count as a friend after we'd left. The stink of pot is everywhere. The beer's always tasted like bicycle oil and the packets of sandwiches on the bar counter are generally not only on the turn but in a race to get out of the back exit first. But Lisa-Marie has little hesitation in marching me in through its protesting doors and insists on getting the drinks. 'Just to thank you for being there for me tonight,' she says. She gets herself a white wine. I tell her I really only want a coffee and she orders me a large Americano. Large is understating it. Two handles and inside the cup this Caspian-Sea-sized accumulation of brown liquid.

We sit down side-by-side on a leather settee in one of the more sparsely populated parts of the lounge bar. I drink to her getting off the charges. And she drinks to finding a new solicitor, one who'll do an even better job than I've done. She puts her glass down but then picks it up again almost as quickly. 'Oh, just one more toast,' she says. 'To my lovely new friend.' She jerks the glass in my direction.

I hoist my vessel from ground level and allow her glass to nudge against it.

She puts her drink down on the table and leans back on the settee. I find myself doing the same. She's gazing into my eyes.

'You were good,' she says. 'Really good.'

That's not true. I wasn't really good at all. I was okay. I was average. I can't boast of having done anything during the

22

interview, whether by way of making clever interventions or of chiding the inquisitor for her interrogatory excesses, that has positively advanced my client's interests in any way. In my mind it's just been another bog-standard interview, one of a multitude it's been my dubious pleasure to attend during the past however many months. Lisa-Marie's words are flattery, no more, no less. But I'm a human being and as a human being I don't care to find the words to refute them. 'In what respect?'

'There you go again,' she says. '"In what respect?" I love the way you talk. Love it.'

I know now I should be trying to stop the HGV ride that started outside the custody centre. My foot wanders over to the brake once more and I check my mirror in anticipation of swerving into the slow lane.

'Lisa-Marie…'

'Just Lisa's fine,' she says. 'Or Li if you like. That's what my mum calls me.'

'Okay, Li,' I say. 'I'm flattered you think so highly of me. But I don't…don't…can't think what to make of it. I mean, you don't really know me at all. I don't know you at all. Your background, your family, your work, anything.'

She bursts out laughing. 'Oh, my days, you're so the lawyer,' she chortles. 'Get all the evidence together, take statements from witnesses, see if there's enough there to make you like me. Life's not like that. If that makes sense.' She gulps down some more wine.

I lift the monstrosity in front of me and take a sip from the south shore of the Caspian. 'Okay.' I say. 'I'm not after your life story. I don't know…maybe just…just tell me one interesting thing about yourself. Your life.'

'My life's not interesting,' she says. And as she says it the laughter lines disappear from her face, and her eyes become clouds of grey. 'It's crap. Not like yours I bet. Always has been crap. I'm a crap person. I hate myself. Always hated myself.' She takes another gulp from her glass and bangs the glass down on the table in front of us. 'I've got a heroin addiction, I'm an alcoholic, I've got four kids, all taken away from me. The last one was at birth. Social were sitting in the maternity wing. They're like, as soon as the baby's been born, they're taking it

23

straight off of me. And they did. Literally straight off me. I called him Nelson. I've cried for him every day. At least with the others, I've seen them grow up a bit. Never got the chance with Nelson. Does that make sense?'

'Haven't you tried to get him back?'

'I've kept on asking social,' she says. 'But no. I get to see him once a fortnight. At his foster mum's. Not the same. It's my fault. I don't deserve him. Don't deserve anything really.'

'At least you've got a good mum,' I say. 'A generous mum, anyway.'

'You know what.' She picks up her glass again. 'She's the only person who's ever loved me. Really properly loved me. You know who she named me after?'

'I'm guessing Elvis' daughter?'

'Right. Right first time. You're so clever. That's why you're a lawyer.' She digs me in the ribs.

I can sense the speedometer needle rising again. 'Not that clever.'

'Cleverer than me.' Now she's stroking my arm.

I need her to stop, need her to stop now. I need to be lifting my hand and snatching her hand away. But my arm has turned to stone. 'What about brothers and sisters?'

'I've got an elder brother…I guess we get on okay. When he's not in jail. And a half-sister. But I don't see her. Not seen her since I was six.'

'Your dad? He still around?'

She sighs and gazes down at her wine glass. 'Never knew him. All he's done is just send me money. As though that makes up for everything. I'm guessing he's like, if he just keeps sending me money, more and more money, then that's as good as being there for me. He is generous, I'll give him that. He even paid the deposit on my flat. But if I had the choice, right, between him paying that and him putting his arm round me and telling me he loves me I'd go for that. Even if it meant sleeping in a frigging cardboard box. If that makes sense.'

'What about the father…fathers of your children?'

She scowls. 'Every bloke I've been with, it's always the same,' she says. 'They just want me for the sex and don't give a toss about me. Just use me. No love there at all. Not real love. I

24

fall for it each time, try to be nice, know what I mean…I'm like, if I care for them they'll care for me, you know, as a human being, someone with feelings, if that makes sense, but no, next thing I know they've got me bladdered and got me in bed and next morning I'm hating myself because it's my fault. None of the dads wanted to know when I got pregnant with their kids. I don't know where any of them are. They don't want to know. So, yeah. That's my life. Crap. Does that make sense?'

The coffee's cooling now. I begin to make more meaningful inroads into the accumulation of fluid in front of me. It gives me thinking time. I try to recall my dating years. Things I asked. Things I told myself I mustn't ask. 'Okay,' I say. 'Tell me one thing you enjoy. That you like. Could be an interest, could be a band, could be a film, or film star. Anything.'

She drains the wine in her glass, then turns to me. 'I don't think I'm very good at this game,' she says. 'Look. I'm not like that. I don't have, you know, interests, hobbies, pastimes, whatever you call them. I don't live life like other people do, if that makes sense. I'm chaotic. That's what they all say about me. Doctors. Nurses. Shrinks. Even my own brother. When he's not in jail. Chaotic, that's me.' She reaches out and places her hand in mine. It's like a charge of two thousand volts. 'I'm sorry,' she says. 'You're doing great. I like it. You can keep asking stuff if you like.'

'Okay, one last one,' I say. 'Tell me something, anything that you've achieved. Apart from motherhood. And you've got to answer.'

Now her smile broadens and she moves closer to me.

'I have achieved something.' She emphasizes the word "achieved" as though she's trying it out for the first time. 'Tonight. I've met a bloke who sees me as a human being. Who respects me for me. Does that make sense?'

She swings round towards me, her hand still in mine, and I feel the leather of her left boot against my knee and my calf. Her face, her smiling face, is staring directly into mine.

Then my phone goes. I let go of Lisa-Marie's hand and reach for it.

Emma.

'What's going on?' she demands. 'I thought you'd be back ages ago.'

'Interview was late starting. Not long over. I'm on my way.'

'So's your dinner. Will be on the table in five minutes. It's looking forward to seeing you.'

I put my phone away, edge my right leg from the rub of the boot leather and gaze down at the rest of the coffee. 'Look. I need to go,' I say. 'You've got my business card and email. Be in touch. Thanks for the coffee.' I rise to my feet.

Go now, Matt. Don't linger. Just get out. Back to your dinner. Your home. Your wife.

'Aren't you supposed to shake hands?' she asks.

'I think we've kind of done that,' I say.

I turn my back on her and head for the door. Moments later, I'm walking out into the November night.

I stride off towards the car park along the deserted street. A damp mist cloaks the night sky.

It's only as I arrive at the car park that I remember I've not got the car. That I'd come up here by bus.

I get out my phone to check the time of the next bus. I don't want to have to call Emma for a lift but I'm not waiting around here all night.

I'm just bringing up the app when I hear the hard bang of footsteps on concrete.

The next moment I feel a hand on my arm. It's not the firm hand one might expect of a prospective mugger. It's gentle and cosy, warm and caring.

I turn to face Lisa-Marie and fix my eyes on hers. And in her eyes there's an intensity and a soulfulness and a neediness I can never remember seeing on Emma's face even when we felt at our most unstoppable and inseparable.

'Can I see you again?' she murmurs.

'I don't know, Li.' The burning lava of being wanted, properly wanted, needed, loved, now meeting the cold dull waters of real life and real expectation and real common sense.

'I'd like to cook a meal for you. I'm quite a good cook.'

I can feel the steam of her breath and can see the patches of saliva on her lips.

'I don't know that I can, Li. I'm sorry.'

26

Now go, Matt, for pity's sake.

But my feet are glued to the pavement and now the cold dull waters evaporate in an instant. My arms are round her neck and I'm allowing my lips to play across her cheeks until they meet with her lips. Then my tongue enters her mouth…

2

I get home and find Emma in the kitchen removing a plate of shepherd's pie from the oven.

'Matt, I'm really seriously peed off.'

'I told you the interview was late starting. Then the bus got delayed.'

'I could have come and collected you.'

'I didn't want to mess your evening up.'

'I wouldn't have minded. You know that.' She puts the meal on the table in front of me and sits back down. Her empty plate's in front of her. 'Always the same. I do us a nice dinner and we end up eating it two hours apart.'

'I can't help it if things get delayed..'

'You could at least have told me a bit sooner.'

'Not always easy to tell.'

I sit gazing over my plate of food, waiting for the next line. The line in which she asks what it is she's not supposed to know. A friend of mine once said that a woman always knows if her partner's up to no good. Something about partner's body language, speech pattern, and speech rhythms. Up till now I don't think Emma, who's always been very good at reading my body language, would have suspected anything for the very good reason I've done nothing to make her suspect. But I know if the grounds for suspicion are there, she'll find them with the efficiency and expertise of a top-class motor mechanic looking for faults in a Rolls Royce. We used to joke about it. I told her she'd probably know I was in an affair even before I did. We'd have a titter.

Only these days it doesn't seem quite so funny. And in the light of what's been going on less than half an hour before it seems less funny still. I remember the priest that married us having us over to the vicarage for a pre-nuptial pep-talk. During our meeting he likened a marriage to a fine building, comprising many rooms, each one requiring to be cared for and properly maintained. If, he said, you're prepared to keep an eye out for snags, do the necessary work to whichever room or rooms need it, and take preventative measures to forestall future problems, the building remains not only habitable but enjoyable to live in. But if you don't bother, and let nature take its course, the building will become rotten. It won't necessarily all rot at once but bit by bit: firstly an upstairs room, then a downstairs room, then maybe another upstairs room, until it ends up having to be pulled down altogether. "If your marriage is to survive, you've got to want to look after each room," he'd said.

I know I should be wanting to do that. And I think I do want to. I think I care for Emma too much not to want to. I think. It's not just the fear of recriminations: to begin with, the items most dear to you, your phone, your laptop, your iPad, tumbling out of the upstairs window, and as a grand finale following the marital collapse, the bill for the whole thing, the bill that makes you wish you'd kept all those McDonald's hot drink loyalty tokens as that's the only way you're going to be able to afford to keep yourself warm at night. It's more than that. It's about love. The love I have for her may have changed, just as the nature of our relationship may have changed, but despite what's just happened with Lisa-Marie, perhaps even because of it, I want to start to rebuild. I think those rooms are worth keeping and the rotten sections worth treating and I think I want to call in the surveyor and assess what's needed for a proper repair job.

I think.

Anyway I don't just think, I know that I'd be a disaster at managing an affair. A proper affair. I'm not much good at keeping guilty secrets and I'm not a great liar either. Which is ironic, I guess, given the amount of lies I'm constantly told by my clients. That's the big difference between my IP work and my criminal work. In the IP department, I was dealing for the most part with basically very honest, hard-working, enterprising types who were terrified at the thought of antagonising the big boys. But in the criminal department I'm acting for people who I know won't be too ashamed to tell whatever falsehood it takes to exonerate them. Ethically I'm not allowed to be party to what I know to be lies but unless the client tells me outright they're lying, all I can do is probe them as to their truthfulness. "Prove I'm lying, then," is their stock response to any challenge on my part to the veracity of their instructions. And if nobody can prove they are lying, well, it's worked for them and they'll think it can work for them again. On the strength of my dealings with my criminal clients I should be the world's expert liar. But I guess that as far as I'm concerned, it's like watching Tiger Woods in his prime. Instead of taking tips from him on becoming a world-class golfer the realisation of the depth of the chasm between him and the rest of us just makes me, at any rate, feel even more inadequate and the possibility of emulating him even more futile.

I lift a forkful of shepherd's pie into my mouth and as I digest it I allow myself to look into Emma's eyes. I reason that if she suspected something I'd know by now.

'Phone call for you a little while ago,' she says.

No. Can't be. I can't have given Lisa-Marie my private number by mistake. Or can I. Please, no. I can hardly permit myself to draw breath. 'Oh yes?'

'Your dad. Couldn't get you on your mobile. Inviting you up to see him and Karen this weekend.'

'I'm invited? What about you?'

'I'm working, aren't I. All day Saturday. All day Sunday. All day Monday till late. Unless by some miracle they've actually got round to changing the shift patterns.'

'I thought that had been done weeks ago.'

'Well if they had, I'd have told you.' She gets up from the table taking her empty plate with her. 'Last thing was, they were going to tell us this weekend. Pigs might fly. Anyway, you're on your own.'

'Okay.'

'Alan says can you ring him tonight to let him know.'

'I'll do it. Later.'

'Do it now, will you. I don't want you keeping me awake. Again.'

'Sorry.'

She goes out. I'm just loading my fork again when she comes back. 'Oh,' she says, 'Almost forgot. Karen says George can't wait to see you. Asks you not to be late for his birthday party.'

'Birthday party.'

'That's right.' She looks me in the eye, sighs and shakes her head. And without a word she turns and walks out again.

*

My dad lives in North Yorkshire and because Emma needs the car for work on Saturday I'll have to take the train. I decide to get a very early train out on Saturday and return on Sunday after lunch. Not only does the early start save me a few quid but it also allows for more time in York, where I have to change trains, on the Saturday morning. I've always loved York with its Minster, its Jorvik museum, its ancient walls and gates, and its network of alleys known as snickelways. I check with Emma that she doesn't object to my getting up, and thereby almost certainly waking her up, at an ungodly hour on Saturday. She's well used to being woken because of the nature of my work but somehow it seems unfair for it to happen when it doesn't have to. In fact she's fine about it; she just asks me to make sure I do some shopping on Friday as she won't have time over the weekend.

That's all good. The trouble is that when I go online I find all the affordable Sunday afternoon train seats have gone. If I book onto the one train that's got availability, I won't be getting home till a quarter past one on Monday morning. That's if all the trains are on time. So I think again. I've some leave owing and having secured Emma's agreement I ask Danny if I can take Monday off and come home then. Danny asks if I can do him a return favour and help him out at the police station on Friday evening when he's on call for own clients. Deal. It backfires on me to the extent that I'm stuck at the nick till ten past eleven on the Friday and I'm not home till nearly half past. But all that's forgotten as I travel north next morning.

I'm in the city by ten and for the next three hours I wander, and I snack, and I shop. The three hours pass far too fast but at least there's the prospect of more time in the city on Monday, and it's the thought of that that sustains me as I climb aboard a local train to the town nearest dad's home village. I call him as the train approaches my stop, and he says the kettle's already on and birthday party guests are starting to dribble in.

If they lived nearer I suspect I'd see them most weekends.

31

And that would certainly reduce my weekly shopping bill. Karen, my stepmum, may not be a cook in the Jamie Oliver class but if quantity and generosity of portion size were all that mattered she'd be crowned Masterchef before the new series had even started. She has a natural talent for plain home cooking. And today it's clear she also has a natural talent for birthday party food. As I look across the dining room I'm surveying fields of the stuff, from cheese straws to mini sausage rolls, from fish paste sandwiches to jellies and tubs of ice cream, and in the centre, a birthday cake the size of the Royal Festival Hall…I'm already wondering where I'll find room for the lamb casserole and cherry pie and custard Karen promises will follow when George is put to bed and it's just the three of us.

I don't think it was just the cooking that attracted my dad to Karen. I suspect he was looking for someone different from mum. I think the polite word for mum was conventional. Mum had been born towards the end of the last war; she'd grown up in a strict household and had gladly embraced the same spirit of self-discipline and restraint. She met dad, a year younger than her, at college and they led a quiet, settled life in rural Kent. Then came the attack. A vicious cancerous attack that grabbed her body and spat it into a premature grave. That was twenty-one years ago. For a long time dad was unwilling to recommit, fearful perhaps of another dose of hurt and worry and anguish which had attended mum's final months. But I'm sure he felt a sense of relief. Although on the surface he'd seemed happy enough with mum, I do believe that in reality he felt stifled. After mum died he stayed put and stayed widowed for a few years then when he retired from his career in insurance at the age of sixty he decided he needed a fresh start and moved from Kent, where all his roots were, to North Yorkshire. He'd not been there a month when Karen came along. They met by chance at a pub in York, and although she was exactly half his age they clicked at once. She'd been born in Hertfordshire into a working-class family, and had lost both her parents to illness when she was in her early twenties. After they'd passed away she realised she was bored in Hertfordshire, her life was going nowhere, and having loved childhood holidays in Yorkshire, and realising the cost of living there was so much less than down south, she decided to move to Leeds. She'd worked for herself as a make-up artist, not earning much but surviving and loving the Leeds social scene. She did young. She dressed young. She had a passion for things young people did, and left ageing for others to do. Dad may have been sixty but he was a young sixty, still sporting a fine head of deep ginger hair and, helped by his muscular build and six feet something in height, having a commanding and impressive presence. The two of them started dating, began cohabiting within six months and got married two years after they first met. They struggled for a while financially – Karen's work never paid her that much and a lot of dad's savings went on doing up their house – but they made economies and took some sensible advice and now they get by.

Fifteen months after their wedding Karen fell pregnant. It wasn't the easiest pregnancy but there were no major concerns and Daisy appeared, two days early. Dad said it was the greatest thing that had ever happened to him. People are prone to exaggerate at times of extreme emotion but I believed him. I knew why it meant so much to him. Their first child. His first daughter. A sister for me. Anyway, all was well during the early days, but when Daisy was four weeks old she developed breathing difficulties. The doctors weren't worried. They said it wasn't a problem. With sighs of relief all round, normal service was resumed. Daisy was fine until she was eight months old. Then, quite out of the blue, the breathing problems returned. Only this time they seemed far worse. And one morning, Dad's in the shower and Karen comes in screaming her head off, yelling that Daisy's turned scarlet and is gasping. They rush her to hospital. She never came back out again.

Dad said it was worse, much worse, than losing mum. I was his only child and I'd often said as a child how I'd have loved a little sister. He so wanted a sister for me as well as a daughter for him. He said it felt like a double bereavement.

They tried again. Even though the doctors reassured them that there was no reason why Daisy's condition would re-emerge in another child of theirs, I was convinced it was a huge risk. But two years later, seven years ago, George was born, and he thrived. He's thrived as a baby, and he's thrived at pre-school, and he's thrived at primary school...something very, very special about him.

And there's something special about Karen today. She may now be approaching her mid-forties but she could pass for late twenties, or maybe, this afternoon, even early twenties, with her Radiohead T-shirt and ripped black jeans, and her jet-black shoulder-length hair bunched up to reveal a brace of tattoos and circle of coloured beads round her neck.

I begin to regret my earlier snacking on top of a big breakfast as there's precious little room for any of the party fare, never mind dinner. For the sake of appearances I force down a couple of mini sausage rolls, at the same time exchanging pleasantries with George's old reception class teacher, Polly. I think there's a law that states that all reception class teachers should have happy sounding names, preferably ending in ly. Mine was Sally, Emma's was Dilly, Karen's was Billie. Of course teachers, whether they're reception class teachers or "A" level teachers, aren't supposed to have favourites but Polly has never made any secret of the fact that all the time he was in reception, George was her number one. And I know she's not just saying it. There was something special between them. She says as much to me now and I say all the right things back. Then I find room for a fish paste sandwich and Kirsty, the mum of George's sometime best friend Jamie, manoeuvres her way up to me for a chat. I ask after Jamie who's now moved schools. He misses George a lot, she says: they were best buddies, inseparable throughout their time together at St Anne's C of E. As I down a probably ill-advised mouthful of chocolate cake following the blowing-out of the candles and a spectacularly tuneless chorus of *Happy Birthday To You*, I'm approached by a woman who takes me for George's dad and Karen's husband. She won't let me get a word in and she prattles on for so long that I've not got the heart to disabuse her.

By the time the party guests have gone I feel I need some fresh air and some way of offloading the calories. So it's on with the running gear and out into the declining light. But even though darkness is on the march, there's sufficient of the day

34

left for me to make out the heather-clad tops of the North York Moors and the distinctive volcano-like summit of Roseberry Topping. And despite the skyline being swallowed up by the remorseless tide of early November nightfall, there's still something mesmeric and captivating about the Yorkshire air, and two hours later I find I'm still going. The two hours' running brings me to a village some four miles from dad and Karen's house where there's a real ale pub. It's only after my third pint that my phone goes and it's dad asking me to move my backside so I can get home in time to say good night to the birthday boy.

I hurry back and the three of us make our way upstairs to George's room. The view from the window on a clear sunny day is one of the most perfect I know. It's a partially wooded hillside and in the autumn the trees turn a hundred shades of red, of ochre, of rich yellow and rich brown, and on a clear day the tops of the Moors provide a stunning backcloth. The room feels lived-in and loved. On top of the pine wardrobe rest a heap of board games and a family of soft toys from across the animal kingdom, while the bookshelves groan with the works of Roald Dahl. At the window sits a table with a scattering of paper and crayons and pencils and rubbers and sharpeners and rulers. It's as though there'd been an explosion in a stationery shop. But it's George's room and we wouldn't change a thing.

By the dim bedside light I see no movement from between the duvet and mattress. Karen turns to us and mouths 'He's asleep.' I watch as she smooths the pillow and adjusts its angle. Then she leans down for a goodnight kiss.

'Sleep well, little angel,' she says.

Dad and I follow suit then leave Karen to have the last word. She's still there as Dad and I leave the room.

I walk downstairs with dad and we re-enter the lounge. We exchange glances.

'Thanks, Matt,' he says with a smile. 'I know Karen really appreciates it.'

*

A mostly lazy Sunday, albeit with a bit of garden football

35

thrown in, helps me recuperate following the hectic Saturday, and, assisted further by Karen's Monday morning fry-up, I'm revitalised, determined to make the best use of every second of the two hours I've got in the city before travelling home. But they still don't seem nearly long enough and in the end I'm having to dash for my train.

It's only when I'm on the train that I wish I'd come home last night after all. I'd have had a lot more of the train to myself. The service I've opted for is crammed and it's noisy. Seated next to me is a harassed mother and two evidently pre-school children who I'm guessing are on their way to London to compete for the Scream Most Likely To Be Heard In Shanghai award. I'd hoped to get a bit of work done but that's never going to happen. My phone signal is intermittent and I decide to forget that too and turn my attention to the *Metro* newspaper. I can just about cope with the quick crossword but that's about as intellectual as it's going to get. So I turn to the paper's Escape pages and a report on the joys of night life in Port Moresby. But, as my science teacher used to tell my mum and dad on parents' evenings, nothing's going in.

We're hurtling through Grantham when my phone goes. Emma.

'Matt, you never shopped on Friday, did you.'

My heart slumps towards the carpet beneath my feet. I've no defence. But clearly going no comment isn't an option. Not with this particular interrogator. 'I was in the police station,' I try.

'Don't give me that. Please, Matt. There's an Asda the size of the Isle of Wight yards from the police station. You can't tell me you didn't have a spare quarter of an hour.'

It'll have to be the wounded puppy. 'I'm so sorry, darling. I just...kind of let it slip. It was busy on Friday night. Just didn't...really sorry.'

'Sorry enough to make sure you shop on the way home? Because I won't have time today. And believe it or not, last time I checked, there were no shopping fairies to be had for love nor money.'

She likes her fairies, Emma does. Her drawing my attention to lack of existence of, or lack of easy availability of, certain species of same, whether it's shopping fairies, washing line fairies, or switching lights off fairies, is integral to each and every critique of my competence around the ancestral semi.

'Of course, darling,' I hear myself say. 'And I'll cook tonight as well. Leave it with me.'

'Can I really trust you? Really?'

'Of course.'

'You'd better not mess up.'

'I won't.'

'Well, that would make a nice change. Oh, and by the way...'

The boy opposite me decides on another audition piece. Whatever Emma was going on to say to me is lost in a maelstrom of high-pitched yelling and equally decibel-rich maternal remonstration.

By the time the performance is over, and I'm able to engage with my wife once more, said wife has hung up.

I think about calling her back but thinking about it's as far as it's ever going to get.

Once more I recall that priest before our wedding. He said a lot, did that priest, ahead of the big day. It's Emma's fault: she, not me, was the one wanting the church ceremony. But now something else he said is ringing in my ear. "Just be nice to each other and you'll be fine."

Made it sound so simple. Too simple. If said at the wrong place at the wrong time, it would have invited a suitably terse response.

But he was right. Of course. Because now that Emma's stopped being nice to me and with every conversation is serving up increasingly generous portions of irritability, resentment and hostility, with a few teaspoonfuls of sarcasm added to taste, I can feel the pretence and the denial surrounding the real state of our relationship slipping down the plughole, while the bath plug itself enjoys a well-earned holiday in Blackpool.

Lisa-Marie may not have my private mobile but I have hers. I give her a call. No reply. Then and only then do I remember something she mentioned to me the first time I saw her at the nick. That it's generally a waste of time to try calling her before around 3.30pm. It's to do with whatever she's on. She'd prefer to be texted.

So I text her.

"That meal still on? x"

We're careering through Hitchin when my phone bleeps.

"Tomorrow night at 8 my place. Veggie lasagne to die for xxxxx"

"Perfect. Can U confirm your address??xx"

We're pulling into Kings Cross and there's another bleep.

"Still GFF 88 Slimwood Parade in east brighton xxxxxx"

"CU then xxx"

"Can't wait presh xxxxxxxx"

*

I make a Brighton-bound train at King's Cross by seconds, but I've had to sprint to catch it and I'm panting and wheezing most of the way to East Croydon. I feel disgusting and probably smell disgusting.The weather, bright and sunny in York, has deteriorated and although it's not raining, yet, the skies are now grey and heavy and a moody, spiteful wind's got up. It's blowing into my face all the way from Brighton station to our house. There's food to be bought and cooked, but the priority is a hot shower, after which I'll be able to face the supermarket. At least I've ample time. It's just coming up to four when I get in. Emma always works till late on Monday and won't be home for another three hours.

As I get into the hall I can hear Candy Staton blasting from next door and curse Neil, our neighbours' son. He does this every day when he gets home from college. Of course the moment his parents return from work he'll stop but he doesn't afford the same courtesy to Emma and me. So just now the young hearts are not only running free but doing GBH to my cardrums.

I need the shower straight away. I hurl my clothes onto our bed, grab a fresh towel from the airing cupboard and thirty seconds later the warm cascade obliterates the muck and the sweat and the travel-weariness. Our shower has a personality all of its own, sometimes scalding me and at other times replicating the National Service recruit's first morning ablutions with ice cubes thrown in for no extra charge. But today it must have mistaken me for Goldilocks, or at any rate baby bear, because it's all just right. I usually reckon to have half the *Magic Flute* overture finished by the time I step out. But today as I switch the shower off the overture's done and we're well into the first aria.

I go back into our bedroom in order to change into some clean clothes. I'm just getting my shirt on when there's a gust of wind and I hear a door bang downstairs. Sounds too big a bang for the kitchen or the lounge door. Has to be the front door slamming in the wind. I was sure I'd closed the front door properly when I came in but I suppose if I can forget to do the shopping there are other ways in which the gaps in my evidently leaky memory are equally likely to manifest themselves. I hurry down to check the door which is now tight shut and seems to have suffered no obvious ill-effects from the blast of November air.

I return to the bedroom and see my phone isn't still in my back trouser pocket where I thought I'd left it, but on the bed. I don't understand it. I'm sure I've not had it out since I got home. I don't see how it could have fallen out. Maybe Danny was right. He told me not so long ago he'd done three or four 24-hour police station duties in a week and he said by the end he was so out of it he'd got to the stage of putting his pants on the wrong way round. I remember thinking at the time that I was surprised he'd been able to find a pair of pants that he could get his legs through in the first place. And the vision of his struggling with a recalcitrant G-string and the vast acreage of buttock remaining exposed to view while he looked for something to put over it was to blight my appetite for days afterwards. But I can see what his problem was and maybe the demands of the job and the extensive travelling of the weekend are getting to me as well, and in ways I couldn't have thought possible.

First priority after I've dressed is to delete all the texts to and from Lisa-Marie. The detail's easy enough to remember: Number 88 at 8. Next priority is to enjoy a cuppa. After that I get on my bike and go to Tesco, choosing something a bit tastier, albeit pricier, than we'd normally have on a Monday night at home. It'll be a nice surprise for Emma. I've always believed that the unexpected treats are the best. Even now, at this critical stage in our marriage with my finger poised over the self-destruct button, my instincts make me want to please her. They make me want to see sunshine and warmth return to her face. They make me want to see the grey clouds of exasperation and boredom lift from her eyes. They make me want to be persuaded that my emotional as well as physical future lies with her and not with an alcoholic heroin addict under police investigation. And they make me want to be able, once the unexpected treat is over, to pick up the phone and tell the alcoholic heroin addict that tomorrow's veggie lasagne is off.

Trouble is, I know my limitations. I'm more of a well-meaning cook then a well-able cook. If I cook, I try to make sure that it's not a case of fifty shades of brown but that there's some greenery in the overall ensemble, and that in fact there's a variety of colours and vitamins, as little processed meat, sugar or salt as possible, and as few saturated fats and additives as possible. I try to avoid convenience foods, I aim for a variety of dishes rather than the same thing each time, and I like to experiment a little. But something usually goes awry somewhere. That's the trouble – it's never the same thing each time and I never know what it's going to be. I may get the quantities hopelessly wrong; I may omit an ingredient I believed to be unnecessary but which turns out to have been essential; I may not give it enough time in the oven; I may cook everything to perfection but leave half of it stuck to the baking tray. And as night follows day, my efforts are rewarded by Emma with the full Simon Cowell or Craig Revel Horwood treatment. I've learnt to give up saying that at least I've tried.

Emma's always back from work by seven and ready to sit down to eat almost immediately. As I remove the food from the oven at six fifty-eight, by jingo I think I've got it. It smells good and it looks good: the red and green peppers stated in the recipe book to be optional have given sparkles of colour to the mixture. And as a sample spoonful hits my tongue I can feel my taste buds doing a Highland fling of gratitude.

I'm setting the food down on the worktop when my text bleeps. Emma. "Don't forget, won't be home till half past."

What does she mean, don't forget.

Then I remember her call on the train and the bit at the end I never heard. And for just a moment I want to pick up the dish with the cooked food and throw the whole thing out onto the street.

Steady, Matt. It's okay. Just pop it back in the oven on a low heat. Not difficult. It's what you've seen her do. Keep calm.

I return the food to the oven, then wait.

Emma's as good as her word. She is home by half past. She comes in and sits down at the table.

'Surprise,' I say.

'That sounds ominous,' she says. There's not a trace of a smile.

For the second time I remove the food from the oven. And even I, the well-intentioned but well-unable cook, can see that the mixture I'm about to serve to my wife is, just like the FA Cup, not what it was. What thirty minutes ago was a joy to the senses has become a stodgy morass. The sweep of vibrant colour is now a compost heap of decaying greens and moribund reds. And the taste buds' Highland fling has given way to a funeral dirge on bagpipes stiff with mould.

'Well, I'll save you the bother of saying it,' Emma says. 'At least you tried.'

*

It would have suited me to have either been in court or in the police station all next day. But on this particular Tuesday I'm not required in either. Instead I'm stuck at the office with Danny, who's having one of his panicky fits because of the lack of business. Danny stresses when it's busy but probably stresses even more when it isn't. There are rumours today of another round of legal aid cuts. Danny, never one to understate things if he can help it, says if these cuts are then translated to our salaries then given the lack of work we soon won't be shopping at Sainsbury's but at the food bank. And the client shortage isn't just bad for the firm but today it's bad for me because it's giving me too much time to think. With that excessive thinking time come the doubts, and the guilt, and the fear and the

41

stupidity. It's true that morally speaking it would make no difference if Lisa-Marie were, rather than wasting her life away in an alcohol and heroin-fuelled haze, in the running for sainthood – save I suppose that if she were, she might at least have the sense to stop the juggernaut in its tracks before it smashes my marriage to pieces. But, as I keep being forced to remind myself, it's her very lack of saintly virtues that brought us together to begin with and which throw into the mix an uncertainty and unpredictability that is toxic and dangerous and insane and terrifying.

And yet if it were all snatched from me the fear of what would be left is greater still.

It'll be the first time I think I'll ever have ventured to this part of Brighton. I've heard of it, and indeed a goodly number of my criminal clients hail from it. Which in itself is enough for me to decide against driving there. And in view of the steady drizzle floating down from the heavens, I fancy the idea of cycling it even less. So I'm taking the bus to get there, and probably a cab home.

It's been easy enough to tell Emma I'm on 24-hour police station duty. There's never any pattern to them so that's not going to cause the slightest northward movement of her eyebrows. Rather than come home first, I've stayed on at the office. Otherwise she'd be asking me why I didn't take the car. I tell her the police have just rung to say they're ready with a case I supposedly picked up a few hours ago, four Poles arrested for a mass brawl in some back alley in Peacehaven. In truth, this is the one scenario I always dread when I'm on police station duty: a multi-hander violence investigation. When it's shoplifting, possession of drugs or drink-driving, for instance, then generally speaking the facts speak for themselves. But where violence is alleged, and there are a number of suspects, there may be issues around identification, provocation, self-defence, and worst of all, the possibility of finding I'm conflicted and having to stop in mid-flow because the guys I've been asked to act for are all blaming each other. And of course if they're Poles some if not all of them may need an interpreter, with everything having to be translated, meaning the whole exercise will take up to twice as long as it would normally. So I

42

explain to Emma that I could possibly be tied up with this case all evening and maybe even through the night. I hope I'm not tempting fate by using this as my fictional scenario and that it won't happen for real next week. Mum was in no doubt. "If ever you feign illness you're just asking to fall ill for real," was something she told me more than once. I may not be feigning illness but the principle is the same. And the feeling of discomfiture arising from the nature of my story to Emma, with all the fate-tempting possibilities that arise from it, isn't assuaged one iota by the speed, or lack of it, of my bus journey into the eastern suburbs of the city. I'm counting the sets of temporary traffic lights and in the twenty minutes we've been on the move I think it's up to four. That would be a good question for the Eggheads. What is the collective name for a group of temporary lights. Is it: A, an irritation, B, a vexation, or C, an infuriation. Sorry, Kevin, you're wrong. Trick question. It's all of them.

The loudspeaker in the bus is announcing my stop as the next stop. I leap to my feet and walk to the exit door, arriving there just as the bus comes to a halt. The door slithers open. I'm shaking so much I lose my footing on the steps leading off the vehicle and crumple into a heap on the adjacent pavement. I'm not hurt thank heaven and my only thought is get up as soon as possible and hope the sniggering urchins at the back of the bus haven't seen the performance.

The bus disappears and I brush myself down. I'm a mess. Which I guess is kind of appropriate. It reminds me of what one of my old work colleagues said. Affairs are always messy. They're not the glamorous business the average reader of the *Metro* Guilty Pleasures pages might expect them to be. Forget the fast sports car, the swanky restaurant, the king-size four-poster. Forget the romance, the fun, the love, the laughter, the excitement. Even if you think you've found pockets of it within the mess, the aforesaid colleague told me, it's impossible to get rid of the smell of mess. A smell which will stay long after the mess itself has been cleared up. He should know. He was seeing another woman within two weeks of getting back off honeymoon. As I set off towards Slimwood Parade I'm shaking my head at the stupidity, the idiocy, and the crassness, searching, as I am, for that glamour, fun, romance and love in a November drizzle among soulless, characterless streets built by soulless, characterless town planners. The stench of the mess is overpowering.

I've allowed way more time than I really need and I've about half an hour to kill. I spot a mags and fags-type establishment, just off my route, and wander in, hoping to while away a few minutes by browsing at the mags. A grey-haired man of Asian appearance stands by the Pot Noodle department asking if he can help me. No, just looking, thank you. I pick a TV listings magazine at random and study its contents. I see they're starting a rerun of Ted Rogers' *321* on Challenge next Friday. Worth watching if it's one of those where the couple win nothing but a dustbin, if only to see the looks on their faces. But I think I'll pass on tag wrestling from Connecticut at half past two on Sunday morning. And I decide not to send a good luck card to the latest actress to be written out of *EastEnders* especially as "although we can't tell you what happens, we can't rule out a return for her character in years to come." I close the magazine but it's as if I've been robbed of the ability to apply my muscles to the task of replacing it in its rack and it's in an almost robotic state that I wander over to the grey-haired man, present the magazine to him and then shuffle out of the store before he can ask me whether I'm wanting to buy it.

I take a deep breath. I try to tell myself nothing has happened, nothing may happen and even now it's not too late to ensure nothing will happen. But the noise from the opposition party, the party which tells me that if nothing does happen I'm looking out across a deep, dry pit of empty loneliness instead, shouts it all down.

I've run out of any other possibilities for pre-match entertainment but it's still not even twenty to eight. I don't want to be early. Really don't. It was one of the first rules I learnt about dating. Too early is too keen. I decide on the simple expedient of walking at half my normal pace. But there's something inside me that seems to want to fight it. Doesn't help that it's downhill almost all the way. It's no good. I'm going to be getting there early and that's the end of it.

Slimwood Parade has nothing on the face of it to justify its name. There's certainly nothing or nobody on parade. No shops, no square, nothing. And I see no slender stretch of trees. It's just another residential street, like the multitude of residential streets around it, with two long rows of closely-packed brick terraced properties looking out onto lines of double-parked cars and vans. It's striking only in its extreme ordinariness.

I make my way up the street. I'm not alone. There's someone else, a woman, walking the street but she appears to be absorbed in her phone. It's seven minutes to eight when having walked a hundred yards along the street, and being guided by the harsh street lighting, I find myself at a door of peeling and faded yellow with the number 88 hand-painted on the door in peeling and faded red. On the right-hand side of the door, there are two long white buttons, one above the other, the bottom labelled GF, the top FF.

I just stand there for a while. I'm not going to press the button a second before eight o'clock. Assuming I resolve to let the madness in, these are my final seven minutes of sanity. But even within those minutes, I feel fear. I smell fear. I can even taste the fear. Fear to the left of me, fear to the right of me, fear within me. Fear of what it means if I walk through the faded yellow front door. Fear of what it means if I turn my back on it.

Then I push the button labelled GF.

Nothing. No answer.

I push the button again. No answer.

Perhaps I've misread the text and she lives in the first-floor flat. So I push the button labelled FF. No answer.

Perhaps the mechanism's broken. So I knock. I can feel the door move in response to the knock and I daren't knock any harder for fear the door will come away from its hinges and smash to the ground.

So I phone.

'Hallo?' Her answer. A slurred, lazy hallo.

'Li? It's Matt. I'm outside.'

'Outside?'

'Your flat.'

'Wait, is that the time. It's not is it, oh, look, listen, I'm sorry, right, I'm sorry, sorry.'

'Where are you?'

'Dog and Partridge.'

'Where's that?'

'Uh?'

'I said where's that?'

'Clayton Street...listen, you know what, I'm so sorry, I'm really sorry. I just...I...you know what...sorry, sorry...'

'Clayton Street? Is that near?'

'Yeah, not far. Not far at all. Not that far. Listen, yeah, I'm sorry, right...'

'How far?'

'Two, three minutes away.'

It may be two or three minutes by car but not on foot. It's at least fifteen minutes, this time it's uphill all the way, and there are at least another six Slimwood Parade clones that have to be negotiated first. And then when I have negotiated them I wish I hadn't. The Dog and Partridge makes the Half Moon seem like the Ritz. It looks as though it received its last coat of paint to commemorate the accession to the throne of the Queen. Victoria. From the odour in the so-called lounge bar it seems clear that the landlord regards the ban on smoking in closed public places as just something that applies to other people. The colour of the carpet is something I wouldn't have expected to see outside the walls of H Block at the height of the dirty protests. And by the expression on the barman's face you'd think he's either expecting an imminent Martian attack or is one digit out on a Euromillions jackpot.

I look around me and it's clear that one thing the management don't have to worry about, well not tonight at any rate, is overcrowding. Three men sit round a table, their eyes fixed on their phones, none of them saying a word. A middle-aged woman in a puffa jacket capacious enough to conceal most of the Isle of Man converses by the fruit machine with a slightly younger woman who sports a red boob tube and short white skirt, her heavily varnished toes poking out of matching white sandals with stiletto heels. And there's a man, in his twenties at a guess, who with stubble-encrusted face stands draped over the bar in mid-mutter, while lengths of wire extend out of his ears and somewhere into the interior of his hooded jacket.

And then I see Lisa-Marie. She sits in a corner of the lounge bar on a low sofa with a narrow table in front. Her hair's lost its joyful frizziness and has more grease than John Travolta. She wears an olive-green vest top with her bra straps on show underneath, and she's teamed the aforesaid vest top with light grey jogging pants and scuffed green trainers. She's not alone. Seated next to her, to her left on the sofa, is a man who looks roughly her age, dressed in a fleecy black top, blue tracksuit bottoms and scuffed black trainers. His skin is dark, and both his physical appearance and his accent as he exchanges words with her suggest he may be of West Indian origin. But what strikes me about him more than anything is a great mop of brown hair, lots of it, crammed onto the top of his head. It's a one-man ecosystem. It's enough for a whole Sunday night series with David Attenborough. His right arm extends so that it's behind Lisa-Marie's neck. There's no overt intimacy between them but there's certainly contact between their reclining bodies. As I approach he draws his right hand back then follows the example of the phone students and transfers his attention to his own electronic comfort blanket. On the table in front of him there's a quarter-full bottle of Smirnoff. He puts the phone down then picks up the bottle and takes a swig from it. Then he replaces the bottle and slumps back onto the sofa.

Lisa-Marie doesn't move in response to my coming to her. I crouch down to her level and we engage in a clumsy embrace. Then she shifts across the sofa to make room for me on the right-hand end. The effect is that she's now sitting in the middle and she and her companion are closer still.

'I kind of thought you were cooking for me,' I say to her.

'Oh yeah. You know what, I'm sorry, sorry, s...s...so sorry. Look, listen, we could go get some Chinese. Plate of chips. Whatever.'

She leans towards the Smirnoff guzzler who's grabbed the bottle again, apparently ready for another intake.

'Hey,' she says, 'gimme the bottle, you pig, s'not yours.'

And a moment later she's snatched it from her companion as a starving tigress might seize a piece of meat from her mate. Her eyes are wild, her focus on the alcohol in front of her scarily intense. She takes a gulp, then brings the bottle to the table and slaps it down so that the remaining liquid dances and spins and cavorts within the wall of glass. 'Sorry. Not introduced you. This is Jazz. Jazz, Matt, Matt, Jazz.'

I find myself reaching across her to shake hands with him. He mutters something inaudible. He doesn't smile.

'Jazz is a mate,' Lisa-Marie explains. 'Good mate. Really good mate. Really fu… Ooh, sorry, nearly swore there, mustn't swear in front of Matt The Lawyer or he'll get upset and I go to jail cos I'm a bad person.' The last two words are delivered twice as loudly as those preceding them. But every word is running haphazardly into the next like out-of-control vehicles on a patch of ice. 'Cos I drink and take lots of drugs. Drugs and drugs and drink and drugs and drink and more drugs. And I hurt people and get hurt myself and all my kids get taken away and it's cos I'm this really bad person, if that makes sense.' She digs me in my ribs. 'You know judges are lawyers, right.'

'Er, yes, that's right.'

'Are you a judge?'

'No,' I say. 'I'm not senior enough. I wouldn't want to be a judge.'

'Oh dear, have I put my foot in it? I have, haven't I, cos I'm like, you're a judge and you aren't, oh, sorry, sorry, sorry, look, listen, you know what, just ignore me okay.' Each word, each syllable, not just colliding with the next, but ricocheting and banging into the one behind. 'Anyway I think you'd make a great judge.' She grabs the bottle and empties its remaining contents down her throat in two more gulps. 'And then you could be my judge, and you'd be like, Lisa-Marie, she's not really a bad person, she's actually a nice person, too nice to send to jail, so we'll just give her a slap on the…slap on the…oh, wait, what is it, slap on the…'

Then she belches.

I've never been a belcher. With me it tends to come out the other end. I have known some people who belch, but their emissions of wind are always discreet and the reaction is usually one of embarrassment. Not with Lisa-Marie. Her belch has the discreet quality of a charge of wildebeest.

Everyone in the lounge bar falls silent. Then there's an explosion of laughter. Laughter that seems to cause the walls of the Dog and Partridge to shake. Laughter that goes on long after the thing has ceased to be funny.

I wait till normality is restored. Then I turn my head to my left.

'Listen, Li,' I say to her. 'I don't think I...' And I really don't know what I'm expecting to say next in order to finish that sentence. But there's no shortage of candidates is there, Matt. Don't think you should ever have thought you could pull this off successfully. Don't think you ever really stood a chance of getting this damaged woman to operate on your wavelength, to your set of values. Don't think you belong here. Don't think you realise how good Emma really is for you, how it's not too late to put the love back into your relationship. Don't think you can't start this process right now. Starting with the next bus home...

'Don't think you what?' she says, slamming the bottle back on the table.

I get up. 'I'll call you,' I say.

'Don't you wanna Chinese?' she demands.

I shake my head and mutter a negative. But I don't look at her. I walk straight out of the lounge bar and back onto the street.

The drizzle's got heavier. I can feel it and I can see it by the streetlights. A keen breeze slaps the branches of a nearby soggy-leaved silver birch. Even though it'll be downhill most of the way, I can't face trudging back to the bus stop. It'll have to be a cab.

It's a long time since I last needed a taxi and I can't find any cab numbers stored in my phone. I've no wish to linger round here but multitasking's never been a strength of mine and the need to fiddle with my device compromises my ability to proceed as rapidly as I would have liked. And suddenly I'm aware of footsteps behind me, steps much faster than mine. The footsteps get louder and moments later, as I get level with a brick wall to my right, there's a bang on my left shoulder.

I turn to my left and Lisa-Marie's sofa companion, Jazz, is standing there. He holds a glass bottle in his left hand. It looks very much like the same one he and Lisa-Marie were drinking from just now.

'What you playing at, bruv,' he mumbles.

'Sorry?'

'The way you walk out like you do. Disrespect. Where are your manners, man.'

He's gazing into my eyes, his face poised no more than six inches from mine. With the wall directly behind me, there's nowhere to run. Every bone inside me is rattling. 'I'm sorry,' I say.

'You what?'

'I'm really sorry.'

'I thought you's a lawyer, man,' he says. 'You is a lawyer, huh?'

'Mmm hmm.'

'Then you's a man of big words, impress the judges and the juries.'

I say nothing.

'Well aren't you?'

I nod. Safer not to disagree. 'I suppose,' I say.

'Then why you's saying only sorry? Sorry, sorry, sorry. You wanna defend yourself more than that, man.'

There's no pride left in me to destroy. 'I'm scared.'

'You scared of me man?'

I nod once more.

'You right to be scared of me.'

He throws the bottle to the ground. It smashes. Before I can react, he's picked up a piece, a piece with edges sharp enough to pierce the skin of a brontosaurus. Then with his right hand he's grabbed me by the shirt collar and yanked me back up against the wall. And with his left hand he's brought the piece of glass towards me.

I'm pinned. I can't move. I try to move but I can't.

Time stops. So often I've speculated what, when, how, why, where my last hour might be and what I might do when I reached it. But now this guy Matt, who stopped believing the moment his mum disappeared into the churchyard of St Margaret's, has no idea what he's supposed to do or think next.

'Nobody disrespects Jazz,' he whispers.

He's still gripping my collar. I can see the glass coming closer. It must be no more than three inches from my Adam's apple.

I'm going to die.

I scream.

Then above my scream I hear a smash.

He points to the ground and I can see a fresh array of glass fragments lying at our feet. Then he shows me his empty left hand.

'I...I thought you were going to kill me.' I can feel tears beginning to course down my face.

Still keeping hold of my collar he pulls me away from the accumulation of wreckage. The shards of broken glass crunch beneath the soles of my size 10's.

'Listen man,' he says. 'One word of this to the cops and I go to your boss and tell him about you and Lisa-Marie. I tell him you's overfamiliar and you, out on your ear, then you's not the big clever lawyer any more, you get me?'

'Yes, I get you.'

'Now go. Run. I never wants to see you again.'

He jerks me forward and releases his grip.

I start to run. To sprint. Twice, three times my normal running speed. I reach the end of the road and plough on along Folkington Avenue and down Alciston Rise. I don't know where I'm heading and what's going to happen, but I'm telling myself that for now I should just separate myself from the scene as quickly as humanly possible. Keep on running and somehow it will turn out all right. Alciston Rise gets steeper and steeper on its descent, and I'm going faster and faster, unable to find a way of slowing the pace, and then there's an uneven paving stone and my foot catches the edge. I feel as if my whole body's been lifted from the ground and I'm flying. Then in what seems like minutes but is maybe just half a second I'm coming in to land and, with my forehead taking the brunt, my eleven-stone frame crashes to the floor with the force of what seems like a thousand earthquakes.

3

It's not enough to knock me cold. My head's hurting but the pain isn't unbearable and I'm still aware of what's around me. Only I'm not sure that I can trust myself to get up and walk on without bits of my body coming away from the rest of me and dropping onto the pavement. So for a while I lie there in a morass of indecision.

There may be streetlamps nearby but the night feels thicker than the complete works of Proust. A drizzle is continuing to waft down from the November night sky while a pall of mist has created an impenetrable barrier between the earth and the stars. In the night and the drizzle and the mist there's only silence. Nobody comes. Nobody passes.

I make my decision. To try and lever myself up and then take stock of the situation. See if I'm able to move meaningfully from this spot.

With pain coming from muscles in my body I never knew I had, I'm able to get up onto my feet.

Seconds later I'm crumpling back onto the floor. And this time I've made contact with something sharp and piercing and digging right into the palm of my right hand. It could be broken glass, it could be a nail, it could be a fragment of a pranged motor vehicle, but whatever it is, it makes me scream.

It's an involuntary scream. It's not a conscious cry for help. Even if it were it would have been wasted. For as the echo of that scream disappears into the muck of the night, it's not elicited as much as one pair of rushing footsteps.

I need my phone. But it's in my back pocket and I simply haven't the strength to undertake the manoeuvring necessary to prise it out.

This next scream will be a cry for help.

But as I gear myself up to wake not only the good residents of Alciston Rise but yak-herders in the Khangai Mountains of Mongolia, I hear the sound of squelchy, rubbery soles on damp concrete. They're building in volume. I glance upwards, and by the light of the nearby streetlamp I see a woman approaching. I can tell she's seen me and moments later she's standing over me. I guess she's in her early sixties. She's wearing a long dark coat, her greying curly hair largely but not wholly concealed beneath its hood. Small beads of sweat rest on her age-worn cheeks and neckline.

She doesn't bother with pleasantries. She cuts to the chase.

'Can you move?'

'I can try. With your help.'

She may be smaller than me but she's generously built and is able to support my weight as I haul myself onto my backside.

'How did it happen? Someone done this to you?'

'I fell. I was running and I tripped.'

'I'll get you an ambulance.'

'Honestly, no. I'll be fine.'

'You won't be fine if I don't get you an ambulance.'

And I remember nothing more until I wake up in St George's Hospital.

*

She's there beside me when I come round. Her name's Lorrie. L-O-R-R-I-E, she tells me. Short for Lorraine. Lorraine McEwan. But everyone calls me Lorrie, she says. Despite her Caledonian name her accent's south London. Apparently she'd watched as I was lifted into the ambulance, and she'd held my hand as I was wheeled into A & E. And she says she's been sitting with me ever since I lost touch with the world in general and the joys of Alciston Rise in particular. She tells me that she and the staff have between them have managed to get in touch with Emma. Emma in turn has said she's on her way, and will be with me as soon as she can.

My injuries actually aren't that bad. They don't require operating on. I'd call it discomfort rather than searing pain. Most of the discomfort is to my head, my neck and my right hand. I'll be staying here tonight and if there's no change for the worse by the morning I'll be able to go home then and recuperate there. The doctor I've spoken to has asked me what happened. Above the sound of the clatter of the trolleys as the nurses did their evening rounds, I've explained I was simply running for a bus and caught a loose paving stone. In the absence of witnesses there's nothing or nobody to refute that.

But when Lorrie and I are alone she asks me if it's true.

There's no fight left in me. My defences have been blown to fragments. I tell her everything. And as I tell her, the tears are dribbling across my cheeks.

Now Lorrie's putting an arm around me. She's doing more than that. She's folding me in an embrace. I know she won't tell on me and the truth can stay confined within whispering distance of my bed.

*

In due course Emma arrives. As she does so, Lorrie says she has to go. She gives me her number in case I want or need anything from her. I tell her I'm sure I'll be fine. She introduces herself to Emma, explains who she is and why she's been with me, then goes off. Now it's just Emma and me.

She kisses my cheek and places a fleeting hand on my arm.

'Thank you so much for coming,' I say.

'I'm still your wife,' she replies. Businesslike. Matter of fact. 'How are you feeling?'

'I'm okay,' I say. 'They're just going to keep me in tonight then I'll be able to go home tomorrow.'

'Good,' she says. There's no smile. No warmth. Not a whiff of sincerity. Throwaway is nearer the mark.

She sits down on the bedside chair. 'So how come you got such a bang? Were you running?'

'Mmm hmm.'

'Why?'

'For a bus.'

'From the police station?'

'Mmm hmm.'

I sense a trap but maybe my head isn't right because I can't work out how to avoid it. It's wrong-footed me.

'You were never at the police station, were you, Matt.' Her voice is low in volume, respectful of the surroundings. But the lack of decibels is more than made up for in sheer intensity.

Thing is, though, she can't prove it. Only Lorrie can. And

she won't tell anyone. I have to keep spinning the web. Have to. 'I was.'

She looks around her. It so happens that at this particular time there are no others in sight: no other patients or medical staff. And having looked around her, she's now upping the vocal power. 'Think hard about this next bit, Matt. I'll try again. You're weren't at the police station. Were you.'

'I just said I was.'

'So if I showed you a video of your walking up Slimwood Parade in Brighton and standing outside number 88 you'll be able to tell me that's someone else altogether. Just happens to look quite like someone we both know.'

And suddenly there are no words.

'You're thinking, how does she know,' she says. She's staring straight out across the ward, not engaging with my eyes at all.

Still no words.

'My new hours, Matt. The ones I told you about when you were on the train. I guessed you couldn't hear. Or weren't listening.'

I'm waiting for the storm to break and it's worse in some ways than the storm itself. A nurse chooses this moment to come and, begging my pardon for interrupting, to ask if I need another pillow or a hot or cold drink. I manage the merest shake of the head. Then the nurse disappears and it's just us two again.

'You mean you were at home yesterday afternoon,' I say.

'Little tip, Matthew, darling. You ought to take your phone into the bathroom with you. Silly leaving it unattended where anyone might find it.' Then a smile. Rather, a patronising smirk. The smirk of the poker player with all the cards.

Please Emma, just get on with it.

Still she smirks and says nothing.

I've a choice. I can feign a sudden relapse and hope Emma will show a collector's item hint of humanity and either call back the nurse, postpone the inquisition or both. Or I can beg for mercy.

In fact there's no choice. For before I've even sorted out the relative merits of each option in my brain, my mouth's done the deciding for me.

'Ems, nothing happened. I swear. It was a stupid mistake. I see that now. Really, nothing happened. It's all over. She was a nightmare. I could never bear to look her in the face again. I'm sorry. I'm so, so sorry.'

And at last the main event. 'Do you really think that makes it all right?' she cries. There are flames of anger in each syllable and I can feel them licking at every square inch of the ward around me. I expect the conflagration to prompt, if not the clangour of the fire alarms, then at least an invasion of medical staff. But it seems they've had a better offer. It's still just us.

I shake my head. 'Not really, no.'

'For heaven's sake, I'm not stupid. You've just lied to me. Lied. One lie after another. You exchanged texts with this girl and you went to her wanting more. Too bad it didn't work for you but there it was. You wanted it, were prepared to get it. Veggie lasagne, wasn't it? And whatever it was you had planned for afters. Right?'

I say nothing.

'I'll ask again. Right?'

I manage the faintest of nods.

'Do you care so little for me?' She's still seated but now she swings her body towards me and looks straight into my eyes.

'Of course I care for you,' I say. 'But there just seems to be so little love between us these days. Yes, I wanted some love, and there was someone who I thought could give it to me. It was stupid. I've been stupid. Look. I see this as our wake-up call. It's not too late. I want us to try again.'

'Oh yes, try again now the bit on the side's proved to be such a washout.' She sighs and taps the fingers of her left hand on the bedpost. 'Listen. I need a moment, okay.'

Now she gets up from the chair and wanders away down the ward out of sight.

I dare to hope that she's giving herself some thinking time, and that she's going to be persuaded I deserve a second chance. It's something I argue in court on behalf of many of my clients. He or she deserves another chance. Of course they've had a hundred another chances previously so I never expect to be believed. But this is different. This is me. I'm a first offender.

I've never strayed before. I'm stuck in a hospital bed. I deserve sympathy. I don't deserve condemnation.

But as my granddad used to say, you don't get what you deserve. You get what you get.

The nurse has returned to my bedside. She may not have heard my conversation with Emma, but she seems to sense that it's not okay. That I'm not okay. She renews her offer of pillow and liquid refreshment as if that'll make it all okay. I shake my head. She asks if the pain's got worse. I can't fault her bedside manner. I just don't need it. I shake my head again. She goes away and I'm on my own in the half-light with the sound of the clatter of trolleys, the smell of disinfectant mixed with floor polish, and the all-pervading aura of institutionalism. Of being in a place nobody would ever ask to be or want to be.

Suddenly I'm tired. Crazily tired. My whole body is now expressing its discontent. My right hand, which took the full force of my second crash to the ground, is grumbling. My left leg is having a whinge. And my head is contemplating a letter to the *Daily Mail*. I'm too tired even to weep for the pain. I don't even know if Emma's coming back. I guess there's nothing to lose by trying to sleep. I pull the covers over my head and lie there. Lie there for goodness knows how long. But as far as entering the Land of Nod is concerned, my online visa application has been rejected.

Then I hear footsteps getting louder and I pull back the covers to see Emma coming towards me. This time she sits on the bed and looks straight at me.

'I'm sorry, Matt. I really am.'

She doesn't look sorry. She doesn't sound sorry. 'What do you mean?'

'I've had to forgive so much. So much. But I can't forgive this.'

'What are you saying?'

'What do you think.'

'Look.' I take her hand. Willing her not to snatch it away. She doesn't. 'I've been an idiot, okay. It was wrong. So wrong. All wrong. And the second I realised it was wrong I got out. Don't you want to know how I got hurt?'

She shrugs.

57

'Her mate, she had this mate, after I've left he's come after me. He's held a broken piece of bottle up to me. I really thought he was going to cut my throat with it. And I ran. Ran as fast as I could. And I tripped and fell. Lost consciousness. Ended up here. So you see. I've been punished.'

'All right, so you have. But it doesn't change a thing. Whether you got your end away or not, whether you got hurt or not, that isn't the point, is it.'

'Can't we just call it a idiotic mistake? Move on from there?'

'We're moving on all right.' And now she does take her hand away. She's still sitting on the bed but she's staring out into space.

'Sorry?'

Her voice quietens and her pace slows. 'I've been doing a lot of thinking lately, Matt,' she says. 'Wondering if I'm to blame in some way for how things are between us. Keep coming back to the same conclusion. I hate having to say this, Matt, but...'

'Tell me.'

Now her eyes are filling with tears. 'And you won't want to hear this, and it'll probably hurt you like hell, but I'm going to say it, and I should have said it ages before, and if I had...oh, look, I'm useless at this, but...'

'Tell me. Please tell me.'

'It's you, Matt. You're selfish. Completely selfish.' She emits a sigh as deep as the Grand Canyon. 'There. I've said it. And I mean it. I'm sorry but I mean it. You don't care about anybody but you. You look after number one all the time. Okay. You're not lazy. You're motivated and I like that about you. You're good at what you do. Or you seem to be. But you just live in a big bubble. You never really care about anything or anyone else. Certainly never care about what I want.' The last few syllables disintegrate amidst the sobs.

'I don't think that's quite fair, darling.' I take a tissue from the box by my bed and pass it to her. 'I can think of times when I've asked you what you've wanted and I've done my best to...'

'I'm not talking about going out for meals or drinks down

58

the pub or where we go on holiday.' She gives her eyes a perfunctory wipe with the tissue, throws the tissue down and stands up, folding her arms. Her eyes are now fixed on the ceiling. 'I mean things that matter. Long term. Matter to me. Matter to us. Or should matter to us.'

I don't need to ask her what she means by that.

'Listen, darl,' I say. I take her hand again. She doesn't try to struggle free but she's still not looking at me. 'I accept I may have tried putting you off starting a family. I did understand that you might want....'

'Oh, for crying out loud, why do you have to talk like a flaming lawyer all the time.' And now she does snatch her hand from mine, and the fire returns to her voice. '"I accept, I did understand."' Now she's pacing round the bed, her arms folded. 'That's half your problem, Matt. You live in your own world and think you can get by in it by hiding behind your legalese and your cold legal logic. It brings out the worst in me, I know that. Because each time you do it it makes me want to knock you down, prick your balloon, belittle you. I'm the loser so you may as well lose as well. I wasn't sure till tonight. Was always wondering, hoping that maybe we had a future if only you could be bothered to work for it. And work at it. But now you've done this, I'm afraid there's nothing left. Nothing.' She stops pacing and looks towards me. 'I'm leaving you, Matt. I know it's a crap time for you but when's it ever going to be a good time. I'm going home to pack all my stuff then I'm going to mum and dad till I can sort out a place of my own. I'm taking the car. I'm sure they'll sort a cab for you when you're ready to go.'

*

After she's gone I try to get some sleep but for a long time I can't. The pain on its own isn't keeping me awake but I can't help reliving, over and over again, all that's happened since leaving the office last night and if anything's going to make my head start throbbing again it's the memories that those hours have triggered. And now, at two in the morning, six hours after my marriage-wrecking campaign took off, I'm the one in need

59

of the tissues. Then, far too late for my liking, nature takes over.

I feel my appetite coming back as breakfast appears and I manage a bowlful of Shreddies and a slice of toast. I'm also able to get hold of the office and call in sick. One of the nurses asks if I'm okay to get home. I tell her I quite fancy a walk but she says that's not a good idea and suggests that if I can't get a lift I should, like Emma said, take a cab. But somehow the thought of being dumped outside my now empty house by a stranger feels worse than making the whole journey on foot. Then I remember Lorrie. The one who found me. The one I could confide in. The one I could cry with. The one who offered me further help if I needed it. The one who cared.

She's there with her car soon after nine. I explain everything that's happened and she insists not only on driving me home but seeing me indoors. She says in other circumstances she'd stay with me longer and make sure I was properly okay, but she has other commitments so she can't. She offers me what she says is a very poor second best, namely the promise of a friendly and sympathetic telephone voice if I need one. In the meantime she checks there are people I can talk to if I want, and tells me to go back to the hospital or my GP if I start feeling unwell again. Then she embraces me and in the love and warmth of that embrace I remember what it was like to have a mum. I've not had that feeling since mum slipped away from us.

As Lorrie's leaving I suggest coffee and cake in town on Saturday as a thank you. She tells me she'd love that, but she's going to be tied up pretty much all of this weekend so can we make it next Saturday the 17th instead. I ask where in town she'd like to go. 'Come round to me,' she says. 'It's cheaper.' I tell her that wasn't really the point and I was wanting to treat her. She tells me my company will be the treat.

*

I've never been a lazy person. Nor a particularly untidy one. So it's no great shock to be faced with the cooking and the cleaning, the washing and the ironing. I can do all that. I could never do it to Emma's standards, but I can still do it. I can cope with fiddly little plumbing jobs and suchlike, and I've always managed our household finances. The practical side of things is fine.

What isn't fine over these early days of separation is the silence when I get home, assuming absence of Glastonbury-esque racket from next door. It's the silence of singlehood. The silence that accompanies getting in from whatever I've been doing, closing the door behind me, and finding myself alone. Before Emma and I got together I could handle that silence. Now it scares me. Perhaps that's because with it comes a feeling that nobody in the world actually minds or cares what I'm going to do once I am home. I don't do community things, voluntary work, amdram, choirs, residents' associations. I've always said I'm too young for all that. As for leisure interests, yes, I run, and I cycle, but neither of those have any great appeal after dark. Beyond a liking for a good TV drama, which hardly counts, I've never been one for indoor pursuits once I've put my clients down for the night. In some ways now I'm wishing I was. There was this guy at school who was into stamp collecting. It was an absolute obsession of his. I was one of the nasty kids who taunted him. I remember telling him he'd be sorry when he grew up with nothing more exciting to look forward to after work than applying his tweezers to a specimen from Gabon, and only then it dawned on him that everyone else had a life except him. As Spooner might have put it, I had him down as the last warring banker in town. Yet I heard recently he was married to a fashion designer, living in one of the posher London suburbs and about to become a father for the third time. If he were to bump into me tomorrow he'd be asking me who's the warring banker now.

I've rung dad, of course. I spoke to him almost as soon as I got home following my discharge from hospital, and I've called him over the weekend as well. I don't tell him about the events that led to my hot date with the paving stones of Alciston Rise. I just tell him I was running for a bus. He's not good on the deep stuff but says all the right things as I knew he would. Shame about Emma but maybe it's good for you both to have some time apart, decide what's best in the long run. You're old enough and sensible enough to know what you're doing. Any time you want a Yorkshire-shaped break, it's just a phone call away. And go back and take a photo of that paving, and send it to the council. You never know, there may be a bit of compo for you there.

But even as I speak with dad and he's filling my head with positivity, and all the stuff I need and want to hear, I know this is still only the honeymoon period.

With so much silence around me, I'm thinking back more and more now to Jazz. Did he really mean to kill me. Was he capable of killing. Had he killed before. If he was intending to kill me, what was it that stopped him. For hours and hours on the Sunday after it all happened, I'm thinking, what would it have been like to die. To not quite quote from Old Man River, I may be tired of living but I'm scared as hell of dying. Then I find myself singing snatches from that song, and those words in particular, over and over again, and I can't seem to make it stop and that's scaring me even more.

I agree with Danny that I'll do some of his 24-hour police station duty shifts, both general duty and own client, hoping these will help fill some of the silence and concentrate my mind on other things. It'll also bring in some extra cash, which I'll certainly need when Emma bless her decides to start tightening the screws, assuming that's the way it's going. So here I am on my first extra shift, willing one of our regulars to get out and effect a ram-raid on a jewellery shop or two, and then turn themselves in. But on this particular shift, not one would-be client succeeds in attracting any interest from the good old boys and girls in blue. Day turns to evening turns to night, and I'm lying sleeplessly in bed with nothing to quell the noise of that silence.

Amid the silence, fear is starting to claw its way in. Fear around Lisa-Marie. Owing to the decline in workload Danny's paranoid about any potential client slipping through our fingers. If we pick one up as duty solicitor at the police station or at court, he'll be wanting us to make sure that they sign up with us and that we see their case through to conclusion. Lisa-Marie's a case in point. I've picked her up as the duty solicitor and it's a potentially excellent earner for us. All the time things stay as they are, I'm safe. If the police decide to take no further action I'm safe. But if she's to be re-interviewed or charged and taken to court, well, that's when it'll emerge whether or not she's shopping elsewhere. Now I'm sure Lisa-Marie didn't mean it when after the re-interview she said she was sacking me. Even if she didn't, though, there's no reason why she might not have decided to vote with her feet and instruct someone else. And if she has done, Mr Latte Breath is likely to want to know why. I dare say I can concoct an innocent-sounding reason why. But even if he swallows that, it won't be the end of it. I can see it now because he's been through the same routine before. Several times. He'll pull up a chair next to me and sit himself down on it the wrong way round. I don't know if he got that pose out of some third-rate American middle management manual or if he's been watching too much of Ricky Gervais on UK Gold. I suspect the latter. For, like Ricky Gervais' David Brent, he clearly thinks he can be all things to all men, the manager and at the same time the friend, the Obergruppenfuhrer and budding bromancer, the businessman and amiable buffoon. He'll kick off with a pleasantry and enquiry about my well-being. Then will come the homily in which he'll express his disappointment vis-à-vis the lost client, and his fear that if we continue to lose clients we'll lose the criminal department. He'll cite the closure of the family department two years ago because it wasn't paying its way. "And that was damaging to us in crime because when our existing family clients took their family business elsewhere their crime went with it," he'll say. "Makes sense for one firm to be doing the lot. Once one piece of the edifice falls away, other parts can so easily start crashing down as well." Yes, thank you Danny, I know the script pretty much off by heart. Then another squelchy handshake, or, if I'm really unlucky, a ruffling of my hair, and back to work again..

But supposing Lisa-Marie does want to stay with us. It won't just be a hot potato for me: it'll be a hot potato topped with double helpings of butter, melted cheese and coleslaw and half a hundredweight of baked beans. Granted, she might, throughout her dealings with our firm, remain the soul of discretion. The events immediately following the re-interview might remain a close secret between us. Jazz might be happy to stay out of the picture. As a result, the whole episode might go undiscovered by my delightful superior. But that's an awful lot of mights. I don't know what the collective name for several mights is but it only needs one of those mights to become a might not, and I'll be before the Ellman Rich People's Court being forced to explain to Reichsprotektor Letwin why the danglier parts of my anatomy should be allowed to remain attached to the rest of me

I know I should be telling Danny everything. I should be insisting that I did nothing Lisa-Marie didn't consent to and took no improper advantage of her or of her situation. But it's just like with Emma the other day because the right words won't come at the right time.

Then my thoughts turn to Emma. I've not entirely given up hope of her coming back. I get that if she doesn't want to, she doesn't want to. But I just want to know one way or the other. I've tried phoning and texting her but she won't answer, neither will her parents, and she's not contacted me at all. I've no idea whether that means she's having second thoughts or whether she's now been in touch with Rottweiler, Rottweiler & Rottweiler, with the muzzle manufacturers' strike into its tenth week, and the next thing I receive containing any input from her is going to be on their headed paper. "We look forward to hearing from you or, if it's easier, just sign everything over to us and we'll do the rest. Assuring you of our best attention at all times." Though at least such a letter would constitute proof of acknowledgement of my existence. As night turns to day and the week goes on, I'm beginning to wonder why I continue to exist at all. I'm dreading the phone going and Lorrie telling me she's got to cancel our coffee date on Saturday. The only reason for getting out of bed at the weekend snuffed out with a single snatch of Mozart's 40th Symphony in G minor. I never thought meeting a woman some twenty years my senior for a hot beverage in suburbia might be so precious. It's pathetic. It's just a few days in my life and I can't handle it.

I trudge home on the Friday evening and as I'm inserting my key in the lock the phone goes. It's got to be Lorrie. But no, it isn't Lorrie. It's dad. He and I may be in regular contact with each other but tend just to dwell on the banalities and trivialities: the cricket in Australia, the village art festival Karen's helping to organise, or the planning application he's just been copied into which if successful will soon have next door but two's garden swarming with alpacas and nanny goats. This evening he's ringing to invite me to Yorkshire to spend Christmas there. It's an easy answer. I know I'll be well looked after. I know dad will be kindness itself, continuing to say the right things just as often as I need to hear them. And I know that Karen will already be stirring the Christmas pudding mixture, will be blowing the dust off her grandma's trusted recipe that produces the best mince pies in the district with enough to go round until February the 15th, and will be eyeing up the assembly of blissfully unsuspecting free-range turkeys in the barn at Hambleton's Farm.

But it is, can only be, a temporary respite, and when it's over, it'll be back to the sound of silence of singlehood.

*

I've arranged with Lorrie to get to her house at eleven. I'm still without a car and I doubt if I'll be in a position to afford another one. I've used my bike on the two occasions this week I've had to go to the nick after the buses have stopped. I try to look on the positive side and tell myself it's a healthy option, though I'm not sure I want to make a habit of pedalling through monsoon conditions at three in the morning, particularly having regard to the dodgy state of my sprockets. I contemplate cycling this morning but following my exertions during the week I just can't face it, especially as I've flowers and a bottle for Lorrie to bring with me. Besides, the forecast is for it to start cold and get colder. In fact an early burst of the perennially wrong kind of snow can't be ruled out, and a dusting on the heights of the South Downs is certainly worth a flutter at Ladbrokes.

I go online to check buses. Only one bus service runs anywhere near Lorrie's, with two services each way per hour on Saturdays. The closest stop to her is a five-minute walk away, and a bus is due there at three minutes to eleven. I might get away with it. But with Brighton traffic being what it is, there's every chance that it may be delayed and not arrive till gone eleven, and I don't want to risk being late especially as Lorrie's told me she's going out for lunch. The bus before that is exactly half an hour earlier. I decide on that one and hope that I can do better at killing time than on the night I threw my marriage out of the window.

The bus decants me just short of the Redgate Road junction, beside a small parade of shops and eateries amongst which is a café, Coffee Unlimited. It looks, on the face of it, unlikely to feature in the next *Michelin Guide*. An A board parked outside offers FREE COFEE WITH ALL SANDWHICH'S 9-11. The smell coming from inside reminds me of the pong which I generated when, during my university days, I attempted to create what I believed to be a ground-breaking full English breakfast incorporating sweet-and-sour pork and grilled Turkish Delight. But now icicles are beginning to form on my hands and I need thawing out. I go in and order an Americano with hot milk, and sit down with it as close to the hot air blower as I can.

Despite the offer of free cofee, whatever that particular taste treat might be, precious few folk seem to be taking advantage. The functional wooden chairs and tables and the less than adventurous range of foodstuffs on offer suggest it to be a place where people come for a short sharp caffeine-and-cholesterol boost rather than as a happily anticipated and rewarding interlude in their busy lives. In fact of the eight tables, just three are occupied, each by lone individuals engaged in deep and meaningful interaction with their phones. One is a grey-haired man in a grey overcoat with a bowl of matching grey liquid in front of him. One is a lanky youth who despite the conditions outside sits in long shorts and flip-flops, taking occasional slurps from a can of Pepsi.

The other is a woman in, I would guess, her early thirties. She's roughly my height, maybe a little shorter. Not much. She sits at the window at right-angles to me. She has curly golden hair that ebbs and flows and tumbles to her shoulders, the gold of her locks complemented by the gold of her cheeks and her neckline. She wears a jumper whose shade of warm rich green is redolent of the exuberant leaves of a chestnut tree in May. Her legs are encased in jeans of soft blue denim over which are polished black flat-heeled knee-high boots. A leather-looking jacket covers the back of her seat. Her bag rests on her table.

I try to keep my eyes off her but I can't.

4

She puts her phone in her bag and I dare to hope that she might look around her and acknowledge my presence with a smile, however slight or fleeting or polite that smile might be. But she's gazing out towards the far wall, seemingly lost in herself. Her hands rest on the table in front of her and my eye is caught by the jewellery on her ring finger. The sparkle of the gold of the band and the stones that cluster together beside it would, given the right light conditions, spark off a sunglasses shopping spree all over Brighton.

Emma and I have been together so long that I've almost forgotten what it's like to don my tin hat and step out into the dating minefield. But I do remember that when I dated in my twenties, those women I set my sights on tended to come ring-free. Now the present-day reality is banging on the door. Here's this woman, the one whom I'm trying so hard not to fix my eyes on, seemingly happy enough to demonstrate her marital status to anyone who might care to look. Of course she may not be happily married. She may be miserably married. But the fact remains that someone else has got to her first. And she wants the world to know.

That's what it's going to be like Matt, so get used to it. Take this as your first valuable if not especially enjoyable lesson. If you're to restart this game, you've got to be prepared for the ones who you fall in love with at first sight to have already fallen in love themselves and to remain deeply in love. To have had the big wedding, the big marquee and the honeymoon in Mauritius, and now to have a great marriage, liberally sprinkled with sexual adventure you thought only existed after ten o'clock at night on Channel 4. To have produced at least one darling offspring and to have settled into one of Brighton's leafier suburbs with the most pressing concern facing them on leaving the house for the morning school run being whether they'll have time before work to check their twitter feeds.

I sit nursing my coffee and gazing at the clock, hoping that in the race for the former to lose any pretence at drinkability and the latter to reach five to the hour, the latter will romp home at seven to two. At least if you ask for a takeaway coffee you get a plastic lid which keeps the heat in longer even though it means the potential for a whole load more waste killing off a whole load more of our innocent sea creatures. As it is, it has to be the much more eco-friendly placing-the-saucer-over-the-top-of-the-cup routine. But it's not worked. The coffee wasn't piping hot to start with and if it stays unconsumed for even five more minutes it'll be attracting interest from ice-skaters. It's only just gone a quarter to eleven and I look down and my cup's empty. The maitre d' spots the empty vessel and is asking if sir wishes a refill.

The woman, the one with the golden hair and the gold band, has put on her jacket and is now making her way out. No smile. No acknowledgement. Brutal. But as Bruce Hornsby so rightly proclaimed, that's just the way it is. The way it may be for days, weeks, months, years, forever.

The offered refill isn't free and I say no to another cup and decide to make a move. Thus a choice presents itself, between walking slowly or arriving a bit early. It's Slimwood Parade all over again. Except this morning it's not really a choice: the cold will keep me moving fast however much I might want to dawdle. I leave the café and find myself walking past the bus stop. The same one at which I disembarked nearly half an hour ago.

The woman with the golden hair is standing on her own, presumably waiting for the bus, presumably the bus I'd originally thought I might get away with catching. As I make to walk past her, she looks straight into my eyes.

Harriet gets nowhere near it. Nowhere at all.

And from nowhere come words. My words. 'I hope your coffee was hotter than mine.'

She looks at me as though I'd just stepped off the set of *The Zombie Diaries 3*. 'Sorry?'

'Your coffee. In the café. I was there just now.' I point back to the establishment in question. 'Hope it was hotter than mine.'.

A glimmer of recognition wafts over her face. 'Oh. Yeah. Sorry. Miles away.'

She gazes past me. I turn and look in the same direction and realise she's looking up at the live information bus departure screen. Against the next advertised bus is the word DUE.

So that's it. Seconds, and that's if I'm lucky, to find some way of engaging with a woman who by the jewellery on her ring finger seems happy to tell the world that someone else has got to her first.

'Long journey?' I ask.

'Not that long.' And at that moment the bus draws up by the stop.

Now she smiles at me. 'Sorry. Got to...got to get on. See you.'

See you. As if. As if the person to whom it's directed is actually meant to believe it. No. That person stands there and watches as the person who says it boards the bus and without as much as a wave is whisked away into the pool of her own life, her own being, her own time and her own space.

Grow up, Matt. You didn't come out today to indulge in behaviour of sixteen-year-olds. You came out to recognise the kindness and love and selflessness of someone who came to your aid as a result of your...oh yes. Indulging in behaviour of sixteen-year-olds.

Enough.

*

I walk fast and it is exactly eleven when I find myself ringing Lorrie's doorbell. That bus, the one that carried the woman with the golden hair and the gold band out of my life, would have been just fine after all.

It's a modern detached house. You wouldn't call this the most sought-after part of Brighton but maybe it is sought after by those who want the space and the privacy but who haven't the dosh in the bank. As I reach the house I can see the grey tower blocks looming behind, as though poised, like in some sci-fi movie, to advance upon and then swallow up the more agreeable dwellings in their shadows. Both sides of the road are stuffed with cars and I can see they're not the latest models. But the street itself has little moving traffic and the thin green

69

verges are dotted with saplings. They may still be modest and diffident and vulnerable but I like them. I see in them a desire to create leafiness for future generations and also to provide some soul for those who pass by or get up to this each morning.

I ring the bell and a moment later the front door opens and there's Lorrie. Her face has the glow of a summer evening in Provence and her eyes could illuminate Sydney Opera House. Despite the cold outside she's dressed as though it were summer. Orange T-shirt, denim dungarees and black clogs. She gives me a hug. I can feel the love before even crossing the threshold and feel it even more as I come inside. Everything is warm, tidy, cared for. And to judge by the number of philosophical musings on plaques hanging from the wall in the entrance hall, starting on the left with SEIZE THE DAY right round to LIFE'S NOT ABOUT WAITING FOR THE STORM TO PASS, IT'S ABOUT LEARNING TO DANCE IN THE RAIN, it would seem she's single-handedly keeping the gift shops of Lewes and Alfriston in business. She takes the flowers and bottle and thanks me, then ushers me into her front room, and I sit down beside a coffee table on which is a tray with a jug of fresh coffee and another jug of steaming hot milk. There's also a cake which is another tower block but this one is a riotous tower block of what looks like a mix of strawberry and raspberry and lemon and chocolate and cream.

Lorrie disappears for a moment. I can tell she's walking around from the bang of her clogs on the floor. She returns with a bowl of sugar lumps. She moves a newspaper to make extra room on the coffee table, and appears to be about to sit down when I hear what sounds like a shrieking sound from another room.

'Sorry,' she says. 'Help yourself to coffee. I'll be back in a sec.'

Even on the carpet in the front room her clogs bang as they hit the ground and continue to bang as she walks away. There's more shrieking. I just sit there. I'm wondering if I should offer my assistance, but it's as if my bum's glued to the seat. That's me all over. Doing what Emma knew I did so wonderfully well. Staying in my own bubble. Letting someone else deal with whatever it is. Not getting involved.

The sound of banging clogs gets louder and Lorrie's back in the front room.

'I told you to help yourself,' she says. 'Can't have the coffee getting cold, can we?'

'I was...I was a bit worried for you,' I say.

It's left to her to pour the coffee and gouge two slices, one half the size of the other, from the mountain of sugar and saturated fat that lies in front of us.

'No need to worry,' she says. 'I've lived with it eight years. This is one of his better days.'

'His?'

'Jake. I'm his carer.' She hands me the plate which bears the larger slab of cake. 'I think you're going to need a fork, aren't you.'

'It's fine. I can manage.'

'Good luck.'

I try to pick up the slab with my fingers and it's only now that it dawns on me that the fork would have been the better option. Half of the mixture slips through my fingers and back onto the plate, while another substantial dollop, clearly opting for the softer landing, decides to make acquaintance with my trousers. And that leaves only a few token segments to find their way up to and then between my lips.

'I'll get you a fork,' she says.

She goes out and I hear another shriek. Before Lorrie told me what, or rather who, it was, I might have dared to hope it was perhaps a somewhat excitable family pet. The fact that the owner of the yell appears, from what Lorrie says, to be another human being serves to dull the tang of the flavours of my portion of the monster concoction before me. There's more banging of clogs. The shrieks get louder and more urgent. The last words I hear are Lorrie's. 'Stop it. Stop it, Jake.' Loud but not shrill. Clipped, brisk staccato. It seems to work. For now at least. The shouting stops.

Eight years.

There's further clog dancing and a moment later Lorrie appears with two forks. By now I've completed the clearing-up operation and save for some rogue crumbs which have somehow got lodged between my crotch area and the seat of my

71

chair, all the surviving pieces have been winched to safety. An immediate inquiry has been launched into the cause of the disaster and an assurance given that lessons will be learned.

For a few moments there's silence as we both work our way through the contents of our plates. It's Lorrie who finishes hers first.

'Lovely flowers, Matt. My favourites. You needn't have.'

I think back to the number of times my mum said that, or similar, when people gave things to her. You needn't have, she would say; you really shouldn't have bothered, I wasn't expecting anything. I see mum's eyes in Lorrie's. I'm beginning to see her heart in Lorrie's as well. For a moment I'm lost for words. Easier to let her talk.

'Tell me about Jake,' I say.

Lorrie laughs and looks at her watch. 'How long have you got, Matt,' she says. 'All right. The potted version. Jake is the son of some very good friends of mine. Both became very severely disabled. Mentally and physically. His mum died nearly four years ago, his dad's…well, I hate to say it, but basically he's a vegetable. Well, I don't know, nobody knows, quite, if there's some inherited condition, but Jake is very severely autistic. Right at the bad end of the spectrum. He's had it from a child. And it's got worse. Some children grow out of it, but not Jake. You name any of the worst symptoms of autism, he's got them all. Fixations on activities, tick. Lack of co-ordination and clumsiness, especially around inanimate objects, tick. Specific routines and rituals, double tick. And aggression, rage, noise…full house. All of which we could just about cope with. But for the other issue.'

'You mean there's more.'

'Just a little.' There's no self-pity, no anger, no resentment. She might be talking about the groceries she needs when she's next in town. She smiles as she talks. I can feel the smile in her voice as well as on her face. 'His fixation with routine means always wants to do things in a certain way at a certain time. And he had this routine of going down to the corner shop to buy a paper at exactly the same time each day. Had to be the same paper, so he mustn't be late or they might be out of it and nobody would ever hear the end of it. Well one morning, eight and a half years ago, he's running slightly late. Like about two minutes late. I think he'd had a mishap when he was shaving. Anyway he's determined not to be late to pick up his paper and he's walking a lot faster than usual. He gets to this road crossing and there's a van coming but he just walks straight out in front. Thinking the van will stop for him. They usually do. But this one doesn't.' She laughs. 'I'd always thought everything I'd heard about white van men was just a lot of baloney. But this was classic white van man. Never even slowed down.' She demonstrates the force of the impact by smashing her left fist against her right palm. Even the demonstration causes me to flinch backwards. 'Jake suffered very serious injuries. They're inoperable and he's stuck in a wheelchair. He can use his hands, which is a mercy, although even that is a struggle, but unless they can find a miracle cure, he'll never walk again. He's certainly not well enough to get around on his own. And his frustration just made his autism worse still. He was a very distinguished academic, brilliant lecturer, but he simply became impossible to work with, impossible to employ. So his career, his mobility, all that's gone now.' She sits back in the chair and shakes her head. 'And he never did get his paper, poor man.'

All the time she's talking I can feel the smile in her voice as well as on her face.

'So how did he end up with you?'

'My husband had done a disappearing act. Some floozy in Northampton. My children had left home. I was only working part-time and I was lonely. I suppose there's the cheesy bit as well, wanting to give back. And it was about this time that Jake's mum and dad became incapable of caring for him. So I volunteered. I've been a carer all my life, in various guises. I know it's a cliché, but I love people. I don't do books and clever stuff. My dad was a window cleaner and I went to the worst comprehensive in the south. I'm not educated. Pick stuff up as I go along, always have. I always knew I'd end up working with people, not computers or books or accounts. Anyway, Jake came to live here. That became my career, in effect. Or rather, he did. I get benefits for him, of course I do. He's comfortable, so am I. A lottery win would be nice, but till that day dawns, we muck along okay financially. On top of that, his mum left me a fair bit in her will but really more as a thank you rather than as financial provision. Money's not the problem. The problem is keeping him quiet. Keeping him happy. And that's a full-time job in itself.'

'Does anyone help you?'

'I do have lots of support, yes. There's this woman who'll care for him every Wednesday, and most weekends. His sister comes down but only if I'm desperate. She needs to be near her dad, and, I've got to say it, I can't stand her. She can be quite nasty. And I've got three or four other people to come and keep him company, take him out, or house-sit if I'm out or if I've wanted a few days' respite. There's one in particular. She's very good. She'll take him to this park where there's a little bird sanctuary and she gets him to identify all the different species. And on hot days they'll go to the beach. Loves sitting in his wheelchair on the pier with his Brighton rock. He's got such a sweet tooth. That'll be the next thing. His teeth all falling out.' She gazes down at the newspaper on the coffee table. 'I guess it's an ill wind. I've had to spend more time under my own roof then I ever thought I would. I've learnt basic DIY. Saved myself a fortune on handyman's bills. Can fix most things round the place. I succumbed and got a decent phone and spend a lot of time on that. Skyping my kids. You Tube. The dreaded social media. Never thought I would, but...and if I ever get bored there's always the Su Doku. I'm getting pretty good at it. And Wordsearch too. I think I'm running out of words to search for. May have found them all. Oh, and I belong to a choir. Meets Mondays. Can't always get along but I enjoy it when I go.'

'And Jake's had autism all his life?'

She nods. 'There was always something not quite right about him as a child. He was amazingly good in some subjects at school, dreadful in others. No co-ordination whatsoever. Got horribly bullied. His parents kept on having to change his school. He was a maverick. Quite normal in some respects but you only had to go a bit below the surface and you knew there was something different about him. Mostly not in a good way. But there are some things he's remarkably good at. You've just got to tap into the right part of his brain.'

74

I pick up my cup and down the remnants of my coffee. 'And there's no chance the autism can get better?'

'He's had enough people working on him, poor love. We got contacted by some specialist in Massachusetts who said he could cure him. Providing we could find the four billion dollars he was asking for. It was some pioneering treatment or other, it had a name which I can't remember other than I'd have got at least hundred points if I'd got it down in a game of Scrabble.' Another burst of shouting tears the air in half. 'I'm exaggerating. Wasn't quite as much as four billion. But it might as well have been. We tried a crowdfund appeal but that never got anywhere near it. We've been on local radio once or twice. Tried to raise awareness of how severe the condition can be. Trouble is, so many other deserving causes. Cancer, Parkinson's, MND...so many people wanting to cash in on other people's compassion. Has to stop somewhere.' She winces as a series of fresh shrieks get in amongst our earlobes. She rises from her chair. 'I think he knows I've got company. He hates that. He's worried it's going to mean things don't happen when they should. Routine, you see. He'll be good as gold once you're gone. Not that I want to hurry you away.'

'Don't you resent him for all the demands he makes?'

'You never resent the people you love, Matt.' For the very first time the smile in her voice fades. 'Excuse me. I won't be a mo.'

She goes out.

I should be sitting there filled with admiration for her self-giving, her loving acceptance of both her situation and his, and the way she sees Jake as a human being deserving and needing love and not just as an object of pity. But all I've taken is a polite interest, an interest demanded of me by the fact that she's helped me get back on my feet, has welcomed me into her home, and has now produced this edible timebomb for my delectation. And in a few minutes I'll be setting off for home, leaving it all behind me, with relief rather than loving empathy as the predominant sensation, probably the sole sensation, that trickles over my consciousness. It all comes back to you, Matt, doesn't it, and probably will always come back to you. It's how it affects you. You're not actually that interested or concerned in this man, are you, just mildly irritated that his yelling is putting you off your refreshment and is causing his carer to be stamping about the place like a Prussian army general on the eve of battle. And despite his carer having all mum's attributes and possibly even more, you wouldn't want to come back within a mile of her front door for fear of what he might do to you if he saw you with his own eyes.

I summon up enough decency to stack the used plates and cutlery and place it all on the tray with my empty coffee cup. There's still a little liquid left in Lorrie's but it looks stale and muddy and I add that to the tray too. Then I sit back down, pick up the newspaper and glance at it. Sure enough, it's open at the puzzle section. She's made good inroads into the Su Doku but the fact that she's got two 9's in the far left-hand column is going to come back to bite her at some point. Below the Su Doku is the bridge and chess. When I was in the IP section of Ellman Rich what now seems like decades back, there was a colleague who'd offer me his newspaper when he'd finished it, and I used to go straight for the chess puzzle. White to play and mate in however many moves against any defence. I usually got it right. A legacy of chess at school where I used to do rather well. We had matches against neighbouring schools and I was a regular on board 2. I think I only lost twice in a dozen matches. And seeing the bridge column in said newspaper always reminded me of mum who loved the game. She wasn't much good at it but she had the gift of refusing to take it seriously and I always thought that was the best attribute of all. She used to laugh when taken to task by one of her bridge friends for making a cockup in the bidding as she often did, confusing her Weak No Trump convention with her Geneva convention or whatever. And she wasn't much better when it came to playing the hand. "Always get your trumps out," she'd be told. "Under the railway arches of London you'll find crowds of bridge players who didn't get their trumps out." Considering that I think the most mum ever lost in an evening's competitive bridge was 68p, neither she nor I were ever too worried for our family's financial future. Not in that regard anyway. Back to the chess. This one, White to play and mate in four…

Lorrie's back again. I wonder whether to tell her about those two 9's. Something tells me not to. I smile at her and pop the paper back on the coffee table.

'You trying to fill in my Su Doku?' she says. 'That's a hanging offence in this house, I'll have you know.'

I shake my head. 'I was looking at the chess column.'

Lorrie's eyes, bright as they already are, seem to acquire even greater luminosity at the sound of those nine syllables. 'Do you play, Matt?'

'Not now, I don't.'

'But you did?'

'Used to be pretty good. Probably a bit rusty now.'

Still standing, she grips the shoulder straps of her dungarees and jiggles them around. She takes a deep breath. 'I wonder if you'd like to give Jake a game.'

I freeze. 'Um...'

And I'm sure she can tell I've frozen. She laughs.

'I don't mean today,' she says. 'But maybe if you could come again...'

I'm searching my mind for something, anything, that means I couldn't. 'The only thing is, Lorrie...' And I'm sure she can tell I'm searching. But this time I can't see her bailing me out. She's looking directly at me. She wears a slightly mischievous smile. She says nothing. I stumble on. 'I'm...I've got...likely to have a fair few Saturdays on call with work...'

'Doesn't have to be Saturdays, Matt. Could do a Sunday. Evenings good too. Thing is, I'm rubbish at chess. Jake mashes me every time. In fact I get so mashed I'm waiting for someone to come in with the bangers. It's not helping him. Sometimes he even gets shirty with me for not trying hard enough. He's got nobody else to play chess with. A game with a good player would stimulate him – and doctors say anything that stimulates him is going to help him.' She sits down and folds her arms over the bib of her overalls. She's no longer smiling. 'Matt, I can't force you, and I know you must be a busy guy. But might you? For me? Perhaps?'

In chess parlance it's checkmate. Or should be. But I'm still sitting there, spade in hand, wondering where to burrow next in the hope of chancing on an escape tunnel.

'Listen, Matt. There's no pressure,' she says. 'Call or text me

77

sometime. You know where I am. And I'm going nowhere.' She looks at her watch. 'Really sorry, Matt, I think I'm going to have to break up the party.'

I rise to my feet. I look more closely into her eyes. They're the same colour as mum's. In just that split second I dare to believe that a part of mum has come back to me through those eyes and it's her that I'm standing in front of just now.

She puts her arms round me and I put my arms round her. For a few moments we stand in her front room in close embrace and I don't want it to stop.

Then, as we stand there in a kind of togetherness I thought I'd lost for ever, there's another shrill cry.

'Quarter past twelve,' says Lorrie. 'That'll be his apple juice time.'

*

Lorrie's said there's no pressure but the reality is that it's weighing on me like a pair of elephant hooves. I may be able to put off the evil day for a bit, based on Danny's request to me to cover a few weekends at the police station. But the diary remains empty on Sunday, 16th December. I think to myself that if I go for that date then at least it'll be over and done with before Christmas. And then I ask myself how can I possibly treat it as something to be over and done with, and even though my self-esteem has plunged off the diving board in recent weeks it's not only hit the water but is sinking further into what seems like a bottomless abyss.

I phone Lorrie from the office on Monday and arrange to come and play chess with him at 11am on the 16th December.

She says I'm a star.

I wish I was a star. If I were prompted by love, by caring concern for Jake, by a wish to help this hideously damaged man in his quest to claw back a smidgeon of self-respect and self-worth from the burnt-out shell into which his conditions have put him, I might be considered a star. If I were motivated by a real, genuine, heartfelt desire to give Lorrie some respite, some space, and, when it came to the chessboard, to save her from becoming a bit-part player in the next sausage and mash meal, I

78

might be considered a star. A modest, ineffectual star in a modest, ineffectual galaxy, that sheds less light and lasts for a shorter duration than a cheap supermarket battery, before being eaten by a black hole, never to come to life again. But still a star. No. It's guilt. It's all guilt. And guilt isn't the stuff of which stars are made.

After speaking to Lorrie, I'm just beginning work on a trial I'm defending next week when the phone goes again. It's DC Janman,

'Okay,' she says. 'Lisa-Marie Williams.'

A chill rushes across my cheeks.

'No further action.'

I punch the air. 'Thank you,' I say. 'That is brilliant.'

'I've not finished,' she says. 'No further action on the shoplifting. But we're charging her with possession of heroin with intent to supply, possession of crack cocaine with intent to supply, and possession of cannabis with intent to supply. She's getting a summons to attend court on 11th January.'

5

I don't normally go for a run after it's dark but I do so tonight in the hope I'll tire myself out so much I'll actually get some sleep.

And it works in the sense that as soon as I switch off my bedside light I've gone straight off.

But it doesn't work in the sense that I'm awake again at ten past three and simply can't get back off again after that. I never have a problem with loss of sleep if I'm on police station duty. It goes with the territory, and it brings its financial rewards. But I resent deprivation of shuteye when, like tonight, I'm not on duty, and therefore there are no potential customers waiting at the nick, hoping for me to effect a throw of the dice which yields for them a get-out-of-custody-centre-free card.

Then I think to myself I may as well make use of this period of unwanted consciousness by formulating a plan. And at ten to five or so I think I have one. Four hours later, I'm putting it into action.

Step one is a call to Fargoes, another firm of solicitors in the city. They're Danny's Private Enemy Number One. Not because they're cowboys. If they were, someone would call time on them, and/or their dissatisfied customers might end up coming to us instead and we'd be only too happy to get the instruction and take the money. No, Fargoes arouse Danny's hostility because they are so good. If anything, they're victims of their own success. They're often so busy out there getting results that there's nobody available when I want to talk to them. But I've chosen my time well today. I'm told Craig, one their best criminal practitioners who also deals with child care law, is available, and I'm passed to him straight away. Without revealing details of my indiscretions, I explain what I need from him and he says he'll be delighted to help.

Step two is a call to Lisa-Marie that afternoon. I can't risk being overheard so I go outside into the street and call her from there. By some miracle she picks up.

'Hi presh,' she says.

'You okay?'

'Bit crap to be honest. Jazz tried to knife me.'

'He what?'

'He was round his flat, nah I mean I'm round my flat, no, I'm round his flat. We're just you know, having a nice evening, if that makes sense, then he's like d'you wanna sleep with me and starts coming onto me and he's, no, I'm effing telling him I don't wanna, and I'm, I mean he's grabbed this kitchen knife and I'm running screaming out of his flat and calling the police.' The words are queue-jumping and jostling for position and falling over one another in their anxiety to get up to the front and out of her mouth.

'Have they found him? Arrested him?'

'I dunno. I dunno. I guess maybe they have, if that makes sense, I've not heard or seen from him after. Anyway, lissen sweetie, I'm really sorry, right, really sorry, sorry for that night, I was drunk, I didn't know what was going on, what Jazz was up to, does that make sense?'

'Li, they're charging you with drug offences. In court on the 11th of January. Possession of heroin with…'

'I know presh, I know all that, that police lady Janner whatever she's called she's come round my house and told me, right, and I'm like what are my chances of keeping out of prison if I'm found guilty, right, and she's like she's not allowed to give advice and I'm like I can't do prison and it's just going to make me worse, my problems worse. Does that make sense? You can tell me, I can take it from you, what are my chances of staying out? Scale of one to ten?'

The conversation, having gone downhill so quickly, is now careering out of control. I need to do something or it'll be crashing into the piste-side *Ski Sunday* cameraman. 'Li, just listen to me a second. Are you listening?'

'Yeah, yeah, sorry, yeah. Go on.'

'We need to talk about who's going to act for you at court.'

'Well you are, obviously.'

'Li, I can't. Not after what happened. If my bosses found out about it it's curtains for me.'

'But I want you.'

'I'm sure you do, but it's not going to happen.'

81

'I could go to your boss. Tell him none of it was your fault.'

Even the thought makes me want to bring back my mid-afternoon chocolate Hobnobs.

'That's not going to happen either. Listen. I've sorted out someone else to act for you. At Fargoes.'

'I don't want them, I want you. How many more times.'

I can feel my strength and resolve disintegrating inside me with each syllable. I'm conscious how frighteningly little I've got left to play with. To be precise, one single card. If it doesn't win the next trick, I may as well go to Danny with my freshly-ironed white flag.

'Suppose he could get Nelson back for you.'

'Nobody could do that. Last couple of visits to his foster mum's, they went tits about face. And I'm still drinking too much, I'm still taking stuff I shouldn't be. Not ready. Don't think I ever will be.'

'This man is a genius,' I tell her. 'I know from experience he's reduced hardened social workers to quivering mounds of jelly. Reunited mothers with children they never thought they'd see again. You want Nelson back, don't you.'

'It's all I ever think about.'

'He can do it. I can't. That's the thing. I don't do family law. This guy at Fargoes, he can do the whole thing. Fight to get you off your drug charges and fight for Nelson. It's all interlinked, don't you see. Better for one firm to be doing the lot. I really advise it, Li.'

'You're the lawyer, you tell me.'

'I am telling you.'

'I dunno…but no, look. If you're telling me I ought to….'

'I am. Really am.'

'Well, I mean, if you think…look…yeah.'

'You're okay with it?'

'Yeah…yeah, do it.'

'It's a yes?' Suddenly I feel like a hapless auditioner on one of the more contemptible commercial TV talent shows.

'Just said didn't I.'

'He can meet you in his office on 12th December. 4.30. It's in the middle of town. Very easy to find. Can you do that?'

'Suppose. Just make sure my mum knows so she can remind

me, okay.'

My eyes are watering with relief. 'No problem. Look, Li, whatever happens, I just want to say all the best for the future. Fargoes are supposed to be really good. I'm sure if anyone can get you off, they can. If anyone can get Nelson back for you, they can. No hard feelings, hey.'

'Okay, thanks hun.'

'And please don't call me again, okay.'

'What?'

'I… I can't risk it, Li. Not after what happened before. It was wrong. Not professional.'

'You did nothing wrong, presh.'

'Not in your eyes, maybe,' I say. 'But…just don't, okay.'

'Yeah, I get it, yeah.'

I hang up.

Step three is easy enough. Phoning Craig and sorting out the admin. I tell him I'll ping the papers through and he agrees to let me know if there's anything missing or any conflict which emerges which means he can't act after all. Heaven forbid.

Then it's step four. The yukky part. Telling Danny. I need to get in first, before he finds out for himself that we've lost Lisa-Marie as a client. And find out he will. He checks these things. If for one moment he gets wind of the fact that I let him find out, without forewarning him, it'll be the full five-star treatment. Me sitting at my desk, him either kneeling down on the floor next to me or sitting on the chair the wrong way round next to me. Then he'll get going at me. Properly. This isn't just a tuppeny ha'penny shoplifting or minor bust-up in a pub car park, Matt, old mate. These are serious drug offences. From your excellent notes she has a runnable defence. Crown Court trial. Major sentencing exercise if found guilty. Vital business for our firm. A huge earner. And we've lost it and you hoped I wouldn't notice.

Here endeth the lesson. The choir will now sing the Te Deum.

So it'll have to be the extra-large coconut milk latte, his current special treat favourite, and luxury lemon muffin, with luscious liquid lemon filling, at my expense. Since the start of September previous purchases of said beverage and comestible have earned me at least three days' leave at short notice and the joy of being relieved of a particularly messy four-day multi-handed assault trial. I pray it might do its magic again at this of all times. I tell him that it's with the greatest regret that we've lost this client but given the circumstances, namely the need to link ongoing family proceedings with criminal proceedings and the inevitable overlap of relevant evidence, it's understandable. I tell him I know he won't like it going to Fargoes but there's nobody else to whom I could safely and confidently entrust the case in question. I add that I've asked Craig to email me if there are any problems.

It works. He grimaces when he hears who now has the case and reminds me again of his plan to post an atomic bomb through their front door once he receives his online delivery of uranium from NATO headquarters merchandise department. But he acknowledges these things happen and Fargoes hold out her best hope of success of any firm in Brighton in having her little boy returned to her. And through gritted teeth and a lingering aroma of coconut milk he accepts that it makes sense for the one firm to be dealing with it all. I ram the point home. With the closure of the family department, I tell him, there's always a risk that we're going to lose business in precisely that way. Isn't that right Danny and would you like me to pop out and get you a second luxury lemon muffin seeing as you've already scoffed the first one.

We don't speak of it again. Then on the last day of November he goes off on leave for two and a half weeks. And the angst that has surrounded this whole business disappears out of the door too.

*

It's Sunday evening, two days after Danny's departure for the more exotically located branches of KFC and Starbucks across the globe. Since my secondment to the naughty side I've never loved Sunday evenings. But at least tonight I know that when I'm back at work in the morning I can enjoy the fact of the criminal department being transformed into a McFlurry-free zone and continuing to be so for the next fortnight. As Sunday evenings go, I've known worse.

The phone rings and it's Emma.

'How are you?' she asks. The three syllables come with all the tenderness of an army drill sergeant at morning parade.

How do you think I am, Emma. You've not been in touch at all and haven't picked up when I've tried to ring. You dumped me when I was still recuperating in a hospital ward and I had no fight to properly defend myself against your charges. And I'm still searching in my piggy bank for the two million pounds I suspect you're going to be asking me to stuff your Christmas stocking with. So yes. Great.

'Surviving, I guess,' I tell her.

'I know I've not rung. Things have got...well, interesting for me, if that's the right word. Been on a bit of a rollercoaster.'

'What do you mean?'

'I've met this guy.'

'Oh. Right.' Again perhaps she's fortunate to catch me in a reasonably agreeable frame of mind. In other circumstances my anodyne response might well have been substituted by one rather less charitable. Took your time, didn't you. Your side of our bed still warm. Might you not at least have discussed the way ahead with me first, possibly even considered some counselling or mediation, before starting on your window-shopping.

'I didn't mean it to happen. I was just out for a drink with a girl friend from work and while she was in the bathroom he came over, started chatting. Went from there. He's...well, he's...'

'All the things I'm not. Go on, say it. Better in the kitchen, better in bed.'

'Certainly better in the kitchen. Does great things with eggs.'

I don't know if she's trying to lighten the mood but if she is she's going to need to improve on that. 'What does he do?'

'I forget his job title. Something quite big in aviation.'

'What's his name, Jumbo?' The floods of jealousy are already lapping at my back door and I'm right out of sandbags.

'Zachary, actually,' she says. 'Zak. He gets a lot of free air travel. Him and his guests. We've had a couple of trips abroad.

I had some leave owing, see. So that's why you've heard nothing from me. Just haven't had the chance. Anyway, we've become…we're close. So. There's your grounds.'

It's all happening too fast. 'What do you mean, there's my grounds?'

'What do you think I mean? You're the lawyer. I don't know, you could have gone to bed with half the women of Brighton, but you've not owned up to it, so I thought I might save you the trouble. I can give you dates, times, places, whatever you need.'

'You can spare me that for the moment.'

'Fine. Well, I'll ping you my solicitors' details. Perhaps you can give me yours. Assuming you're not self-representing. Then we can get it all moving properly and start talking about the money side. I've put some proposals together.'

The clinical callousness of it momentarily robs me of my powers of speech. Our marriage dismantled in one easy lesson.

'Did you hear that?' she says. 'I've got some proposals for you. Hopefully a straightforward clean break.'

And now I do find my voice. 'So…that's it, is it. We're finished, then, are we?'

'I'd have thought so, Matt, yes.'

I'm waiting for the sorry. I'm waiting to hear her say that, far from blameless though I know I've been, she still cares. Cares about me, cares about my feelings, cares about my future.

But it looks like it's all been cancelled with not even the promise of a replacement bus service.

*

We're now into December and the weather, while unseasonably mild, is also abnormally wet. I blame the summer. It was too hot and dry and, as mum was wont to say, nature will always seek to redress the balance. Besides, did we not all complain that it was so hot and so dry and we desperately wanted some rain. So should we not be delighted to see the rain. Much-needed rain which replenishes our aquifers and reservoirs and brings the green back to those dirty brown lawns and verges. No. We're not delighted. We moan. We say there's now too much rain. The drains can't cope. There's nowhere for the water to go. Too many new-builds. And now the media are stirring it up. The *Daily Star* is promising this will be the wettest winter on record and it won't stop raining till May. While the *Daily Express* invites us to look forward to Christmas Day gales of 110 mph to add extra zest to the cranberry sauce.

Danny's not due back till the Thursday 20th but we've spoken on the phone while he's away. He's allowing me to take the Thursday and Friday of that week as leave. Dad's happy for me to come straight up on the Thursday; it's massively cheaper to travel to North Yorkshire by train on that day than the days immediately following, so Danny's doing me a big favour. Although the office shuts on the Friday 21st and doesn't reopen until 2nd January, we as a department have to provide standby cover for own clients, plus we have our 24-hour duty slots, but Danny's also said he'll swap out my stints, leaving me work-free every day from the 20th December to 1st January inclusive. So I can enjoy just under a fortnight up North. Dad's delighted. He says I work too hard. He then goes on to tell me what's in store during my time up North. It starts with the bring-your-own-chilli-con-carne evening at Mark and Sean's the day before Christmas Eve, and ends with a village New Year's Eve party in the Memorial Hall with live band, dancing and hog roast. In between there's the full works on Christmas Day, turkey already in the freezer, followed by the traditional Boxing Day all-you-can-eat buffet with cold meat platter at the village inn. Then Karen's invited her journalist elder brother Steve and his wife Vikki from their home in Norfolk for lamb casserole the day after Boxing Day. I can see that by the time I'm ready to return home on New Year's Day there won't be any animals grazing in the fields round the village since we'll have eaten them all in the meantime.

But first it's the chess game with Jake.

The day fixed for it is in fact, thanks to duty swaps, the only guaranteed work-free day I've got this month before I go away. It's the day I'd have otherwise set aside as my Christmas shopping day. I may not go in for the spiritual side of Christmas but I love the pre-Christmas atmosphere in the centre of town. I think it's more precious now. We all know how the growth of online shopping has had such a negative effect on the traditional High Street shops and what business leaders call footfall. But close to Christmas the High Street fills again with people who realise they've presents to buy and find that Amazon can't guarantee delivery before the big day. The streets become crowded like they always used to be. And I love it. I love the decorated shops and the street entertainment and the sound of the carols and the smell of the roasting chestnuts mingling with the scent from the woodstoves. As a result I've always planned to have a full shopping day in mid-December, soaking up the festive atmosphere. Emma, who's never bought into it, has been happy enough to let me go alone. I follow the same routine each year, taking the same route round town and stopping off at the same places for refreshment, the day always ending with Earl Grey, buck rarebit and jam doughnut at the Mock Turtle tearoom.

But this year it can't happen. And all because of a chess game. A chess game with a man who needs to be scraped from the ceiling if his wretched carer is more than 23 seconds late with his morning pop tarts. A chess game with a man likely, in his rage, to blast my ears to kingdom come if, when we get down to the contest, I gain as much as a single pawn advantage.

I can't do it. I simply can't do it.

And I decide I'm not going to do it.

I rationalise it. Easy enough to do. I tell myself that this is always a horrible time of year for me because of my bereavements. It may be over twenty years ago that we lost mum but it still hurts just like it hurt then. At Christmas the pain of loss is so much greater. I tell myself that the Lisa-Marie business, including what Jazz did to me, has put me under considerable additional stress. And as if all that wasn't enough, my darling wife has only just now abandoned me for a wannabe Richard Branson and is probably at this very moment, having touched down with him on his private landing strip in the Seychelles, about to start nibbling at his award-winning frittatas. So, I say to myself, if the world has sent to me, by special delivery, this succession of well-orchestrated kicks to the teeth, with toecaps of red-hot steel, and there's no decent dentist within a radius of 50 miles, what do I owe the world. Besides, there are other chess players in Brighton. Must be, if you look hard enough. I'm sure that if Lorrie googled Chess Clubs and refined her search appropriately she'd come across half a dozen budding Kasparovs and Botvinniks not two hundred yards from her front door, all delighted to demonstrate their prowess at the King's Gambit or the Queen's Indian Defence, particularly if a Black Forest gateau the height of the Shard was waiting for them at the end of it.

I don't want to cancel by text or email. Although I may be more coward than Noel I'm not a cruel coward. But nor can I face speaking to Lorrie and being made to feel like a cruel coward. So I come up with a compromise: a Christmas card to both her and Jake, wishing them the compliments of the season and explaining simply that I'm unable to do the chess thing and hoping we can remain in touch. I explain I'll be away in Yorkshire over Christmas with my dad and his partner and coming home on New Year's Day and maybe we can do another coffee then and it should be my treat next time.

My conscience still doesn't feel it's received the final rubdown following the application of the polish. So the night before the day on which we were due to play, the day which is now available for my Christmas shopping, I ring dad for support. And he says everything I need him to say. Yes, you're quite right, Matt, it would have been a risk, it hadn't properly been thought through, and besides, these days one's got to be very careful, you might have a case against his prime carer if you've been left alone with a vulnerable or mentally unstable individual without proper procedures having been followed, and yes, it's a pity that in these Health-and-Safety-conscious days everything has to be risk assessed, but I wouldn't want you as my son being placed in danger and if you need anyone to back you up I'll be pleased to help.

But that doesn't stop the Mock Turtle's jam doughnut turning into rabbit droppings in my mouth.

*

I catch the 2pm train out of King's Cross on the Thursday

20th. I'd rather have got an earlier one but this is way cheaper than pretty much anything else the same day, and in any case, as I remind myself, I've nearly a whole fortnight's holiday ahead of me. We're just pulling out of Doncaster at around five to four when my phone goes. Danny. He's full of apologies for disturbing me but there's a query on a blackmail case I've been dealing with. He says he's happy to sort it out himself but needs to check my emails and for that he wants my updated password. I've no reason not to let him have it, so I give it to him. I've nothing to hide. He says thank you a hundred times and wishes me a merry Christmas. I return the festive greeting and, having hung up, I return to You Tube. In no time I'm in York, sitting in Bullimore's tea room and enjoying their house special, Borrowdale teabread and Lancashire cheese. Less than ninety minutes after that, I'm home. My proper home.

*

It's Christmas Day and it's just family. Us and us alone. We'd agreed the timetable at the weekend. Stockings first thing, smoked salmon and scrambled eggs for breakfast, then a walk, and lunch on the table at 1. Breakfast and walk have come and gone. Now it's lunch with presents to follow.

I'd helped Karen wrap her prezzies for my dad and George last night. For dad, it's a new Black & Decker. Hardly romantic but the old one's on a state pension and has just put in for its free television licence. Dad's become a DIY junkie in his old age. Even stuff that doesn't really need fixing is getting his treatment. I can easily see him first thing on Boxing Day morning finding something, somewhere, that needs a screw, and applying his new tool with gusto.

And for George, it's a football. It was his birthday weekend when an over-enthusiastic goal kick sent the previous ball soaring up over the stands towards the heavens, to land...well, according to popular rumour, it was last seen nestling half in, half out of a bush on the central reservation of the A64. Karen had gone shopping and found a replacement which wouldn't disgrace the turf of Old Trafford, with a price to match. 'But he's worth it,' she says. It comes in a square-shaped, lavishly illustrated cardboard box – well, given how much she's paid for it, it ought to come in a solid gold casket – so once it's wrapped it won't be obvious from its shape what it is.

But first it's lunch. Karen does this sort of thing so well. I don't see her as a replacement mum by any stretch of the imagination. I would never want to be mothered by her. In any case, she's only a year my senior. One big difference between her and mum is that she's tactile. Mum was very reserved in that regard. She hated the touchy-feely stuff. Hated it. In church she couldn't stand the bit where you all had to shake hands with one another. She told us she'd sometimes deliberately sit miles from anyone else so she didn't have to. But Karen finds any excuse to give me a cuddle or a peck on the cheek. On the lips it was this morning after a cherry brandy plus two top-ups. She wears a light green and white hooped rugby shirt and black trousers, plus heels which bring her up to my height. I offer to help her serve the turkey. She smiles and says she can manage. There are big portions for Dad and me. She knows how to keep her men happy. A smaller portion for her. 'George won't want much either,' she says. 'Never mind. More for the rest of us, hey.' She smiles again.

We sit down and say grace. Dad and I know mum would have wanted us to keep doing that whatever our standpoint on life and the universe might be. Then we raise our glasses to absent friends. That's the bit that we find hardest. We don't mention names. We don't need to. Then Dad clears his throat, and thrusts the metal serving spoon into the bowl of Brussels sprouts with unnecessary vigour. A moment later we're talking about tonight's telly and whether Steve and Vikki's journey the day after tomorrow may be affected by the forecast deluges for East Anglia courtesy of Storm Nathan. Or is it Ethan. One or the other.

We make respectable inroads into the mountain of food but we're forced back to base camp. Dad and I help ourselves to what's uneaten on George's plate so we can all claim membership of the clean plate club, but the bowl of sprouts is still over half full and the base of the dish containing the roasties is still groaning so much under the oppressive weight of unconsumed carbohydrate it's exciting interest from

Amnesty International. We decide to delay the Christmas pud till later.

Now it's prezzie time.

The first one's from George for me and it's a box of Quality Street. Nice one, George. Thanks mate. I reciprocate with a wall map of the world to hang in his room. It was Karen's suggestion: she assures me he's always had a lively interest in geography and foreign countries. George has got Karen her favourite brand of shower gel, while dad is the proud recipient, from his son, of a six-pair pack of indestructible socks. Karen was saying only the other day that dad had run out of socks without holes in. He knows his stuff, does that boy.

Then it's presents from the adults to the adults. I produce a bottle and a cricket book for dad, and perfume and a celebrity cookbook for Karen. No prizes for originality for any of that, but no complaints either and their visual and verbal expressions of pleasure appear genuine enough. There's a Fitbit from dad and Karen to me – I'd dropped enough hints – and dad's got Karen a blue zip-up jumpsuit which she'd chosen herself in York a couple of weeks ago. She insists on going upstairs to change into it. A few minutes later she's back with it on. 'Hopelessly impractical,' she laughs. 'Means I have to strip naked every time I want to go to the loo.' But it's clear from the beam on her face that she loves it. So do I. Then it's dad and his drill, and sure enough he promises he'll destroy our Boxing Day lie-ins at a single press of a button.

And lastly, George.

To our dear George, the tag says. With much love from Mum and Dad.

I've never seen hands tear with such random delight at the carefully Sellotaped seasonal paper. Mum would have had a fit. "Brand new paper, that is," she'd say to me. "If you don't tear it you can use it again." But her valiant attempt at helping to save the planet was always doomed to failure, in our household at any rate, and it would have been no more successful today. The final piece of wrapping falls away and there it is. The Wembley Wonder it's called. Further intense activity is needed to free the ball from the box which once it's served its purpose is then hurled aside. And there's the ball itself. Then comes the ritual smelling and feeling. The squeak of leather against clammy excited hands. The first bounces of the ball on the carpet. And then the shrill cries of excitement as, notwithstanding the declining light, the ball gets its first outing on the field – well, the garden. There's certainly no thought of taking any risks with long shots. Some precision ball control and classy lay-offs will have to do. Using the time-honoured jumpers – well, Christmas jumper and old coat – for goalposts, I stick myself in goal and surprise myself with my early distribution skills. But basically I'm a rubbish player, always have been, and I can do nothing about the three shots which whistle past me. And although there was a suspicion of handball about the last I'm not going to delay proceedings by calling for the video assistant referee.

Eventually darkness forces the blowing of the final whistle despite our playing only two of the five minutes of added time. Karen, still wearing her jumpsuit, comes over and rescues the coat while I put my Christmas jumper back on. She puts her arm round me.

'Thank you, honey,' she says.

'What for?' I ask.

'You know what for,' she says. 'Entering into the spirit. Helping to make today special for all of us. Being there for us. Putting a big smile on his face.' She gives me a kiss. 'You will keep coming up to see us, won't you.'

Then she kisses me again.

*

The next week flies past. I can't believe how much we're cramming into each day. I don't want to leave. I want to stay. Dad and I have never got on so well. And with Karen I'm having to be careful because I'm thinking she may be developing more than just stepmotherly affection towards me. We all embrace the various gastronomic events that dot the period between Christmas Day and the end of the old year. Steve and Vikki battle their way from Norfolk through the floods for lamb casserole, and Steve boasts, as he often does, of the number of stories in his paper which have made it into the nationals and onto national radio thanks to his seemingly endless contacts with the "right" people. Vikki is quieter but relaxed and easy to talk to. She explains her sister Alison's just divorced and got herself a new place with her grown-up son in Surrey, close to the Sussex border, and asks me if I have any ideas for good places to visit in Sussex should she ever be at a loose end. I oblige her with a couple of dozen. We play lots more with the new football. Dad wipes the floor with us at Scrabble. I get my revenge at the pool table in the pub. On the Saturday we go into York for a day's sales shopping and wind up in this massive music store, full of instruments and musical scores. Karen's thinking about taking up the piano but at the prices they're charging for decent keyboard instruments she's going to have to carry on thinking for some time yet. They've started selling vinyl LP's and whether they're newly pressed or second-hand I don't know but there are even some 45rpm records of classical works. I tell Karen that I remember how when I was five or six my dear late granddad would play me 45rpm recordings of Gilbert & Sullivan songs on his gramophone. I don't think I've seen a 45rpm record since. Karen says as she can't afford a decent new keyboard without saving for the next eighty years, by which time it may just be too late to start to become the next Rachmaninov, she'll treat me to a couple of the 45rpm's as a souvenir. Then we adjourn to Betty's, the best teashop in the world, and devour egg and bacon muffins followed by scones, jam and cream. The bill for it puts Karen's keyboard-buying potential back even further. Listening to Betty's' own live pianist will have to do, for today at any rate. Next day we go up to Sunderland. One of Karen's pub friends has secured us all tickets for a football match at that city's Stadium of Light. Karen's become a keen Sunderland fan but her loyalty to the Black Cats, as they're nicknamed, is severely tested when her team go two nil down in the first half hour. But they claw back to 2-2 and with just a minute left to play, the home side's top striker smashes a fierce volley into the top corner of the net. Karen lets out a scream of delight then turns to me and gives me a hug. A moment later when the ref blows for full-time she does it all over again.

In between the family stuff I'm out running, using my new toy. If the weather had been better I might have been wanting to have ventured into the Dales and possibly to have had a go at one of the Three Peaks. But time is limited, and in any case each morning seems to bring the knocking of raindrops against the window, and the whinging of the wind as it has another go at uprooting the fence separating us from Mark and Sean next door. So I stick to the more benign footpaths and farm lanes on our doorstep. I'm not one of these people who gets withdrawal symptoms when they can't get out onto the fells and hills. I'm happy enough just being up here. It's feeling like home: not just dad's house, or dad's village, but the neighbouring villages and countryside too. Dad asks me one evening what time on New Year's Day I'm hoping to get home. I tell him this is my home. He doesn't argue, and in fact says I ought to think about moving up North permanently. It's only crossed my mind a few hundred times in the past week.

New Year's Eve. Dad says he's shivery, has a sore throat and doesn't feel up to going out. Too much footballing in the rain and the cold, he thinks. Blame the new ball, he says. Karen suggests he and George stay at home while she and I go out for a drive into the moors and some lunch. The rain is taking an overdue day's leave and the sun has put in a guest appearance. The landscape is transformed into a symphony of lush emeralds while each river and stream we cross sparkles in the morning sunlight. We drive up into the hills and pause at one of the laybys to admire the craggy summits and the clamour of the waterfalls. Then we drop down from the heights into a valley and there before us is a quaint old town of the kind I thought had been left behind in the world of Enid Blyton. Karen says there are more independent and family-run shops in this little town than in the whole of Leeds and York put together. One of them is a bookshop. I'm not a great reader but I enjoy murder mysteries and Karen shows me a shelf of whodunnits written by a local author and set in her and dad's home area with a number of characters based on people they know. The hand-drawn colour cover illustrations by themselves make the books worth buying, and I end up treating myself to two of them. Then we go to the Italian restaurant Karen has suggested for our lunch, and we submerge our forks in spaghetti strands that if put together would be long enough to encircle Vesuvius. I insist on treating her and my reward is a hug and a kiss on the pavement afterwards. She's wearing the top she wore on Christmas Day and combined it with some leather jeans. It's a great look, complementing her great figure, and I've noticed heads turning in her direction all the time we've been in the town. I'd have been happy to keep pottering around its streets for a good while longer but as we're partying tonight Karen says we need to get going again. As we set off for home, my thoughts are turning to tomorrow when I've got to leave and I'm hating those thoughts. So hating them.

We get back and dad says if anything he's feeling worse, he's not up for the New Year knees-up at the Memorial Hall, and he'll stay at home with George. Karen doesn't try to persuade him otherwise. I think she's rather pleased. She certainly doesn't look displeased. She says she can cancel the childminder and save a few pounds. Then she winks at me and remarks that dad's absence will leave all the more hog roast for us.

She's right. We get there and we tuck in and I'm the proud recipient of three helpings. I'm not a great fan of this sort of evening but having finished my final dollop and been propelled onto the dance floor I find myself getting in amongst it from the off. One moment I'm chasing gay Gordon round the willow, the next I'm stripping the dashing white sergeant. I don't know if it's the blue jumpsuit doing it but everyone seems to want to buy Karen a drink. And if they're getting her one they have to get me one as well. As a result, the longer the evening goes on, the more creative we're becoming with our interpretations of the dance steps and formations. We're not moving; we're cavorting. At one point it takes some nifty footwork on the part of two other revellers to avoid a sequence of collisions which would have resulted in multiple write-offs and a mega insurance payout.

After *Auld Lang Syne* and New Year hugs and kisses all round at just gone midnight, the party winds down very quickly and by twenty-five past midnight we're heading home. Well, in a manner of speaking we're heading home. It's not only the booze doing the talking, it's doing the walking as well. Lurching hand in hand, we take a homeward journey that chooses, like some of the more infuriating Brighton bus rides, to incorporate pretty much every street within a five mile radius of the most direct route. That said, I think the fresh air has been beneficial – to me, anyway. Once we turn the key in the lock and manoeuvre ourselves inside our house, I can at least recall firstly what day it is and secondly what time I have to be up for the train tomorrow, neither of which I'd have had a hope of remembering half an hour before.

Karen pops upstairs and comes back to announce there's no sign of life from either dad or George, and dad is snoring nicely. She puts the kettle on and a few minutes later we're sitting together on the settee in the living room sipping at our coffees. I look towards her and my eyes travel around her face, her eyes of chestnut brown, her jet-black hair plunging down to her shoulders, and her neck adorned with tattoos and beads of all colours and more besides.

'This has been perfect,' I say to her.

'What has?'

'Everything. Christmas. And today. I mean yesterday. New Year's Eve.' I feel a tear on my cheek. 'I don't want it to end.'

She smiles and looks straight into my eyes. 'Doesn't have to. Not yet.'

'Mmmm?'

She moves closer to me on the settee and puts her face close to mine. 'I want you, Matt. Want you now.'

For a moment I can't believe she's said the words. It's not real. I've done another Alciston Rise and banged my head on a paving slab outside the hall and here I am back in A & E. But my head isn't throbbing, I see no medical staff and I can't smell the antiseptic.

I splutter the first words that come into my head. 'But...but you're my stepmum.'

'So.'

'You're with my dad.' And as the shock waves generated by her words begin to spread outwards I start to think. To think fast. 'What would he say? His son, his only child, messing around with his wife.'

'Don't say messing,' she says. 'Makes it sound nasty, dirty. You know I'm not like that, Matt.' There's a sweetness in every syllable. I can't remember when Emma last spoke to me in that way.

The boring part of me begins to assert itself. The sober, rational, thinking-things-through part of me. 'Could we live with it afterwards, Kaz. Knowing we'd betrayed him. I love my dad.'

'It wouldn't change things,' she says. 'Won't affect how we live our lives. Tomorrow you go home. Everything will be just as it was. Me, your dad, George. They won't know. I'm just asking the once. Just now.' She places her arm round me and moves me closer to her. 'Look at us. What a day we've had. Perfect day, as you said. Won't this just be the natural conclusion.' She starts to rub the back of my neck. Wow, my neck. How did she know. How did she know. I should be stopping her. Should be getting up and thinking this through. I should be the lawyer and consider the implications, the ramifications, the repercussions. And having closed my thesaurus I ought to be thinking of dad, and what he'd do if he knew, and even mum, and what she'd say.

But I can't move an inch. Just now I don't want to move an inch.

Then comes a moment of inspiration and lucidity. 'If we do this,' I say, 'and I mean if, I want you to promise me something.'

'What's that?' Her hands are travelling towards parts even Emma hadn't explored since our earliest, wildest days.

'That you'll do what I asked last August. You remember, don't you.'

'Of course I do.'

'And you start straight away. No putting it off.'

Her hands stop moving.

'I don't know if I can, Matt.' Now she releases her grip on me and sits upright on the settee. She shakes her head. 'I'm not sure I can, sweetie. I want to…I so want to…but…'

'Just think how liberating it would be if you did,' I say. 'Think how thrilled dad would be. Think how it could change you. Think of it as a nasty, dirty, soggy rain cloud that's been hanging over you and what a relief it is when the rain falls and the sun comes out and the landscape's fresh and green and 'vibrant.'

'You have a way with words, you lawyers,' she says. 'Look. You go and empty the dishwasher and put these cups in. I'm just popping upstairs. I'll think about it. I really will think about it. If I've gone to bed when you come back, well, you'll know what that means. If I'm back down here...I'll think about it, Matt. I promise.'

She kisses me on the lips. It's not the first time our lips have made contact in the past week but it is the first time I can see the sparks and hear the fizz. A moment later I can feel her tongue in my mouth and feel the electricity as she manoeuvres her hands round my neck and my back.

At length she withdraws her tongue and her hands and with a final kiss to the lips she heads for the stairs.

I stagger from the front room into the kitchen and shut the door behind me. I don't want her thinking I'm watching her as she makes her decision. Then I bring down the flap of the dishwasher. I know that if I simply wanted her for the physical satisfaction she could give me, I could turn round, get her back into the living room, tell her to forget everything I've said and tear the jumpsuit from her body. But I don't want it to be that simple. It can't, it mustn't be that simple.

The dishwasher is crammed. We had a big roast dinner yesterday evening and invited some village friends over to eat with us. I'm thinking, this is taking twice as long as it should, even with the amount I'm having to extract and find homes for. But I know she'll need the time. And so do I. Because even now, even if she agrees my terms, I'm not sure. I'm scared. Scared things might never be the same. Scared that somehow dad will find out. Scared that each time we talk I won't know how much he knows.

At last the job is done. The final spoon is slotted in the top drawer and, with the coffee mugs deposited into the machine, I'm able to close the flap with a satisfying click. I open the kitchen door and walk into the front room.

She's gone. The light's switched off. The only illumination comes from the landing light at the top of the stairs. All is quiet.

I tell myself it's best. Our consciences will remain spotless and shining and should be fine until the next annual service.

There'll be no regrets and we'll wake up next morning ready to get on with our lives as though none of this had...

I see movement out of the corner of my eye. I look up and I see Karen coming down the stairs.

As she approaches me I see she holds a small packet in her hands. 'Thought better safe than sorry,' she whispers. 'And you don't need to worry, he's snoring for England.' She moves her face up to mine. 'So want you, honey. So want you.'

'And I told you what I want from you,' I say. 'You're willing to give that?'

'All of it and more,' she says.

I kiss her.

She grabs my hand and leads me back into the lounge and onto the rug by the fireplace. In seconds I've stripped. Just the thought of removing her jumpsuit is enough and I'm able to rip open the packet and ease the content into position. Then I pull down her zip. I try to do it slowly but in no time I've reached her waist. She kicks off her shoes and pulls down her knickers and a moment later I'm ripping her jumpsuit and her knickers away from her. We lie on the rug, first side by side, our hands playing round and round each others' back, our lips and tongue playing round and round each others' face and lips and tongue. I feel the stupendous pain of her nails digging into my neck and watch her beautiful, exquisite pain as my teeth bury themselves in her shoulders. I want to hold back but I can't. In seconds I'm diving inside her, down, down, a thousand feet down, and my whole body seems to explode with flames of release and delight and joy.

6

Whether it's as a result of the physical exertions I don't know but sleep comes to me so quickly I'm denied the dubious pleasure of lying in bed asking myself what the hell I've just allowed myself to do. And I don't wake till ten to nine when I need to be getting up.

I go down to the kitchen where I find dad sitting eating his Crunchy Nuts. No sign of Karen. I can't look dad in the face and I stand over the kettle wondering, speculating, does he suspect, has he guessed. Has Karen said anything to him in the meantime. But he says and does nothing to satisfy my curiosity. Between mouthfuls he tells me he's checked online and the 10.16 is running and on time. Then he implores me to finish the Alpen, reminding me I'm the only one in the household who likes it and unless I can find room in my suitcase to bring it home with me it'll only be cluttering up the place after I've gone. We sit and exchange a few more superficialities. I oblige him by downing the rest of the muesli then make an excuse and go to find Karen.

She's sitting on her bed, getting a jumper on. I sit down beside her but I don't touch. For a few moments we sit in silence. I'm the first to speak.

'Any regrets?'

'No. Of course not.' She places her hand on my arm. 'And you're not to have any either.'

There's something about the way she's responded that troubles me. It's not so much the words but the tone. Her tone suggests that she sees this as no big deal. A snog behind the bike sheds before double Chemistry. No. My dad's been cheated on, for heaven's sake. The one man I value in my life more than any other has been cheated on. It may not have been my idea but I'm complicit. And the airy, Edith Piaf-esque way in which she expresses her lack of regret just made me regret a whole lot more than I thought possible when I'd put my clothes back on and stumbled upstairs to my bed. I have to make her realise what a big deal it is.

'I'm serious about your keeping your side, Kaz,' I say.

'So am I.' Again I detect a touch of the blasé about her reply.

'I'm worried about what I might do if you didn't,' I say.

And now her expression does change. 'You don't mean you…you'd…' She gestures in the direction of the kitchen.

Of course I wouldn't. Never in a million years. But it's the only hold I have over her. I say nothing.

'Look,' she says. 'I promise, okay. I really promise.'

And now I dare to believe she means it.

She moves her lips towards mine but then I hear the sound of footsteps on the stairs.

At ten to ten we're all in the car heading for the station. The silence is as thick as the mist that's rolled down from the moors. Karen lets out a couple of yawns and announces she'll be going back to bed when she gets home. Then we're at the station. Dad and I shake hands. He and I have never been huggers, not with one another. Karen and I hug, of course. But it's a clumsy, awkward hug, that of the youth after his first date in a suburban coffee shop, wondering who's looking. We make a whispered agreement to speak in the next day or two. A moment later she's released herself and five minutes later I'm on the train.

*

The worst part was always going to be walking into my house. A place I really don't think of as home any more. I'd left my proper home at 10.16 this morning.

I'd hoped that maybe by preparing myself for its banal awfulness, by sitting in the train envisaging that awfulness, I might draw some of the sting. If anything, though, it's worse than I feared. At least there's no rock concert happening next door but that's about the only plus point. It's dark outside, it's so dark inside, and it's cold, so cold. Of course it was going to be cold. I wasn't going to leave the heating on normal settings for a fortnight just so that when I got back I could guarantee stepping into the warm. And I still haven't the technological wizardry to enable me to control my heating remotely. Then inside the door, among a hefty accumulation of snail mail, is the expected communication from Emma's solicitors regarding her preliminary thoughts on the financial side. She's not asking for any more or less than I expected. It's clear this house will be an early casualty but it remains to be seen whether there'll be enough left over for that half-decent-looking tent and ground sheet in the Cancer Research shop window. Apart from that, there's some junk mail, a couple of bills, more junk mail, a building society statement for an account that's been dormant for five years and boasts the majestic total of £12.79 in credit, a separate communication from the same building society in relation to the same account consisting of a proud announcement of the reduction in interest on it from 0.001 per cent to 0.00075 per cent per annum, and…more junk mail.

But the grimmest aspect of the overall return-to-Brighton package is the sense of a house without love and care, and a house with nobody or nothing to make it any more than a convenient place to eat and sleep. Emma and I have always spent our Christmases at home together, and one of the bits I loved was when I went out on my own, maybe for a run or bike ride, then came back and found the tree lights switched on, a log fire burning in the grate, and Emma promising me that if I put my disgusting outdoor clothes straight in the wash she'd cut me a slice of Yule log to go with my mug of tea.

I summon up enough strength to switch on a couple more lights and drop my suitcase down by the washing machine. Then I fall into the nearest chair and my tears could fill Wembley Stadium.

I don't know how long I'm sitting there, or for how long the tears flow. Who knows and who cares. I'm due back in work at nine tomorrow but maybe nobody cares about that either.

I'm thinking back just twenty-four hours. In fact rather less than twenty-four hours. There I was, spending the day and much of the ensuing night in the company of someone who did care about me. We were laughing. We were joking. We cared about each other.

Now I feel there's nobody to care.

Then my phone rings.

I look at my screen and it's Lorrie.

Any other time I wouldn't pick up. Any other time I'd say, well, yes, though I deserve the generous portion of haranguing that's going to be served up to me with a double helping of resentment on top, it can stay in the freezer for another week or two till I feel my digestive system is up to it.

This, though, isn't any other time.

'Hi, Lorrie.'

'Happy New Year, Matt.'

'You too, Lorrie. Look, I'm so sorry. I'm so, so sorry. I let you down, I let me down, I let…' And I'm off again.

'Matt, listen to me.' The same tone of voice I'd heard her use to calm Jake. 'You didn't let anyone down. Not important. That's not why I've rung. Are you free this evening?'

'Er…'

'I just wondered if you'd like to meet up with me. For a drink in town. I'm bored with sitting at home all day being a lonely old git. Thought we might be two lonely old gits together. I've got someone who'll mind Jake.'

Any other time it would be a no. There's unpacking to do. There are at least two loads of washing. Plus four layers of dust to scrape off the skirting boards. And for all I know, following a rat infestation in the loft a year ago, a new colony of rats may have taken vacant possession of the said space and they've invited a hundred of their friends to a house-warming party.

This, though, isn't any other time.

'Let's do it,' I say.

*

I've no idea how much might or might not be open on New Year's Day evening, but I don't need to worry as Lorrie's found a café-bar just off Western Road that she says never seems to shut. My late lunchtime jumbo sausage roll and chocolate chip cookie courtesy of the well-known Russian station buffet owners Ripoffski & Sons still haven't quite finished with me so I content myself with an iced orange juice and tell Lorrie I'll help her with whatever's left of her lasagne.

So that's the easy part.

We sit in silence for a bit. Lorrie, nibbling at her opening portion of the quivering mass she has before her. Me, no idea what's going to come out of my mouth by way of explanation or statement of contrition, but only too aware that both are needed. Needed now.

I decide on the abject surrender card and trust she won't do a Treaty of Versailles on the vanquished enemy.

'You must think I'm such a waste of space, Lorrie.'

'Why must I think that?' She puts her fork down. 'Matt, darling, I'm not your keeper. To borrow from your world, I'm not your judge and jury. I'm not here to criticise. Certainly not to judge.'

'Thing is...last few weeks...'

'I'm not asking you to justify yourself,' she says. 'I didn't meet up with you for that. I met up with you because I like you. So. Forget it.' She breaks into a broad smile. 'Tell me about Yorkshire.'

'I loved it. I miss it.'

'Your dad? Well?' Her smile fades but the care and the solicitousness in her voice are unmistakeable.

'Bit under the weather yesterday. Otherwise great.'

'And his other half? Get on well with her?'

'I slept with her.'

Just like that. I don't know why or how it's come out with such simplicity, such succinctness, and in such a matter-of-fact way. An act that could shove a bulldozer through the heart of the man I love the most reduced to four terse syllables. It could be that the emotional demands of the last twenty-four hours have torn away the wrappings of diffidence and awkwardness to reveal a streak of recklessness inside me, and a resultant outpouring of easy candour. Or it could be that my subconscious is wanting to rattle this woman sitting opposite, this woman who seems impervious to any kind of attack on her internal workings, regardless of where it features on the Richter scale.

Her expression doesn't change. There's not even the merest upward movement of a single hair on her eyebrow.

'Does that not shock you, Lorrie? Sleeping with my stepmum?'

'I don't know, Matt.' She smiles again. 'I don't know the circumstances, I don't know the background. Do you want to talk about it?' She plunges her fork into the depths of the two-ton monstrosity before her and extracts a seething, steaming, smouldering lump of minced beef from which flow waterfalls of melted cheese. 'Listen. If you don't want to, then don't talk about it. I was the one who mentioned her first. We can talk about something else if you like.'

'I want to tell you,' I say. 'It was last night. She wanted it. I wasn't sure. I thought about my dad, what it might do to him. Then I said I'd do it on one condition.'

'Which was?'

'That she started getting professional help for dealing with our son George's death.'

*

Now Lorrie does suspend her fork in mid-air and a chunk of minced beef slides back into the morass with a splash.

And I explain. I begin with Daisy. The respiratory problem which had been dismissed by the doctors as nothing to worry about. Anyway, I continue, after Daisy's funeral, dad and Karen go to the doctor with a view to finding out if there's some rogue gene either of them might have which could mean it all happens again. Karen's quite clear that she'd never want to risk going through the same nightmare a second time. She's said she herself would rather die. But no. Doctors are quite sure Daisy's condition hasn't been inherited.

I'm not convinced. And it's all very convenient not to be convinced. Because when Emma starts getting broody, a year and a half after we married and not that long after Daisy died, I'm able, with perfect sincerity, to tell her what a risk we might be taking. I ask Emma if she could bear to put herself through what Karen did. Emma tells me I'm being paranoid. She points out I'm a lawyer, not a doctor, and in the same way that I advise clients on legal matters and expect them to accept that advice, why can't I accept advice and assurances given by medical experts. In any case if it is a hereditary thing, it is just as likely to have come from Karen's side as dad's so I would have nothing to worry about. Then my skill as a lawyer comes to my aid. I tell Emma what it was like seeing Karen for the first time after Daisy had gone. I relive the day of the funeral. Karen and myself bawling into each other's arms. Dad standing nearby, his knuckles gleaming in his determination not to succumb himself and to prove his stoicism and his strength. The worst days of our lives. Yes, maybe the risk might be small. But would we, could we live with ourselves if the worst happened to us. Emma concedes the argument. And each time she's brought up the subject of children after that, I've been able to use the same argument to put her off again. I've never been keen on becoming a dad and this has given me a ready-made excuse for making sure I never do.

And, of course, as things were to turn out, my argument just got a whole lot stronger.

Anyway, dad and Karen try again and, two years after Daisy has died, George is born. And to begin with all is fine. The pregnancy's been easier, there are no complications round either that or the birth, and George is pronounced A1. No respiratory problems and no obvious signs of issues to come. George thrives at his pre-school, and loves his reception class. Then, twenty months ago, just a couple of days before he's due to go back to school to start his summer term in reception, Karen's in the kitchen and she hears a wheezing sound from the front room where George has been playing. She assumes it's something George is watching on the telly, and carries on. Then she hears a groan. She drops a china dish to the floor with a smash and a moment later she's in the front room. George has gone bright red and can't say a word. Sweat is pouring off his forehead. He's rushed to hospital but like Daisy never comes out.

I thought losing mum was bad enough. Losing Daisy seemed worse, maybe because she'd never had a chance to make her mark on the world. And now it's happened again and I'm feeling not just grief-stricken but angry. Angry at the randomness, the arbitrariness, the senselessness of it all. And I'm feeling that as so much has been taken away from us as a family, what right has the world to take any more from us. So I won't let the world take any more. I look after me, I look after Emma, or at least I have looked after Emma, I make sure dad's okay, and I make sure Karen's okay because now she's part of dad. But as for giving back outside that circle, well, it's not going to happen.

And what makes it all so much worse is that ever since George passed away Karen simply hasn't been able to deal with it. The weeks following his death were the worst weeks of my life. My bosses were very kind and gave me a sizeable chunk of compassionate leave, almost all of which I spent with dad and Karen. Dad and I took care of all the hateful stuff that had to be done, from notifying people who needed to know, to arranging the burial and headstone. We did the lot. Karen couldn't, wouldn't do a thing. Then, ever since, she's been going into these weird phases of carrying on as though George were still alive. Often she'll address remarks to him. Every birthday he's had a party. Every birthday and Christmas he's had presents. When she goes out for a walk, alone, she often tells dad George is going with her. Every so often at mealtimes, there's a place laid for him, and she'll serve up a helping for him and will allow it to sit there. Then at night she'll go up to his bedroom, which she's decorated and furnished just as it would be if he was alive, with just the same sort of books and toys and games that a boy of his age would have, and read to him and talk to him about what she's been doing that day and what she plans to do tomorrow. After a phase of it she says she always feels so much better. But then when she's forced to face the reality of the situation once more, as she must, she gets angry, shouting and shrieking and chucking things all over the shop, or she goes into depressive mode, sometimes shutting herself away and refusing to engage with anyone else.

'Lorrie, it's been awful,' I say. 'I loved George just like she did. The little brother I never thought I'd have. I'd love him to be around me now. Really around me. So much we could do together. So much we could have enjoyed this Christmas. But when she goes into this pretending thing, it's like we're walking on eggshells. The moment dad or I say something that might shatter the illusion, she's yelling at us, telling us that we're not the ones who've given birth to a child that's died, that nobody can get inside the mind of the mother of a child that's died, that's how she's dealing with it, that's how she's coping. But in my eyes it's not coping at all. It's telling me she's lost the ability to cope. The only reason it was so good this Christmas was that dad and I just agreed to go along with it. When we go along with it and play her game, she's back to the old Karen, the one we both love to have around. But something will happen to break the illusion and then you just want to stay as far away from her as possible.

'Thing is, after George died, dad and I went on at her to get help but she always said she didn't need it. Dad dragged her along to some free counselling that was being offered locally and it ended in tears. He got details of some professional counsellors and said he'd happily pay for her to go. I think they went along to one session and Karen walked out after twenty minutes. After that she just gave up. I think dad gave up as well. Easier just to go with the flow, humour her, play along. To be truthful, he's not got a lot of money to throw around. Neither of them have. They get by but couldn't afford to pay silly money only for it to go pear-shaped again. Would just make things worse. Then last August I'd been up there for the weekend and she was being ridiculous. Talking to George all the time. I really did think she was hallucinating. I was actually worried for her sanity. I told her she had to sort herself out. Had to get professional help. And fair's fair, she promised she would. But she didn't. Always some excuse. And there I am, early November, going back up there to celebrate his birthday party. Only the birthday boy no longer exists. It's just like the story of the Emperor's new clothes. People too afraid not to go along with the pretence. And everyone just waiting for some smart Alec to pipe up that he really has got no clothes on.

'I never thought she'd climb down last night. But, you know, we've had this brilliant Christmas and New Year and she and I have been getting on, well, better than we ever have, and yes, we'd had a bit to drink, but when she propositioned me I thought, seize the moment. If she wants me, the way she wanted me last night, she's got to take me as I am, understand how much I want this nonsense to stop. I made her believe that if she didn't play ball, I'd tell dad we'd cheated on him. That's how big this is for us. I just hope and pray that now she's capable of making it stop.'

*

109

It's almost midnight when Lorrie and I leave our table and head back out onto the street. As I expected, it's been left to me to eat most of her meal and we've downed a carafe of red while I've been munching. We've ordered a cab. I may have seen the occasional bus go by during the last half hour but a check of my app confirms that none are or will be heading in the directions we need to go and neither of us fancy walking any distance. There's a chill easterly breeze and it's trying to rain. I've told Lorrie we can share the cab: we'll go to hers first, and I'll pick up the bill for the whole thing. She doesn't argue. Wow, she's actually letting me give her something back to her. I almost feel I should be thanking her for that.

It's weirdly quiet on the street outside. It's as if following party night last night everyone's now wanting to make up for lost sleep, restore the equilibrium and readjust their body clocks ready for work in the morning. And the quiet on the streets, compromised only by the gentle hum of the wind, is reflected in our own quietness. Lorrie and I hardly speak as we get into the cab and head for her home. I think we're both exhausted. We've talked so much and shared so much in the last three and a half hours, not just about my family and about Emma but about her family as well. Her children. Her cheating husband. Jake of course. And why it is that she never seems to win any competitions in her puzzle magazine despite having texted correct entries to every puzzle for the last 73 consecutive weeks. She's convinced it's the same few lucky so-and-so's winning the holidays for two in Malaga month after month. She may not be anywhere near old enough to be my mum but I'd love to think this was how mum and I could have been. Love to.

We sit together in the back seats but we're silent all the way. I glance at Lorrie from time to time. She appears to be absorbed in her own little world. She doesn't seem to be asleep – her eyes are still wide open – but there's something about her facial expression that seems to say she doesn't want to engage in conversation, profound or prosaic.

As we draw up outside her house, she leans forward and speaks to the driver. 'Can you give us a minute, please.'

She motions to me to get out and a moment later we're

standing together on the pavement.

'I've known a lot of people who've had to get over bereavements, Matt,' she says. 'Jake for one. And just saying they're going to get help is the easy bit. Yes?'

'Of course.'

'I told you that when Jake's mum died she left me a fair bit,' she says. 'Not so much for Jake's needs, more as a kind of thank you to me. She trusted me to be sensible with it.' She extracts a chequebook and a pen from inside her bag, opens the chequebook and starts writing. Then she turns to me. 'Matt, listen to me carefully. I want you to play chess with Jake. This Saturday morning, eleven o'clock, would work well, assuming you're available.'

I thought this might be coming. The reasonable price to pay for her undeserved forgiveness. 'Of course, Lorrie.'

'And in return, I'll do something for you. Or rather, for Karen.' She tears a cheque from the chequebook and hands it to me. 'This is for her. With my love.'

And when I see the amount for which she's made the cheque out, I almost keel over onto the pavement. 'Lorrie, that's really kind, but it's far too much.'

'Who says,' she replies. 'I like you and I care about you and I can see what this whole business has been like for you. Must have been ten times worse for your dad. I've had some bad breaks but nothing can be worse than losing your children and thank heaven I've never had to suffer that. This'll get Karen started. Give her maybe a few sessions with someone who knows how to break down her barriers. If it works, great. If not, she's lost nothing.'

'Maybe not her,' I say. 'But what about you?'

She smiles. 'I'm all right,' she says. 'I've got you. See you Saturday.'

She shuts the chequebook and places it back in her bag.

*

I may have been somewhat sleep-deprived the previous

111

night but that doesn't stop me lying awake through the small hours of the new day, Wednesday, long after nature should have taken its course.

I set the price I wanted Karen to pay for an act which still has the potential to blow my dad's security and happiness sky-high. Yet having undertaken that act, I'm now the one who's paying. Again. It's not right. It can't be right. I keep thinking back to that first meeting in Lorrie's house and those shrieks that, until she explained their source, made me wonder if she'd opened the Brighton branch of London Zoo in her back passage. The sounds are coming back to me now. Then I think of those words Lorrie uttered. "I'm all right. I've got you." Manipulative. Controlling, even. I feel I'm being bribed. I feel I'm being bought.

I come to a decision.

After work that day I pop to the shops and buy Lorrie a card. In the card which I've write that evening I don't use words like manipulating or controlling or bribery. I explain that I simply don't feel it right to accept so much money in these circumstances. I've assured her that Brighton is groaning at the seams with budding chess grandmasters, and, following some online research, I've enclosed with the card a list of names and web addresses of chess clubs across the city and beyond. I write that any one of their members assuredly can and will give Jake a much better and more challenging game than I would be able to give him this or indeed any weekend.

To be honest, I feel as though the front wheels of a twenty-ton lorry have been lifted from my upturned backside. Everyone's a winner. Lorrie keeps her money which I was loath to accept in any event. I escape the chess match from hell and avoid becoming the Andy Pandy to Lorrie's puppeteer. And Karen will have to find another way. It shouldn't be a matter for my conscience that her future emotional welfare in North Yorkshire risks being compromised because her stepson doesn't fancy a board game in Brighton.

I've put the cheque and the list inside the card, placed it all in the envelope and sealed it.

I know now this is it. Lorrie gave me a second chance and I've hurled it into the long grass without a Flymo in sight. No more invitations to emulate the Lady and the Tramp and consume Italian cuisine from the same bowl. No more cakes the tops of which require oxygen masks to access. No more helping hands the next time I choose to execute a Fosbury Flop on some badly paved suburban highway.

I have a spare first-class stamp in my wallet and there's a handily placed postbox in the next street.

*

My phone rings and it's dad. He's wanting to know if I got back safely and to thank me for a great Christmas. Then he tells me Karen wants a word and he passes me over to her.

First I make sure she's able to take or has taken herself out of dad's earshot. Then we talk. She assures me dad's none the wiser and she's been able to convince him that her new commitment to professional help is a New Year's resolution. Then I ask her what she's going to do about it.

'There's good news and bad news,' she says. 'The good news is that I've done a whole load more research and found someone who ticks all the boxes. Someone who's a qualified psychotherapist and counsellor and lost a child at a very young age. She's American and lives in Maine but we can have conferences on Skype. We had a chat earlier and she's lovely.'

'And the bad news?'

'I can't afford her. Alan would go mental if he knew how much she was asking for just one session.'

'You can't persuade him, then.'

'I don't want to ask.'

'Karen.'

'Look,' she says, 'Alan may not be a Yorkshireman but as far as money is concerned he thinks like one. I know what he'll say. Transatlantic mumbo jumbo. Waste of time, waste of good chip butty money.'

I sigh. 'Guess you're right.'

'Just wish one of my scratch cards would come up.'

If only they'd called twenty seconds later. By which time I'd have reached the postbox. I've not reached the postbox and the envelope containing the card and cheque is still in my hand.

*

Saturday's one of those days which the weather seems to have forgotten.

It's a nothing day. There's no sun. There's no rain. It's not cold enough for snow. There's no wind. The sky is colourless. An absence of blue, pink, red, grey, black. I suppose white is the nearest contender but that suggests a brightness and purity and positivity, and there's none of that. I've missed the radio weather forecast. Normally the weather babblers on my radio station of choice can turn even the most innocuous of meteorological events into an apocalypse right out of the pages of Revelation but they'd be pushed to have done that today.

Even as I cycle through town there seems to be an aura of nothingness. It's the fifth of January, the first Saturday of the new year, and although every shop seems to have the word SALE in its window the punters aren't biting. I couldn't blame them if they were all still in bed. Perhaps they are. As I head away from the centre towards Lorrie's I realise I'm following exactly the same route that the bus took me when I went to see her last. There may be a quicker route but I've not got the mental energy to find it. And so it is that I find myself passing Coffee Unlimited. I glance at my watch. I've allowed for delays and thanks to the absence of same I find I'm twenty minutes earlier than I need to be at this stage. If I reach Lorrie's early I may be getting it over with more quickly but, if I'm as much as two minutes ahead of the time Jake expected, it may just as easily precipitate the collapse of Western civilisation.

So into the café I go.

And there, sitting at the same table as before, she is. The woman with the golden hair.

The ensemble has changed. Today it's a blue jumper, the blue reminding me of that of the soft evening sky I'd gazed at on an Adriatic beach four summers ago. Covering the upper half of the jumper is a scarf of purple and crimson and yellow. She wears darker blue skinny denim jeans, the lower reaches of which are covered by black ankle boots with chunky heels.

I don't stop to think about it. I walk straight to her table. As I

114

approach, she looks up at me.

'We must stop meeting like this,' I say.

'Sorry?'

'You don't remember me.'

She smiles but shakes her head. 'Sorry, no.'

'I was the one who cared about your coffee. By the bus stop outside. A few weeks ago.'

Now her face lights up. My insides turn into melted butter. 'Of course, yes,' she says. 'I'm sorry.'

'I'm the one who should be sorry. Don't know what came over me. I'm not a creepy guy, honest.'

'Glad to hear it.' She smiles.

'Getting the bus again?'

She nods.

'Fancy another coffee while you wait?'

She points to her cup. 'No, you're all right. Haven't finished this one.'

I wonder where to go next. In every sense. But as I wonder she's speaking again.

'You can come and join me if you like,' she says. 'That is unless you'd rather sit on your own.'

I get a small Americano and sit down at her table. Suddenly I feel I'm the gauche gawky teenager trying to remember the rules. What you should say and what you shouldn't say. And when you say it best when you say nothing at all. That's the bit I kept forgetting. The fool that rushes in where more seasoned campaigners would fear to tread.

'I'm Matt,' I say. 'What's your name? If you don't mind me asking?'

'Fiona.'

'Do you live round here?'

'Sorry?'

I repeat the question.

She shakes her head. 'Just on the edge of Brighton. Falmer.'

'So what brings you round these parts?'

'Sorry?'

You're gabbling, Matt. This isn't the time for a hurled delivery aimed at the off stump. I try moderating my speed to medium pace.

'Just wondered what attracted you to this watering hole.' I gesture around me. 'I mean, it's hardly Central Perk, is it. Work? You working?'

She shakes her head. 'Aromatherapy.'

'Aromatherapy?'

She nods but declines to add any words.

'I'm sorry.' Another schoolboy trait: apologising when you've done nothing to be sorry for. 'So what do you do?'

'I work for a publisher in Brighton.'

'Which one?' Not that the name would mean a jot to me. But anything to elicit a response that means we can start talking like grown-ups rather than year nines in the playground.

'We publish travel books. We're quite small. You wouldn't have heard of us.'

I take a sip of the liquid in front of me. 'Try me.'

'Okay,' she says. 'The Wilbury Press.'

'As in Travelling Wilburys? For travel books?'

'Well done,' she says with a smile. She drinks the last of her coffee and sits back. 'Most people don't get it. I didn't at first. Thought a wilbury was a kind of summer fruit.'

'Please tell me you're not serious.'

And now she allows herself a laugh as she shakes her head. I'm beginning to relax.

'I tried to get a travel book published once,' I say. My confidence is mushrooming with each syllable. 'It was the worst travel book ever written by anyone. It was about getting round Europe by train, you know, the best sights, the best journeys. Trouble was, I knew nothing. Nothing about history, or architecture, or geography...all based on my own experience. Or rather my own prejudice. I wrote about how Athens was a lousy city you wouldn't want to go near in a million years. And all because I ate a dodgy curry there and couldn't move off the bog for forty-eight hours.'

I start to laugh. It wasn't amusing at the time, nor was it particularly funny when I first wrote about it, and it's even more unfunny now, but I want her to laugh back. She doesn't laugh back but her sympathetic smile makes a pretty good second best.

'My husband did the Europe thing,' she says. The ring was a

116

big hint, but there's still a frisson of pain and disappointment as she utters the word. 'He was doing Europe by train. That's how we met. In Prague. I was on holiday with my mum. I don't know if you know Prague but there's this really old bridge over the river lined on both sides with sculpted figures. And there's one which if you touch it is supposed to bring good luck. It's had to be repaired because so many people have touched it. I touched it. I looked round and there's this guy standing there. Peter. Pete. And he looks at me and then the statue and he says "I won't need to touch it now will I. Not now I've seen you." I mean, yeah, most grown women hearing that would chuck up over the bridge but there was something about him that made me fall for it. Fall for him. I came home with mum while he went on touring. But we stayed in touch. Talked most days. Texted all the time. When he got back we got together. That was seven years ago. And then we went back to Prague. On honeymoon. Five years ago.' She glances down at her phone. 'Got to go. Bus due.'

I gulp down the tepid remains of my coffee and accompany her out of the café. As we reach the bus stop she turns to me. 'Been really nice talking, Matt.'

And she brings her face up to mine and plants a kiss on my cheek.

7

The bus has come along at that moment and she's boarded and given me a perfunctory wave. And off the bus has gone and I'm left at the stop, my feet glued to the pavement, my statuesque position arousing irritation from disembarking passengers being forced to find a way round me. But they don't matter. Nobody else matters. Nothing else matters except that Fiona has just planted a kiss on my cheek.

It means nothing. Of course it means nothing. She has a husband and nobody else need apply. But seeing her face in my mind's eye, and hearing the echoes of her voice across this weather-less January morning, and remembering the softness of the touch of her lips, I'm realising it also means everything.

I don't know how I find it in me to haul myself onto my bike and complete the ride from the cafe to Lorrie's. I ring Lorrie's doorbell then glance at my watch and it's with relief that I see it's only two minutes past eleven. It's still two minutes late, which given the weight of responsibility perched on my shoulders is really two minutes too much. But if Lorrie's annoyed at my tardy arrival she doesn't show it. She gives me a hug, tells me I look as though I could do with some immediate sustenance, and offers me a coffee and a slice of lime and elderflower before the chess starts. 'Might help to get the brain juices flowing,' she says. It's an offer I can't refuse and it's not till nearly half past eleven that after two slices of cake and a generous slice of chitchat she invites me to follow her along the corridor to Jake's room.

Everyone's heard the estate agents' cliché, deceptively spacious. But in the case of Lorrie's home that's exactly what it is. This unassuming redbrick house in a street of other unassuming redbrick houses fans out into a maze of corridors, passageways, storerooms, shower rooms, wet rooms, dry rooms, long spells of sunshine rooms. There's no mistaking Jake's, though. It's the one from which I hear cries and shouts just as I've been hearing them from the time of my first bite of lime and elderflower. Lorrie places a reassuring hand on my arm as we approach his door. 'He'll be fine,' she says. 'He's looking forward to meeting you. '

Then she opens the door and ushers me into the room.

The first thing I'm aware of is the smell, a mixture of beeswax and stale sweat. Then I'm struck by the size of the room. It's big enough for Brighton to hold its inaugural Grand Prix. Perhaps it feels larger than it is because of the floor space. I like to think of myself as a tidy person, even though when I do the weekly vacuuming I find myself negotiating my way round the odd potential Dyson-destroyer, from maverick Sugar Puffs to cleverly camouflaged teaspoons. But by comparison with what I'm seeing now, I should be putting myself forward for a special Christmas edition of *Strictly Come Grimebusting*. A vast acreage of floor stretches ahead of me, uncluttered by even the merest hint of fluff. As I begin my journey across the bright green carpet, I see it's flanked on my right side by a neat assembly of black box files and then on both sides by bookcases that stretch from floor to ceiling. Lorrie may not have qualified as a librarian but the city library, if not the British Museum, could certainly use her. Hardback general fiction all in one place, paperback science fiction all in one place, sitcom DVD's lining two shelves and not daring to mingle with the TV docudramas. Then beyond the last bookcase to my left, I pass a doorway, and through the half-open door I notice a bed with plain brown duvet and a wheelchair parked beside it. Continuing towards the far end of the room, I approach a plain wooden desk which is empty apart from a chessboard with the pieces prepared for the start of a game. Facing the desk are two upright chairs, one looking to the window, the other with its back to the window. Immediately adjacent to the one with its back to the window, and also facing inwards, is an armchair covered and upholstered in stark images of royal blue and white which might have jumped straight from the pages of Laura Ashley.

And in the armchair sits a man.

It's hard to tell his height in his seated position but I guess I've a couple of inches on him, no more. He wears a dark pinstripe suit with a crisp white shirt and plain blue tie. His hair is dark, with a neat bald patch on top: a shallow dewpond on a

119

downland summit. His cheeks have a complexion that seems almost too ruddy, as if plastered with heavy stage make-up. A neat area of stubble decorates his chin. A pair of thick dark spectacles rests halfway down his nose. His greeny-blue eyes look straight into my eyes. It's the look I last saw on the face of a particularly aggressive prosecuting counsel about to cross-examine one of my clients and rip his case to shreds.

'Jake, sweetie, this is Matt,' says Lorrie. 'He's going to play chess with you.'

I reach out with my right hand. He draws back from it as though he thought I was going to slap him with it.

'You're late,' he snarls. He pulls back the left sleeve of his jacket to reveal his watch. 'You were meant to be here at eleven. I was ready for you at eleven.'

'That's my fault, darling,' says Lorrie. 'I thought he should have a coffee before you started.'

'Let's get on with it, then.' There's querulousness, anger and frustration rooted in every word. Lorrie helps him off the armchair and onto the upright chair next to it, and once he's in position he motions to me to sit on the one opposite.

'I'd better go,' says Lorrie. 'Leave you to it. I'll be around.'

She may be under the same roof but "around" is still way too distant for my liking. Instinctively I turn to watch her. She walks to the door, and it's like mum leaving me on my first day at school. I continue to watch as the door closes behind her. And as I watch, I hear a shout of 'Hey' from behind me. I turn back to face my chess opponent.

'We're starting,' he barks. 'You need to concentrate.'

I'd expected to introduce myself, ask how he is, ask if I can get him anything, maybe tell him a little bit about me. But such pleasantries don't appear to be on his agenda. He's nominated himself as White, meaning he kicks off the game, and he's already advanced his king's pawn two squares towards my territory.

We play out the opening moves and glide into the middle game with no obvious advantage to either side. The pace isn't unnervingly brisk or stiflingly sluggish. It's how I used to like to play during school lunch hours with the suet pudding and custard still lying heavily on my inner workings. I'm very aware it seems like a long while since I last did this. But as the clock ticks on and as I continue to marshal the battalions at my disposal, stuff starts to come back. Not the suet pudding and custard, or should I say the lime and elderflower, but an understanding of tactics: when to go on the offensive and when to stick my head back beneath the parapet. He's clearly no grandmaster, but he's nobody's pushover either and he seems to identify and snuff out, without breaking into a visible sweat, my less than wholehearted attempts to get inside his chessboard personal space. I remember reading somewhere that a bad plan is better than no plan at all. Perhaps my best plan just now is to refuse to rise to his outbursts of gamesmanship: his making of each move by slamming down the piece in question on its new square; when taking one of my pieces, his swiping away my piece as though it were infected with the latest superbug; and when it's my turn to move and I'm wondering what the hell to do next, his inhaling and exhaling like a hedgehog with laryngitis.

My left knee suddenly feels stiff. The stiffness is possibly a legacy of the effort needed to only get here two minutes late. It's his move and he's taking an age over it so I decide to get up and wander around. I remember the guy who always had the top board in our school chess matches would do the same while his opponent was contemplating what to do next. Stretch the legs, let the eyes focus on something else…

'Sit down.'

He's gazing at me and pointing with his finger to the chair I've just vacated.

For a moment words, rude words, lots of rude words rush to form a queue at the edge of my mouth. Who are you to tell me how I can, can't conduct myself. There's no clause in the arrangement with Lorrie that stipulates that player A the party of the first part must hereinafter unless compelled by the exigencies of surrounding circumstances remain in a seated position in the area on the plan hereto attached as and when required by player B the party of the second part. Why can't you be grateful that you're getting a game at all and can you really be surprised if with such Stalin-esque standards of hospitality and tolerance nobody else is coming to play with you.

I sit down. But I can't compose myself. I realise I have allowed his tactics, such as they are, to get inside my head. I gaze at the board and all I see is just black and white wooden pieces. Bishops who are doomed to spend their lives walking in a diagonal line. Kings whose great age and infirmity will only allow them to transfer their persons to an adjacent square and never further. And pawns who, like frontline troops at the mercy of their all-too fallible commanders thirty-five miles behind the lines, are never permitted to drop back on pain of court-martialling and death by firing squad for cowardice in the face of the enemy.

Jake advances his knight into the middle of the board. At first sight it doesn't look like his best move. As a result of it, I could initiate an exchange of material that would put me a pawn ahead. I go through other options in turn but the exchange strategy looks the best, and after several minutes of intense deliberation I'm about to execute it. And this is where his psychological tactics have their effect. My hand is moving towards my black-squared bishop, the immediate deployment of which is needed to set the exchange in motion. But robbed, as I am, of the capacity to think like an adult human being, I'm now asking myself whether in fact the exchange of material is such a good idea after all. It suddenly looks questionable at best, potentially unsound at worst. I permit myself a further five or six minutes' thinking time, all the while aware of the increasingly thunderous look on my opponent's face. The words "Get on with it" are imminent. And fearful of the force of his anticipated imperative, I come to a decision. Which is to change my mind. I abandon the proposed exchange and material gain, and adopt a passive neutral approach, pushing a hopeful pawn a couple of squares north of base camp.

Jake jerks his head towards me and leans forward. 'You're not trying to let me win are you,' he growls.

I can feel the beads of sweat coursing down my right earlobe. 'N...n...no, of course not, Jake.'

'Because I can't bear being patronised. I don't let anyone patronise me. Get that?'

Just play along with it, Matt. Save the clever ripostes for when you're back out on your bike and yell them at the unsuspecting occupants of Heavitree Avenue. 'I promise I won't patronise you, Jake.'

'First you breeze in late, now you're making stupid moves deliberately. I don't like it. I won't have it.'

He, like me just now, takes his time to deliberate. Then he picks up his queen. To say he makes a move is an understatement. It's Operation Barbarossa, it's the noise and the clamour and the violence and the devastation of a million infantrymen and a thousand tanks and the thundering hooves of a hundred thousand horses. The lady, guided by her adrenalin-fuelled general, sweeps down the board and crashes head-on into one of my hapless bishops. The Church has often been criticised for failing to give a more positive lead on social issues. And this representative of the Church is clearly fated never to lead anyone or anything. He's dispatched into outer darkness, wailing and weeping, and is now queuing up for a set of teeth that he'll be forced to gnash till kingdom come, and beyond.

'Check!' yells the general.

I regroup and gaze at the board with a fresh focus. And it doesn't take more than a minute or two to see I could capture his queen with my king. I look for the catch. There must be a catch. Has to be. But after several minutes of looking, I still can't see one. There seems to be no reason why I can't eliminate his most powerful piece of weaponry from the field of battle. So I do.

And of course Sod's law dictates that barely has Her Royal Highness left to take an early bath than I realise I've been had. I've been the victim of a sacrificial attack. And now a queue of pieces appear at my monarch's doorway to take Her Majesty's place. An inquisitive white rook. A capricious white knight. And a white bishop whose brand of Christianity seems a good deal more muscular than that of my own weak-kneed cleric. There's no escape. I'm zugzwanged, as they probably don't say very often in Hemel Hempstead.

Bearing in mind the histrionics that accompanied the placing of my king in check, I can hardly bring myself to contemplate those that will attend the final rapier thrust. Nor does my mean-spirited self particularly want to give him the satisfaction of inflicting that thrust. So I place my thumb and forefinger on my king and lay him out flat on the board.

'Black resigns, then.' There's no triumph in his voice. It's the petulant voice of the bad winner.

'I'm afraid so.' I extend my hand towards his. 'Well done, Jake.'

And just like when I last offered him my hand, an hour or so back, he won't take it. He stares down at the board. Then up at me. Then out to space. I'm now wishing I'd given him the satisfaction of inflicting the checkmate. But what's done is done, and we've had our game, and it must be time for his 12.38pm visit from Lorrie with his pre-Saturday lunch aperitif, and…

It comes without warning. They come without warning. His hands, whipped from the armrests on his chair, fly over the board with the speed and focus of a Pershing missile. The next moment they're gripping my neck.

'You let me win! How dare you let me win!'

'I didn't, Jake. I promise.'

'You let me win! You know I'm rubbish so you let me win and I hate you! I'm going to kill you!'

And now I feel the stinging pain as his fingernails set about the skin around my collarbones. At the same time he's pushing and pulling my head forward, back, forward, back. Now he's got me by my neck and he's tightening his grip. I can feel the tears of pain on my eyes and am powerless to fight back because with the intensity of the pain I've forgotten how to fight. I try to shout. I try to scream. But whatever he's doing to me is gradually reducing my ability to muster any half-decent vocal response. All right Jake. You've beaten me at chess and you're beating me at the strangulation so can you just let go. But he doesn't let go and now he's shouting, yelling. His shouts and yells seem to be getting fainter, I'm sure not because their decibel level is diminishing but because my consciousness is beginning to ebb and even if he hasn't sucked the breath out of my insides it's only a matter of time before my head's separated from the rest of me and I'm scared, so scared…

'Stop it! Stop it, Jake! Let go! Let go!'

Not my shouts. Lorrie's. And they have the desired effect.

The pressure lifts. The stinging stops. The chains drop away. Jake's hands return to base. Jake sinks back into his armchair, his shouts and yells giving way to panting and wheezes resembling the death throes of an ageing steam locomotive. Gradually they become slower and more laboured and die away altogether.

Then there's silence.

'Say thank you to Matt for coming to play with you, Jake,' Lorrie says.

*

Lorrie cuts me another slice of lime and elderflower. 'How are you feeling?'

I apply another layer of cold cream round my clavicles. 'Lorrie, he was going to kill me. He would have killed me.'

'And you would have been killed doing something for someone else, which is as good a way of going as any other.' She puts the slice on a plate and passes it across the coffee table.

Part of me wants to answer back. To tell her she's a callous, unfeeling bitch. To ask her how she can have the audacity to think what she's just said, let alone say it. But something stops me. Maybe because I can't argue with the truth of it. 'Has he done it to you?' I ask.

She doesn't answer. Maybe she feels she doesn't need to because he's so obviously done it so often. She points to an area of neck just below my right ear. 'You need to do that bit. It's still very red.'

'Lorrie, you shouldn't have to put up with it. It's not right. You should do something. Before he...before...' I look up at her face and she's smiling. I can guess what she's thinking. It's not right, no of course it's not right, but so much that goes on in this world is not right. Suppose she were to "do something," as I've just put it. What might that mean. It might mean giving up on him. Giving up on the love. Giving up on the hope. Possibly surrendering him to an existence of institutional misery. Of course she shouldn't have to put up with it but I know that once I finish this family-sized portion of lime and elderflower and

125

leave, she will keep putting up with it. And I won't have to. There's no point in carrying on with my sentence because there's selfishness etched into every character, every dot, and every speech mark. It's all about me, and I just know that Lorrie knows it. My speech strikes the buffers and announces that all passengers should change and proceed to platform 4 for onward connections.

But she's Lorrie so she doesn't flinch.

'I absolutely get you,' she says. 'And if it's any comfort, pretty much everyone who's met him for the first time says the same thing to me afterwards. And of course I've a big advantage. I know him. I live with him. We live together. I don't see it as putting up. It's not like say putting up with the Germans if they'd invaded during the war. I chose to have him, after all. We're both human beings. We both have needs. We both have feelings. We can both be challenging and we can both be quite nice. Just like you, just like anyone else. I mean, yes, of course, Jake's a bit different. A bit more hard work. And yes, sometimes if he's going off on one I might be tempted to hurl something at him. But then when I'm wondering what to hurl at him, I stop and ask if my reaction says just as much about me as it does about him. It's not all one way, see. I mess up sometimes. Don't forget I've had to pick it up as I've gone along. I don't have a degree in behavioural science. My degree's in muddling through. When you've been doing this as long as I have, you get to know what's going to rattle his cage. What's going to make him irritable and sulky. And what's going to make him happy. What makes him laugh. Yes, he does laugh sometimes. I tell you, Matt, it's the most beautiful sound on God's earth. More beautiful than the dawn chorus. More beautiful than the sound of raindrops kissing the leaves during a dry summer. When I hear it, it makes all the tricky bits worthwhile. It's not putting up. It's living. Life.'

Still the self-pity refuses to quit the scene. 'I guess it's just a shame I've only seen those tricky bits,' I say. 'I think he hates me. Just sees me as patronising him. Wanting to lose to him on purpose.'

'I know you were never going to lose on purpose,' she says. 'And I know that deep down, he knows that too. You're not stupid. I know you wouldn't have gone soft on him. Not deliberately. He's a good player. Useful player. Never going to set the world on fire but good enough to make you think about your next move. You were playing for some time, weren't you. You were making each other think. That's great. He'll have enjoyed it. He might not have said so, but he'll have enjoyed it. And I promise you he doesn't hate you. Won't hate you.'

She sits back in her chair, still looking towards me and smiling. And as I apply another blob of cream as Lorrie suggested, I'm sure I know what's going through her mind and I can almost hear what I'm sure she's tempted to say. You're quite enjoying this melodrama, aren't you, Matt. The martyr who's given up his precious weekend off work to do a stint of community service and gets rewarded for it by being verbally harassed and abused and coming within a whisker of being garrotted. But don't expect any OBE notification to pop through the post just yet.

'Listen Matt,' she says. 'I really appreciate your doing this today. Really. You didn't have to. I couldn't blame you if you hadn't. But you did, and I'm grateful. Really so grateful. The neck thing wasn't part of the deal. So this is for you. To pass on to Karen. Give her another session or two maybe. If she doesn't want it, maybe donate it to a children's hospice.'

She reaches for her bag and takes out her chequebook and pen, and moments later she's placing another cheque into my hands.

It's a cheque for the same amount she'd given me on New Year's Day.

'It's too much,' I tell her.

She smiles. 'Let me be the judge,' she says. 'Or Karen. Or your dad. Or George himself, if you believe in all that.'

Granted, the wretched individual for whom Lorrie cares may have threatened to terminate my stupid futile existence somewhat ahead of schedule, but her fresh gift is still way out of all proportion to the time and effort I've put into it. And worse, it's way out of all proportion to the love and care I've put into it. I'm asking myself if I've put any love or care into it at all. I'm not sure I have. Suddenly I feel like Al Capone.

'I don't like to accept it, Lorrie,' I say,

She rises to her feet. 'I'll go and find an envelope for it,' she says. 'And you'll want a tin for the rest of the lime and elderflower.'

'Are you sure?' I say. The cheque's still in my hand.

She smiles and looks down at the cheque and then she looks up at me. 'You can bring the tin back when you come again next Saturday.'

As an example of impeccable timing it puts Rolex to shame.

She disappears then returns a few moments later with the promised envelope and tin, and escorts me to her front door. As I make my way out into the weather-less January air I turn back to her. It's something I need to be sure of before I do entrust my battered neckline to Jake's tender mercy again in seven days' time.

'Lorrie,' I say. 'What he did to me…he's done that before, hasn't he.'

'He has been violent before, yes.' A cloud covers her face.

'So it wasn't just luck you came in when you did. Was it. You knew what he might do so you were waiting outside. Just in case. Weren't you.'

For a moment her expression doesn't change. Then she smiles and nods. 'Yes, Matt, my dear. I was waiting.'

*

I ring Karen straight away and tell her about the further windfall which is on its way to her. She tells me she's already fixed up two Skype meetings with Jessica, the first of these being tomorrow evening, but in the meantime they've had another phone chat and she feels she's making progress already, even before the proper stuff's got under way. With the second cheque she says she'll be able to arrange at least two more Skype sessions.

Then Dad's called me on Tuesday to confirm safe arrival of the cheque and report that Karen's first session has been a huge success. But he accepts they've only just begun. 'If Karen's full recovery is the Taj Mahal,' he says, 'we're only just coming off the M25.' He's got mixed feelings about it: he loves the fact that she's got off to such a promising start, but is fearful that if she wants to keep it going for a sustained period, it's not going to sit well with her long-suffering bank manager. Nor his. Karen was right. There's more Yorkshire than Kent in him these days. I tell him I'm sure it'll sort itself and moments later we're chatting about England's dire first innings in the current Melbourne test match. We'd agreed at Christmas that their middle order needs sorting out.

But the fact is that every time I see from my phone that it's him calling I'm wondering if this is it. If this is That Call which reveals that he knows everything, either because Karen's guilt has got the better of her or through some intelligent deduction. Come now, dearest. What was the medicine you took that did the trick. Not just a New Year's resolution was it. Oh yes, New Year's Eve. The night you and my son, my own flesh and blood, went partying together. This after you and my son, my own flesh and blood, spent the day together. This after you and my son, my own flesh and blood, were kissing and cuddling at every conceivable opportunity all the time he was in your line of vision. No. Not just a New Year's resolution. Something else around the turn of the year, wasn't there? Just as Jake said, Black resigns. Or to put it another way, so busted.

I can't recall the last time dad got angry with me. Really angry. He certainly never has done since my teenage years. And I know he would have hated ever having to be angry. He doesn't do anger. He never really has done anger. That's why That Call would be so scary. I don't know what would feel worse: his stepping out of character and shrilling obscenities down the phone, or his trying to keep a lid on his emotions and coming over all weird and unnatural and still trying to talk cricket. But none of it's happened. Not yet. On the contrary, he's being so nice to me, clearly thrilled about Karen, delighted at my somewhat unorthodox fundraising activity, and anxious for me not to be too downcast or demoralised now Emma's jetted off with Mr Virgin-I-Don't-Think-So Atlantic. All of which makes the prospect of That Call scarier still. The physical distance between us, far from making it easier, is promoting and fuelling the dark uncertainty. Dad may have a trusting nature but he's not stupid. Sometimes I think Karen underestimates him.

At least I'm adjusting back to the new normal. Returning to the empty house in the evenings – I simply can't think of it as home any more – is still hateful but it's bearable. I don't love my work but I tolerate it and I don't think I'm too bad at it. I'm now up to three trial wins out of three since the start of the year and I've got a couple of clients out on bail who deserve to be rotting in prison. Danny's being almost likeable and we find ourselves chatting and laughing together. And on Thursday as I'm leaving the office Geoff, one of the partners, asks me if I've got a moment then tells me the partners are delighted with my crime work and delighted with me. Could not do better. The IP work's apparently taken a downturn and unless it picks up again significantly it's unlikely I'll be transferred back in the foreseeable future, therefore the partners hope I don't mind staying in crime. I smile and tell him what he wants to hear. That's fine, Geoff.

But it's not ideal. The long hours involved may help keep my mind off other stuff, but it's like a drug, withdrawal from which brings its own perils. I realise just how tired I'm getting. By Friday afternoon the rigours of the week have caught up with me and all of a sudden I'm wishing my Saturday was free. Completely free. Free from chess enthusiasts stashed away in the less fashionable corners of coastal towns and skilled in the art of unarmed combat. But it has to be done and may have to be done for a few more Saturdays yet if I'm properly to repay Lorrie for what she's allowed Karen to have. There may be no legal obligation but it's an obligation I'm feeling, just the same. Besides, there's the F factor. I'm still pretty much a stranger in Fiona's eyes and she's the married woman. If I've somewhere nearby to go after seeing her, it legitimises the time we may enjoy together. There'd certainly be no other excuse for visiting that café, in all probability shortlisted for the Community Zeroes awards, Least Appetising Hot Drinks category, and as such the last place on earth one would choose for a decent shot of caffeine. I've acted for enough clients being investigated or prosecuted for stalking, and I've no wish to become one of those clients myself. And if to avoid any accusation of stalking her, I'm having to tell her I'm on my way to play chess with a homicidal maniac, perhaps I should be seen to be going on my way to play chess with a homicidal maniac.

*

It's sunny on Saturday morning so I'm back on my bike and again find myself outside the café a good twenty minutes ahead of time. I keep telling myself not to be disappointed if she's not there. Her precious Pete may have whisked her off for a winter break in the Canaries. Other circumstances may have forced a change of routine. Or she may already have me down as a stalker and has decided to seek out the nearest Costa in the hope of enjoying a cup of coffee that actually tastes like coffee. On the strength of what I experience as I enter the café this morning, nobody could blame her for seeking a more agreeable beverage. The Smell of the Day is smoked haddock mingled with burnt baked beans, while the guy behind the counter, who moves with the grace and finesse one might expect of a drunken diplodocus, has pounced on me the moment I've come inside and is inviting me to try a taste of today's special. He points to the plate containing same. It looks more brown than Derby and more fatty than Arbuckle. I confine my order to a small latte. Then I turn round to the tables to see if she's there.

She is.

She's dressed just as she was last week and I'm liking it even more this time round. She's nursing a cup of something grey-brown. And she's looked up at me. She offers a brief smile of recognition. Without waiting for my coffee to be made I go over to her and I'm planting a kiss on her cheek.

'Okay if I join you again?' I ask.

'Go ahead.' She smiles again but the smile seems to be tinged with sadness.

'You okay?'

'Missing Pete, I suppose.'

The coffee arrives at this moment, courtesy of Mr Diplo. 'You forget. Is not waiter service,' he says. 'You meant to wait and take it yourself.' He places the cup down on the table with a plonk, a kind of plonk that I guess is reserved for plonkers like me. Then he waddles off.

'You are a glutton for punishment coming to this place,' I say. Then I set about pouring back into my cup the not insubstantial amount of coffee that thanks to the plonk has been set free from its interior.

'I know,' she says. 'Aromatherapist again. Bit of a wait for the bus.'

'So what's Pete doing today?' I linger a fraction too long on the P of Pete and at once I wish I hadn't. I seem to be regressing. More teenage stuff, this, and I hate myself for it. Get over it, Matt, the girl is taken, accept her for who she is and what she is.

She doesn't react. 'Sailboarding and surfing,' she says. 'Gone off with a couple of mates to Cornwall. Set off half three this morning.'

'Half three?'

'Mmm hmm. Stop for breakfast somewhere round Exeter, should be out on the water by now. Few beers at the pub, bit of lunch, out again on the water early afternoon, set off for home by four, back by half ten.'

I take a mouthful of the liquid in front of me and wish I hadn't. 'Long way to go for all that.'

'He says it's worth it. Says you won't find better surf anywhere else in the country.'

'Exhausting.'

'He loves it.' She picks up her cup and slurps at its contents. 'Could have got very good at it but for the one thing he loves even more.'

'Mmm?'

'Rugby,' she says.

I wouldn't say I was a great sports fan. I may enjoy kicking a football about with dad in the garden but if I'm going to follow anything it's cricket. Dad adores cricket. He loves watching it, and he actually played it till quite recently. I've sat with him through a goodly number of Test matches on the box. I've been to a couple of them with him as well. But he and I are united in our loathing of rugby. I've always hated it. I was forced to play a bit of it at school and every second of it was hell. The excerpts I've seen during sports bulletins on telly haven't changed my opinions. It's brutal. It's messy. It's muddy.

132

It's too disjointed, too stop-start. And I've never understood the rules. I'm not sure anyone who hasn't played it understands the rules, and probably half of those who do play it don't understand the rules. But the real reason I've continued to loathe it is that in my single days it was invariably played by the other halves of women who were attached and I wished were not. Harriet, darling Harriet, was one. It seems to have been an unwritten law moving through my life with me. If I fancy a girl slash woman, her boyfriend slash lover slash husband will be a rugby player. Here we are again.

And now it's getting worse. She's getting out her phone and showing me scenes from the life of this guy, this blond macho man. Exhibit C1 hyphen 3BA, the one with his rugby gear on, his knees filthy and the obligatory blob of perspiration on his brow. Exhibit C1 hyphen 3BB, a pic of him sent to her from the summit of Snowdon during last August's triathlon. I've never seen him before and am probably never likely to but I hate the man. I so hate the man.

She's just shown me the one of him on Fistral Beach, Newquay, in his bright orange speedos when she announces that's all we've got time for in this edition as her bus is due in two minutes.

My latte disappeared several minutes ago and the only taste in my mouth now is that of bitter defeat. If this is her way of telling me that much as she likes my company there's only one man she really wants to have anything to do with, best to take the hint and have done with it.

'I'd better go as well in that case,' I tell her. I rise from the table. She's still seated.

'Before you go,' she says, 'you told me you'd written this crap travel book.'

I nod. 'Crap it certainly was.'

'Next time you're popping by my office…would you like five minutes for me to tell you how to make it…a bit less crappy?'

I don't get it. Don't get it at all. It's barely seconds since she was flinging herself at the altar of speedo kid. But before I can respond she's doing the responding for me.

'If you popped by next Thursday at about half past one I

could be standing by with my mop and bucket,' she says.

Still not getting it. My tongue's certainly not getting it. 'If…if you're sure you want to,' I splutter.

Now she's looking at her watch. 'Wow, I need to run,' she mutters. She empties some more liquid grey-brown into her throat and slams down her cup which sets the unconsumed contents dancing up the china walls that were confining them. 'Really nice to meet up. Hope to see you Thursday.' She reaches in her bag, extracts a small piece of card and drops it down on the table in front of me. 'This is me,' she says. I glance at it and see the name Fiona McKenzie-Wallace on it, plus title, Assistant Commissioning Editor, plus landline number, plus mobile number. The next moment, Fiona McKenzie-Wallace is kissing me on my right cheek, and another moment later she's gone. Leaving me with the small matter of finding my crap travel book by next Thursday.

Or, if I can't find it, writing a crap travel book by next Thursday.

*

Lorrie agrees it's best that Jake and I don't start off on the wrong foot by a repetition of my tardiness from last week, even though she accepts it was really her fault for plying me with comestibles ahead of the game. She promises this time that refreshments will be served after the main event. I tell her that's fine by me. I'm sure I'll enjoy today's *Great British Bake Off* audition piece, cappuccino and chocolate fudge cake, all the more if ordeal by chess board is behind me rather than in front of me. She ushers me into Jake's room as soon as I've given her my coat.

Don't let him get to you this time, Matt. Think of what's already fallen into your lap this morning. And think of what Lorrie's done for Karen and for George's memory. So much has been given to you and you're not being asked to pay a lot back. Are you.

Lorrie promises that she'll be in the next room, and for the duration. I'd prefer the same room, but she assures me next room's as close as it needs to be. And I do get a grunted hallo from Jake. It's perhaps too much to expect him to take my proffered hand but when I see the sweaty shine on his palm I've no undue difficulty with his rejection. The chess pieces are all set out and from the way they've been done I don't need to ask who's White and to whom it thereby falls to get proceedings under way. It's me.

I move the pawn in front of my king two squares forward: e4, in the language of chess. Head down, get on with the game, get through it, keep reminding yourself that...

'You're not going to let me win!"

It's not a question. It's a statement. It's a chilling reminder. Jake hath spoken. One bad move, one blunder, a single question mark after a single manoeuvre, and I have to pray that when Jake kicks off in response, Lorrie hears my bleatings and is through that door with half a hundredweight of Shredded Wheat inside her.

Focus, Matt. Focus. Suet pudding and custard. It always seemed to taste better on Fridays and I can recall that Friday taste now and it's helping me. Soon I'm a pawn ahead. Of course material advantage isn't everything but when I become a bishop to the good, I feel I might just come out of this without needing to order a new collarbone off Amazon. He's got a new set of mannerisms for today, of which the most predominant and by no means the least unappealing is the growl and/or the snort he emits when I make a move that weakens his defences. As his defences weaken, the swagger of his pieces about the board is replaced by something altogether more diffident and apologetic. When he effects a capture of one of my men – never resulting in any strategic gain for himself – the ruthlessness with which the captured material had been hurled into oblivion last week is replaced by tentativeness, as though he himself knows he is going to be repaid with interest. As I might have expected, he's taking an eon over each of his moves. But as I've no major plans for the rest of the decade, and as long as Lorrie's going to reward me with something out of the glossier pages of Mary Berry, he can take as many eons as he likes. I think I can beat him.

The game continues and yes, I not only think I can beat him, but I know I am going to beat him. My forces are encircling his inadequate defences and unless he can summon up a Dunkirk-sized fleet of little ships, his men have nowhere to go.

Two moves later, I put his king in check and it's game over. He only has one move that gets him out of check, but it's only delaying the inevitable. It's mate next move.

I know he won't want to give me the satisfaction of checkmating him. He'll want to dictate the agenda. He'll decide when the game's over, not me. I'm not expecting him to make the only move available, and sure enough he doesn't. He just sits there, glowering at the board, continuing to growl, continuing to snort. He must carry on doing that for a good five minutes.

I should guess something is coming when his growling and snorting stop, and are replaced by a momentary silence. I look up at him and see his face reddening and his eyebrows twitching. The next moment there's a shriek. My instincts cause my hands to rise straight to my neck. But his hands come nowhere near my neck. They grip the board. And a second later the board, together with all the pieces left on it, has taken off without taxiing or obtaining clearance from the control tower. Knights, pawns, kings, queens whistle over my head. One black pawn bounces off my forehead and cannons into the comparative safety of my lap. Other pieces aren't so lucky and a series of bangs and cracks signify their crash-landings before the words "brace, brace, brace" have had the chance of being unleashed and the respective cabin crews have been able to yell at their passengers to pull down their oxygen masks.

Then the silence. Then the whimpering. Jake's whimpering. His shoulders tremble and his face gets ruddier with each sob. Because this time he can't accuse me of letting him win. This time I made him lose.

He's without doubt the most aggressive, selfish, self-pitying, self-obsessed, petulant man I've ever met. And yet here I am getting up and walking round to his side of the table and I'm putting my arm round him and telling him it's only a game and how we'll have to do it again and call it the decider. I don't expect him to reply or react and he doesn't.

After my attempt at consolation I go round and pick up the board and the pieces then begin the hunt for casualties. All is safely gathered in save for one pawn. One wretched black pawn. Could be anywhere. My fear is it's rolled into one of the narrow horizontal gaps between the bottom shelves of the bookcases and the floor and got stuck out of reach. There is, however, one place where I've not looked but is potentially accessible: a wider, vertical gap between the last bookcase to Jake's left, and the neat pile of box files. If it's not there it's probably lost for good.

But by a miracle, that's exactly where it is. I just need to move the box files a tad to get my arm in to recover it. And that is my tactical undoing. Rather than dismantle the pile one by one, starting from the top, I decide to try and push at the bottom box file and hope those above move with it. Sure enough, the pile obligingly jerks in the desired direction, but as it does so, the top two box files come away from the rest and crash to the ground, spilling papers all over the floor.

He'll kill me. Lorrie may intervene to forestall another strangulation attempt. But he'll find another way. I know he will.

I look up at him. He's still whimpering, not looking at me at all, but preoccupied in Jakeworld. Maybe if I can put the papers back before he's had time to find his automatic pistol I can have the death penalty commuted to a life sentence.

There are too many papers on the ground for me to pick them all up at once. I grab my first handful and am about to put them into one of the box files when I see, on the piece of paper sitting on top of my handful, the BBC logo. It's a printed copy of an email.

I shouldn't be reading it at all. It's none of my business. But I can't stop myself.

Dear Jake,
Your email's been forwarded to me by Head of Religious Affairs Broadcasting.
I certainly am unaware of anybody who like you has attempted, or I should say is attempting, to learn and recite the whole of the Bible by heart. I think I can safely say that this would be a unique and unprecedented achievement, which is certain to attract widespread media attention, not just national

but potentially worldwide.

In answer to your question, then, yes, we would in principle be extremely interested in featuring you on at least one of our Sunday morning BBC Radio 2 Sunday Breakfast programmes and, as you suggest, the ideal time for this is once you have memorised all of it and have organised performance dates. I am delighted you have established contact with us and we look forward very much to conveying your fantastic talent to our Sunday morning audience.

Please keep in touch and let me know how you get on.

Best regards
Stewart Pimlott
Producer – Sunday Breakfast

8

Then he looks up.

'Leave that alone! Leave that alone! How dare you! How dare you! Get out!'

I may be at the far end of the room and safe from his tentacles but the force of his yelling threatens to knock me off my feet.

Amid Jake's yelling the door opens. Lorrie. She walks to Jake. She doesn't rush. She doesn't hurtle. There's calmness written all over her face.

'Stop it, Jake. At once. Stop. Now.'

It's just her normal speaking voice, without a hint of urgency or desperation, and it does the job. He stops. I'd love to know what her trick is. But I guess that's where her years of experience come in. She's able to make the whole thing look effortless. It's like a world-class tennis player routinely acing an opponent or killing a point with a delicate dropshot. In Lorrie's case, it's just lots more love. Far fewer balls.

Then she turns her attention to me and the misbehaving box files and contents thereof. 'It's all right, Matt, love, I'll deal with those later. Game over?'

I nod. 'My turn to win today.'

'Well done. Tie-breaker next time. Come on. Coffee time. Go into the front room and help yourself. I'll be there in a few minutes.'

And in a few minutes she and I are sitting, coffees in front of us both, she with a token sliver of her latest cholesterol showpiece, me with a Mount Vesuvius-sized slice of aforesaid cholesterol showpiece, duly extracted from the main article. I couldn't blame the base of my plate if immediately beforehand it felt like Pompeii, nerving itself for an outpouring of lava of mixed sponge and cream, fearful there will have been insufficient time to evacuate the women and children.

I extract, consume and digest one of the more solid corners of the concoction. 'I'm so sorry about the mess I made in there.'

'Don't apologise, for goodness' sake. It's high time I threw it all out. So you saw some of the BBC correspondence?'

'Couldn't help it.' I apply my fork to the centre of the mixture in front of me, and watch in stupefied impotence as sticky brown rivulets race each other to the edge of my plate. 'It's good, though, isn't it? Keep him out of mischief?'

She leans across and passes me a tissue. 'Blob of something cakey on your hooter,' she says.

'Sorry.'

She waits till I've removed it then takes a deep breath. 'I don't allow many things to give me sleepless nights, particularly where Jake's concerned. But this did. He started memorising chunks of the Bible. Years ago apparently. Maybe even in his mid-teens. I mean, it's not something you can pick up in a couple of years. Anyway, one morning a while back, he said, completely out of the blue, he wanted to recite the whole caboodle from memory. In public. And this was where I made my big mistake. Classic own goal. I humoured him. Left him his elevenses and told him I'd hear him do the whole thing, word-perfect, with his afternoon tea. And when I marched in with his scone and butter and his Earl Grey at five twenty I got half the book of Genesis. The world created in seven days. Adam and his apples. Jacob wrestling with a pillar of salt. Joseph going online to order his technicolor dreamcoat.'

I cram another forkful of naughtiness into my mouth. 'So what happened?'

She peers at my face. 'You've missed a bit. Just above your lip. Every morning he'd be telling me what chunks he was going to learn or bone up on that day. And, idiot that I was, I said I'd test him at the end. I didn't need to test him. He was pretty much flawless. But he insisted I listened. Said there was no point in reciting to himself. He saw me as his mentor, his partner in the task. He said he couldn't do it without me. Testing him, correcting him if need be, and crucially, applauding him when he got it all right. And as the days went by, and he was absorbing more, the testing was getting longer. What started as two or three pages became eight, nine, ten. And I saw them getting longer and longer still.'

'But you didn't put your foot down? Tell him you didn't

have time?' I'm so absorbed in the story that I've not even attempted to take remedial action with my tissue.

She starts laughing. 'If you could see yourself in the mirror,' she says. 'I knew that extra tub of cream was a mistake.' Then she sits back in her chair. 'This is what I mean about the sleepless nights, Matt. There he was, thriving on the challenge. He found a purpose in life he thought he'd lost. Saw it as his reason for getting up in the morning. Maybe even a way of getting back at those who thought he was finished, who thought he had no live left worth living. I know he used to attend church when he was younger. Never talked about it much, never really discussed religion at all. Certainly not with me. But anyway, that may have influenced his choice of task. I don't know whether he thought that God, some God, any God, was underpinning it, but when he put his mind to it, got into the zone, it really was as though there was a spirit in him. He just got carried away with it. Building up more and more in his brain and, make no mistake, his accuracy was astonishing. His brain is unique. He goes completely blank with some tasks, but this one, wow. And I saw his eyes sparkle as he warmed to the task. He got through the whole of Genesis, all fifty-two chapters or whatever, then Exodus, and actually I didn't mind a lot of that. Plenty of action. The burning bush. The plague of locusts. The Ten Commandments. But I don't know how well you know your Bible, anyway, not long after the Ten Commandments, it's page after page, chapter after chapter of laws and rituals. The foundation stones of the Jewish religion. Hugely important, I'm sure. But believe me, I started to lose the will to live. We got past that bit and on to lots of wars, and battles, and good people, and bad people, and the Lord popping up where you least expect him...sorry, that's a bit flippant, but that's how it seemed. But then he'd insist on going back over, and I used to dread the Ten Commandments coming because soon after I knew we'd be back into the laws and the rituals. Do not cook a young goat in its mother's milk. Have them make a chest of acacia wood, two and a half cubits long, a cubit and a half wide. Build an altar of acacia wood, three cubits high. And then he'd get his cubits mixed up and insist on going back over till he'd got it right. I knew I was that close to doing to him what he tried doing to you. All the time, though, he was building up

141

more and more material. All the names. So many lists of names. Some impossible to pronounce let alone learn by heart. I was just waiting for his brain to explode and millions of little letters to fly out across the room. He'd reached the psalms by now and I did like listening to the psalms, the poetry, the images, the humanity. so I sat them out. Then came Proverbs, and Song Of Songs. They were nice. Lyrical. Accessible, I suppose. But after that it was Isaiah, and that was going to be sixty-six chapters. Followed by Jeremiah, another fifty-two. When I saw those two looming, I told him. I said I couldn't do it any more and I wanted him to stop. I said if he wanted to learn it for his own pleasure, fine, but I wasn't going to be there to listen to it. It was becoming almost a full-time occupation, sitting with him hour after hour, day after day, while he spewed out this stuff. I'm afraid that's how I saw it. I suppose I don't disbelieve in someone or something more than us, but as an adult I've never been to church, I've never heard the Bible read except at weddings and funerals, and it never resonated with me. I told him that too. I told him it might actually also be for his own good if he stopped. I didn't want him putting weeks, months, years into this juggernaut only to realise at the end of it that it had all been for nothing. For no purpose. I did think, even if he retained it all, there was no way he was ever going to get to recite it out loud in one go. Certainly not to me, certainly not to anyone else, whether in a public arena or not. I tried to explain that with his brain, there was so much he could do, so much potential inside him, that he could share with others and still feel he was doing something genuinely worthwhile. I honestly had no idea what that might be. I mean, yes, I was flannelling big time, but I was prepared to do whatever it took.'

'And you lived to tell the tale.'

She smiles. 'With Jake, bless him, one tantrum's very like any other,' she says. 'But you know what was far worse?'

'What?'

'It was seeing the sparkle go out of his eyes,' she says. 'He was never happier than when he was learning the Bible.' She sighs and I detect the slightest quiver in her voice. 'And I stopped him.'

*

Only after our conversation about Jake's Biblical heroics do I share with Lorrie the good news about Karen. Then I tell her I'll be back the following Saturday for the deciding chess match. She says there's really no need: he and I have won one game each, it's honours even, and she was only joking when talking of a decider. I suspect that she regrets being quite so generous with her chequebook and she's trying to put me off coming, perhaps assuming that I'll be expecting another pot of money which in reality she can't afford. I suspect she may not have given me the second cheque but for Jake's attempt on my miserable life. So I do the diplomatic bit. I tell her that for the money she's already shelled out it's the least I can do to play one more match, with no further cheques expected or wanted, and call it a day. I can see relief breaking out all over Lorrie's face. She says in return she'll use her contacts to try and obtain some sustainable help for Karen to follow up the professional sessions she's having, and she hopes to have some names for me next time.

Having got home from Lorrie's I spend much of my Saturday afternoon looking through all my old personal papers and files at home to see if my travel book is among them. It's the only book I've ever written. I do actually remember the name of the publisher I sent it to. World View Press, they called themselves. The duly rejected script wasn't just returned. It came back on the rebound. I'd been warned it might take three months for a decision on publication to be made. I can't imagine this one would have been polluting the submissions editor's desk for more than about three and a half minutes. I'm quite sure that it is, as I suggested to Fiona, the worst travel book ever written by anyone, and I can't believe she will disagree. But I need to have it when I see her on Thursday or she'll think I've been wasting her time at best, or have been dishonest or disingenuous at worst. I can see the indictment now. Pursuing a course of conduct amounting to harassment of another in that you wilfully visited her place of work clutching not the promised manuscript but a great big wodge of fresh air.

I know I wouldn't have thrown it away. I put too much work into it for that. But the fact is that although in my paper chase this afternoon I've discovered letters and documents I never knew I had, and other letters and documents I did know I had but wish I'd never had, this particular piece of paperwork seems to have crept under the radar and drifted away into oblivion.

There's one last hope. Dad. I was living at home when I wrote the book and it's just possible he may still have it. I give him a ring and he says if my book was anywhere in the house it'd be in the loft in a big cardboard box. The box, he's explained, has become a giant repository for unwanted paperwork he's not known what to do with, all of it dating back to when he and mum were together. He's said he's been meaning to sift through it, with a view to filing stuff that's important or useful, and recycling or shredding the rest, but just hasn't had the inclination, let alone the energy, to do anything with it. A classic rainy-day job, really, he's said, and certainly low priority. He says if he's got time he'll have a look after lunch tomorrow.

Then on Sunday Karen rings. She wants Lorrie's address so she can send her some flowers as a thank you. Then she says that as Alan had a hot date with his Black & Decker this afternoon he hadn't fancied a trip to the loft and she'd gone up there instead. But then she'd seen how much was inside it and she'd suddenly remembered there was a really good film about to start on the Sky movie channel. She says she did have a quick skim through the material towards the top of the three billion items of paperwork and although there was no sign of my book, there were some bits of my mum and dad's family history which she says would certainly be worth looking at another time. So, yes, one day she says she'll have a closer look, definitely, but sorry, not just now, ok, and she asks me to wish her luck for my next Skype session tomorrow night.

I hang up with a sigh of disappointment. But given what she's going through just now I can't blame her for not feeling up to playing a paper version of *Where's Wally*.

*

I've an idle few minutes at work next morning so make a start on recreating my magnum opus. In fact it's not quite as

144

difficult as I feared. Frankly I could write the first words that came into my head and the literary quality would still be higher than that of the original. But then I'm forced to abort my mission. Danny's ambling in, clutching a piece of paper bearing some inky scribble. His face is suffused with disapproval. And that before he even knows about my need for an extended lunch break on Thursday.

My conscience shouldn't be troubling me. I spend far too much of my supposed free time engaged in work-related activity, a good deal of which I'm never going to get paid for. But that still doesn't stop me reacting to his advent like a schoolboy being caught for cribbing his neighbour's maths homework.

'Hi Danny,' I say. 'How are you.'

'Not great, as it goes, Matt.' He lowers his voice. 'I was summoned to a partners' meeting on Friday evening. Basically I got the third degree. They put me through hell. Ruined my weekend. I've hardly slept since. There I was, up there in room 101 at quarter past seven on Friday night, when I should have been halfway to London. They were demanding I explain why our crime workload is continuing to hurtle through the floor and was last seen heading for Grand Central Station, Canberra.'

'If they're not committing the crimes or the police aren't catching them, that's not something we can do much about,' I say. Just as I've said pretty much every time he's moved his overweight body and underweight memory round to this topic of conversation.

'They're suggesting the work's there but we're not getting a big enough piece of the pie,' he says. A grimly apposite metaphor as far as he's concerned. 'Anyway, I reassured them we've our fair share of duty slots. So they're suggesting we're losing clients after we've acted for them as duty. And next thing, muggins here is forced to undertake a check of every duty case on our system, live and concluded, whether we picked them up at the police station, whether we got them at court, and make sure we've been following them up and haven't lost them without a watertight reason.'

'I bet that'll take a while.'

'It already has taken a while.' He pulls up a chair and sits down beside me. 'I was away at the weekend so I've been at it since five thirty this morning. And I'm sorry to say this, but I've identified three cases of yours where there seems to have been no follow-up. If I tell you what they are, perhaps you can tell me what actually you have done.'

I step up to the crease and wait for the first delivery. Since I know this is a hobbyhorse of his I keep a careful personal record of each one of my duty cases and as a result I'm confident of swiping all his bowling to the boundary. But one can never be sure there won't be the odd bouncer, dangerous and unplayable, in the general mix.

'First off, Andrew Bell. You attended the police station on 10th December. Released under investigation. Nothing since.'

A slow ball, duly dispatched for four runs. 'I rang the officer last Thursday, should have a decision in a fortnight, rung the client and explained. Just hadn't quite got round to doing the attendance notes yet. On my to-do list for this morning.'

'Okay, thanks for that. Next one, Leonardus Zagurskis. Court duty case 17th December. Sent to Crown Court on bail, next hearing this Wednesday.'

The bowler's clearly learned nothing. Another inviting delivery and again the ball skims across the pitch and into the car park. 'His supporting papers for legal aid funding only came through on Friday. Should get a decision today and I've got counsel provisionally booked.'

'Super, thank you.' He's still right next to me and for one ghastly moment I think he's going to stick his bingo wings round me. 'We're a good team, Matt. I really like working with you, you know that. Just one more to go and I'll get out of your hair. Last but not least, dramatic tension-building pause...Lisa-Marie Williams.'

Just the mention of the name is enough to make me jerk upwards in my seat. I only hope there's so much of his stomach obstructing his line of vision that he won't spot it. 'Police station interview, 23rd October,' he intones. 'Re-interview 30th October, charged and bailed to attend court last Friday – and nothing. That's two and a half months, Matty.'

Worse than mate.

'She's gone over to Fargoes, Danny. I spoke to you about it

before Christmas. She's had her children taken into care and she really wants the youngest one back. I know Craig's a red-hot family lawyer and as he does crime as well, makes sense for him to do all of it. Don't you remember our conversation?'

'So she's being represented by Fargoes now.'

'As far as I'm aware, Danny, yes.'

He knots his brow. 'What do you mean, as far as you're aware? Do you think that'll satisfy the partners? Matt, either she is or she isn't. She goes to Craig or she comes back to us. Doesn't she. I mean, the only reason you'll have given it to Craig was his expertise in both areas. You said yourself. Can't think of anyone else you'd be prepared to entrust the case to. This would be a huge case for us to lose. And I'm kind of getting you really don't care whether we lose it or not.' Now the bit which means I know I'm in trouble. He comes and kneels down beside me. 'So, I've got to ask you again, Matt. Is she with Fargoes or isn't she?'

A faster ball, yes. I obviously can't say a hundred per cent that she's continued to instruct them. All I know is she's no longer instructing us. But the long run-up prior to final delivery has given me thinking time and I'm able to respond with a sound defensive stroke.

'It's fine Danny. Craig and I agreed he'd email me if there was a difficulty but I've not heard from him since I sent him the papers.'

'No email?'

'No.'

'So you're saying she'll still be with Fargoes, okay. So I can go back to the partners, tell them there's no issue with us losing clients for no good reason, and everyone's happy. Yes?' He allows himself an extravagant nod of the head and almost as a kneejerk response I'm smiling and my head's nodding too.

Next moment, his arm's sliding round me. And the McMuffin fumes are now borderline unbearable.

'Matt, you know what. We are a great team. Better than that Fargoes lot any day of the week. Shall we drink to that with a coconut milk latte? My treat?'

'Not for me, thanks, Danny.' But I'm not going to squander the opportunity presented by his sudden display of largesse.

'Tell you what though. I could use a day off on Thursday.'

'Consider it done.'

*

Three evenings and a morning are hardly long enough to complete a work of travel reportage to the standard of Paul Theroux or Patrick Leigh Fermor but, as I was kind of reflecting on Monday, such a description could never have been applied to my original work in the first place. I've little compunction about embellishing some of my experiences and inventing others. Dad's convinced that half the stuff on travel bookshelves is made up anyway. Nobody's going to know any different, he says. Obviously I've not had time to prepare a whole book: I've rattled off two chapters and I'll explain to Fiona that it's sample material and I can make more available if she wants it. I obviously need to make it look twenty-five years old and well-fingered and I end up putting as much effort into that as into the work itself.

Fiona's office is down a narrow mainly residential street just off Western Road. I ring the bell adjacent to the nameplate and she's the one who answers. She's wearing a baggy red jumper, short frayed denim skirt, black tights and green low-top Converses. But while the ensemble may lack the pzazz of those of the last couple of Saturdays I know I want to be with her and to get to know her just as much now as then and I'm hating Pete just as much now as then.

She kisses me on the cheek and I kiss her on the cheek, then she suggests we go out for coffee in the café down the next street. Any cake is likely to be a disappointment after the culinary Everests laid on by Lorrie over those last couple of Saturdays so I opt for a cheese scone and am presented with a creation of about the size of a beach ball. I slice it open and out crawls a mixture of cheese aromas, from creamy Camembert to solid Red Leicester, from robust Stilton to Roquefort where you can almost hear the bleating of ewes on the hillside and the accordion in the cobbled town square. It's while I excavate butter from the ten-cubic-metre dish of the stuff that's also been presented to me, and begin applying it to the interior of the monstrous foodstuff before me, that Fiona, who's gone for the more prosaic clingfilm-wrapped fruit flapjack, flips through my written work. Then she puts it down next to her plate. I've enough tact not to ask her opinion straight out. And she doesn't seem to want to offer one.

So we talk. I'm not wanting to talk about Pete. I'm wanting to talk about her. So she tells me about her. She tells me she's thirty-five, was born in France but came to England at the age of six, and settled in the New Forest where her parents still lived. Then she went to university in London and stayed there for her first publishing job before moving to Brighton and getting a publishing job there. She says she's always loved books and that's what led her to the publishing world. I ask her about her weaknesses. I often feel you can tell a lot about people from that. She says that apart from the normal vices, too much wine, too much chocolate, her big weakness has been social media addiction which she says got so bad that she sought medical advice and she's now closed down her social media accounts altogether. Now she just communicates by the spoken word, email and text. Then she asks me about me. I tell her about me and Emma, and about a letter just received from her solicitors which has reminded me firstly I need to put our house on the market, and secondly to remember to keep peeling off and retaining the loyalty stamps, tokens and stickers from my takeaway coffees. I tell her about my work and about Danny and the time he'd had one large fries too many and couldn't get inside the door of the court to continue a trial he was defending. Yes, that's invented, but it makes her laugh. And I find myself inventing more stuff about Danny because I'm prepared to do anything that'll make her laugh. The time races, and it's Fiona who ends up looking at her watch and saying it's time she was back at the office.

I look down at the script. Then I look up at her.

'Is there any hope for it?' I ask.

'I'd love to think so,' she says. She's not looking down at the script. She's looking across at me. 'I love your enthusiasm, and I love your style and your humour. I'm excited. I wasn't sure but came at it with an open mind and, yes… let's take it to the next stage.'

'Brilliant,' I say.

'But as for the script, I'd forget it if I were you.'

*

Another Saturday, another chess match. Fiona says she's likely to be supping another weekend helping of Diesel oil *chez* what we have now rechristened the Bus Stop Barista and I'm welcome to join her if I happen to be passing. But we also agree that there's no point really because we're mates, and when mates meet up they go to baristas who serve liquids that are actually fit to drink. We've agreed we'll meet at the Horse Guards Inn just after work on Monday and possibly go on for a bite to eat. Of course I've had to ask if Pete minds and she's said he'll be working away so he'll be none the wiser. So. I'm now the guy she doesn't want her guy knowing about. I shouldn't be smiling to myself. Really shouldn't. There's another reason to smile; having put the house on the market with Smithson's, I get a call from their top man Andrew Sherman, who says he knows of possibly six couples who could be interested and I should have a buyer before the end of the month. It may be a few days sooner if the snow promised in the long-range forecast holds off.

I decide on pedal power again for my journey to Lorrie's this morning. Despite what Fiona and I have agreed it's tempting to stop off en route and spend a few precious moments at the café with her but maybe it's the knowledge that the kiss and embrace we shared on Thursday is never going to be as good today, because when I cycle past the bus stop the temptation has melted away. I don't want to stop off. I just want to get on with this game of chess. I'm actually ten minutes early. 'He won't like you being that early,' says Lorrie. In relation to me, I can't think of a single thing he does like so I reckon I've probably got nothing to lose. I don't say all that out loud but I'm sure she knows what I'm thinking. Best to humour him, she says, and go in at the agreed time. After today you probably won't see him again, so just go along with it once more. Sit down and have a quick look at the paper, and you can have your milk and biscuits after. And please thank Karen from me for the lovely flowers. She really didn't need to.

At eleven precisely, having once more done my informal risk assessment by ascertaining that Lorrie will be in the next room, in I go. There's Jake and there's the chessboard all set out ready, with an empty wooden box next to it. The way the pieces are arranged it's clear I'm playing the black pieces. He's seated in his upright chair ready to start. He glances up at me as though I'm something rather unpleasant that got itself attached to a shoe on Brighton beach. Instinctively I offer my hand. Like the last time and the time before he doesn't take it.

'What's the point!'

Many philosophers have uttered these three syllables during the course of human history. But unless they were in Sao Paolo wanting to test the effectiveness of hearing aids being worn in Chorlton-cum-Hardy I can't believe they have ever been delivered with such force. And if I knew I were condemned to spend every Saturday morning at 11am for the rest of my life sitting in this room, facing these thirty-two wooden chessmen, with this ungrateful, surly individual glowering at me from behind them, I'd probably yell something back. Instead, knowing it won't matter after today, I just sit there and smile. Not expecting him to go on.

Only he does go on.

'If you win it makes me feel a failure and it's one more blow to my head in my sad pointless little life.' With each word he utters his face is reddening, and the foam round his lips is hurtling in my direction in sharp angry drops .I'm wishing I hadn't surrendered my jacket to Lorrie when checking in. 'And if I win I can't get past the possibility that you've let me win. How do you think that makes me feel.'

'I promise I won't let you win, Jake.'

'How the hell do I know that!' He's starting to cry, unleashing a succession of sobs boxing and coxing with snivelling of such generosity that I wonder if he's secreting the next month's water supply for the entire city up his nostrils. 'I used to be this super-intelligent guy and had this great life and now I've still got the intelligence and all it's doing now is frustrating me, because it's going nowhere except round and

151

round and in on itself and I hate it. I hate it. I ruddy hate it. I want to die. Someone let me die.' And he takes a handful of chess pieces from the board.

I can guess what's coming. An onslaught of wooden monarchs, clerics and horses, propelled into a kind of warfare to which, outside the classrooms of my early teenage years, they would have been wholly unaccustomed. I duck down in my seat and put my hands up around my face...

Nothing happens. There's a silence for perhaps a minute and a half. I dare to uncover one of my eyes and now I see him, not hurling the pieces into space but picking up the wooden box and emptying the pieces into it, one by one, from out of his hand. Even that operation doesn't go entirely according to plan, and I can only watch as the occasional pawn evades his grasp and slithers away. I rescue the rebellious pieces and add them to the box. When he's finished, he shoves the box to one side, then folds the board in half and flicks it away to his left.

'That's that then,' he says. 'I think we call that a draw, don't we. Honours even.'

I don't know what he wants me to say. So I just nod and smile.

'Won't you want to be getting along?' he asks. 'We've had our decider. In a manner of speaking. You don't want to be sitting there any more than you have to. I mean, come on, who in their right mind would want to?'

I can't work out if this question is another purely rhetorical one. 'People who want to help you,' I hear myself say.

And then I wish I hadn't said it.

'Exactly,' he retorts. 'When I was well people came to see me because they liked me and knew I had something to offer them. Now people only come because they want to help. To do their bit. Their good deed for the day. Don't tell me I can't spot it, can't see it coming, because I see it a mile off. If that's all I've got to look forward to, just being the object of charity...I want you to go. Now.'

'Sorry?'

'You heard. Just get out. Get out! Get out!'

For a moment I stay seated. I'm thinking he doesn't know what he's saying, and in my naivety I'm trying to convince myself that by staying put I'm showing that I care and want to help and there might be ways of turning all this round.

'Go! Now!'

His yells are as savage and uncontrolled as his first words to me when I came in. But maybe they just seem louder to me than they really are. Because although I expect Lorrie to come in and do what she does best, she doesn't come in. I'm not frightened for my safety – I've retreated out of reach of his arms and hands and I've no reason to suppose he's got an AK47 hidden beneath his chair. But a dark, cold fear seems to grip me all the same. It's not the fear that Lorrie may chastise me for failing to complete the match. It's the fear that I may somehow be accountable. I've never shared mum's belief in a day of judgment. I don't subscribe to the prospect of long lines of resurrected bodies, each waiting for their Maker to decide whether to issue them an e-ticket through the Pearly Gates or whether to dispatch them to their own special brand of eternal torment, be it a pit of fire or literally endless repeats of *Loose Women*. But I now find myself asking, what are we put on this earth for if we're not to be accountable, somehow, somewhere, to someone, something, for our actions. If Lorrie, who doesn't practise a faith and has only the vaguest belief in a supreme being, has taken it upon herself to effectively sacrifice her life for this guy, is she not accepting her own accountability to someone or something. And I'm under no illusions: if this whole Jake business has been some form of test, an assessment as to my ability to make a positive difference to the life of one or more other human beings, it's a test where I'd probably get one per cent for writing my name and that's my lot. Too late to pick up any more marks. The exam's over. Leave your paper on the desk and depart from the examination room in silence.

I take one last look round the said examination room. I take one last look at Jake, slumped over the table, his shouting having given way to barely audible yammering. I look up at the acres of books on the shelves. Directly in my line of vision, four tiers up from the ground, I see a book of bright red leather, the spine of which gleams in the light of the sun as it pours in through the window at the end of the room. I pull it out of the shelf. It's a Bible. The New International Version.

I open it at random and find I've turned up the beginning of the book of Job.

'Jake,' I say to him. 'Just start the book of Job will you, for me, please.'

It's as though the rain has stopped and a strip of blue sky has parted the grey clouds. Jake looks into my eyes but it's not the piercing, condemnatory look that has become his default expression when favouring me with any more than a passing glance. I hardly dare to say it but he looks pleased. He looks happy. 'Job, chapter 1?'

'Job, chapter 1.'

'"In the land of Uz there lived a man whose name was Job. This man was blameless and upright; he feared God and shunned evil. He had seven sons and three daughters, and he owned seven thousand sheep, three thousand camels, five hundred yoke of oxen and five hundred donkeys, and had a large number of servants. He was the greatest man among all the people of the East."'

It's word-perfect. 'That's amazing, Jake.'

'Thank you.' And he smiles. 'Shall I carry on?'

9

He carries on through the first chapter, and then the second. His face is fired with enthusiasm and motivation. For the first time I begin to see how far this extraordinary guy could have gone in life if the fates had given him the chance. The accuracy is spellbinding. There may be the odd insignificant error, like "broken in pieces" rather than "broken to pieces," but nothing is left out, nothing is transposed, and the delivery is smooth, controlled and steady but never too slow or too laboured. Crucially I find myself getting lost in the narrative rather than worried for him. That in itself is the best compliment I could give him.

After four chapters I suggest we call it a day. Well, a morning. I don't think I've ever had so much scripture hurled at me in one go. The odd snatch at a wedding or a funeral, but never in this quantity. The wedding snatches have tended to be of the joyful, lyrical variety while the funeral snippets have offered hope and consolation. None of that today, though. In the third chapter Job is cursing the day of his birth, and demanding that blackness overwhelm the light of day. In a strange sort of way, it seems relevant to our times. Here, on these pages, is a human being overwhelmed with despair. "'I have no peace, no quietness; I have no rest, but only turmoil.'" From my day job – no pun intended – I know there are enough people around today who are just the same. It's powerful, compulsive stuff. But after consuming those four chapters I'm beginning to get slight pangs of indigestion and I ask him if we can leave it there for today.

'When can you come back?' he asks. 'Tomorrow?'

I need to think fast. 'Maybe not tomorrow. Could be difficult.'

'Please, Matt. Soon. As soon as possible. I've learnt so much, I need to show it off.' He offers his hand to me and smiles. 'Thank you. Thank you so much.'

I almost dance from the room.

Lorrie's in the kitchen and I can't wait to tell her. The Day

This Excuse For A Man Made A Difference In A Good Way. It's like coming home and telling my mum I'd come top in my end of Year 8 French exam.

'That's a Cheshire cat of a smile,' she says. 'You won the decider then.'

'We've not been playing chess,' I tell her. 'He didn't want to play chess. We found something he'd much prefer to do. We've been doing that. He loved it.'

I see a raising of her eyebrows. 'You mean cards?'

'No. Not cards.' My smile is broadening with every word.

'Monopoly? He always beats me at Monopoly.'

'Not Monopoly. Not a game. Think...mental challenges.'

For a moment her calm, relaxed expression remains. Then, in an instant, her face does a passable impression of Niagara.

'Oh, no. Please, no, Matt. Not the Bible.'

'Lorrie, he loved it.'

'I'm sure he did, Matt. But....' She puts her hand to her face and stares down to the ground. 'Don't you see what you've done? Didn't I make it clear when we last met?'

'I know, Lorrie, but...'

'Do you know, Matt, that's the thing. I told you, didn't I, it's not much that gives me sleepless nights, but this Bible business did, and I sorted it out. So, just when I thought I had my life back, and my sanity back...' The words stop to be replaced by an all too audible sigh.

'I'm sorry. I'm really sorry.' My smile has long disappeared and is now believed to be on a Qantas flight to Adelaide.

'He won't just read and memorise for his own amusement. He needs someone to listen. Says there's no point without that. Now you've stepped in and he can smell blood. Don't you see?'

'Lorrie, I'm so sorry.'

'All I asked was you to play chess with him. Didn't I make that clear to you? I never asked you to do anything else for him. If you'd said no to the chess, fine, I could live with that. If you'd walked out when he went off on one, had a go back at him even, yep, I'd get that, you wouldn't have been the first, certainly not the last. Just chess, Matt. Just a game of chess. All you needed to do.'

'I'm sorry.' The apology needle's got stuck in the groove.

'I know you meant well, but you should have thought it through, remembered what I said. You're a bright guy, brighter than me in all sorts of ways, so couldn't you just have brought a bit of brightness to bear here. Spared a thought for what it meant to me. Not a lot to ask? Is it?'

I've never seen her like this before and it's turning me to jelly. She invites me to adjourn to the front room and to sit down. Somehow I make the journey. And when I've sat down she pushes a plate with a potentate-sized slab of a chocolatey-looking extravaganza in my direction. Then she sits. For a few moments she says nothing but I can hear her deep breaths and see how the colour of her face has darkened from cheerful pink to distracted puce.

Then she speaks.

'Matt, forgive me, I'm sorry. I shouldn't have. You've seen the state of him. You did what you thought would inspire him. Make him happy. Of course I understand that.'

I don't know what's harder to deal with, her initial anger or her climb down. Because again she's seizing the moral high ground and speaking the voice of reasonableness. I could respond to her temper by walking out. I can't walk out on her niceness and her understanding.

'He loves his Bible, does Jake,' she continues. Her face lightens. 'Always has. I respect him for it so much and I love the fact it brings him to life. Puts him in touch with what he's lost. And when you asked him to recite – oh, I'd have loved to see him. See the way his face would have lit up…' She sighs.

There's a but coming, and I know what's going to follow behind it: it's whisky to the alcoholic, she'll say, a shot of heroin to the druggie. He's been weaned off it once and that for his own good and, just as importantly, mine. Now, thanks to you, she'll tell me, he's had this taste and he's going to want more and once he's had more he won't be satisfied with that either. It was all sorted, resolved, dealt with, and now, this one thing which caused his carer sleepless nights, is an Issue again with a capital I – a capital bigger than Tokyo.

I can't bear to listen to her saying it and I'm about to spare her the bother. But she's already one step ahead even of that. The sunshine disappears from her face again.

157

'Straight choice, Matt, love. Either he has to accept this was a one-off and it's never going to happen again. Which means having to tell him. Or, you take it on your shoulders. Start coming here however often you can spare. Sitting listening to this sacred verbal diarrhoea, hour after endless hour. Bearing in mind that the longer you let him do it, the harder it will be to call time on it. You've got to be prepared to be in it for the long haul. In it until he gets to the last page. Until he can say he's recited the whole shebang from memory and he has an audience who can vouch for him.'

I bite into the cake. The sponge is just the right consistency. It's moist and rich but won't create a Pennine-style peat bog in my stomach. I don't doubt there'd be plenty more cake on offer on that long haul. But I'm under no illusions. I'd be rushing in where Lorrie, even Lorrie, this carer above all carers, feared to tread. Her explosion of ire is still ringing in my ears, more frightening for its rarity value. Forget being the hero of the hour, Matt. Remember who you are. Remember who you are not.

'I think the one-off thing is better,' I tell her.

'Good boy,' she says. 'I'll go and talk to him after you've gone.'

'Lorrie, I'll tell him. My responsibility.' The words are out before I've had the chance to think them through.

She puts her fork down and looks straight at me. 'Sure you're up to it, Matt?'

I don't know that I am. But I've said it.

'I've got to, Lorrie.' I take another bite of cake. And another. And another. Moreish doesn't do it justice. This could, almost certainly, will be my last Saturday morning spent in this way. I'm hating to think this could, almost certainly will, be my last slice of cake under her roof. As mouthful number four, or is it five, goes in, and then down, I look up at Lorrie and I'm aware that she's watching me. She's smiling.

'I wish my children had your appetite,' she says. 'I always end up with a freezer full of cake after they've been here. Now, about Karen. I've spent quite a lot of this week on Twitter, and texting and googling pretty much everyone I know. Try to sort something out for her that's sustainable, that'll follow up the professional work. Sorry it's taken a while but I've been wanting to identify the right person, the right help. Anyway I've linked up with someone who's been through exactly what Karen has. Done all the being in denial stuff. I've spoken to her and she is brilliant. She's not a professional, won't want paying, anything like that, but she really does seem to know what she's talking about and she'll be happy to give her as long as she needs, as often as she needs. Phone, Skype, whatever suits. And on top of that, if Karen wants a friendly ear she's always very welcome to call me.'

*

Fifteen minutes later, I'm back in Jake's room. I'm there alone with him: I've told Lorrie I want to do this on my own. I don't want spectators. Sitting out of reach of his roaming paws, I tell him that I think his memory is astonishing and I've loved listening to him, but both Lorrie and I are just too occupied to be able to give him the time he needs to demonstrate his skill, quite possibly unique in this country, or indeed in the world. If he can do this, I tell him, he must be capable of other, more manageable, less high-maintenance stuff which will still make him feel valuable, both to himself and to others. I tell him I hate having to say all this, and I know he won't want to have anything to do with me after today, but it really is best in the long term and I can only crave his forgiveness and his understanding.

Twenty-five minutes later, I'm leaving Lorrie's house having promised to come back on Tuesday night and carry on listening to him reciting the Bible.

I've told Lorrie I've agreed to play him at Monopoly. I lay on the flannel. Three for the price of two at Boots flannel. I tell her I loved Monopoly when I was a kid but mum and dad always seemed to lose the will to live after the first five hours, and since then I've never met anyone else who wants to play it. But she herself has mentioned Jake always beats her at the game so he must quite like it as well. It's win-win, I tell her: we're going to be playing a game we both enjoy, I'm giving her some more me-time in return for her efforts on Karen's behalf, and the Bible gets put back to bed.

And I think she actually believes me.

*

Monday has never been my favourite day of the week. I read somewhere that the third Monday in January is what's known as Blue Monday, the day of the year when people generally feel at their lowest after the excitement of Christmas has worn off and with the arrival of credit card bills they realise they're now having to think about paying for it.

But this is a great Monday. My phone rings on my way to work and it's Danny saying he's gone down with something, he feels diabolical and he will certainly be off work today and tomorrow, possibly all week. A whole week without the stench of McDonald's getting in amongst my office, my files and my nostrils. Result. Then during the afternoon Andrew Sherman rings. He tells me he's got three viewings organised already. The first one's tomorrow evening when I'm out. I've left a duplicate key with him and tell him just to get on with them. The asking price has been set some way above the supposed ceiling price for our street, but he's advising me not to accept a penny below that asking price because somebody will be happy to offer it. So maybe, just maybe, it'll be the Millets Basic Starter tent and sleeping bag, plus two-year warranty, after all.

Then this evening it's Fiona.

We meet up at the Horse Guards Inn slightly west of the city centre for a drink at the bar then at my suggestion go into the dining area for something to eat. She's all in black tonight, a plain black top partly concealed by a black leather jacket, and a long silky black skirt. Over our dinners – gammon for me, plaice for her – we talk. We talk about everything, from cycling to the criminal law. Then when I tell her that my chief interest, as far as the law is concerned, is intellectual property, she tells me that in her second and much of her third year at uni she dated an IP lawyer in London. She mentions his name and although I've never met him or dealt with him I have heard of him. She says he was obsessed with IP and discussed quite a few of his cases with her. As a result she says she knows a bit about it. So to test her I go through some of the basic concepts of IP with her and it's clear she understands them all.

All the time we're talking about her, she doesn't mention Pete once. I don't either. And I don't talk about Jake and Lorrie. It just doesn't fit into the framework of our conversation. I guess if she'd asked me whether I did any community or voluntary work I might mention it. But she doesn't. I guess if there were no other things to talk about I might mention it. But there's plenty of other things for us to talk about. I tell her about Emma, and about my family, and the little half-siblings that never made it. As I talk about George she's putting her hand on my arm. We talk IP some more. Then I try and lighten things up by going back to the Mont Blanc of lard that is my immediate boss. I've developed quite a good impersonation of him in one of his more insufferable moods and I make her laugh when I try it on her. And the more we talk, and the more we laugh, and the more we find we have in common, the more in love with her I know I am. Right at the start of the evening she's told me she's meeting a girl friend for a drink in the city centre at half past nine. Out of the corner of my eye I see a wall clock and I hate the fact the hands on it are moving so fast towards zero hour. I want so much longer. I want forever.

The location of the pub where she's meeting her friend is off my route home but I tell her I'll walk part of the way with her. We set out along the street, and how it's happened I don't know but we're walking hand in hand. The sky is clear but there's a chill wind blowing straight into our faces. A present from Moscow, the forecasters have been calling it. The start of a cold snap that's likely to bring snow to all areas by the weekend. This wind is just the giftwrapping.

We get to the point along the street where our ways must part: I've to turn left and she's going straight on. I point to the left and tell her that's my route. But I'm still holding her hand. I turn to face her and my grip on her hand gets tighter. As it tightens, I know I can't avoid the P word any longer.

'Can you help me with something,' I say.

'Go on.'

'I got the impression that time in the café that you were still very much in love with Pete.'

She doesn't say anything for what seems like minutes. Then she speaks, in a gentle whisper. 'Let's not, hey, Matt.'

She releases her hand and puts her arms round me. And I put my arms round her and gaze into her blue eyes. It's happening again, just as it happened with Karen exactly three weeks ago. There's the same physical attraction. Yet there's also the same caution, springing from the realisation that Someone Has Got There First. It may not be my dad this time, it may be someone I've neither met nor wish to meet, but he's still Got There First. I try to tell myself, surely it has to be different this time. Surely I deserve the break this time. No. Doesn't work like that. And I'm asking myself if, as far as Fiona's concerned, I'm fated to be the sideshow, to be part of the fun of the fair but then to be packed in the box once the vicar's drawn the raffle and the marquee's been dismantled.

But it's clear that, from the four syllables she's just uttered, I'm to be left in ignorance on this one. And something's telling me not to pry, but rather to dance to her tune and to enjoy the present.

For a few precious moments we remain locked in embrace. Then our lips make contact. Then our tongues.

I'm the one who withdraws first.

'When can I see you again,' I murmur.

Again, there's no immediate answer. Our tongues engage again. But this time she's the one who retreats. She pulls her whole body away from mine. 'Matt, I need to go, I'm really sorry. Text me tomorrow, okay.'

We allow ourselves one more kiss on the lips and seconds later she's gone.

10

We text each other the following morning, and in her text she tells me Pete's away this weekend and not back till Monday. We agree it would be fun to go out together on Sunday, enjoying a decent bike ride followed by a meal, preferably a Sunday roast. I offer to come round to her with a change of clothes: I tell her we can then have our bike ride, change into something cleaner, drier and smarter when we get back to her place, and go into town on the bus. She says it's a lovely idea but she's got decorators coming this week and the place will be a mess, and while she appreciates my chivalrous intentions she really has no problem lugging her change of clothes round to me. She also points out that a lot of the best pubs in the city don't serve roasts after about three on Sundays and we don't want to be clock-watching all the time we're out. And that leads me to advocate an alternative: she comes to me, we go off on our ride but break somewhere for a light pub or café lunch, then I'll cook for her in the evening. I add it'll be nice to do some entertaining in my house before being turfed out onto the street. She's fine with my suggestion. I stop short of inviting her to stay the night. If it happens it happens.

At lunchtime I plan the route. It won't be a massively long one – she's told me that there's only so much her backside can take – but it's full of variety with great views to the sea and the South Downs, and two quaint and picturesque villages in Rottingdean and Firle. Our main destination and lunch stop will be Alfriston, a large historic village with an excellent choice of cafes and pubs.

Then I check the weather forecast for the week ahead. I see the forecaster licking his lips as he prophesies that temperatures throughout the next 7 days aren't expected to climb above two degrees Celsius anywhere south of Watford Gap Services, and although at the moment there's uncertainty about the precise detail it looks as though there will be snow for many southern areas towards the end of the week. It doesn't take long for the tabloids to begin to turn the screws of sensationalism. For headlines there are all the usual ghastly puns: Snow laughing matter, It's a freeze country, Flaking out, White out of order. With them come the scare stories. Transport networks will be crippled. Essential service provision will be paralysed. Panic-buying epidemics, fuelled by good old social media, are already starting in some parts of Kent, with no toilet roll to be had for love nor money.

Karen calls during the afternoon. She says she's had another first-class session with her American counsellor; this will have been her third meeting, with one final one due next week. She's already made contact with the woman Lorrie recommended, and their sessions should start in a fortnight. She says she's so grateful to Lorrie for her help and her offer to lend a listening ear but she thinks she may be okay without that. Everything, she says, is going in the right direction. So it's in good spirits that I set off for Lorrie's, going straight there by bus after work.

Lorrie throws open the door and gives me a customary hug. She'd suggested I get there thirty minutes before our appointed time so she can ply me with high tea. I used to love high tea as a child and today's doesn't disappoint: shepherd's pie with a field of French beans, chunks of crusty cob either to accompany it or to follow, and then fruit cake. Lorrie's full of apologies that the cake isn't home-made. Shock horror, hold the front page, it's shop-bought. I joke with her that I'll refuse to eat it on principle. She says if I don't want it she won't be offended and she'll be going past the food bank next morning and they can have it if they want. She seems particularly relaxed tonight, and when I tell her so, she reminds me she has a day off from Jake on a Wednesday, and she's already looking forward to some puzzle time. She passes me a magazine open at what she says is the latest Su Doku she's working on, which has got her completely stuck. But I'm cautioned not to give her any hints. I glance down at it. I give her ten out of ten for effort, but less than one out of ten for neatness. I think she's tried all the numbers between one and six for the third square in the top row. Just a quick glance shows me it should be a nine. If she worked that out, she would then solve the rest of the puzzle in ten minutes. As it is, she'll probably need all most of tomorrow to undertake the necessary remedial work. Even then it may

164

have to go back for further repairs.

After tea I make my way along to Jake's room, where Lorrie has told me I'll find the Monopoly all set up. It strikes me I've not troubled to ask Lorrie to be there or thereabouts in the event of a further histrionic outbreak involving blizzards of Community Chest cards or Old Kent Road hotels going into orbit. Perhaps I should have asked her. It would have made our deception a little more convincing. I'd been wondering earlier if Jake himself might have said something to her to make her realise we wouldn't in fact be playing Monopoly at all. But I reason that if that was the case I'd know by now. I walk across Jake's room to the table, and a quick glance confirms the game is indeed ready to play, from the allocation of our Monopoly money to the presence of the boot and the iron on the starting block.

Then I say hi to Jake.

All of my previous visits have begun with his trademark scowl, but this evening the scowl is replaced by a broad smile. He says hello in return, takes my proffered hand, pumps it as though we're congratulating each other on getting to the top of Everest, invites me to sit in the chair opposite and produces the Bible which is open at the start of the Gospel According To St Luke.

'Not Jobbing today then, are we,' I say.

I'm taking a risk. I'm questioning his choice of scripture and I'm indulging in an infantile play on words. I expect a slap, or worse. Maybe the Good Book itself will be hurled in my direction in a type of punishment not infrequently meted out by dad's geography master. But no: there's no slap and no low-flying religious text. Rather, there's a civil response.

'I've been learning up Luke,' he says. 'Matthew and Mark are in the can. I'm finishing Luke this week, starting John I hope next. So let's get on with Luke tonight.'

Before we start, I take the precaution of rearranging the Monopoly bits and pieces to make it look as though we're in the middle of the game, just in case Lorrie should appear when we're supposed to be hard at it. Then and only then do I look down at the open Bible. Keeping my finger in the page at which the Bible was opened, I flick back to the contents page from

165

which I note that Luke is well into the New Testament. I'm no Bible scholar but I remember enough from my Religious Studies lessons at school to recall that the Bible is split into firstly the Old and then the New Testaments. Our RS teacher may not have imparted much material to us between onslaughts of paper darts and surreptitious Mars Bar consumption sessions but I know that he said an easy way to remember the number of books in the New Testament, to wit 27, was to multiply the 3 and the 9 representing the 39 books of the Old Testament. That was fine if you remembered there were 39 books of the Old Testament. It all comes back now; well, some. I seem to remember the Old Testament was way way longer than the New Testament, and was full of Charlton Heston-type episodes, with floods, human sacrifices, kings living to be over 900 years old, plagues of frogs, cities in flames, pillars of salt, and burning fiery furnaces. And then came the altogether gentler New Testament with, I seem to remember, its Sermon on the Mount, feeding of the five thousand, and water becoming wine. My brief flick back to the contents page confirms that the New Testament is indeed significantly shorter than the Old Testament, and if Jake has completed the Old Testament he has broken the back of the task and it should be a brisk canter to the finishing line.

I jest, of course. Luke's Gospel still has twenty-four chapters and the very first of them has eighty verses, with some further chapters later on boasting upwards of fifty or sixty. It's no pushover. Still, Jake negotiates, with no real fuss, the opening chapters with the familiar story of the shepherds abiding in the field keeping watch over their flock by night. It brings back memories of primary school nativity plays. The plum parts were reserved for final year pupils. I duly reached the final year and looked forward to it being my turn but I was called away for a jab just as auditions for the leads were taking place. As a result I ended up as 6th Shepherd, and any theological, spiritual or existential significance attaching to the events we were portraying was thereafter kicked into touch as far as I was concerned, never to be thrown back into the field of play. But Jake brings it back to life for me in an instant. Then he's moved on to the maturing of Jesus into a young man, challenging the

166

elders of the Temple in Jerusalem. After that comes John the Baptist and his diet of locusts and wild honey; I doubt he got that from *Woman's Own* or Weight Watchers. Then towards the end of the third chapter, I can see a killer coming. It's a genealogy, that is, a list of names tracing the ancestry of Jesus to the Lord God himself. There's nothing that would instinctively lead you from one to the other. I can see by the expression on Jake's face that he is nerving himself for this list. He takes a deep breath and dives in. He decides on the preferred ripping-plaster-from-skin method. In other words, doing it at a hundred miles an hour, presumably on the basis that to pause to think too hard about it would increase the risk of it all going horribly wrong. It's flawless. And as he reaches the end of the list, a broad smile breaks out across his face. He doesn't need to ask me if he's got it all right. He knows he has. Before I can applaud, he's going straight on into chapter four. He's the consummate professional.

He's good.

By the end of chapter six I can see he's beginning to get tired. He's left nothing out, but errors, mainly transposition errors, are starting to creep in. As he draws breath, ready to start chapter seven, I suggest to him he might like to stop. For a moment his facial expression darkens and I wonder if in a few seconds I've undone all I've done so far in getting him to see me as something more than an unwilling instrument of charity. I'm waiting for the yell. "You sit there. I'll tell you when I'm stopping and nobody else will." No: like a ray of sun momentarily blocked by a chunk of fair weather cloud and then beaming down to earth again when the cloud has passed, the light and alertness in his face soon returns. 'I'd really like to finish the first half,' he says in kindly tones. 'Can you stay for that?'

Ouch, I think: another six chapters. I glance at my watch and actually it's not as bad as I thought. So far he's been just under fifty minutes and he should only need another fifty or so to reach the end of chapter twelve. I tell him yes, I will stay, but why don't we both have a break and some refreshment before ploughing on. He seems ok with that. I ask him what he'd like to eat and drink then take his order to Lorrie in the kitchen. I assure her that he's the wizard of the Monopoly board: I explain I've landed on Park Lane, checking into the second hotel he's constructed on that thoroughfare, and it's about to bankrupt me unless I can get on particularly friendly terms with my mortgage lender. She tells me I'm a saint, and congratulates me on keeping him so quiet. I'm a bit worried that we've been occupied so long that we're interfering with normal routine, but Lorrie assures me he ate before I came and I can stay as long as I want. She says she'll get him sorted after I've gone. I collect the requested eatables and fruit juice and return to Jake's room, making a few more adjustments to the Monopoly board to reflect my now terminally impoverished state. Silence reigns for a few minutes as he champs his way through three Jaffa cakes. I've never seen such contentment and serenity in his face. It's as good a time as any to start engaging with him properly. It strikes me we've never actually had a conversation. We've interacted, yes, but have never exchanged more than a few crumbs of information about one another.

'Can I ask you something?' I say.

He frowns at me over his spectacles. 'What?'

'It's about your Bible memorising.'

And again the cloud of suspicion is transformed into the blue sky of relaxed confidence. 'Ask away, Matt.'

'When did you start?'

'I've been learning bits ever since I was a boy. Retained it. Not sure why, I just did. But the idea of learning all of it came to me about six years ago. I thought, I need a project I know will make me feel I've done something special, something different with my life. And this came to me. I don't think anyone in this country has done it or is likely to. There's no conclusive proof anyone in the world has done it. Not all at once. I know it's crazy. But I knew that if I did it I'd be remembered for it. It's what we all want, isn't it, Matt. To be remembered for something. And I'd be remembered as the man who learnt the Bible. So I started preparing. Opened the book at Genesis, creation in 7 days, and off I went. And pretty much every spare moment I was either recalling stuff I knew already, or learning, learning, learning, and more learning. But then I thought, I need someone with me. A prompt, mentor, call it what you will, someone to help me, encourage me, someone to bounce it off, as I'm building up the stuff I'd remembered. I'd not got round to thinking who I'd recite the completed Bible to, where I'd do it. That could wait till I'd got it all learnt. All I wanted in my preparation stage was just one person. I asked Lorrie and she agreed. I went through huge chunks of it with her. Must have been, what, two thirds of the Old Testament. Then she told me she wanted me to stop. Told me there were better things I could do with my time. Like playing cards. Doing Su Doku puzzles. Feeding the ducks on the Trinity Street duckpond.'

'Or chess.'

'Truth to tell, I'm not that keen on chess.' He picks up Jaffa cake number four. 'I don't like it any more than I like Monopoly. I pretend to like it because it makes her happy. Keeps her quiet. But it's not what I do. It's not who I am.' He points down at the Bible. 'That's what I do. That's who I am. Now if I want to do it I have to do it all on my own.'

I'm confused. 'So you're saying you can prepare on your own? Don't need Lorrie?'

He frowns and punches the table. 'I've done my best,' he says, 'but I can't do it on my own. Not any more. It feels meaningless, not without someone listening. There's no feedback, no support, no encouragement. Never going to get to recite it all out loud to anybody, anywhere. That's what I've been wanting. To learn it, rehearse it with a mentor, prompt, whatever, then do it all in public. And I could never organise that without help. Help I'm never going to get. After Lorrie pulled out I tried, heaven knows I tried, to go it alone, but I've been hating it. I got to this last Christmas and I realised I was going to have to give it up. Hardest decision of my life.' He reaches out and places his hand over mine. 'Maybe you could give me what Lorrie can't. Or won't.'

I'm lost for words. To accept would be to boldly go where even Lorrie has never gone before. To refuse would be like cutting off his oxygen.

'I want you to think about helping me, Matt, all right.' He withdraws his hand, and takes a deep breath. 'I want to do it all, Matt. I'm going to do it. One day. Recite the lot. Out loud. In front of other people.' He sits back in is chair. 'I used to do stuff in front of other people. Loads of stuff. I lectured. On psychology, psychoanalysis. Not just students. Experts from all over the world. I loved it. It was like a drug, the buzz I got from standing in front of a room full of people, sitting, hanging on each word. I never needed notes. I just knew the stuff. I lived for the attention, the laughter, the applause...then I had my accident and they threw me out and it all stopped.' He looks into my eyes. 'Matt, I was somebody once. I was respected. I was an...an authority. People listened to me. Now nobody listens. When people stopped listening to me, when they stopped thinking I had something to say, when they stopped appreciating me for what I could offer...that was when I started to die.'

I see tears in his eyes. In my own mind's eye I can see an oak-panelled lecture theatre and Jake standing in his gown, pacing back and forth across the stage, never once needing to glance at the lectern, captivating, enthralling his listeners with his dazzling rhetoric, stunning the world of psychoanalysis with the force of his unassailable arguments. Then, I look across at what's left. I see only a sad, lost man with so much still to say but nobody to say it to.

'They'll listen to you again, Jake.' It's as cheesy as an online order for Gorgonzola. But as I see the smile that these words elicit, a smile as broad as the Champs Elysses, I might just have told him he was being offered the key to the Ark of the Covenant.

'I want to do it all, Matt,' he says again. 'Start to finish. Before I die.'

'Would be a bit difficult to do it after.' Why did I say that. It's the sort of silly, flippant comment I might share with Lorrie over her latest ozone-layer-touching cake. It's inviting not just a shout but a screech of censure.

But no: he gives me another smile. It's as if the moment he applies himself to his Bible learning not only does he acquire the ability to communicate rationally, but his humanity is restored.

'You're not frightened of me any more, are you Matt,' he says.

*

I listen to him for not six but ten more chapters: four extra for good behaviour. Then I tell him I have to leave as I can't risk missing the next bus. There is some truth in that: having checked the bus times I'd be in for a very long wait if I didn't make the one due in twenty minutes. But the real reason is that I have had more than enough of St Luke fed to me by now. I also explain I can't come this weekend; I don't bother him with the reasons but they're solid enough. I've agreed to do a 24-hour police station duty on Friday and inevitably there'll be cases I pick up on Friday which don't get sorted till Saturday. On Sunday it's Fiona. But barely have I told Jake that I'm unavailable at the weekend than he's made me promise to phone as soon as possible to agree when our next session can take place; he says at that session he plans to recite the whole Gospel to me, plus John's Gospel depending on when I return. Then and only then does he allow me to leave and we say goodbye. I go back to Lorrie and tell her that our Monopoly is over: I explain he's not only squeezed me completely dry but got me put on a worldwide credit blacklist, while he, jammy so-and-so, has bought a third Park Lane hotel and is holidaying in the Antibes on his rental income from the waterworks. She hugs me and force-feeds me another slice of the much-maligned fruit cake. The food bank's lost out after all. Lorrie wraps the rest in tin foil and tells me to take it home to eat in front of *News at Ten*. I tell her I'll ring her when I've come off that blacklist and am once more legally permitted to own and draw rental income from real property. She says there's absolutely no hurry and she couldn't blame me if I said I was never coming back. We hug and we kiss and we're all smiles.

But as I hasten towards the bus stop, my smile fades. For it's now, only now, back out on the cold street on a cold hard moonlit night, that I start to think rationally about what I might be letting myself in for as a result of being so encouraging to Jake in relation to his Bible-learning endeavours. I may not have committed myself to anything specific, but I've said

171

nothing to disabuse him of any notion he may have that I'm prepared to support him. I've even said that people will listen to him again. If I were on trial for inciting him to unleash excessive quantities of sacred text onto an unsuspecting public, that assertion alone could be interpreted as a damaging admission, serving to bolster the prosecution case against me and increasing the likelihood of a guilty verdict. I'm thinking, suppose I do agree to provide the mentoring he wants. At once, the realisation of the magnitude of that task hits me like a lorryload of granite. I'm thinking back to my conversation with Lorrie ten days ago when she told me how many whole books of the Old Testament she'd already had to listen to before she told Jake she couldn't take any more. There was Genesis, Exodus, Psalms, Proverbs, Song Of Songs, and shedloads of others besides, I don't doubt. I've heard just two thirds of a single book and my resolve is flickering. For a moment I panic.

Then on boarding the bus I'm struck by an idea. I could suggest to Jake that he deliver a public rendition of the very portion of scripture he's just been spewing, the Gospel According To St Luke. It's a favourite with many: those shepherds, no room at the inn, that Good Samaritan, and the Prodigal Son. They're crowd-pleasers, all of them. He reckons the complete gospel, which he wants to perform to me in full next time, will take three hours, once he's perfected it. He may be able to trim this time down still further. Although I'm no churchgoer myself, I know there are churches all over Brighton, and I'm thinking that one of them, maybe more than one, would welcome the prospect of a possibly unique presentation of this portion of scripture to their congregation over the course of an afternoon or evening. Of course the logistics will pose a significant challenge. Three hours is still a long time for people's posteriors to be in contact with the cold, hard pews that I assume still to be the lot of modern-day church attenders. But we can work round that somehow, whether it's a bulk order of cushions or an interval with stiff gins all round. In practical terms Jake's never, bless him, going to be able to recite the whole Bible, with all the mentoring assistance and organisational headaches that would entail. But a single, much-loved, book of the Bible is doable. Jake's hard work will have borne fruit; with the extensive plaudits which his word-perfect rendition will have earned, he will have that appreciation he's told me he misses so much. In a further burst of inspiration, I'm thinking that perhaps we can film it and upload it to You Tube so his efforts, and the resultant applause, are available to him to watch back as often as he wants, and can be enjoyed by others too.

As for Lorrie, well, she won't need to be involved at all, save for ensuring he gets him to and from the venue in one piece; since I'm happy to be his mentor, there'll be no risk of her getting sucked back into listening to him for hour upon hour, day after day, as she felt obliged to do before.

It's perfect.

As I sit on the bus, the phone goes. It's Andrew. I have an offer, way in excess of the asking price. They're cash buyers with no onward chain. The only condition is that they must have vacant possession by the end of February or the deal's a no-no.

I ask Andrew's advice. He tells me if he were me he'd be biting their hands off.

That'll do me.

*

As prophesied, the cold snap continues. The skies remain clear and blue throughout Wednesday, Thursday, Friday, and into Saturday. The bad news is that the wind has been and is coming straight from Russia, intensifying by the day. It's bringing with it an unwanted late Christmas feast: the Moscow Monster, the tabloids are calling it. Today, Saturday, sees the appetiser in the form of barely tolerable frigid air, with wind-chill bringing temperatures down to minus twelve degrees Celsius. Tomorrow, Sunday, late morning, the main course arrives at our table. Twelve inches of snow will fall across Kent, with the snow spreading, albeit in slightly less generous quantities, to all parts of Sussex as the afternoon goes on. The pudding course comes with the Monday commute: following the snowy blitzkrieg, there'll be a hard frost that will react with the packed snow to render most roads and pavements

173

impassable. The city's bus company are already warning that they might not be able to run any services on Monday morning at all. It's no surprise when Fiona messages me asking if we're still on for tomorrow's bike ride. I wonder if there's a dollop of subtext there, in the form of an unspoken challenge. Pete, the all-round sporting supremo, wouldn't let a little inconvenience like an Arctic-style blizzard interfere with his itinerary, so let's hope you're not going to either, Matthew Chalmers. I reply at once saying it'll just mean an extra pair of gloves and one more layer of thermals, the vat of coffee and sausage sandwiches at the Jolly Teapot will just taste a whole lot better, and I relish the more testing cycling conditions and the payback in the form of a landscape transformed into a white winter wonderland.

In truth I'm praying the forecasters have got it all wrong.

I wake up on Sunday and gaze out of the window. Again there isn't a cloud in the sky and I'm beginning to think we may be all right. I go to my phone and get the latest forecast. It seems the snow's enjoying a bit of a breather somewhere in the Ardennes and may struggle to get to us in Sussex until late afternoon, especially if the French air traffic controllers are on strike again. I've certainly no intention of still being out in the late afternoon so I'm not hugely worried, and remain unworried despite receiving a text from Fiona, shortly after my checking the forecast, to the effect that she's running late. Anyway when she does appear, half an hour later than previously planned, I'm pleased and relieved to see she's clad sensibly: she wears a sturdy cycle helmet, thick yellow woollen scarf, thick green coat, matching thick green gloves, black corduroy trousers and trainers. Functional has to rule today, well, until we get home at least. We exchange a cursory kiss on the lips then I tell her we should get going at once to ensure we're back well before the weather does its worst. The plan is to follow the coast road to Seaford via Newhaven, turn inland to reach Alfriston which we should make in time for a lunch at about 1, then head back along an inland route to Lewes past Alciston and Firle. At Lewes, depending on the time and our state of fitness, we can choose how much of the route back to Brighton to cover by train and how much to cycle, bearing in mind there are trains from Lewes and Falmer. I've deliberately chosen a direction of travel which means we battle with the wind for the early part. Then when we get to Alfriston we can relax, knowing the wind will chase us home.

Having set off at eleven o'clock we make our way from my house down to the coast road, picking it up by the Palace Pier. There's then an uphill slog to the Marina entrance, beyond which things level out a little and there's a clifftop cycle path available all the way from here to Rottingdean. As we follow the cycle path, enjoying grandstand views of the Marina and the sea under clear skies, I keep looking to the far horizon, as if by gazing alone I have the power to repel the grey clouds that carry the Moscow Monster on their backs. We drop down to Rottingdean, one of the prettiest villages in the county with its Kipling associations, and we permit ourselves a five-minute detour to see the house where the great man lived at the start of the 20th century. Beyond Rottingdean there's a big climb, another descent to pass Saltdean with its splendidly restored Lido, and then a murderous ascent to Telscombe Cliffs and Peacehaven, two sprawling and largely forgettable coastal settlements. But beyond Peacehaven there's a long and exhilarating descent to Newhaven where beyond the river Ouse it's a low-level ride to Seaford with just one modest rise and descent, and a fine view to the pre-Norman church at Bishopstone. We reach Seaford at 12.30 and we've only another three miles from here to Alfriston. I'm pleased at how well we've done. My only regret is we've had no real chance to talk thus far. In fact my only communication with Fiona has been to look back periodically to check that she's not lagging and that she's all right. And each time she's smiled and given me the thumbs-up. Her face glows with contentment. But I can see that face getting redder and more wind-blown each time I look at her. And the last three miles from Seaford to Alfriston are tough, involving a massive descent and punishing climb. At least the surroundings provide more than adequate compensation for the hard work, especially the views to the Cuckmere River as it snakes its way southwards from Alfriston towards the sea. We arrive in Alfriston at one o'clock exactly.

Alfriston is full of history. My favourite building, among the tile-hung, flint and timber-framed constructions on the High

175

Street, is the 16th century Star Inn, its ceiling timbers decorated with carved animals. On the street corner beside it is a large red lion, the figurehead of a 17th century Dutch ship, pilfered from a wreck off the Sussex coast. It's such an unusual and photogenic feature. I also love the green at the top end of which is the 14th century parish church of St Andrew, known as the Cathedral of the Downs. I remember mum, dad and me doing a running race across from the church on one side to the timber-framed 14th century Clergy House on the other. I was told there would be a prize for the winner. I won, and my prize was mum feeding me the fascinating information that the Clergy House was a Wealden yeoman's house and was the first purchase of the National Trust. I'd have preferred a bar of chocolate and said so.

Having battled with the cold and the wind all morning, however, neither Fiona nor I are in the mood for sightseeing. The priority is hot food and drink and we decide on the Jolly Teapot on the east side of the square. A real fire crackles in the corner of the dining room, and the smell of seasoned logs burning in the grate competes for nostril delectation with the aroma of freshly-baked bread. We need the hottest thing on the menu and in response to our request the waitress brings us twenty-fathoms-deep bowls of soup and chunks of warm loaf with ramekins full of creamy butter. As Fiona and I tuck in, we relive the scenic highlights of our ride so far, then we talk about places we've cycled to and places we'd like to cycle to. I want us to be visiting them together. And it's the fact I want us to be visiting them together, and my making it clear that I'd like us to be visiting them together, which means I have, somehow, to confront the absent figure, the one standing in the way, the one who Got There First.

By now we've finished our soup and we've moved on to coffee. The armchairs either side of the fireplace, occupied by others when we arrived, are now empty and the waitress invites us to take our coffee to those armchairs if we so wish. The fire is burning as brightly as it was when we arrived but the glow is as a feeble spark compared with the glow I see on the face of the woman who is beside me.

We settle in our chairs and I'm trying to think how to raise the question of that absent figure. I'm lost in thought for two or three minutes and she's the one who speaks first.

'I need to ask you something, Matt.'

'Go on.'

'Well, you know Pete told me he was away with work this weekend.'

'Right.'

'He told me he was going to be staying and working in York. He forwarded me his online hotel booking form so I knew where he'd be. You know York pretty well, don't you.'

'Oh yes.'

'Well, I've not told you this, but before Pete went to Europe and met me, he was seeing a girl called Lucy. They were very close. He was crazy about her. Then she left him for another guy. Broke Pete's heart. Well, last year, we found she'd split with that guy. And I remember him telling me she'd got herself a flat in this place called Stamford Bridge. I wasn't that interested, really. She was history. He'd moved on. I didn't really give a monkey's.' She sits forward in her armchair. 'Is Stamford Bridge close to York, Matt?'

'Just a few miles away. Like, the next village.'

'Honestly?'

'I know it. I've visited it.'

Her head drops. 'I should have known it, Matt,' she moans. 'What a fool. What a stupid fool.'

'What's wrong?'

'I always thought Stamford Bridge was in London,' she says. 'You know, as in football ground. Chelsea's home ground. Or Fulham's. One of them. Just assumed this Lucy had moved to London. But yesterday when I had the radio on, I don't know why, it could have been a quiz or something, they were talking about the Battle of Stamford Bridge in 1066. And they said it happened in what's now Yorkshire. Well, don't you see?'

I nod. 'He won't be doing much work while he's in York, in other words.'

'I am so flaming stupid.' She takes a slurp from her coffee cup. 'I'm quite sure he knew I'd have no idea about this other place called Stamford Bridge. He must have taken me for such a mug.'

177

Now the lawyer in me comes to the fore. 'York's a big place, Fi,' I say. 'It could just be coincidence.'

She shakes her head. 'He's never ever been to York with work before,' she says. 'I did a bit of googling about the company he works for. They've not got an office in York. Never have had. Thing is…and I know you'll say I'm probably being ridiculous – I've kind of always believed in karma. Here I am, going on dates with you behind his back – and this is my punishment. My husband, the guy I thought would never cheat…Matt, I think he's been lying to me.'

'I so hate liars,' I say. Even more I hate the hypocrisy inherent in saying it because I know there are times I've lied. We all have. Sometimes we lie for the best of motives, but we all do it. We're all liars. Now, though, on this bitter Sunday afternoon in a café in a chocolate-box East Sussex village, is the time to hate them.

'I think we may be in trouble,' she says.

Still the lawyer refuses to leave the court room. 'It's only a couple of weeks since you were telling me how good you two were.'

'I think I was trying to convince myself, to be honest. Talking myself into believing it was all good. The more I said it, the better suddenly our marriage would be. Five years is a while, Matt. A lot of my friends who got married about the same time as me, their marriages are breaking up. Have broken up. I was determined it wasn't going to be the same for us. I've always tried to love him…always tried to do my best for him…I guess the best isn't always good enough.'

Now she gets out of her chair and kneels at the foot of my chair and places her arms round me. I can feel her shaking. 'Matt, I'm scared.'

'You don't need to be scared,' I say. 'I think Pete's a fool. But it's his decision and it's his loss. You're with me now and I'm going to look after you and I'll never ever leave you. Do you trust me?'

She looks into my eyes and a broad smile envelops her face. 'Of course I do.'

'Hold my hand,' I say.

She withdraws her arms from round my back and places her

hands in mine.

'And you want to stay with me?' I say. 'Be together with me?'

She nods and smiles again.

'I love you, Fi.'

'I love you too, Matt.'

And the kiss that follows is the best ever.

*

We emerge from the café and I reel back in shock. The blue sky has gone. In just the time we've been sitting indoors, the azure mattress above the village has been covered by a sheet of whitish grey. The wind squeals and moans and howls. I can feel fragments of white in the air, teasing, testing the waters, ready to signal to its millions of companions to join it in smothering the Sussex countryside, and blanketing us as well.

I'd planned a more adventurous roundabout route back to Lewes avoiding the main road, following a byway above the villages of Berwick and Alciston as far as Firle, and then a minor road immediately below the green tower that is Mount Caburn. But I daren't risk narrow or rough roads and the priority is our safety. So the main road it has to be. The wind is helping us now, carrying us along, goading us forward. But there's no cordiality in its currents of razor-sharp air. We're the naughty children who've had the temerity to venture out today in defiance of good sense and now we're being sent home with a slap on the wrist and a warning not to do it again. We need just forty minutes to cover the nine miles to Lewes. I'm beginning to relax again. The random flakes are still random and still flaky and the sky is still light enough to make me think that the main event is going to await our return home. So I suggest to Fiona that even though we could get a train back from Lewes we press on, using the cycle lane parallel with the main Lewes to Brighton road.

Then no more than ten minutes out of Lewes, the sky darkens and it's as if a great bath plug has been yanked from the grey mantle above us. There's suddenly nothing but white and it's coming at us from all sides. In minutes, the dark tarmac beneath our wheels and the wheels of the cars that hurtle past on the adjacent carriageway is buried by a wintry carpet that's getting thicker by the second. I'm shaking, not from cold, but from fear that I'm not just needing to take care of myself but the woman to whom less than an hour ago I pledged my love. I permit myself a glance behind me. She's still there but the glowing enthusiasm that characterised her battle with the wind on the way out has been replaced with an expression of anguished determination. I think about turning back to Lewes and get as far as stopping my bike and reversing it. The wind almost blows me off my feet and chunks of snow hurl themselves into my eyes and threaten a Panzer-style invasion of my nasal cavities and earlobes. There's no way I'm subjecting either of us to taking on the wind as well as the snow. So on we go as before. I tell myself what I always tell myself when adverse weather catches up with me towards the end of a ride, that every turn of the pedals is a turn closer home. But as we battle up the hill past the South Downs Way junction at Housedean Farm I'm scared for Fiona, scared that she won't have been schooled in cyclists' optimism. It's with a gasp of relief that I reach the crest of the hill, see Fiona is still tucked in behind me, and realise that it's a simple downhill canter past the university buildings to the sanctuary of Falmer Station.

Simple downhill canter. Matt, you twerp, how could you have been so crazily complacent. The lying snow has turned the pavement into a ski run. As we progress downhill, my brakes can't stop the slide of the wheels and I'm forced to use my feet to regain control of my machine and my destiny. But as my speed lessens my ears are stung by the sound of screeching from behind me and then alongside me. I can't work out if it's the sound of a human being or the sound of a bike. But whoever's made it or whatever's made it, what I'm seeing is Fiona, evidently lacking the experience and capacity for quick thinking, careering past me. A moment later, she's swaying to the right and then lurching to the left. Her wheels, deprived of any traction, skid off the path at an angle of forty-five degrees. A moment later she's hurled from her machine and is catapulted into the air before crashing to the ground with a thud while her cycle, choosing a different direction altogether, smashes into a nearby bush.

Thank her lucky stars, she was protected by her cycle helmet and doesn't seem to be hurt. She rises to her feet in seconds and shakes off the snow hanging from her coat and trousers. I ask her if she's okay. She says she's fine and she's more concerned about her bike. I pick it up and examine it. It's clearly not rideable – the chain's broken and one of the pedals has smashed – but at least it's manoeuvrable and it's a short walk with the bikes to Falmer Station. I've lived in the area long enough to know that trains from here, even on Sundays, are frequent. What's more, I've checked and there are none of the dreaded rail replacement bus services out today. I tell her we'll be back in central Brighton in no time and we can work out how to get back to my house from there.

Which all sounds fine until we get to the station entrance and find that owing to a weather-related incident in the last half-hour, all services between Lewes and Brighton have been suspended with immediate effect. And on checking my app I find that within the last ten minutes a decision has been taken to pull all bus services in the city until tomorrow morning at the earliest.

Meanwhile the snow is continuing to cascade from the sky, its intensity clearly discernible against the glow of the orange light shining on the station forecourt, and I'm expecting a burst of Aled Jones' *Walking In The Air* at any moment.

An idea strikes me and I turn to Fiona. 'You live in Falmer, don't you.'

'Mmm.'

'Far from here?'

'About…fif…twenty minutes' walk.'

'What if we go to your place.'

She shakes her head. 'You've got no change of clothes.'

'I'm fine in what I've got on.'

'And I've got no food in.'

'Doesn't matter. We'll grab a pizza, whatever.'

'Matt, we can't.'

'Why not?'

'I told you. I've…we've got the decorators in.' I can see her face in the orange light and her cheeks, already a generous shade of red, seem to acquire a fresh, darker layer of red with each syllable she utters.

'It's only a bit of wet paint.'

'It's more than that, Matt. House is in a complete mess.'

'I don't mind that.'

'Well, I do.'

'Your safety's the main thing,' I say. 'Our safety.'

'We just can't, that's all.' Worry lines are playing all over her forehead.

'Is there a problem?'

'For crying out loud, Matt!'

It's the first time she's addressed me with such volume and such anger. And I feel a chill inside me because it sounds just like Emma. I can't do Emma any more. I want to love again, and to be loved by someone who doesn't do things like Emma did them.

But as I stand there, gazing at her, my body shaking from the cold and now from the fear, her face transforms. The anger melts away in a moment. She starts crying. Tears dribble down her deep red face. 'Matt, sweetie, I'm sorry. I didn't mean to snap, I really didn't. Please forgive me.'

She wipes the tears from her eyes, wraps her snow-flecked arms around me and a moment later we're kissing through the snowflakes, our cycle helmets still perched on our heads.

*

In the end we manage to get a taxi, but only after contacting five other firms which haven't wanted to know. The driver who does condescend to come and collect us says he can't accommodate our bikes, which we end up having to secure in the bays outside one of the university buildings, but is still happy to charge a fare that's way over the odds. As Fiona's insisting on paying it, though, and won't be persuaded otherwise, I don't interfere.

It's a hairy journey back to my place but we get there, stagger inside and collapse in each other's arms. We take off our coats and regroup with mugs of tea and slices of cake. Then

I suggest to Fiona that she might like to change out of her cycling clothes into the clothing she's brought with her. She says she's happy to stay as she is. There's nothing wrong with the baggy grey pullover that removal of her coat reveals, or the corduroy bottoms from which the last vestiges of wintry mix have now been brushed. I tell myself that if things turn out as I hope they will, I'll need to get used to the baggy and workaday as well as the style and the glam. Perhaps this is her way of reminding me of that. I leave her with a second mug of tea while I go upstairs and prepare the bed. Then I come down and we light some candles, switch off the lights and curl up with the DVD of *Titanic*. I think I last watched it with Emma from start to finish three weeks before we got married. I would have liked to watch the DVD again. But as Emma, ever the down-to-earth one, reminded me, forcefully and irrefutably, it's on one of the freeview channels practically every Bank Holiday weekend of the year, so why bother. Fiona's seen it as well but she says she loves it and would never get tired of it. We sit on the settee, side by side, hand in hand. As the film progresses, Fiona keeps very quiet. Thank heavens. If I'm enjoying a film I like to do so in silence. In fairness Emma was always good like that too. It's Karen who's the shocker in that regard. So yes, it suits me that Fiona remains silent and does so pretty much throughout the first half of the film.

I wait till we've got past the nude painting scene just before the eponymous vessel's meeting with the friendly passing iceberg, then suggest an intermission for more substantial refreshment. Fiona says that she doesn't want to be too late, so perhaps we can eat and watch at the same time. I'm happy with that: Fiona had told me not to go overboard, no pun intended, so I'd gone for convenience over cordon bleu. I do the necessary microwaving, and in no time our plates of food are on our laps and it's back on with the film. Then as the waters envelop the ship, and as I hold on to Fiona's hand, so my sense of anticipation and excitement is washing round and over my body at the thought of what awaits us. I want the film to end and am just willing Leonardo to get on with it and sink into the icy waters. He seems to take a lot longer about it than I remember from my previous viewing. And it still feels like another two transatlantic voyages could have taken place in the time it takes to draw proceedings to a close. But close they do. The music stops, I flick the telly off and it's just us, our hands still clasped in the flickering candlelight.

'I so love you,' I say.

We kiss.

'I so love you too, Matt.'

We kiss and kiss.

'So want you,' I say.

We kiss and kiss and kiss.

'Let's go to bed,' I say.

'Can you just give me a second, Matt. Just need the bathroom.'

'Sure. First right, top of the stairs. Bedroom's next one beyond that.'

She gets up from the settee and leaves the lounge. I put a light on, blow out the candles, then take the dirty plates and cutlery out to the kitchen and throw them in a bowl of water with the rest of the washing-up. It can wait till morning.

I'm curious about what the weather's doing. I'm hoping Fiona will be happy to stay the night but if she really does want to go home I'm concerned about how, and indeed whether, she'll make it. It could be that the worst of the blizzard is over, but equally the cessation of the snow earlier may just have been a temporary lull and we could now have moved to something altogether more apocalyptic. I open the back door and a blast of cold air smashes into me. Having picked up the pieces, I walk out into the garden.

And it's as I walk outside that I feel as though I've been carried into a different, gloriously different world. No snow is falling; the small back lawn is blanketed in white but above us is a sea of stars, and the sky seems awash with effulgent glitter. I want to reach out and grab a handful, and come back for more. The stars are shining and the woman I have learnt to love is waiting.

I come back in and close the door and let the warmth of the kitchen embrace me once more. Then I make my way upstairs to the bedroom.

It's empty.

I go back out to the bathroom and knock on the door. There's no answer. I try the door and it opens. She's not there either.

I call out to her. She answers. But her response comes from the lounge.

I go back to the lounge and she's standing there fully clothed. She's got her scarf, coat and gloves on and has her cycle helmet in her hand.

'What's wrong?'

She bursts into tears. 'I can't, Matt. I can't.'

I put my arms round her. She grabs them and pushes them away.

'Fi, what the hell's the matter?'

She shakes her head. 'I don't...can't...'

'Is this Pete? Have you been talking to him?'

She shakes her head. 'I just think we have to stop this now.'

'What do you mean, stop?'

'I mean we just don't see each other again. We say we've had a great time but we can't go on.'

'Not even as mates?'

'Would never work, Matt. We'd always want more.'

'And you won't give more?'

She shakes her head. 'I won't. I can't.' Now she places her arms round me and kisses my lips. 'Thank you Matt for everything. Now I've got to go.'

'You can't go out in this.'

'Got to.' Her lips barely move.

And before I know what to say next she strides to the door, opens it and disappears into the frozen night.

11

For a moment I just stand there, crushed by disbelief and bewilderment. Then I get moving and in a few strides I've reached the pavement along our street. But the wasted seconds are fatal. There's no sign of her. I figure she's likely to be heading for the city centre so I turn right and start to run. But in the light of what's just happened I've forgotten that the pavements have been transformed into ice rinks and all that's missing is Torvill & Dean and a burst of Ravel's *Bolero*. Without warning the concrete underneath me seems to disintegrate and the next moment I'm crashing buttocks first to the ground. A glance at the scoreboard indicates I've scored a token 1.5 for originality but a resounding minus five for star quality, and even taking the public vote into account I'm almost certain to have to go through the rigours of the elimination dance-off.

I'm not injured. My inside is doing cartwheels at a hundred miles per second, and my pride is more bruised than the bananas on special offer outside the Happy Mart in Lindisfarne Drive. But I'm able to haul myself up onto my feet without the need for any Lorrie-esque acts of kindness and a few minutes later, aware of the impracticability of continuing my search, I'm back inside my house and slumped on my bed. I try phoning Fiona but it's no surprise that she doesn't answer.

I try to tell myself that Pete was always going to be a massively complicating factor. And even if he'd been out of the picture from the start, Fiona and I had only dated two or three times. This wasn't a long-term romance within which we'd made vows of life-long commitment. As the Carpenters nearly sang, we'd only just begun. But then I think how that song continues. Sharing horizons that are new to us. Talkin' it over, just the two of us. So much of life ahead. It's the thought of what we could have enjoyed together that prompts the tears that irrigate my pillow.

Somehow, I don't know how, I get some sleep but it's no surprise to wake up and see from my phone that it's still only five to four. I lie there till half past five then decide to get up, get ready for work and go back out to Falmer to collect my bike and wait until she comes to pick up hers. She told me yesterday evening she planned to collect it first thing this morning. I've made up my mind I'll wait as long as I have to.

It's still dark but from what I can see by the streetlamps there appears to have been no more snow in the night. I pour myself some cereal and go online to find that because of the dangerously icy conditions there will be no trains until eight at the earliest, and although a limited bus service is operating, the buses will be confined, for the time being, to routes in and around the city centre.

I decide to set off on foot. I can cut round the centre of the city and pick up Lewes Road which I can then follow all the way to Falmer. If a bus comes along, it's a bonus, but even if no bus does appear I'm still hoping I can get there well before eight. I'm wearing my work suit and a pair of shiny red wellies that I found in the cupboard under the stairs. I think Emma got them online, found they were too big for her and never got round to returning them. They actually fit me quite well. They wouldn't win any plaudits on the catwalk but they do their job, saving me from further episodes of dancing on ice, and even without mechanical aid – I've not seen a single bus since I set out – I'm able to make it to Falmer with no difficulty. I look at my watch and it's still only twenty past seven.

As I approach the spot where we parked the bikes I rehearse what I'm going to say to Fiona. In essence, I've two main points. Point one, that if she's got this close to being unfaithful to Pete she's clearly got a problem with him and if so, and if Pete is himself faking business trips in order be with the woman he really wants, isn't it better that she just gets out of their toxic relationship so that she and I can be together. Point two, that yes, our relationship has blossomed in a very short time but there's been electricity there from the start; unless I've done or said something wrong, and/or unless I've missed something, we have such a great future ahead of us and while she may feel nervous about committing to me in the bedroom we know we belong together so let's just take it gently at first and allow the physical aspect to follow when the time is right.

187

Then I turn the corner to arrive at the bike racks and see that her machine isn't there any more.

*

I try to ring Fiona again and there's no reply. I text and there's no reply. I walk to her office and ask to speak to her but I'm told she's called in sick and in any case is likely to be working from home for most of this week.

By now the exertions of my walk to Falmer and my bike ride back into the city are beginning to bite. I'm starting to get pain from the part of my backside that took the greatest part of the impact during my impromptu ice-dancing of the previous night. I'm not ill and I've previously gone into work feeling far worse. Throughout my legal career I've only had half a dozen days off sick, all when I was genuinely ill. I've never before taken a day off sick when I've not been genuinely ill. But I've made up my mind I'm going to take one now.

I phone Danny and tell him I've got a bad stomach upset and won't be in. I don't expect him to like it. I was supposed to be doing a trial at Brighton Magistrates' Court this morning. Well, I say that, but we've no defence and the client's only running it because he thinks his ex-wife, whom he allegedly struck during an argument in the street, won't turn up. If she does, he'll go guilty. If she doesn't the prosecution will drop it. So it won't be a trial at all. But even before I tell Danny all that, he's turning on the sympathy tap. Poor you, he says. Lot of it about this time of year. You just lie there, get better, and we'll look forward to seeing you when you're up and about. He couldn't have been nicer. Here he is under so much pressure from the partners and he can still take time out to care about his colleague. I feel another coconut milk latte treat coming on. My treat.

*

I must try texting Fiona twenty or thirty times during the course of the day, and emailing her a dozen times. I've acted for clients who've been done for harassment after sending half as much. I suppose the difference in my case is that my texts have

188

been civil and my emails constructive, covering similar ground to what I'd rehearsed on my way to Falmer. I don't want to antagonise her. I want her back. I keep thinking on those words I was preparing to say to her, and in particular "unless I've done or said something wrong...unless I've missed something." I want to know what that something is. Just twenty-four hours back we had what I thought was a fast-developing relationship, a strong relationship with love and trust and interdependence and lots more love sprinkled on top. She told me she loved me. What is the something that means that all that's gone and there's now just silence. I think back through everything I've done and said to her in the course of yesterday. I reach out to try and capture the memory of just one stupid, inadvertent remark that might have suggested to her I should be chucked aside at the close of yesterday's play. Nothing springs to mind. I think back through what she said about Pete. I claw at the rock face for the recollection of a single observation she made by that fireside that suggested that, notwithstanding his antics, her place was still with him rather than with me. In the end I'm forced to give up. Trouble is, there's no genial quizmaster about to put me out of my misery by revealing the solution and the name of the lucky winner.

As I prepare my evening *haute cuisine* fare of cheese on toast – the meal I reserve for occasions when I can't be bothered with anything any more – I try and tell myself that life's like that; it's a mistake to seek to adopt a rational lawyerlike mentality and think that because it's all so unfair I'm entitled to seek some sort of relief. But it's not long after the final mouthful of cooked cheddar and burnt Warburton's thick-sliced has disappeared into my interior that another three texts have rolled off my production line, and with the management having offered generous overtime rates, the workforce are set to continue operations for many more hours yet.

*

I've never believed in taking any sleep-inducing medication and I don't do so tonight. I'm kind of trusting that as I got so little kip the previous night, my body will now be compelled to

189

take control of my restless mind and provide me with much-needed rest from this brutal world. My trust is rewarded in part. I nod off almost immediately I've extinguished my bedside light. But I'm awake at four thirty after five hours' slumber and that five hours proves to be all I'm going to get.

I'm in no great rush to get back to work but at the same time I can't allow myself the luxury of another day's self-pitying self-examination. I've a complicated Trading Standards sentencing case at Brighton Magistrates' Court this morning and I wouldn't want to have to dump that on anybody at short notice. I'm back at my desk at just after eight, ploughing through yesterday's emails and reminding myself of the main points of the plea in mitigation for the sentencing. A favourable outcome – anything that ensures the client goes out of court by the public exit will be classed as favourable – may just help me to decide my existence isn't as stupid and pointless as I think it is right now. And just reflecting on that stupidity and pointlessness brings the tears back up again. Which is why at the unmistakeable sound of Danny approaching along the corridor – nobody else in the office moves about so ponderously and inhales and exhales so audibly in the process – I have to dash to the loo so that he won't see me crying.

I dry my eyes, compose myself and walk back out into the corridor. I've not had the displeasure of seeing Danny for a week and a half, and I'm sure he'll be wanting to touch base with me sometime today. So as I return to my office, I'm expecting him to be there, maybe at Judy's desk if she's not in yet, or, if he really wants to get up my nose, doing his David Brent pose on a chair he's pulled up next to mine. But he's actually nowhere to be seen.

My phone goes again. 'Hi, Matt. Rob here.' Robert Kenworthy's the practice manager. I don't have much to do with him as a rule; I've always found him okay but he has a reputation as a stickler and I know he's not popular with some of the secretarial staff. 'Can you please attend my office at nine thirty.'

'Sorry Rob, I can't. I'm due in court in fifteen minutes.'

'We've arranged Martyn to cover that.'

'Rob, it's quite a complex case. I really need to cover it

myself.'

'See you at nine thirty, Matt.'

I put the phone down and I'm sure my heartbeats could be heard in Colorado.

Normally I try to avoid Danny as much as possible but I need to speak to him now. I need to find out from him what's going on. I think back to the last few months, and his extreme concern about our falling workloads and question marks about the viability of the crime department. If the department's under threat, he would know something. He must know something.

I dash to his office. He's not there. I call his mobile. There's no answer.

For the second day running I'm trying to be rational. It's only a few weeks since Geoff's complimentary remarks, on the back of my run of good outcomes. Nothing to worry about.

Except there's everything to be worried about.

I can't bear to be sitting at my desk and it's as early as ten minutes past nine that I'm making my way upstairs to Rob's office. Wanting it, whatever it may be, to be over as soon as possible.

I reach the office, knock on the closed door and immediately hear Rob's voice. 'Bear with us, will you.' So there I am, for the next twenty minutes, standing there outside the headmaster's study, wondering if I should have brought an exercise book to shove over the seat of my boxer shorts.

At nine thirty exactly I'm invited to enter. I open the door and there's three of them in there: Rob, Danny, and Max Rich, the senior partner and grandson of the firm's cofounder. Max rarely makes an appearance these days and I can't have spoken to him in the past six months. He gives me an affable nod. The other two seem to be going out of their way to avoid my eye.

'Sit down, Matt.' Rob's lips hardly move as he says it.

I sit. For a few moments, nobody says anything. I'm left to sit and gaze through the window at the watery blue sky and puffy white cloud of the world outside. A world that with minimum warning seems to be closing in on me with the purpose and force of a Russian armoured division.

'Matt, I'll come straight to the point.' Rob again. 'Allegations have been made against you that you are in breach of the firm's disciplinary policy in two respects. Are you familiar with the existence and terms of that policy?'

I've not opened it since it was issued to me. 'Yes, of course.'

'It's said that first of all, on 30th October last year, you engaged in unwanted sexual activity with an existing and vulnerable client, Lisa-Marie Williams, following a police interview in relation to matters of possession of class A and B drugs with intent to supply. Do you understand that allegation?'

'It wasn't like that, Rob.'

'I'm not asking if you accept it. I'm asking if you understand it.'

I nod.

'It's said that secondly, on 14th January this year you lied to and thereby deliberately misled your immediate superior, Danny Letwin, on two issues: firstly by telling him an email from Fargoes stating they could no longer act for Lisa-Marie Williams had not been received when you knew it had, and secondly, by claiming that Fargoes had conduct of Lisa-Marie Williams' file whereas in fact they had not. Do you understand that allegation?'

'It's a stitch-up,' I mutter.

'Do you understand the further allegation?' For the first time Rob's looking straight at me.

I nod again.

'Do you wish me to refer you to the specific clauses in the disciplinary policy that it is alleged you have violated in these discrete instances?' Rob asks.

'No, thank you,' I whisper.

'I beg your pardon?' says Rob.

For a moment I'm tempted to shout it so loud that their collective eardrums drop off the face of the planet. I remove that item from the programme and replace it with a shake of the head.

'These allegations require to be formally investigated,' Rob continues. 'You will be notified of a date and time at which to attend an investigation meeting when you will be given your opportunity to put your case. If the case against you is found proved, you may be required to attend a disciplinary hearing. We have given considerable thought to what should happen

192

while the investigation is ongoing. Because of the serious nature of the first allegation, involving as it does the possible commission of a criminal offence, suspected abuse of a solicitor-client relationship, and the potential for compromising the good name of this firm if the matter became generally known, we have decided we have no alternative but to suspend you from the employment of Ellman Rich on full pay pending completion of the investigation."

*

There's more. A lot more. Rob, bless his incongruous yellow towelling socks, assures me that my colleagues will take on my outstanding cases and police station and court duties. How kind and thoughtful. Then he goes all Blue Peter and provides me with something they'd prepared earlier, namely a suspension notice, plus a separate formal notice of requirement for me to vacate the office within thirty minutes of service on me of the aforesaid suspension notice. Completing the contents of the party bag, and also thrust into my less than grateful palms, is a printed schedule of my rights and obligations during the period of suspension.

Once I have all these documents, they invite me to leave.

I'm well used to acting for clients who've received sentences that have blown their livelihoods, and thereby their lives, sky-high. I'm used to being with them during the minutes following the imposition of the sentence. And I'm used to finding the right words to say to them. I've never thought that one day I might be on the receiving end. As I wander downstairs and begin placing my personal effects in my bag I feel as though all of this must be happening to some nameless client, and that having closed his or her file I can carry on as normal. But then I remember I have no client. I am the client. It's all mine.

There's nobody else in the crime department. Judy's mailed to say she's been called to the nick and Martyn's up at court. Danny's presumably still in the star chamber uncorking the champagne. Nobody's there to witness my packing and logging off my computer. When I'm done, I leave by the front door.

I'm walking off down the street when I hear the sound of hurried footsteps. I turn round and see it's Liz, one of the admin support staff in the probate section. One of the obligations attaching to the suspension is that I'm not to contact directly or indirectly any staff member other than those responsible for undertaking the investigation. For a moment I think about doing what I should be doing which is turning my back on her and walking on. But there's agitation and upset all across her face and the next moment I'm in her arms.

'I'm so sorry, Matt,' she says. 'So sorry.'

'What do you mean?'

She removes her arms. 'I had to type up Danny's notes. I know what this is about. I can't believe anyone would make up stuff like that. About you.'

'What stuff?'

'You mean you don't know?'

I say nothing.

'Look,' she says. 'Swear to God you won't grass me up. I'm sworn to secrecy.'

'Of course.'

'He got a call from some woman. Lisa-Marie Williams, just before Christmas. She told him her new solicitors had withdrawn and wanted you instead only she wasn't allowed to ring you. And she said she couldn't really see why you couldn't act for her as you'd done nothing wrong, nothing at all. Then he asked her what she meant.'

'And what did she say?'

'Danny's written that…oh, Matt, I know you'd never do anything like this. She must be crazy. And that lot' – she gestures back towards the office – 'are crazy to even think she might be telling the truth. It's awful.'

'Go on.'

'She…she says after her interview at the police station you sexually touched her on the pavement. And she hadn't consented to it.'

*

I guess the only good thing I can say about the next few

194

weeks is that I'm able to keep myself so busy that occasionally, just occasionally, I forget that it's the worst few weeks of my life.

I keep trying Fiona but still nothing's coming back. I've gone round to her office three times but I'm told she's either unavailable or away. When I attend there on a fourth occasion, I'm advised that they don't want to see me again and if necessary official steps will be taken to ensure they never will. Naturally I've tried the Bus Stop Barista on a couple of Saturdays but perhaps it should come as no surprise that there's no sign of her there at all. I've had plenty of experiences with girls in the past which could be described as a word rhyming with bitty, but none of them get close to this. None of them have caused me to shed as many tears, shout as many oaths when for the umpteenth time her phone goes to voicemail, and seek so many estimates from specialist restorers to carry out the necessary remedial work on my heart. I know I could talk to people about it. People like Karen or Lorrie. Maybe even Emma. Trouble is, I know what they'll say. That Fiona was, still is, a married woman, and if you're going to play with that sort of fire it's not only your digits that'll get singed. That it may not be anything I've done wrong and indeed she may be the one with the problem. And maybe she's one of those girls who talk the talk and flirt the flirt but are careful never to commit and are programmed to shy away just as things start to get serious. I reason that since I know all this, it's hardly fair to waste other people's time getting them to regurgitate it. They'd doubtless be telling me to move on. But I remember what a friend of mine said after coming back from an island beach holiday where he'd not moved from his hotel for the entire fortnight he was there. I asked him why he'd not gone and explored the island which was one of the most scenic in the Mediterranean. "What's the point," he said. "The hotel was perfect. The food, the pool, the bedroom, all of it. I was happy there. Why move away from perfect. I'd only have been disappointed." I know I'd not known Fiona long but she seemed perfect and I can't move away from her either. Once more with feeling: she told me she loved me. So I'm still crying, and I'm still swearing, and as for sticking the broken pieces together, I can't even find the glue to

195

effect temporary repairs.

I can't bear to hang around the house all day every day. One of the more unpleasant aspects of my unwanted idleness is finding myself once again at home when Neil is in but his parents are not. And even though his evident current favourite band R.E.M. can't be said to create intolerable offence to the average pair of eardrums, there's only so much of losing my religion or so many shiny happy people that I can take, and I'm quite well aware that everybody hurts, thank you very much. Some more than others. So I go for bike rides, and I sit in town nursing Costa coffees, and I go to the library's upstairs reference section. I've not been told I'm prohibited access to the electronic legal manual and case-finder that Ellman Rich use so I deploy it to read the latest IP cases online, wanting to keep up-to-date on the relevant law. I'd love to think I might do some more of it one day...but oh look, that's not one, not two, but three fat porkers all with their pilot licences looping the loop just outside the first floor window.

And in the midst of all this there's the divorce finance. Things are progressing well; Emma's actually become more reasonable and co-operative and we're working towards a finance settlement that means that Brighton's shop doorways won't need to be graced with my presence on a nightly basis after all. That said, there's no way I'm going to be able to afford to buy a place of my own, and while I've been round a few rented properties, they've either been too expensive or they're places I wouldn't recommend to sewer rats. Emma's come round while I've been out running and has removed the rest of her personal effects, and it's left to me to box my things up ready to go into storage or accompany me to my next abode, delete as applicable. Of all the hateful aspects of the disintegration of my existence, this is probably the one I hate most. Each piece of furnishing, each item of clothing, each book, each CD seems to bring back memories of our unstoppable days and the pain seems to increase rather than decrease with each newly-filled packing case.

Of course I've kept dad updated in relation to all my issues, without going into too much detail, certainly not about the Lisa-Marie business. He's said I'm more than welcome to come and stay with him and Karen whenever I want or need to. But I fear that every time I'm under their roof now I'll be just one Betty's high tea and one Sunderland win away from a repeat of New Year's Eve. We may have got away with it once but I can't risk it again. I tell him I'll keep his invitation in mind and we go on to talk about England's latest cricketing one-day debacle.

*

In due course I'm invited by Ellman Rich to attend an investigation meeting. I'd wondered about getting legal advice but I feel I need to know exactly what's alleged before I decide if it's worth the expense. I may be able to manage on my own. I'm surprised and gratified that the investigator is Geoff, the one who complimented me at the start of the year. Of all the partners at Ellman Rich he's the most likeable, and, in fairness to him, he goes through every piece of the chronology with commendable care. He explains that Lisa-Marie had phoned the office on the day I'd gone up to Yorkshire for Christmas, and Danny had spoken to her. She'd said that Fargoes had withdrawn their representation because the perpetrator of a knife attack on her, who was at that time in custody awaiting trial on the matter in the Crown Court, was an existing client of theirs. That had then prompted her request for us to act instead and also prompted her to tell Danny about the sexual touching incident. Geoff asks me if the sexual touching happened. I tell him yes, it did, but she fully consented to it. She may not have expressly said so but she'd been flirting with me from the moment she'd arrived at the custody centre; she'd come after me once I'd left the pub, asked me if she could see me again, and didn't recoil when I kissed her. She responded, shall we say, positively. I therefore reasonably believed she was consenting. And she's accepting that I did nothing wrong, although as Geoff says, that's open to more than one interpretation. I add that such contact she and I did have, even if it could be regarded as sexual, involved no touching under clothing. He asks me what I'd done. I said I'd embraced her, French kissed her and rubbed her breasts with my hands, over her jumper; that was all. Which is true. Geoff doesn't suggest

197

her recall was any different, but asks me to confirm she required an appropriate adult for both her police interviews and by definition therefore she'd been assessed as vulnerable. I tell him that was the police's call, not mine, and I never saw myself as exploiting her all the time we were together. In fact I was the one putting the brakes on. Or trying to. He asks me, as I knew he would, if I recall being spoken to by Danny only a week before about overfamiliarity with clients. I nod. It's just getting worse with every second I'm sitting there. Geoff then moves on to the second business involving lying to Danny. I'm on stronger ground here. I tell him that although Danny will never admit to this, I am convinced that Fargoes emailed me saying they were having to withdraw, and Danny, having obtained my password from me the day I went up north, opened the email using my account, printed it and deleted it. He then trapped me into implying that Fargoes were still acting.

Geoff thanks me for my help and promises to expedite matters, but says he will need to talk to Lisa-Marie before any decision is made. Then he's bidding me farewell and I'm walking out of his office feeling as tall as a Borrower.

*

.

All of the above has served, temporarily, to eliminate Lorrie and Jake from my agenda. I feel bad for both of them: for Lorrie because she's Lorrie, and for Jake because he'll think he's had his mentoring hopes raised and then squashed. But eventually I've phoned Lorrie, I've told her about my employment and accommodation issues, and I've asked her if she and Jake can bear with me for the moment. Of course she's fine about my predicament and says if I need a chat, or a sympathetic ear, we can make a return trip to Lasagne City. It's good of her to offer but I don't want to go there, not yet. I don't want her to think I'm unable to get through my life crises without running to her for help each time. The schoolboy who's grazed his knee in the playground and needs a bandage and a hug. I've got my dignity and my pride. I guess it's silly really. I take the tactful option and tell her I'll be in touch to fix something up when my head's a bit clearer. She says that's fine, adding that she'll speak to Jake and tell him there won't be any more Monopoly with me for the moment. Sure enough, she rings me back the next night and says she's had a long chat with him, explained that I've got personal issues at the moment, and therefore our time together, board games and all, is having to be put on hold indefinitely. I'm convinced Jake is going to have blown our subterfuge wide open, but I guess he must be a lot cleverer than I'd given him credit for, because she says nothing to make me think she's uncovered it. I ask her how he took it. She said he shouted, and yelled, and shouted some more, and threw a book across the room so it fell to pieces, and banged the table, and slapped Lorrie in the face. So yes, she said. He'd taken it better than she expected.

Then she's asked me if I've got somewhere to live and I tell her I still haven't. It's now the 22nd February and I'm due to vacate by the end of next week. Then she mentions that she knows of a woman in the choir she sings with on a Monday night who may have a room to let. Lorrie explains that Di, that being her name, has been widowed for four years and she likes the company that a lodger brings. Lorrie says she's lovely but a bit scatterbrained. Her current lodger is apparently leaving the area this weekend so the room will now be vacant. Apparently Di is quite particular but Lorrie assures me that anyone she, Lorrie, personally recommends will be welcomed with open arms and a fanfare of trumpets.

I ask Lorrie for Di's number. No need, Lorrie replies: she tells me I can come along with her to choir this Monday and be introduced then. In the meantime Lorrie will ask Di to hold the room open for me. I tell Lorrie I can't sing. Lorrie dismisses that as a trivial detail.

*

Monday doesn't start well. There's a hold-up at my buyers' end and having hoped to exchange contracts today I'm now told there's going to be a delay of possibly a week. Then there's an email from Rob at Ellman Rich stating that Lisa-Marie, who apparently remains on bail awaiting trial at Lewes Crown Court on the drugs charges, is unwell and due to go into hospital for an op on her liver. Frankly I'm amazed she's got any liver left to do an op on. But anyway it means she's effectively out of the picture till the end of March and consequently there'll be a delay in the completion of the investigation. The email tells me I remain suspended on full pay until April 1st when the matter will be reviewed but it's likely that my suspension will simply be extended to a date after that. While the delay is infuriating, it does at least buy me more time to decide whether to get representation for any disciplinary hearing. Just now, I'm inclined not to bother. I feel I've enough understanding and know-how to represent myself. I don't know any employment law specialists and I'm not sure I could trust whoever it was to say what I want to say and in the manner I want to say it. I just feel it'll sound much better coming from me.

Tonight is choir night. I'd spent the weekend wondering if choir attendance was too big a price to pay for securing a roof over my head and I'd seen a couple of places advertised that looked as though they might do instead. But I'd checked them both out and I didn't love them. And not for the first time since I was hung out to dry with clothes pegs strategically placed to do damage to areas where the pain would be remembered most, I feel lonely and decide that tonight at any rate I could do with nice people round me.

Community choirs seem to be springing up all over Brighton just now: Just Sing, Voices Together, Voices Fantastic, the Mindfulness Chorale, to name just a few. I've seen ads for all these over the past four days alone. The same words pop up every time: new, vibrant, exciting, unity, purpose, brotherhood, sisterhood, changing lives. The consistent images in my mind's eye, when I see the ads, are of super-enthusiastic singers dressed in crisp white shirts and deep red sashes, toothpaste-ad smiles on all their faces, with a repertoire consisting of loud, brash crowd-pleasing anthems, and super-inspirational, super-motivational conductors yelling "You smashed it, guys." It's the sort of thing you get as a tailpiece to the teatime local television news so that when you switch off you're left thinking the world's not such a bad place after all.

Trouble is, I think someone forgot to tell the Whitedean Methodist Singers. Lorrie tells me as we arrive together that they've been going eighty years. And as I look out at the folk walking across the car park towards the hall, I suspect a good few of the founder members are still in it. The hall in question adjoins Whitedean Methodist Church, some ten minutes' walk from Lorrie's; Lorrie explains that a number of the choir attend that church but membership is open to everybody and adherence to the Methodist creed isn't an entry requirement. As soon as I enter the hall, I can see the flaky paintwork and smell the decay and neglect and the cat's pee. Looking round it, I guess that the last redecoration took place when you had to pay three shillings and sixpence for a dog licence. Two of the six light tubes are flickering, and at least two of the windowpanes have cracked. At least it's warm, heating being provided by a line of blowers all pumping out more currents of hot air than a Party conference but creating so much noise in the process that I doubt we'll be able to hear ourselves think, never mind hear ourselves sing. But whatever deficiencies there are in the surroundings are more than made up for by the warmth and effusiveness of the welcome. Clearly any singers aged under 70 are seen as rare birds indeed, and I've lost count of the number of twitchers hurrying to focus their binoculars on this rare and unexplained phenomenon, the Lesser Spotted Man In His Forties. Within ten minutes I've shaken hands with a Ken, and a Maurice, and a Vera, and a Kathleen, and a Mavis, and an Audrey, and all those names you never now see in the *Times* top baby name lists or on novelty stands in card shops. There may not be many punters present tonight – I count about thirty altogether, no more than eight of whom are male – but the ones I speak to are lovely people with hearts that are more golden than a summer sunset, and already I'm being asked if I want to join their Wednesday afternoon bridge class or next Saturday's coach trip to Kew Gardens. I have to explain that I'm here purely as an invited guest and lack the necessary entry requirement which is to be able to sing. Maurice, like Lorrie, seems to dismiss this as a minor technicality. He explains to me that they do three performances a year: a traditional classical concert in March, a concert performance of a Gilbert & Sullivan opera in July, and a Christmas variety show, complete with pantomime sketch, in December. Then he says that one of his fellow tenors has recently fallen off his perch and I'm just waiting for him to ask if in the light of that I'll be available later in the year to take the role of Widow Twankey. At this stage I've still not met Di and indeed am destined not to meet her this side of the coffee break, for as I'm chatting with Maurice a tall balding red-faced man, well into his seventies by the look of him, calls the meeting to order. After saying a prayer he directs the assembled clans to turn to the start of the Durufle *Requiem*, reminding them that the concert's in just three weeks so they need to be thinking about getting some of it right.

I've never learnt to sing, let alone read music. Maurice insists on providing for me my own copy of the musical score, but I've not the heart to tell him the little dots on the page are as intelligible to me as Fermat's Last Theorem in Irish Gaelic. I decide to try to get by simply through copying what he, Maurice, is singing – which would be a good plan if he, Maurice, were able to stay in time with the rest of the choir. As it is his rates of lateness with each entry compare unfavourably with those of even the most underperforming rail operators. But while he, and others around him, may not be up to BBC Symphony Chorus standard, nobody could fault their community spirit. In the announcements that precede the coffee break, choir members are being invited to help at this coming Saturday's church bazaar, to sign up to manning the choir stall at the Portbridge Road Spring Fayre, and to sponsor Daphne and Letitia in the Three-Legged Brighton Prom Walk next Sunday. While it may all lack the dynamism and exuberance of the new community choirs, it's full of decent, kind, well-meaning people, reaching out to the community in love.

We duly break for coffee and Lorrie introduces me to Di. She must be around eighty, I guess, but she's maintained a good head of light brown fluffy hair and has an almost perpetual broad smile which suggests to me she's at peace with the world and herself. She asks if I'm happy to come round and look at her accommodation straight after tonight's rehearsal. I say I am.

Her house is just five minutes' walk from the hall. And three minutes after I've stepped across the threshold I know I want to come and live here. There's a warmth about it and not just physical warmth. The house is clearly well looked after and well maintained. It's simply but imaginatively furnished. It's tidy and devoid of clutter. There's more than enough room and cupboard space to store my day-to-day bits and bobs, and the rest can stay in storage for as long as I need. The room comes with its own kitchenette so I can cook and eat whenever I wish. The road outside the window seems quiet and there's no pub, shop, eatery, business premises or anything else within sight that's obviously likely to generate noise or antisocial behaviour. And besides it being an easy cycling commute to the city centre, the nearest bus stop is apparently just another five minutes distant. It's perfect.

Di has diplomatically gone to the loo while I've been looking, but when I come back downstairs I can hear the kettle on and the sound of footsteps in her kitchen. I go and join her there.

'What do you think?' she asks.

'I love it.' I guess I shouldn't appear quite so keen. A lot of prospective landlords might take advantage of such overenthusiasm but even though I've only just met Di I'm quite sure she's not like that.

'Thank you.' Then she takes a deep breath and her smile fades. 'Oh dear, I feel awful about this. The truth is, Lorrie did phone me and tell me about you but I totally forgot. Me and my memory. There's another young man who came in this afternoon and he said he'd like the room as well but he wasn't sure he could afford to pay the deposit. I'm waiting for him to ring me to let me know. I do feel that I ought to give him first refusal.'

Great. I've just spent two hours of my existence which I'm not getting back sitting listening to senile and often tuneless warblings in an environment that wouldn't be tolerated by refugees from a Middle Eastern war zone. And for what.

I let my silence express how I feel. Di and I stand there, wordlessly. I don't want to look her in the eye. I suspect she feels as awkward as I feel narked. But I'm not going to bail her out.

'Did you like the choir?' she asks.

'I think you're lovely people,' I tell her. 'I think you do fantastic work. And you made me so welcome. Having said that…' And with my irritation comes a candour which, had things gone more favourably tonight, might have stayed away from the party. 'If I'm being honest…'

'Say it, please, Matt.'

'For a start, the hall stinks. Literally. I don't know how you put up with it. It's not just that. Everything felt so rundown, so stagnant. It just wasn't a pleasant experience. Nothing there that would ever make me want to come back.'

She doesn't flinch. Her smile returns. 'I know,' she says. 'But you can guess the problem. Can't you. There just aren't the people. Not in the choir, not in the audience either. And without the people there isn't the money to do things we'd so love to do. If we did them, we'd draw others in. Classic vicious circle really. You know, ten years ago, maybe less, the choir used to be twice this size. But people have just stopped coming. I can't remember when we last had a new person join. And if they do, they don't stay. Nobody seems to want to get involved, commit to anything, join anything nowadays. Too busy with their blessed technology. It's just the same in church. Our congregation's about a third of what it was, I don't know, fifteen years ago. We've lost a lot of folk just recently. People get ill, or housebound, or they die, or they move away, and there's nobody to replace them. And we're not loaded. We're not a wealthy church. It's not an affluent community. We could do with a windfall. The hall, and the church as well.'

The words are out of my mouth before I've had the chance to stop and think. 'I've got an idea,' I tell her.

Ten minutes later the room's mine.

*

Over the next two days I complete the clearance of the house and move into Di's, then on the Wednesday night I'm round at Jake's. I tell Lorrie I just want a chat with him and she's fine with that. I don't think to discuss my plan with her first. I take her support for granted. She's warned me not to make him too tired as he's been out during the day, and he's not long got back. But when I tell him that in a few weeks' time he'll have the opportunity to do a public rendition, entirely from memory, of the Gospel According To St Luke in the Whitedean Methodist Church, in aid of badly needed church and hall repair funds, his face could illuminate the Amex Stadium.

After I've left Jake I go to Lorrie. I find her in the kitchen, sitting at the table with an open Tupperware box of what look like flapjacks in front of her. I come straight to the point. I tell her what I've offered to Di and in turn what Jake has agreed to do. I explain that I've reflected a great deal on Jake's extraordinary gift that I inadvertently tapped into last month. I make no mention of the Great Monopoly Deception. I do point out that the recital, as well as raising much-needed cash, will give Jake the recognition and attention he craves; if he's fated never to do anything similar again, he will at least be able to say he's had one go at it. I tell her I'm happy to mentor him throughout the process and she won't need to coach him. It's all the stuff I said to myself on my way home after I saw the guy last. I've said it even better than I thought possible. Matt, you're a genius. I now fall silent and await Lorrie's words of delight and gratitude.

'It's out of the question, Matt, dear.'

The bluntness of her response almost knocks me back against the wall. 'I'm sorry?'

'It's not possible. End of.'

'Can I ask why?' There's a certain diffidence in my question. I feel as I do when the magistrates have decided against me, torn as I then am between, on the one hand, respect for the bench and, on the other, the prospect of my client berating me for neither openly criticising their decision-making qualities nor demanding a rethink.

'You'd better sit down and get one of these inside you.' She passes me the box, a plate and a serviette. I take them then I extract one of what look like flapjacks from the box. It's not just a square with a lot of oats cemented together. The exterior of the structure is studded with nuts and raisins, and the whole edifice is half coated in chocolate. It's indecency on a plate where in the long term the only real winners will be the dental surgeons and implant manufacturers. I take a bite and crumbs go everywhere. Everywhere. Lorrie smiles and, producing a dustpan and brush, makes passable inroads into dealing with the devastation. Then she sits down again.

'You ask me why,' she says. 'Two reasons, Matt. One, he's not done any public speaking in more than eight years and he may simply not be up to it. Something may go wrong and cause him to lose it big time. It could be a car crash on a grand scale. And I would be held to account as his carer. And as for what Maggie would say…'

'Maggie?'

'His sister. I'm sure I mentioned her to you once. Lives in Buckinghamshire, near their dad, comes down when she can. Which isn't often. Thank heaven. She's two years older than he is, and very protective of him. She's always asking after him, how he's getting on. I'm sure she'd live closer if it wasn't for the dad. Probably will when he pops off. Anyway, if she got an inkling we were plonking Jake in front of an audience, like some exhibit at a zoo, she'd go berserk. She might even accuse me of being unfit to care for him. He might end up in some ghastly institution.' She gets to her feet and makes a mug of coffee which she then passes to me. 'So that's objection number one. But even if we got round that, there's objection number two. Which is mine. Because let's say it was a triumph. And, yes, I get it could be. If it was, he'd be wanting more.'

'That's the beauty of the scheme,' I tell her. 'Even if he never got to do more, whatever happens to him, he'll have the consolation of knowing he did some of the Bible to an audience. If he wants reminding, we can record part or all of it for him, upload it to You Tube, whatever, he can watch it back as often as he wants. So it'll satisfy him. He'll have done what he wanted.'

She sits back down and shakes her head. 'I know Jake. Once he'd tasted it, he'd be like Oliver Twist. He'd insist on another performance. Some other part of the Bible. The Psalms. All one hundred and fifty. 1 Samuel, 2 Chronicles, Three Kings, Four Candles. All the time, justifying it by saying what a success it had been first time out. He'll be bending my ear so much it'll snap in half. Not your ear because you won't be around. My ear. I tell you, he's the most single-minded person in the universe. He wouldn't let it go. Even if I refused to listen to him rehearse he wouldn't let it go. On at me morning, noon and

206

night. So there we are, Matt. Whichever way it goes, it won't end well. Implosion, and Maggie comes down on me like a ton of bricks. A stormer, and it's more of the same please.' She places a lid on the Tupperware box and somewhat theatrically shoves it to one side. There's a mixture of alarm and disappointment written all over her face. 'Matt, don't get me wrong. I love that you're so concerned for Jake and wanting the best for him. But I really wish you'd spoken to me before going to him. Really do. I know you meant well, sweetie, but all we've done now is raise his hopes. Falsely.'

I want to argue back. I want to tell her that the Bible has become his lifeblood only she can't see it because while she thinks she's acting in his best interests she's actually treating him like an errant child who's been eating too many Yorkie Bars. I'm picturing Jake's disappointment. I'm picturing Di's distress that I secured the room in her house under false pretences. I'm picturing that wretched cash-starved choir, hall and church. But I can't argue back. I'm now the one who's zugzwanged.

I put the flapjack down. Not quite true. I let it drop down. I want her to see it drop down. I want this little gesture to show I'm not her puppy. I want her to know this is exercising me. I want her to know I have a voice in this too and more importantly that Jake does.

'Lorrie…'

'Matt, I can see you're angry.' Her voice is calmer now. 'I can see you're anxious. I'll talk to him. Let him down gently. Explain that you meant well but there were one or two aspects that quite understandably you hadn't appreciated.'

I can feel my cheeks warming with my anger. 'Suppose I didn't want him to be talked to. To be let down.'

She doesn't answer me for a moment. Then she reaches out and takes my hand. 'Matt, sweetheart, you can walk away. I can't. Do you understand?'

I concede the merest of nods.

'You're a star for trying, my love, and I tell you, you've got a lot further with Jake in two months than most of the healthcare professionals he's had looking at him across eight years. Text me if you've got a morning free. We'll do coffee in town.'

'Okay.' Not what I came for, but okay.

'Or you can always come with me to choir.'

'Lorrie, I'd rather stick pins in my eyes.'

We embrace. Then I get up, tell her I'll see myself out, walk to the front door and, closing it behind me, start dragging myself up the road.

But before I lose sight of Lorrie's house I stop and allow myself to take what I guess could be my very last look at it.

And even though I'm separated from it by a good thirty yards I hear, coming from the house, a yell. A yell that crashes through the stillness of the February night.

Jake's yell.

I walk back to the house and ring the bell. Then I hear footsteps and Lorrie's opening the door.

'Lorrie.'

'Yes, Matt?'

'I want Jake to do this. I'm going to see Jake does do this. Whether you like it or not.'

12

She doesn't kick me in the face. Nor does she promise to throw me off the top of the i360. What she does do is tell me that she wants no part in it and I will have to make the necessary arrangements to get Jake to the church and safeguard his welfare all the time he is there; if the escapade as much as threatens to assume the physical form of a certain pomaceous fruit, I will have to bear full responsibility; moreover should the success of the occasion result in the aforementioned Jake even hinting at the possibility of a future performance I will be the one required to advise him of the impossibility of same and thereby compelled, in advance of my so advising, to procure and don a suit of protective clothing of such defensive capability as to shield me from any perceived risk of homicide or grievous or actual bodily harm consequent on my so advising.

Oh, yes, and I'm the one who will have to tell his sister that it was all my idea.

It would be all too easy for me, carried away by the excitement of the moment, just to agree those terms and get off home, regarding Lorrie's lack of outright resistance as the victory, and rejoicing that we've laid the ground for the whole thing to go ahead. I not only want but need Jake to go through with this. If I turn my back on him now, not only will I be letting Di down and probably facing immediate eviction as a consequence, but it'll be as if everything I've done for Jake so far has been a sham. As lawyers we speak about our clients having their day in court. I want him to have his day in court. A day when he becomes somebody again. A human being again. When people listen to him again.

But I don't agree those terms. I don't agree them because I know, and I'm sure Lorrie knows, there's no way I could stick to them. I have the presence of mind to tell her that I'd like time to reflect on what she's offered and I'll call her in the morning. And I'm so glad I do. Because when we speak on the phone next day, she's mellowed. She says she's prepared to support him in his recital. She'll escort him to the venue and will see that his physical needs are met both prior to and during the performance. And she'll tell his sister, if but only if she gets to find out, that she, Lorrie, consented to it and as his primary carer she is responsible for it happening.

'Just one thing I ask from you,' she says. 'You make it a hundred and ten per cent clear to Jake, before the event, that this is a one-off. There can, and will, be no repeat performances. And unless he agrees to this, and agrees not to badger me any further once he's done, there can be, will be, no performance at all.'

'It's fine,' I tell her.

'Well, it may be for you,' she says. 'But before you commit yourself, just think about me, will you. Please. You must understand this is a huge leap of faith. I don't doubt he'll agree to your face. But even then, I've no idea, and you've certainly no idea, whether he'll stick to it. And if he doesn't I'll be the one picking up the pieces.'

I hang up and suddenly the optimism and the triumph have ebbed away to be replaced by the guilt and the self-doubt. Lorrie has given Jake everything. I've given him next to nothing. And here I am poised to take a step which threatens to slap an extra-large sack of potatoes around her creaking shoulders. While I walk away. Again.

*

A little while later that day I'm struck by a thought. Di. She knows Lorrie better than I could ever hope to. And she, and her little community, will be the ones to lose out should I decide Jake can't be trusted. So I ask her what I should do, all the while hoping, so hoping, that she'll tell me what I want to hear.

'I thought Lorrie might react like that,' she says. 'Don't forget I've known her a long while. I've met Jake a couple of times but not well enough to know how he might respond to all this. So I've been praying about it. Chatting with him upstairs. And what he seemed to be saying during our chat was, there's a choice here. One, it never happens, and we never know how it might have worked out. Or two, we give it a try and place it all in his hands. In the Lord's hands for him to do with it as he wishes. Maybe reach out to people who've never heard the good news. Give them the chance to absorb it and to give back through their gifts. And trust in the Lord that Lorrie won't get hurt afterwards.'

'And what does him upstairs recommend?'

I think I hear a chuckle down the phone. 'It's a tough call, Matt, dear,' she says. 'It's a big risk. But whatever or whoever you believe in or don't believe in, sometimes life's about taking risks.'

*

It's all sorted very quickly. A conversation with Lorrie, then Jake, then Lorrie again, then Di, and we're done. Mothering Sunday March 31st , just over four weeks away, starting at 2.00pm, in Whitedean Methodist Church. The Gospel According To St Luke.

*

Geoff's been on the phone again. He says he shouldn't really be ringing me and this is all off the record but apparently Lisa-Marie has contacted him and made it clear that she's not going to co-operate with the investigation, hospital or no hospital, and if that part of the case against me fails, that 'only,' in his words, leaves the lying allegation. I'm convinced, and I'm sure he is too, that that part was just a makeweight anyway. He says he can't comment on where all this leaves me, but when I put the phone down I'm confident I'll be back at work soon and all this will be just a ghastly memory. I've been dithering about getting legal representation for any disciplinary proceedings but decide there's definitely no need. I know I can manage.

March arrives. Completion on the sale of the house duly takes place, albeit a couple of weeks later than scheduled. Emma and I are pretty much agreed on a financial settlement, and the divorce itself is going through with no bloodshed on either side. But beyond that call from Geoff, there's nothing more from Ellman Rich. I'm beginning to wonder if Lisa-

Marie's changed her mind and she is going to assist the investigation after all. Trouble is, I've no idea what she might say. She might tell it as it is, that it never got beyond a fumble outside the pub after the police interview, a fumble she invited and one hundred per cent happily went along with. On the other hand, if she's high on whatever her poison is at present, she could come out with enough to put me in another police interview, this time with me as the client. But I trust Geoff not to have raised my hopes inappropriately and also tell myself he would be phoning me again if there'd been a change of plan.

I visit Jake for some practice sessions. He doesn't need them. He's word-perfect and not only is he word-perfect but he's injecting life and vitality into each line. And I discuss publicity with Di. We agree we need to start with her church and choir, given that they're likely to be the most supportive folk of all. I've tendered my resignation from the choir after that one attendance, and although I think technically I was a guest that night rather than a card-carrying member, I make Di laugh by telling her I've probably set the record for the shortest membership in the choir's history. Di tells me that there was one guy who turned up at the start of a rehearsal and left after fifteen minutes never to be seen again. But she concedes that my being tone-deaf, while not actually a disqualifying condition, might hamper my usefulness to the war effort and probably wouldn't enhance the enjoyment of those forced to sit within a radius of at least twenty feet of me. Anyway, as far as plugging Jake's *tour de force* is concerned, she agrees to look after the church and choir side of things, while I undertake to go further afield, travelling by bike to get advertising material round to all the city's churches. I've also agreed to approach the local radio station and newspaper. I decide to do this on the 14th March, two and a half weeks before the event. If I pitch in too early, people will have forgotten about it. If I leave it too late, diaries will have filled up. It's a delicate balance.

A glance at the map shows the multiplicity of churches all over Brighton, and I'm confident that even if only a third of them support the venture, either by providing a presence or some dosh, we, or rather Di's church and choir, will be quids in. But it doesn't take long for reality to pop the party balloons. Of the first ten churches I try, five are locked, two are boarded up, one comes complete with a guard dog from which I'm forced to retreat before it eats me, one is stewarded by a woman who if anything has a more voracious appetite than the guard dog, and one has become a dry-cleaning establishment. My only success, if I can call it that, is with a Seventh Day Adventist Chapel, which while also bolted does at least have an outside noticeboard on which there's a convenient spot to pin my poster advertising the event – subject to said event not being overtaken by the forthcoming imminent return of our Lord as promised in the poster immediately adjacent.

Having had so little reward for my two hours on the saddle, I can't face any more and after a lazy afternoon I decide on an alternative strategy, to be implemented next day: the email. But my efforts in this regard bring no more success than my endeavours on two wheels. Perhaps it was naïve of me to fail to foresee the possibility that the email addresses on the relevant websites might be anything other than up-to-date and accurate. But it's still disappointing that a good one third of the emails I send boomerang back to me, so speedily and unerringly that I'm thinking of patenting them and emigrating to Australia. Another one third generate autoreplies promising that my email will be considered as soon as possible but warning that I may not receive a response for up to fourteen working days. And as far as all the rest are concerned, it's majestic silence. Well, not quite all. I do get a response, from a woman who says the whole thing sounds completely wonderful and she would certainly come along, bringing a posse of admiring friends and relations, were it not for the fact that she has now relinquished her position as St Saviour's church secretary and has taken up residence in San Antonio, Texas.

While the combination of boomeranging and the surge of autoreplies is at its height, I try phoning the local radio station. I speak to a pleasant woman who, after I've given her all the details, says they'll try and mention it during each of their next three Sunday morning God-slots. But they also advise me that, with Easter approaching, the event will be just one of many Church-related events vying not only with each other for precious airtime, but with other items of far greater spiritual and philosophical significance such as weekend rail engineering works and the previous day's non-league football results. As for the newspaper, I'm told the man who handles this sort of story would certainly be fascinated to hear all about it, and would be bound to give me a full-page spread with action photos, were it not for the fact that following a mishap on the Jungfraujoch, he's had to put his crampons to bed for the next six months, and will be off work for eight weeks at least.

I feel I'm running out of options. In fairness, I do get some emailed replies over the next week and a half, the respondents saying they'll try and support it if they can, but as far as the majority is concerned, it's a silence that could be heard in Abuja, Nigeria. Di says she's had some interest, although not as much as she hoped; she's also spoken with one of her church friends who's active on social media and who promises to put the word about by those means, although she concedes that most members of the congregation if asked what Whatsapp was would hazard a guess that it was a children's card game. The result is that on the Wednesday before the recital, with Jake virtually word-perfect and yearning to get out there and strut his stuff, and the arrangements all in place, including the provision of refreshments, we have a guaranteed audience of…four.

So I'm spurred into yet further action. I go round to the local radio station in person and more or less demand to have a slot on the programme going out on the recital day. I don't know whether the guy I speak to is genuinely impressed with my zeal or genuinely fearful for his safety, but I get the result I'm after. I'm given a telephone interview slot at around ten past eight on the Sunday morning. Then at Di's suggestion I phone Brian, the pastor at Whitedean Methodist Church and ask to be allowed to make an announcement at the start of the morning service on the recital day. He tells me he would be delighted if I would, and adds that as it happens to be Mother's Day, there's sure to be a really good turnout. I then proceed to prepare the announcement in which I'll be telling the congregation that this is the most exciting Christian-based event to hit Brighton this side of the new millennium, unlikely to be matched again in their lifetime. That is, if there is no truth in the rumour that Brighton is shortly to receive a state visit from Sir Cliff.

*

There's good news and bad news on the day of the recital. The good news is that the phone interview happens, and the presenter tells all her listeners to "drop everything and go and listen to this remarkable guy called Jake" at Whitedean Methodist Church this afternoon. I really think that but for that, I might have been tempted to suggest booting the whole thing into touch.

The bad news is that the interview is immediately followed by the weather forecast which promises heavy rain and strong winds moving in from the west during the morning and not clearing till after dark.

It's already spitting as I make my way to the church for the 10.30 service. It's Mother's Day today, although Di's already told me off this morning for calling it that. Mothering Sunday, if you please. Whatever it should be called, the fact is that this particular festival has pulled in a sizeable crowd. Among them there's a good number of children, though from what they'd have seen after coming in, one would hardly blame the poor mites if they decided to walk back out and turn instead to the worship of the god iPad. The church is, if anything, in a worse state of repair than the hall. There's a smell which mingles dust and wet rot. Floor tiles are missing from the vestibule, turning it into a multiple trip hazard. Inside the church, a further area of seating has had to be cleared because of cracks in the floor, without a MIND THE GAP sign for the unwary. The lighting is stark and almost brutal in some parts of the church but nonexistent in others. And the organ sounds as though its last tuning was cancelled on account of the General Strike. Anyhow, the show must go on, and at ten thirty precisely Brian calls the meeting to order and invites me to come forward. I'm well used to speaking in public but not so used to having my speeches interrupted by youngsters vomiting in rotation along the front row. But I maintain my composure sufficiently to urge the congregation to drop by on the way back from their Mother's Day – whoops, Mothering Sunday – pub and restaurant meals and listen to the memory man at work. There's a buzz of

215

appreciation and interest right round the church and as I return to my chair, Di whispers 'If that doesn't fill the church this afternoon, nothing will.'

But that's before we emerge from the building at five past twelve to find precipitation cascading from the heavens with such intensity that at least two members of the congregation ask me if Jake might be better advised to recite the story of Noah and the ark.

Two hours later I'm back and very shortly after I return Lorrie arrives with Jake. Lorrie suggests that she takes Jake off to one of the side rooms so that he can compose himself and get into the zone, as she puts it, while Di and I as the de facto welcoming committee concentrate on greeting the milling hordes. Meanwhile, two of Di's friends from church have agreed to organise half-time refreshments, consisting of teas, coffees and home-made butterfly cakes, to be served in the unlovely hall. And indeed when I pop to the hall to use the facilities – facilities which clearly could also benefit from a portion of the funds we're hoping to raise – I see a massed gathering of cups and saucers and an assembly of butterfly cakes so large as to dispel any thought that they might be found in Sir David Attenborough's current list of endangered species.

I return to the church and over the next forty minutes we're standing, waiting at the church door for the surge of enthusiasts drawn here by my persuasive words and by their desire to have the key messages of the Christian faith, the very tenets which underpin their lives and may shape their eternal destinies, presented to them as never before. But as to the questions the examiners have asked in relation to the organisational aspects of the day, it seems that the topic of crowd control has been missed off the examination paper. For at two minutes to two, as Lorrie wheels Jake out to begin his recital, there is an audience of...seven. Specifically Di, Brian, Lorrie, a grey-haired woman in a bright green mac, a white-haired couple the male half of which comes complete with Zimmer frame, and myself.

I look at Jake, who's situated with Lorrie in one of the side aisles, and I see a wild, dark look in his eye. As we engage in eye contact he thunders 'Where is everybody?'

'I expect they're on their way, dear,' says Lorrie. 'It is

awfully wet out there. Maybe they're waiting in their cars for it to ease off a bit.'

'I thought you said you'd announced it!' As he yells, he's looking straight into my eyes.

Again Lorrie puts the case for the defence. 'It's been announced lots,' she says. 'On the radio only this morning. And at church today I think. Listen. I expect people will come and listen to bits as the afternoon goes on. I think the weather's supposed to be getting better. Why don't we start.'

It's been agreed that we'll dispense with an introduction or words of welcome. Jake will go straight into the recital, there'll be a thirty-minute break for refreshment after chapter 12, and he'll then resume, aiming to be done by five thirty. We don't want it finishing any later than that, Di had said, pointing out that most of the congregation don't like being out late at night. At the end Brian will thank Jake, invite the audience to contribute to the retiring collection, and conclude in prayer.

Accordingly, at one minute to two, Lorrie wheels Jake into position and then takes her seat in the front row just a few feet away from him. As prompt, I need to be equally close by so I come and sit next to Lorrie, and switch my phone to video mode. I look in Lorrie's direction and she's nodding at Jake and smiling.

'Off you go, then, Jake,' she says.

'I don't want to start!'

I can't look. I've bowed my head and shut my eyes. I think of the cracks in the floor and am wishing a few more would open and gobble me up.

Lorrie to the rescue again. 'Jake, start. Now. Good lad.'

'The Gospel According To St Luke,' Jake says. 'Chapter 1. "Many have undertaken to draw up an account of the things that have been fulfilled among us, just as they were handed down to us by those who from the first were eye-witnesses and servants of the word. Therefore, since...since..."'

Silence.

'I can't do this!'

Lorrie leaps to her feet and rushes up to him. She grabs his hand. 'Jake, my sweet, you can do this, you know you can.'

'Not with nobody in the church. Not with an empty church.'

'It's not empty, sweetheart. Not at all. There's Matt, there's Di, there's…there's…'

'It's not enough. It's pitiful. It's pathetic!'

Now Brian comes forward. 'Jake, it's not pathetic. Just do it. Do it for those of us who are here. Do it for those who aren't.'

'That's right,' Lorrie calls. 'Do it for the choir, for this church.'

'Do it for the Lord!' cries the woman in the bright green mac.

'Amen!' I yell. 'Do it for the Lord!' I amaze myself with my hypocrisy. But it's followed by a surprisingly impressive chorus of Amens from the rest of the economy-size congregation of spectators.

Lorrie releases her hand, and she and Brian go back and sit down. The tension is so thick it could insulate a skyscraper in Archangel. I still can't bear to look in Jake's direction.

Then I hear Jake's voice. '"Since I myself have carefully investigated everything from the beginning, it seemed good also to me to write an orderly account for you, most excellent Theophilus, so that you may know the certainty of the things you have been taught."'

*

There have been so many films based on Biblical themes. But of those I've seen, none have made me believe that I was actually there, amongst it all, as a real live witness to the events, the sights and the sounds. Yet Jake makes me feel that I'm seeing it, living it and breathing it. I'm one of the shepherds terrified by the sudden burst of angelic glory from the heavens on a starlit night. I'm one of the crowd drawn to Jesus, entranced by his wisdom and his parables, and flabbergasted by his ability to feed those five thousand folk on such meagre and unpromising rations. I'm watching as the Good Samaritan binds up the wounds of the man who fell among robbers. I feel the heat and the dust of the road to Jerusalem, and I'm one of those welcoming Jesus into the great city, heralding his arrival with shouts proclaiming peace in heaven and glory in the highest. I feel a sense of foreboding in the pit of my stomach as both

218

Pilate and Herod question Jesus, and I share the despair of Jesus' followers as the common criminal Barabbas is released and Jesus is handed over to the will of the mob. I can hardly bear to watch as the nails are smashed into his hands and feet. I weep his mother's tears as he hangs from the cross. And I share the mixture of bewilderment and heart-burning excitement of those travelling to Emmaus as the risen Lord talks with them on the road and opens the Scriptures to them. Jake has allowed me to lose myself in the story and that is by far the best compliment I could give him. His delivery is assured, devoid of even the tiniest atom of self-doubt, and never once threatened by hesitancy or anxiety. It is indeed like watching a skilled professional at work: never once does he make us worry for him, never once does he divert attention away from the story and on to him. I almost didn't want the butterfly cake break. I worried that after the break he might take a while to slip back into the zone and that his concentration and hence the quality might suffer as a result. I didn't need to worry. If anything he's been even sharper and more focused in his delivery for the mug of tea and the butterfly cake that Lorrie has brought to him. Then I've worried that, near the end, his concentration might slip with the finishing line getting closer. It would have been tragic, too tragic, to take a tumble with just a few paragraphs to go. But he seems stronger than ever in those final lines. Three hours and twenty-five minutes after starting, he reaches the last two sentences. '"Then they worshipped him and returned to Jerusalem with great joy. And they stayed continually at the temple, praising God."'

After he's said those words he looks up and smiles. I rise to my feet and begin to applaud. I look round and encourage the rest of the audience to do the same. All nine of us. The refreshment providers have joined us towards the end, bringing the numbers to a tantalising one short of double figures. And since it is rumoured that a young woman may have briefly popped in, unnoticed by me certainly, early on in the proceedings, that does indeed mean we will have reached the magic ten.

Brian says all the right things. It was mesmerising, he says. Captivating. He claims he's never been so moved and enchanted by anything in his life. He says he's sure that nobody who has shared the experience of this Mothering Sunday afternoon will feel quite the same about the Christian message again. Never mind the small turnout, he's done it for the Lord, and the Lord will love him for it. Then he says a prayer of thanksgiving and asks us to give generously as we leave.

Then I stop filming.

I've promised Di to help with the retiring collection. But before I do, I need to go and congratulate Jake. As I approach him, I see his face has changed. As he was reciting, there was a serenity and, at times, a kind of quiet joyfulness written all over him, as though the Gospel was his alone to impart and he was handing it out to his children like a benevolent grandfather at Christmas. But now I see a wild-eyed fury. His cheeks are burning red and his lips are shaking.

Then the explosion.

'Why did nobody come!'

For a moment I think his yell is going to blow the roof off. I look round and see that those still left in the church are staring at him in stunned silence.

I wonder if Lorrie expected something of the sort. She takes his hand and holds it to her tummy. 'Jake, my sweet, don't spoil it. All right. You've been amazing. Don't spoil it.' Then she looks outwards. 'He's tired, bless him. Thank you so much for coming.'

She lets go of his hand and wheels him towards one of the side aisles. I try to follow but Lorrie seems to have anticipated that as well. She turns back to me. 'Not now, Matt, love. You go and help Di at the door.'

I head for the door and as I'm on my way another burst of verbal gunfire echoes round the church. 'He promised! Promised people would come and listen to me! That's what he said! He said they'd listen to me!'

I can't bear to hear any more. I explain to Di I've got to go. I shake hands with Brian and tell him I'll be in touch. Then I walk out.

*

I walk off down the street and carry on walking, heading for the beach. I need some sea air. The rain has stopped and a feeble late afternoon sun peers through the clouds of disapproval at my hasty escape.

I've switched my phone off. I'm convinced Lorrie will call me any time now, and I'll get the full package. I Told You So. See What You've Gone And Done. It's Fine For You, You Can Walk Away, I Can't. And maybe another I Told You So for the road. All of which she has every right to be saying. Because I'm the one who's walked and she, who never having wanted all this to happen in the first place, is the one who's lumbered. I can see her now, being sodden by the floods of Jake-shaped invective and, having failed to get hold of me, dialling her emergency home insurance hotline. If I were half the person Lorrie was I'd be with her and with the remarkable man for whom she cares, applying the squeegee, soaking up the abuse and the shouting and the screaming, and at least trying to do and say the right things even though they probably aren't.

I hadn't wanted much lunch and just the one butterfly cake was enough at half-time. But suddenly I'm hungry. I change my mind about my destination, deciding instead to buy a Sunday paper and then seek out the nearest McDonald's. I order a big Mac meal and read the paper from cover to cover, then order a quarterpounder meal plus ice cream and read the colour supplement from cover to cover. I must be there a good three hours in the end. I'm hoping that by the time I get back to my new lodgings Lorrie will be chilling out and won't have come after me with a blunt instrument. I'm also trusting Di will have turned in and I won't have to face her either. I'm feeling bad about rushing off from the church, and, as far as Jake's performance is concerned, I can guess what she'll say and I really don't want to hear it. What an amazing recital, she'll chirp, what an amazing guy…but oh, dear, what a shame about the size of the audience. Barely enough from the takings to afford a loo brush for the ladies' bog in the hall, never mind a new ladies' bog. And that'll make me feel even worse that it's turned out as it has, because both the reciter and his carer will be perfectly justified in saying it's all down to me. My concept. My inspiration. My mess.

*

At least sleep comes easily and next morning I treat myself to a lie-in. Then at ten past ten the phone goes. Rob.

'Are you able to come in tomorrow morning at ten?' he asks.

I'm puzzled. Even though I've decided to be unrepresented I should surely have more notice of a disciplinary hearing than that. But before I can query that he's giving me the answer.

'It's not a disciplinary,' he tells me. 'There's not going to be a disciplinary.'

'Thank heaven.' I can feel tears welling up but they're tears of relief. 'Hang on, though. Have things reached a conclusion?'

'Yes, indeed.'

'So my suspension ends tomorrow?'

'It does, yes. So, see you tomorrow then, Matt.'

It sets me wondering. Wondering if mum had it right after all. She believed strongly that if you do good, but expect and wish no reward, good gets done to you in return. I've done my bit, the getting Jake through St Luke's Gospel bit. And this is the good coming back to me, faster than I could ever have thought possible. I can get back to work and start to rebuild my life, one brick at a time. I'm already thinking that maybe I'm better off away from Di and I should just make a completely fresh start, placing everything that's happened and everyone I've had dealings with over the past couple of months into a packing case and never troubling to open it again. It won't all be bad things going into that case. I tell myself I gave Jake a taste of what he craved and that was better than what he could ever have expected. And there is of course the video. I've got some editing to do before I upload it but then I can send him the link and he can watch it again and again and perhaps again after that. Nobody can take that away from him. Nobody would want to.

The sun's shining from a cloudless sky and although there's a chill in the air, everything is freshened by yesterday's rain. I put on my running gear and run all the way to Devil's Dyke. By the time I've got back, I feel cleansed and invigorated and almost feel like turning round and doing the whole thing again.

But there's a shirt that needs ironing and there are shoes that need cleaning for the morning, and my suit jacket's got a mark on the sleeve that needs attention before I get the dinner on. Not that I begrudge a second of the time spent on all of that, now I know normal service is about to be resumed.

At ten o'clock next morning I'm knocking on Rob's door and it's as if the last nine weeks simply haven't happened. It's another Tuesday morning in Rob's office. There's the same watery blue sky and puffy white cloud outside the window as there was all those weeks ago. Seated around Rob's desk are the same three people. And, just like sixty-three days back, both Rob and Danny are seemingly unable or unwilling to engage in eye contact with me. Except of course this time it doesn't matter because there's nothing to be worried about.

I'm invited to sit and do so.

'Right,' I say with a smile. 'Fire away.'

'As you know, Matt,' Rob says, 'the criminal department of Ellman Rich has seen a significant reduction in workload over the past six months. What you may not know is that other departments, including your former department, IP, and also personal injury, have also suffered a downturn in work and consequently profit. It's been necessary to identify possible savings. Let me say from the outset we hoped to be able to achieve these savings without staff reductions. However, regrettably, we've come to the conclusion that the criminal department, while still viable, is overstaffed. We have had to make a decision as to who to retain and who to let go. I'm very sorry to tell you we have decided to let you go.'

13

For a moment I can't actually accept these words have been spoken. I grip the arm of the chair as if by so doing I can hoist myself back into the real world. A world where the words Rob has just uttered were never uttered at all.

'I know it'll come as a shock,' Rob continues. 'We looked at redeploying you back in IP but that department is also overstaffed. You will of course be entitled to a redundancy package and we consider what we are giving you is more than generous. We will also offer you a glowing reference should you seek employment elsewhere. We shan't require you to work your notice.'

'No way,' I mumble.

'Sorry?' There's a mixture of wariness and irritation all over Rob's face as he says it,.

Now my words come freely. 'You can't do this. You've done this because of these allegations. Which is all they are. What criteria did you apply? Are you going to do me the courtesy of telling me? Or are you going to make me take you before a tribunal?'

Rob picks up a folder in front of him and passes it to me. 'You'll find it's all in here,' he says.

I take the folder and hurl it to the floor. 'You've conned me. Cheated me,' I rage. I point my finger at Danny who's studying his paunch with such interest that I wonder if he's doing a degree in it with the Open University. 'He's the one who should be going. He stitched me up. He trapped me. And the reason he trapped me is he's no good at his job and he's jealous because I do a better job than him. Isn't that right, Danny Letwin?'

Danny Letwin says nothing.

'Great, he's a coward as well.' Now I'm on my feet, pacing the room like an advocate in a third-rate transatlantic legal drama. Then I stand right over Danny. 'You know that Lisa-Marie Williams was never going to give you the answers you wanted. You wanted her to say I'd groped her without her consent. You wanted her to say she was vulnerable and scared.

224

You wanted her to…'

'Matt, stop this now,' Rob says. He too gets to his feet.

'Don't you dare interrupt me. That's right, isn't it, Letwin. Look at me. Be a man for once.'

'Matt, you should leave.' Max Rich speaks for the first time.

If Rob had told me to leave I'm sure I'd have found a few more ill-chosen words from my bottom drawer. If Danny had told me to leave I think I'd have punched him in the face. But there's a gravitas emanating from Max which is compelling in every sense. I pick up the folder and walk out.

*

Within hours I'm on the phone to a firm of employment law specialists with a view to challenging the process by which I've been made redundant. Although they're not prepared to act on a no-win no-fee basis, their charges seem reasonable and at this stage they only want a token payment on account for the initial consultation and preliminary letter to Ellman Rich inviting them to reconsider their decision. They'll want a great deal more if it's going to go all the way. But I can't not do it. I can't let Letwin win.

I ring dad and tell him what's happened. He's great, as I knew he would be. He says it has stitch-up written all over it and tells me a friend of his in Kent had exactly the same thing happen to him and took his offending employers to the cleaners. He makes the point, which hadn't escaped me either, that with Jake's recital over there's nothing whatsoever to keep me in Brighton now so why don't I consider moving to be nearer him and getting a job in Yorkshire. He goes on to invite me to stay the Easter weekend with him and Karen and suggests that, given I might want to take advantage of my sojourn in Yorkshire to knock on a few doors, and do some walking or running in the Dales, I stay a whole week, say Wednesday to Wednesday. The events of New Year's Eve are still all too fresh in my mind, but the prospect of an Easter Day lunch, turkey with all the trimmings, and Karen's home-made simnel cake at teatime, has me succumbing in the third round before the referee has officially stopped the fight.

225

Dad also mentions he's going abroad with Karen for several weeks, leaving next month. Having completed the sessions Lorrie paid for, Karen's had quite a few phone and Skype sessions with Lorrie's contact, who recommended she and dad might benefit from an extended break and a complete change of scene. To cut down on costs, dad's managed to secure the loan of a camper van from someone in the village. Basically he and Karen have agreed they'll just slum it, seeing where the mood takes them. 'Will be like being students again,' Dad says. I tell him he needs to be careful. He may be physically fit but you don't get too many people bumming round Europe in their mid-seventies. He tells me not to worry and says as long as he's got Karen he'll be fine. I could never have seen him doing this with mum even when he was a lot younger. Anyway, he says that on top of my Easter visit I'll be very welcome to stay in their house while they're away and asks me to think about it. I've said I will.

I tell Di what's happened and what's happening in my life, but also tell her that I'm not in the right frame of mind to talk about Sunday's recital or to seek to build bridges with Lorrie and Jake just yet, and please can she bear with me if I keep myself to myself. She's brilliant, as I knew she would be, and says that's absolutely fine but if ever I want to talk with her over a cuppa I have only to knock on her door. I've met a lot of people who call themselves Christian but seem to leave what it means to be a Christian at the church door after Sunday worship. Di takes it with her everywhere and never lets it go.

As far as work's concerned I offer myself to various Brighton firms on a consultancy basis, helping them out if there's stuff they can't cover. The money's not an immediate problem: I've enough to survive on, even after the divorce settlement, and with the house selling for more than we thought possible, and the fact that the redundancy payment is substantially more than I expected, I'm not in urgent need of funds. But I need to keep myself busy and ensure I don't forget how to do the job. Unfortunately it seems like I've picked a bad time. The message I'm getting from all my contacts is the same. Workloads are falling, they tell me, and there's barely enough work and corresponding remuneration for existing staff

226

members. Everyone I speak to is perfectly pleasant. Thank you for thinking of us, they say. Yes, we'll certainly bear you in mind if we're short. But after a fortnight I've had nothing apart from one police station callout for a 3.30am interview on a Sunday morning, exactly a week before Easter, and a hopeless bail application in the remand court at Crawley two days later.

And it's at this hearing at Crawley that I think I discover the real reason why I'm not getting the work. The client is a woman in her early twenties, charged with GBH with intent. She's blonde and tall, and, yes, most would say she was very attractive. After she's been remanded in custody pending her next appearance at the Crown Court, I go down to see her in the cells. It's really a courtesy visit, to reiterate her right to apply to a judge for bail, and to ask if she needs me to notify anyone of her incarceration. Then as I wait to be allowed back out of the cell area, I overhear a solicitor speaking to one of the custody officers. I realise he's talking about me. 'I'll bet he was gutted she was kept in,' he says. 'Was probably hoping to give her a good seeing-to in the car park the moment she got out.' Then they both burst out laughing.

I sit on Three Bridges station platform waiting for the train back to Brighton and when the announcer orders passengers to keep well clear of the train coming through on platform 5 which is not scheduled to stop at this station, there's a stupidly large part of me that wants to get up and stand in its way.

*

Next morning I'm on the non-stop train to York. Although it makes sense to go online in search of suitable vacancies, I feel I've nothing to lose by knocking on a few doors, as dad's put it, while I'm in the heart of the city. But if I expected one of central York's IP or criminal law firms to welcome me into their bosom on the strength of my portal-biffing, it doesn't take more than a couple of hours' trudging to be disabused of any such notion. It's all depressingly similar to what I heard possibly half a dozen times in my wanderings round Brighton a fortnight or so ago. I can't believe that news of my alleged misdemeanours will have travelled beyond Watford Gap

227

Services, so I'm drawn to the inescapable conclusion that, as far as central York is concerned at any rate, there really is no work. Over dinner that evening, dad and Karen tell me not to despair and suggest that I might have more joy in a town or city that has less aesthetic appeal for would-be practitioners.

For the moment, though, all that can wait. Next day's Maundy Thursday and an unseasonably warm sun is shining from a cloudless sky. We all three of us go for a drive across the moors and when we return I go out on a sixteen-mile run. Already I'm beginning to feel reinvigorated and more positive. On Good Friday, another scorcher, Karen suggests a return to the town we visited on New Year's Eve, and as Dad's with us this time I'm quite happy to agree. When we get there we find a Good Friday procession in progress. We watch a depiction of the haggard, exhausted Jesus being made to bear his cross through the heat-soaked dust-filled streets and precincts of Jerusalem. I think back to Jake and how he told this part of the story. Despite today's physical spectacle which Jake couldn't replicate, from the weeping of the women to the blood-soaked face of the tortured Christ, I'm less moved by what I'm seeing here than I was by his rendition. And perhaps it doesn't jar as much as it should when as soon as the procession has passed, dad's asking if I'd be interested in going with him to Headingley next week to see Yorkshire take on Sri Lanka.

The heat continues into Easter Saturday, and the forecasters promise unbroken sunshine and top temperatures of twenty-eight degrees Celsius. As we're having breakfast the doorbell goes and it's two women from the village church reminding us of the big Easter morning service in church tomorrow at ten, with Easter Egg hunt for children and celebratory bubbly for all in the churchyard afterwards. I think Lord Sugar could use them both, as their sales techniques are a lot slicker and more professional than any of those I've seen deployed by his would-be business partners. Then we're off to York for the day, *en famille*. It's our big Easter weekend treat: we'll indulge in some light retail therapy and then go to Betty's for high tea, on me. At times we can hardly move on Stonegate, the city's principal pedestrian shopping street. We find ourselves in the music shop again, and this time it's me treating Karen to a vinyl David

Bowie LP, Karen having bought herself a gramophone a few weeks back. She wasn't born until a few years after his space oddity and his starman waiting in the skies, but still worships him.

She has changed, I can tell. She's still flirty, albeit a more restrained, subdued flirty than at Christmas, but more to the point she's talking sensibly, rationally and maturely about the loss of both Daisy and George. I can see for myself, without her telling me, how beneficial the counselling has been. In turn I tell her about Fiona – there's no reason not to – and again I can rely on her to tell me what I want to hear: that there was probably something mentally wrong with the woman, that at least she had the goodness to decamp before it became properly serious between the two of us, that I'm well clear of her, and there is someone out there for me. She never suggests that she might be up for filling the vacant post, but then again she doesn't need to. I remind her how good she and dad are. She doesn't agree or disagree.

We wake up on Easter Sunday and the weather's turned overnight. Yesterday it was on with the shorts and flip-flops – well, for a large number of the trippers on the pavements of York, it was – but today it's macs and sou'westers time. Rain is pouring from an angry sky and we're told it's going to stay like this all day. With outdoor activity out of the question – even the gentler hillsides normally visible from my bedroom window are taking leave of absence today – we all make our way along to St Hilda's for the service that had been advertised so proactively yesterday. Perhaps too proactively because by the time we've got there it's standing room only. Mum used to joke that you could always tell an Anglican congregation because no Anglican ever occupies the front pews. But this morning even that great sacred tradition is broken. I've no doubt the regulars are overjoyed to see their church full. From what dad says I don't think it happens much these days. Perhaps it's the size of the congregation that unnerves the ageing gent charged with reading the Gospel passage. He stumbles over his words, and stumbles again, and he's apologising. For heaven's sake, he's got the text in front of him. I can't help thinking back three weeks and how, even without the luxury of that text to guide him, Jake delivered this self-same passage in a way that captivated me and gripped me so intensely that it came with a ransom demand. But the priest compensates for it with a sermon that might have been written just for Karen. 'What the Resurrection is about,' he says, 'is burying the past, wiping the slate clean, making a new beginning. We can't pretend the bad things of the past never happened, but the empty tomb symbolises their deadness and it's up to us to follow the example of the risen Christ who refused to allow even death to exert a permanent hold on him.' Stirring stuff. It's just a shame that Karen hasn't heard any of it. She's suddenly remembered she's forgotten to put the oven on.

We enjoy the bubbly, served in the church, but keep an eye out for rampaging tots whose egg hunt has been hastily relocated indoors. Then we head home. Dad announces that he's going to take advantage of the lack of outdoor activity by putting up a couple of shelves in his toolshed. Karen busies herself with lunch while I go online and continue my search for the IP and criminal law vacancies that may exist in the region. I've exhausted possibilities in the York area so I'm having to turn my attention to some of the less scenic towns and cities. There is the odd vacancy here and there, although two towns in particular seem to have more vacancies than most. I do some googling in order to find out why that might be. It's could be a coincidence of course, but it seems that one of those towns has made history by being the first in England to boast more charity shops along its main street than shops actually selling new items. While the other has become the first to boast more boarded-up shops along its main street than shops, including charity shops, that are open for business.

Lunch arrives, as does Dad, from the toolshed. The breaking news is that he's only just finished erecting shelf number one and nobody will mind, will they, if he returns to his labours for the afternoon. After lunch he disappears again while Karen and I clear up. I'd toyed with the idea of a run in the rain but a stiff wind's got up now, the sky's darker and moodier than it was first thing this morning, and there's now a yellow weather warning for flooding across the whole of North Yorkshire. I wonder about going back to my googling in search of other places not to want to work in, but as I stand there gazing into space Karen has a suggestion. She reminds me that there's that big box of papers in the loft containing some family history. She suggests we could both have a look at it.

I'm not one of those people who are fascinated by their family trees and I've never done any independent research into ours, but it has to be a better offer than the only other ones apparently available this afternoon. Accordingly, we go up to the loft and having made ourselves as comfortable as we can, we begin to sort through the material, starting at the top of the pile. There's so much there that I'm concerned that we'll be here till long past simnel cake o'clock. The trouble is, it's in no sort of order. There's a bit of family history here, and a bit there, but then the next bit of paper will be a receipted dentist's bill from 2001, and the one after that a schedule of items excluded from a home insurance policy dad took out in 1998, after which there's more family history. Eventually we decide we've done enough sifting but in any case we appear to have plenty to be going on with. We put it all in a big pile then adjourn to the comparative comfort of the dining room in order to try and make sense of it. After possibly an hour's detective work at the dining room table, we've had it confirmed, although I think I knew this already, that dad's dad, my granddad, was called Frederick, was born in December 1920 and had a menswear store in Ashford. We've also found, which I didn't know, that his dad – my great grandfather – was called William, was married to someone called Edith, saw active service in the First World War and was invalided out in late November 1917.

Karen and I are both puzzled as to why he was invalided out. I imagine at least a proportion of those at the Front during those dreadful years must have been glad of an injury that forced them out of battle but wasn't crippling or life-threatening. I wouldn't like to think of my great granddad being in pain. But at the same time maybe he'd sustained whatever injury he had doing something heroic, possibly saving the lives of others. Perhaps our curiosity will be satisfied by the pile of stuff we've yet to reach. This is the thing about family history, as I've heard pointed out. Once you pick up a thread, you want to follow it through. It becomes a piece of detective work, work that's utterly personal and special to you.

We rifle through more bits of paper. Lots relating to Frederick's flourishing menswear store, hardly spellbinding, and, bless him, two love letters he wrote to my gran, who was born a year after him and died just two years before mum passed away. Then I come to a letter which seems to answer our question. It's dated 10th December 1917 and it's from someone called Reg. I read it out loud.

Dear William, I've just heard from Edith that you're back home now. I expect you have mixed feelings. I'm sure part of you would like to be there still, helping us to the victory we know will not be far off. But I know you couldn't have carried on fighting with your lung disorder as it was and I join in the prayers to Almighty God for…

I happen to catch a glance at Karen at this point and I see that her face, relaxed and contented as we were scouring the documentation a moment before, has become suffused with incredulity and horror.

'What the hell's the matter?' I say.

'Lung disorder,' she says. 'Your great grandfather. Alan's granddad. Lung disorder.'

'Seems that way.'

'Lung disorder that invalided him out.'

She's a couple of steps ahead of me and I'm struggling to catch up. 'What are you saying?' I ask.

'Get him here. Now.'

'You mean dad?'

'Who else. Get him!'

There's no time to think. In seconds I'm out of the back door and scurrying through the monsoon across the back lawn to the toolshed. Moments later dad's back in the living room, his expression as placid and serene as Karen's is dark and wild.

'Your granddad had a lung disorder.' She's standing in the kitchen end of the dining room. In her right hand is the letter I've just been reading from. She waves it in his direction. 'Just found this letter he got from some geezer called Reg. Talking about his lung disorder.'

'That's right, darling,' he replies. 'He did.'

'Never mentioned it to me, did you.'

'I may have done. I can't remember.'

'Exactly. Probably years and years ago. Just slipped it in when we were first getting to know each other.'

'What are you saying, darling?'

'For heaven's sake, what do you think I'm saying!' I've never heard Karen speak to him like this before. It's scaring me. 'All those conversations we had with the medics after we lost Daisy. Could we, should we risk another baby. And all the time you knew but still said nothing about your granddad. Nothing at all.'

'Darling, I couldn't see there was a risk. Fred – my dad – had no issues. I haven't. Matt hasn't.' There's no defensiveness in his tone. His calmness doesn't falter for one syllable.

'You just don't get it, do you!' She's shouting now and I see dad taking an involuntary step back. 'You're not an expert. They are. They simply wanted to know the facts, the family history, any possible genetic cause. Didn't you think they needed to know about something like this?'

'They told us it was most unlikely Daisy's illness was hereditary.' His voice is still measured but I can see his face reddening. 'I just didn't think it was necessary to mention it. As I said, I didn't suffer it. Or my dad before me.'

'Who are you to say what's necessary!" She throws the letter to the floor. 'I know you were desperate for a child for us. For a brother or sister for Matt. You knew you should have mentioned it but you didn't want to say anything because you knew if you did, I'd stall. And even though you knew, I told you a hundred times, I could never go through it all again, you were prepared to take that risk. And look what happened. If Daisy's death was hell, how can I begin to describe what George's death was like? How could you be so selfish. How could you. Eh?'

I can't bear to see my dad being put through this. I need to defend him. 'Kaz,' I say. 'Dad never meant to hurt you. It's the last thing he'd ever do to you. You know he's not like that. Supposing he had mentioned it. Would you really have stopped trying for another baby? Knowing that my dad, and his dad, and I, were perfectly fine? And anyway, what's worse. To lose

George when we did or not have had George at all. And if we hadn't, always the thought of what might have been.'

My speech seems to have given dad the time he needs to regroup. 'Darling, Matt's right. You know he is. As for me, well, maybe I should have said something. If you think I should, I'm really sorry. So very sorry. I'm not a secretive person. I've never kept anything else back from you and I would never do so again. And I'm sure you wouldn't. Would you.'

He's looking right into Karen's eyes. There's no malevolence in his tone but there's no diffidence either. It's a straight question. And Karen doesn't answer.

'Would you,' he says again.

Karen steps back. Again there's a silence and then a whispered 'N...no. No, Alan.'

But her hesitation is fatal. 'Darling. Please. Would you.' I detect just a tiny hint of steeliness in dad's tones.

'Nothing.'

I think back to that sermon. Wiping the slate clean. 'Karen, you need to tell him.'

'Matt, I can't.'

'Tell me what, Matt.' Dad now looks into my eye and if anything that's even scarier. 'Are you trying to tell me...you and Karen?'

I nod. 'After the New Year's Eve party.'

He doesn't react. He just stands there, his expression grey and changeless. I daren't look at Karen. But it's my dad and I've got to care about him first.

So I plough on. 'It was just the once. We'd both had a fair bit to drink. It was my last night before going back to Brighton, and I was in a crap place, and my world was falling apart, and Karen was so good to me, and we'd all had such a great time, and I just got carried along with it. I wish it hadn't happened, and I'm sorry, dad, I'm just so sorry...' And I find myself putting my arms around him and holding him in a clumsy embrace. We must stay like that for thirty seconds. Then dad pulls away.

'Let's have some tea,' he says.

We sit in the living room and drink the tea and eat the simnel cake. It may be the best simnel cake Karen's ever made but it might as well be a Happy Shopper 59p apricot sponge. Karen hardly says a word. There's anger and disappointment written all over her face but I can't tell whether she's angrier with dad or with me. She won't look at either of us. Dad seems to be trying to pretend that nothing's changed, that we're all just the same people we were the last time we were eating and drinking together. I've seen dad in a stressful situation many times before. He's had enough of them to deal with. He's not one for tears or histrionics. I've always admired him for trying to find good in any and every situation. The difference is that in the past he's been able to draw comfort and strength from those around him, united as they are in grief and devastation. Now, it's those around him who've combined to destroy him. And his way of dealing with it is to act normal. To ask if I thought Yorkshire stood a chance in this year's county cricket championship. To suggest a couple more places I might try for jobs. To remind us about the Easter Monday curry buffet at Mark and Sean's next door. A landmine's been detonated on his back lawn and he's still tinkering with the motor mower.

After we've drunk our tea and consumed our modest slices of cake, dad, ever the diplomat, announces he's going back out to the toolshed. I don't want to be left alone with Karen. In fact I don't want to be around either of them. Nor do I want to be up in Yorkshire any more. I'd sooner get straight back to Brighton, out of everybody's way. I announce that I need the loo and having left the room I reach for my phone. To my relief I'm able to change my train booking to enable me to return this evening. I then order a taxi back to York station. I'd need a taxi to the nearest station whatever, and it's just a lot easier and quicker to go all the way.

I can't face telling Dad or Karen I'm going. I don't want them to try and talk me out of it. I tell myself I'll message them once I'm safely in the taxi. I can see from the half-open door leading back into the living room that dad's not there, presumably still in the toolshed, while Karen's put the telly on and from the doorway I can see her slumped on the settee. If I'm to disappear without them seeing I need to do it now. It doesn't take long for me to pack and ten minutes after booking my taxi I'm closing the front door behind me and walking out into the deluge.

As soon as we get going I message dad simply saying it's best all round for me to go back down south and I'll call them again in a few days. I wait for the call back or the text but nothing comes.

*

The journey back to Brighton seems endless. Because of flooding the train is two hours late into King's Cross and I'm not back at Di's until ten past one in the morning.

I crawl into bed at twenty past one and switch the light off.

I'm woken by my phone at just before nine.

Karen.

'Hi Matt. I've left Alan. I'm on my way down to see you.'

14

We arrange to meet at the station at two. Thanks, or no thanks, to a signal fault somewhere between Pontefract and Nijni-Novgorod, she doesn't make it down till ten to three. If she's still angry with me she doesn't show it. She rushes into my arms and showers me with kisses. And as she draws back and I see what she's wearing, it's clear that she's dressing to impress. She wears a bright red top, black jeans with metal-studded black belt, and Doc Martens. She also has a suitcase.

I suggest we go for a coffee but she says it's the last thing she needs or wants. She says she's been sitting drinking coffee for most of the past five hours, the sun's shining, and what about a walk. She's been to Brighton with dad from time to time to see Emma and me but she says she's never really explored the city. So, being the gent and wheeling her suitcase, I take her through the Lanes, narrow streets full of overpriced jewellers' shops, then down to the seafront and along the pier. But it's Easter Monday, the pier is crammed with people, our conversation never gets beyond practical small talk and, with me still pulling the suitcase, we end up retreating and following the pavement beside the coast road all the way past Kemp Town and above Brighton Marina. It's only as we walk along the sheer cliffs overlooking the Marina that the crowds thin out and we can talk. Properly. Starting with me.

'You probably wonder why the hell I blabbed on us.'

'I'm glad you did,' she says. 'I've hated not telling him. Hated it. More than you could possibly imagine. Thought to start with I could brave it out. That in time it wouldn't be seen as a big deal. But I've noticed him looking at me sometimes, I can't define what it is, but it's as if…I don't know…he's almost expecting me to come out with something. Something I've kept from him. And then I've thought I can't tell him, not without talking to you, and the moment passes. I am glad it's out, Matt. Thank you for doing what I should have done.' She turns and kisses my cheek.

'Did he chuck you out?'

'Of course not.' She says it in a throwaway fashion as though the question wasn't worth asking. 'That's half the trouble. You know what, if he'd come down on me from a great height, if he'd roasted me alive, if he'd shoved me in Mark and Sean's cooking pot and served me up with the curry...I think I'd have preferred that. Would have eased the tension. But there was none of that. It was as if he was really trying to pretend it hadn't happened. Like me with George. Just talking about banal, matter-of-fact stuff. Like at tea yesterday. That's what I couldn't take. It wasn't natural. It was...well, it was spooking me. And there's me thinking, I've got this to look forward to for the next twenty years maybe. Always that feeling that he owes me something nasty in return. Always the awkwardness. Always those looks. Have you spoken to him since last night?'

'No. Same reason. I can't do the banal any more than you.'.

'Anyway, that's one reason I left. The tension. The uncertainty. Couldn't hack it. Plus, yes, before you ask, I am still angry with him over the other business. All yesterday evening, while he's doing his weird bit, I'm thinking about what I went through with George. I know what you said, that maybe having him was worth the risk. And I get that, I really do. But what I hate is that I never got the freedom to choose. If Alan had said something, we could have gone to specialists, could have got opinions from the best brains...believe me, after Daisy I'd have done whatever it took, spent whatever it took. But no. As you say, we'll never know, but Alan had no right to stop me knowing at the time. It was selfish of him. He was thinking about him, not about me. So, in answer to your question...I jumped. I wasn't pushed. Don't worry, I've told him. Told him we need some time apart. Time to regroup, decide if we have a future. We've both hurt each other badly. I know I'm just as much to blame. But I'd honestly rather be out of it altogether than pretend we're fine. That was my trouble with George. Too much pretending. I'm done with that. I want honesty. So, yes. Better apart for now.'

'How was he when you left?'

'I could tell he was upset. But he was never going to let that show. He just said to let him know where I was, how I was. And to come back soon. Again, you see. Just pretending it was all

238

natural, that nothing odd had happened. So much harder to deal with.' She sighs. 'I really wanted to make it work. Alan and me. Since Christmas, I've tried, really tried, to keep us, him and me, on track. The number of people who gave us no chance when we got together…but now for the first time I'm wondering if our chance has gone.'

*

We carry on walking for a while. Then Karen announces her feet are killing her so, spotting a convenient bench nearby, I suggest we stop. She removes her footwear, and we sit in silence for possibly ten minutes. She's lying back, her eyes closed, her Docs and socks in a disorderly heap in front of her. I'm gazing seawards. I know Brighton Marina isn't loved by everybody but I like the inlets and the luxury yachts and the modern architecture of the maze-like streets. I could sit admiring it for hours. But as the minutes pass, I see grey clouds threatening the dominance of the afternoon sun, and I can feel the coolness of breeze in my hair. I suggest it might be time for us to move on.

'What next, then?' I ask her. 'I mean, where do you go from here.'

'I was hoping you could tell me.'

I don't know what to make of that answer. I'm hoping she's not suggesting we start something between us. Even if I wasn't still in pieces over Fiona I couldn't heap yet more misery on dad. I want her and dad back together. I'm convinced they can repair the damage. If she's come to me as the best available port in her storm, I'm happy to provide moorings but I need her to set sail once the tempest has abated.

'Kaz, I can't have you,' I say. 'I mean, part of me would love it. But it just…just…' I shrug and sigh and trust there's no need for me to carry on.

'It's fine,' she says. But I can tell by the look on her face that for her it's half a world away from fine. 'Let's go, shall we.'

She reaches for her socks and starts trying to pull the left one on. Whether it's because her feet have expanded as a result of the walk I don't know but she's struggling and when she finds herself stuck at Camp Four she calls for reinforcements. I kneel down beside her and manage to squeeze her toes inside. Little by little the woollen wrapper claws its way along the foot and over the ankle, and, grabbing for further supplies of oxygen, surmounts the Hillary Step and plants a flag on the summit. The right sock goes on with greater ease and within a few minutes we're trudging along the clifftops back towards the city.

'I love what you just did for me,' she says. 'Love that you care about me that much,'

'It was only putting your socks on for you,' I say with a laugh. 'It hardly makes me the Milk Tray man.'

'You know I'd do anything for you as well.'

For a moment I want to slap her down, to tell her not to make such big statements when the lives and futures of all three of us are in such a fragile, vulnerable state. Less than thirty-six hours ago she was happily married to my father. Or so I thought. I'm telling myself she's just said these words in the heat of the moment. That way they're easier to understand, easier to forgive. And I can confine myself to humouring her. 'So the Harry Ramsden's fish suppers are on you then.'

We walk in silence for some minutes. Then she reaches in her back pocket for her phone. 'I'll phone my brother,' she says. 'I spoke to him on the train. Told him I might be dropping in on him sooner rather than later. He says I can come whenever. If I get off to London now I should make it tonight.'

We're a long walk from the station but there's no shortage of buses going into town and it's only a short stroll from the cliff path to the coast road and a convenient nearby bus stop. Karen gets through to Steve and yes, he and Vikki will be delighted to have her for however long she wants to stay. Fifteen minutes later we're back at the station, firstly queueing with returning Easter weekenders at the ticket machines, then battling with them for personal space on the station concourse. The loudspeaker announces that the next London train is now standing at platform 5 and we're caught in a wave of bodies heading for the automated ticket barriers.

As we reach the barriers we embrace and we kiss. She doesn't say she loves me thank goodness because I'd have hated to see the look on her face when I didn't say it back. She promises to call me when she gets to the capital. I wonder if she's hoping that seemingly from nowhere I'll produce an extra ticket and will be boarding the train with her. The sort of thing you might get at the end of a will-they-won't-they romcom. The guy who at the very last moment decides to abandon everything in order to be with the woman he now realises he loves. But I'm not following that particular script. I release her from our embrace, and two more kisses later she's on her way through the barrier and onto the train. She gives me a final wave and then disappears with the Bank Holiday crowds.

Where to now. There may be shops selling everything money can buy within a fifteen-minute walk, but I just know that all the shelves with ideas on where to now will be empty with no prospect of a new consignment coming through. I've thought about this often enough during the past twenty-four hours. I've lost my career. I've lost my home. I've lost the woman I truly believed was my soulmate. I've abandoned my dad. Now I've just let go of the woman who I know loves me.

I find myself retracing the steps I took with Karen a few hours ago. I give the pier a miss but once again am heading eastwards along the cliffs above the marina. And it's as I walk that it hits me.

For it to work, I need to ring Karen.

'You know you said you'd do anything for me.'

'Of course.'

'I need you to ask Steve to do something. Something different. Something amazing.'

*

In the morning I phone Lorrie. Just as I expect, there's no anger or resentment in her voice. She says she'd be delighted to see me, and that Jake would be positively thrilled. I arrange to see them on Thursday afternoon. She tells me Thursday is Jake's 40th birthday. I ask her what he'd like and she says his just seeing me will be fine.

I try to stay positive and upbeat during the intervening forty-eight hours. Not that it's altogether easy. I ring my employment solicitors for an update and they tell me there isn't one. There's a lethargy about them which reminds me of the Fiat Punto I had during a particularly cold winter in my undergrad days. But at least I could usually get the Punto to start following a couple of good hard spanks on the bonnet. As for the consultancy, I don't know if Danny's been doing the rounds but the Great Wall Of Silence could in all likelihood be seen from outer space and is already being nominated as a UNESCO World Heritage Site.

I need to keep busy in this mix of negativity so I go for a couple of runs up onto the Downs and do a complete circuit of Stanmer Park. Then on Wednesday night I get a call from Karen. Yes, Steve would be delighted to help. And there's more. Alison, Vikki's sister, has a room free in her new house in Cranleigh, Surrey, and is happy to have Karen until such time as she feels able to make a decision about where her long-term future lies. Alison's son has just left home so Karen's presence as a lodger will help ease the empty-nest syndrome. And although Alison's split from her husband she remains on very good terms with her in-laws who live near Chichester in West Sussex, and Steve tells me they'll be key to the success of what I'm contemplating.

It's all happened almost too quickly. But Steve's one of these people who, on his own admission, actions everything instantly. He says it's the only way to operate and attributes a great deal of his success to responding instantly to correspondence, emails and phone calls. As a result I find myself with something that's forming almost too quickly. I'm still not a hundred per cent sure in my own mind. It may not work. It may be a non-starter.

Until.

Thursday's a sunny warm day. After the deluge of Sunday, high pressure is building, and forecasters are prophesying a dry settled spell which could last weeks. This weekend we're promised a storm, not of rain but of T-shirts, shorts and flip-flops, and consequently lots of bare flesh with generous quantities of suntan oil in exposed areas. I'm due at Jake's at two, and during the morning of idleness that precedes it I go out to buy him a 40th birthday card. Di tells me there's an old-fashioned stationery and card shop just a short distance from her, the sort of shop that's especially vulnerable to the twin

242

beasts of out-of-town superstores and online shopping, and she says it would be nice if I could support it. I find it soon enough, and although the card I finally choose has probably been sitting in exactly the same shelf since the day Jake was conceived, I like the illustration and I like the message. The guy to whom I give my money seems almost pathetically grateful for the custom and he suggests I might like to explore some of the other remnants of 1950's-style shopping in this corner of Brighton. By turning left out of here and first right along Pinemere Street, he says, I'll reach Broadberry Road which boasts several family-run businesses, with owners who'd love to see me and would doubtless love to see my wallet even more. And just after turning first right along Pinemere Street I see a woman walking towards me.

A woman who looks uncannily like the woman who broke my heart eighty-eight days ago.

She's some distance away. Ninety, a hundred yards. And the glare of the sun means I can't focus on her. But the height looks about right. So does the hair colour. And I'm sure I've seen that skirt before as well.

Perhaps it isn't Fiona. But perhaps isn't good enough. I need to be certain it isn't her. I start to run towards her. But there's a side road in the way and I have to stop to let a car turn left to join it.

It may be a stop of only a moment. But that moment is enough. Because once the car's passed and I've crossed over, she isn't there at all.

I wonder if maybe she's walked round the far side of the parked cars. So I check but she's not there. Maybe she's darted off down another side road but I can't see any side roads. Perhaps she's hidden in a garden of one of the properties adjoining the street but I can't see her there either. And as I look over the fence of number 68 someone inside that house is calling out of the window. 'Can I help you.' Code for "What the hell do you think you're up to." I have to abandon that plan as well.

There's a wooden bench near the top of the street. I sit down there and put my head in my hands. I'm still wanting her, wanting to see her, so much that I'm imagining her. I haven't seen her at all.

I hate this. Hate it. Hate what she's done to me, hate what my mind's now doing to me.

Enough self-pitying, Matt. You weren't sure, weren't sure at all, but you know now what you've got to do. Something that's going to effectively take you out of this rotten world with its rotten way of treating people. Something that will tell that rotten world that you have got something about you after all.

Still seated on the bench, I start jotting.

*

I'm at Lorrie's at two precisely and in no time I'm ensconced on her settee with enough slices of home-made lardy cake in front of me to be able to form an edible pavement from here to Tashkent.

We get the small talk over then I start where I have to start.

'Can you possibly forgive me, Lorrie.'

'Not sure where quite to begin,' she says. Her tones are quiet, measured, and unsmiling. 'Shoving Jake into that awful church in front of an audience of minus five. Walking out the second the final curtain came down. Treating us ever since then as though we've wandered off the planet.'

I know I deserve every word. 'I'm sorry.'

Now, only now, does she permit herself a chuckle. 'If you could have seen your face just then,' she says. 'Matt, he loved doing it. Loved every second of it. And if I'm honest, so did I. I never thought he could be that good. I know you were upset. I could see why you were upset. Could see why you felt awkward about ringing me again. But you don't need to worry. Honestly.'

'But what about his outbursts.'

'Oh, any excuse for a good old yell,' she says. 'I think I'd have been worried if he hadn't, if I'm honest. I mean, I'm not going to deny it, he was very upset it was so badly supported. Of course he was disappointed. Never stopped going on about it. He was craving a church full of admirers and all he gets is a handful of old dears and the church mouse. I know you did your

244

best. Rallying the troops. The radio interview. But I speak from experience, I've sung in quite a few concerts with the choir at that church, or in that hall, and some of their attendances have been diabolical. I mean, it doesn't help that the church and the hall are falling to bits round their ears. But even if they were in mint condition, still wouldn't pull them in. Their target market, whatever you call them, are a fair-weather lot. Too hot, too wet, too cold, you've lost them. Got to be Goldilocks weather. Just right.' She chuckles again. 'We did a Gilbert & Sullivan concert one July and they got the leads to wear costume and make-up. I thought the thermometer was going to explode. Must have been at least a hundred degrees in the hall. Greasepaint dribbling down poor old Maurice's face. If it had been fancy dress he'd have won first prize as a waterfall. Audience of six. So all things considered, you didn't do as badly as you thought. Jake's audience outnumbered the cast and in my book that's a good turnout.'

I extract a piece of lardy cake from the top of the tower, 'Just seems such a shame for him never to do it again,' I say.

Now the jocularity seems to go out of her face. It's a light bulb switched off at the wall. 'Yes, Matt. Yes. It would be.'

It's time. I show Lorrie my written musings of a few moments before. The musings in the course of which I've planned that Jake should recite something in public from memory. And not just a single book of the Bible

I've planned that he should recite all of it.

15

Lorrie looks at what I've written and as I bite into the lardy cake I wait for the frown, the shake of the head, and the nervous tap of her feet on the ground as she works out how, as diplomatically as possible, to blast my brainchild to smithereens.

Instead, she smiles. She hands my notes back to me. 'Okay,' she says.

I nearly choke on my cake. 'You mean...yes?'

The smile fades. 'Matt, darling, you won't have known this, but Jake's been very unwell. Stomach pains, vomiting, diarrhoea. Really nasty bouts of it in the last week or two. It feels to me like more than just a bug or an infection. I'm taking him to the doctor if it carries on. It's not just that, although that on its own's a big worry. As I was on my way in with his lunch yesterday, I heard him saying "I want it now." Kept on saying it. I asked what he meant. He was saying he wanted to end it and he was going to find a way of seeing he did. It scared me. Thing is, and this really sounds awful, I could see it from his point of view. He's got these awful conditions, now something else has been shoved in the mix. If by doing this thing he feels his life's still worth living, how can I stand in his way. It's got to be better than the alternative. And that's why, in principle, I'm saying I can live with what you've got in mind. I wouldn't otherwise. I'd be saying it's far too much for him, for you, for me, for my sanity. But now, it is different. I mean, we've got to face facts. If this new thing he's got turns out to be life-threatening he may not get to do it. But for now we just take it one day at a time. All we can do. So...the answer's yes.'

'Lorrie, I'm so grateful,' I say. 'I will be honest. I wasn't expecting you to say yes.'

'I'm sure you weren't,' she says. 'I wouldn't have expected me to say yes. Not till he started Luke's Gospel and really got into his stride. But when he did, then I saw the joy and elation and pride written all over him. Things I never expected to see in his face again. Things I'd give so much to see again. I tell you,

I'm the one who should be grateful to you.' She reaches across to me and grips my hand for a moment. 'I've said yes in principle. The devil's in the detail. We need to sit down and talk about that, yes?'

'Of course.'

We sit for a few minutes, not saying anything. It's only broken by a burst of shouting from down the corridor.

'That's your cue to break the good news to His Lordship,' she says. 'I'm afraid he's Lord Volatile just now.'

I let go of her hand, leave the room and walk along the corridor to Jake's room. I knock and go in.

He's sitting at his table at the far end of the room. Lying on the table in front of him are two birthday cards and some ripped wrapping paper.

'Happy birthday, Jake.'

I extend my hand but perhaps I should have known better. He glares at it. He glares at me. I withdraw my hand.

'Should have knocked!' he cries. 'Shouldn't just barge into a room, you know. Rude. Ill-mannered.'

'I'm sorry,' I say. 'Do you want me to come back later?'

'Don't be so ridiculous. You're here now. Sit.'

'Before I sit, shall I put these cards up for you somewhere?'

By way of response he snatches the cards up and holds them to his chest. 'Leave them alone and sit.'

I sit down, reach into my bag and draw out an envelope containing my card to him.

'Shall I open it for you?' I ask him.

'I can manage, thank you.'

I pass the card to him and he grabs it. But he can't manage, thank you. I've made the mistake of sealing the envelope and as I watch him I wonder if the sealant includes superglue. He tries picking at the flap. Then he starts licking at it, as if moistening it is going to separate the flap from the rest of it. Then he picks at the flap again. And finally his frustration crashes through. He tears at it and rips the whole packet in half.

'Look what you've done!' he bellows. 'Just look what you've done!'

'I'm sorry.'

'Just get out, will you. Leave me to die. I want to die. Today.

247

This afternoon. Born on April 25th , die on April 25th . Nice and neat, uh? That's the only present I want!' He throws half of the ripped packet across the room.

'Jake, before you die...before I die...before I go...'

'What? What now?'

'I've got...got...'

'Spit it out, will you! What are you, some kind of moron?'

The venom in his voice and in his face is crushing me and for a moment I feel as though I'm going into anaphylactic shock. 'I've...I've got something to suggest to you. To put to you.'

'Oh, this'll be good.' He flings the other half of the packet to the floor beneath his feet. 'Of course, you're a lawyer, aren't you. "I put to you, Jake, that you are a dying, useless excuse for a person, someone who once had a place on this planet and paid his way in the world and put in as much as he gave back. But now you're none of those things so why should the jury justify your continued miserable wretched existence any longer. Objection, my Lord. Objection over-ruled. So, Jake Terson. What have you to say?" '

He pauses for breath and I play the single card that's in front of me. 'Jake, you're going to be reciting the whole Bible from memory. Out loud. In public. In four months' time. And I'm going to help you. Every step of the way.'

The transformation is instant. I've been watching a volcanic mix of anger, bitterness, hatred and disdain, liable to erupt and keep erupting at the slightest hint of provocation. The next moment, I'm witnessing a serene wooded hillside on a sunlit autumn morning after a wet night, the trees weeping to the heavens with gratitude and the falling leaves frolicking with carefree pleasure.

'You mean that? You really mean that?' His words tumble out with the exuberance of a child at Christmas, almost unable to believe the big parcel contains the very gift he wanted.

'It's all sorted,' I tell him. 'The whole Bible from memory. Out loud. Something nobody has ever attempted before.'

And now he's saying this is the best birthday present he could have wished for and he couldn't ever ask for a better one.

I don't need to bother to tell him the things I've needed to do or things that have had to happen in order to effect the transformation I've just witnessed. There's the context: my enforced idleness, courtesy of Lemon Muffin Head; my own need for therapy following what Fiona has done, and evidently is still doing, to me; Jake's recent, worrying physical deterioration and suicidal thoughts; and his flawless rendition of St Luke's Gospel, convincing Lorrie and myself that he can perform in a public arena and has the necessary stamina. And then there's the practical stuff, the nuts and bolts: Lorrie's support, without which it's a non-starter; Steve's influence which will ensure the event gets national and maybe even international coverage; Karen herself, who's told me that having decided she's not going off round Europe with dad, she'd be delighted to give whatever practical help that's needed; and the assistance of Alison's in-laws, Richard and Anne, whose local church between Chichester and Bognor Regis in West Sussex will be the venue. It may only be small country church but Steve assure me that that is ideal for the purpose. The church is apparently in an interregnum now but the assistant clergy and churchwardens have agreed to help us in whatever way they can. With the possible exception of the final day, I can't see the event is going to draw huge crowds at any one time; because the recitation will necessarily be over several days, I see there being a steady flow of people dipping in and out, so a big venue isn't necessary. A country church provides intimacy, peace, freedom from outside noise, and, as Steve's pointed out, a comparatively uncongested parish diary which in turn has made it a good deal easier to organise dates and times. I've done some rough calculations based on the length of time it took Jake to recite St Luke's Gospel and it seems we should allow a total of 85 hours' actual reciting. The most realistically Jake can do in a day is seven hours, so we've agreed the recitation will extend over twelve days during August, two blocks of Monday to Saturday with a rest day on the Sunday. Each day will run from 9am to 5.45pm consisting of some seven hours' recital, roughly one hour for lunch and two twenty-minute breaks, one during the morning session and one during the afternoon session.

After I've left Jake I return to the lardy cake and it's not long before, at Lorrie's invitation, I'm making further significant inroads into the tottering tower of the stuff that she's placed on the table in front of me. It's as I help myself to what will be my fourth slice that she dons her gown and wig and embarks on the role of Satan's counsel.

'Before you get started on all this with Jake,' she says, 'you need to realise a few things. Firstly it's really going to take its toll on all three of us. It's a massive ask for him and I've no idea how that'll affect him and whether it may be too much for him. You're going to be stuck with him for hour after hour, day after day, week after week, and you need to think about how you'll cope with that. And if you or he go into meltdown, muggins here will be picking up the pieces and muggins isn't massively keen on picking up the pieces.'

'I get all that,' I say. 'Lorrie I promise I'm the one taking responsibility here. I've got the time. We'll be fine. I know we will.'

She smiles. 'That was the first thing,' she said. 'Second, I've no idea if this new illness is a one-off or something more sinister. You don't mind that you may waste weeks, maybe months, on a recital that's never going to happen? A recital we may have to pull, possibly at the last minute, because he has a relapse.'

'I realise that,' I tell her. 'But...I don't know...I've just got this feeling that his belief, his conviction, his willpower...don't you think?' Desperate for her to think it because I'm not really sure I do.

'I guess it would be a lot easier if we were all like Di.' She picks up the teapot and tops up the content of my mug. 'She'd say if God willed it then it would happen, and why would God not will him to do this beautiful, wonderful thing. But then why did God will him to end up how he is. I go round in circles wondering about it. I just don't know. We can only wait and see. Que sera and all that.' She sighs and smiles again. 'But I'm afraid we may have another problem.'

'What do you mean?'

A layer of cumulus cloud covers the sunlight on her face. 'While you were up seeing Jake, I got a call from Maggie. Asking after him. She phones most weeks. Jake won't speak to her so I'm the spokesperson. I had to tell her about these new stomach and sickness problems of his, obviously. She was all for coming down straight away. I said there was no need, we're taking him to the doc if it persists, but she still wants to see him. Which I guess I can understand. And if she finds out about the recital, if he lets it slip, she'll go ballistic. I've seen her go ballistic before. It's not pleasant. As I said before he did St Luke's Gospel she'd be furious at the thought of him going in front of an audience and what it might do to him. We got away with it but the whole Bible's massively different. Massively.'

'I know that, Lorrie.'

'But there's more. You remember I told you he used to recite great chunks of the Bible to me. What I never told you was that Maggie detested it. She said it was a waste of his time and my time, and I should be taking him out more and doing constructive things that sensible people do. And she had this theory that it was making his autism worse. So if she knew he'd gone back to it...well, if you hear a nuclear bomb explosion in this part of Brighton on the day she graces us with her presence, you can guess the reason. And while I'm clearing up the ashes and fighting the radiation sickness, she'd be shipping him out and we wouldn't see him for radioactive dust.'

'Would it help if I talked to her? Told her it's actually helping?'

She gives me the kind of look I used to get when I came round to see Jake in the early days. 'No, sweetie. Not if you've grown quite happy with the position of your nose in relation to the rest of your face. And you've no particular desire to have it relocated.'

*

During the next couple of days I sort out some admin with Lorrie, agreeing rehearsal times and making some tentative plans to ensure Jake's welfare during the recital itself. Then Jake and I have our first rehearsal the following Monday. We agree there really is no time to lose. We start at the very beginning of the Bible: Genesis, Chapter 1. Off Jake goes. '"In the beginning God created the heavens and the earth. Now the earth was formless and empty, darkness was over the surface of the deep, and the Spirit of God was hovering over the waters.'"

It's word-perfect, as I'd expected it to be. But these are just the first words; they're six lines out of a whole page, the first page of over 1250. It's frightening. It's ridiculous. If I'd been invited to do it I'd probably be thinking about quitting now while I was ahead. Yep, six lines, that'll do me. But I know Jake won't be satisfied till he's done the lot, from here to the final Amen, via the bits which Lorrie, wonderful Lorrie, simply couldn't face having to sit through. And we're still hundreds of pages even from them. What makes it an even harder task for me, the prompt, is that Jake's using different translations at different times. The default text is the New International Version, or NIV, but Jake's explained that a lot of what he learnt when he was younger was from the King James Version while, also in his youth, he got to learn the Prayer Book translations of the Psalms. And just to spice things up further, he's found that in the tougher sections of the Old Testament he prefers to use the Good News Bible. It's all fine for variety, and for his chances of completing the recitation in one piece, but not so good for the hapless prompt with only the NIV for company.

As he moves onwards, already I'm beginning to get an idea of the scale of the task as a whole, and what it's going to be like for me as mentor and prompt. Bed of roses is not the first description that springs to mind. Bed of nails still doesn't really do it justice. Words, words, words. There's words, there's more words, and there are so many words still to come; they're words that as the rehearsals intensify I'll be hearing possibly more than a professor of theology across an entire career. I'm sure at some stage I'll be asked how many words there are altogether. I don't dare to try to find out.

*

Over the coming days, Jake's condition doesn't deteriorate. In fact, he seems to be improving. He has been to the doctor, albeit not his usual one, has been diagnosed with some condition that is barely pronounceable but not terminal, and has been prescribed some medication. Although Lorrie says it's helped, she also says that the Bible learning is really his best medicine. And so Jake and I warm to the task. Effectively, it's like being in work and experiencing a working day. I arrive at Lorrie's at half past eight and Jake and I work together till one, with a mid-morning tea break. I then go for a lunchtime run and sandwich. We start again at two and finish at half past five, with a mid-afternoon tea break. It's a five-day working week, with Wednesdays, which he spends with one of his carers, and Sundays being my days off.

By the middle of June, we've been through the whole of the Bible twice. Even at this stage a great deal of it is immaculate. Lorrie explains that Jake was brought up in a churchgoing household and he would sit and listen to Bible readings and sing hymns and psalms based on Biblical texts, so when he comes to the palatable and the familiar he's doing it with aplomb and with an easy, almost casual confidence. But despite the years of preparation he's done, a good deal of it with Lorrie's help, there have been glitches. And as one might expect, they've come in the more obscure corners of the Old Testament. Even the most devout Biblical student might wonder how some of the stuff made it into the Good Book at all. It's in such sections that he is liable to lose the thread and then will either dry up or go on a frolic of his own, coming out with stuff that could be in a different book of the Bible or a different religious text altogether. And I've learnt to dread the bits where he does go wrong because he'll then fly into a rage and will snatch the Bible from me and yell the correct words out at two hundred decibels before hurling the volume back in my face. His focus is just as scarily intense as I always thought it would be. The twenty-minute tea breaks and lunch breaks are the only times he'll allow himself to stop, and even then if I'm so unwise as to introduce a subject which isn't directly related to the matter in hand he doesn't want to know. He may permit himself a smile and clap his hands when he's reached the end of one of the books, assuming of course he's done it to an acceptable standard. But I can tell from the sweat on his brow, and the heaviness of his breathing, the times when he's doubting himself and his ability to cross the finishing line.

I try to maintain a semblance of life outside. Karen's moved in with Alison in Cranleigh, and we meet up on a few Sundays. More than once she reminds me that but for the events of Easter Sunday she'd be halfway round Europe by now. She's agreed to look after the fundraising aspect of Jake's recital; it's been agreed that half the money will go to research into what killed Daisy and George, and half of it will go to research into autism. Karen is confident that the combination of the publicity Steve's co-ordinating, and her social media activity, will mean we're looking at not just thousands of pounds but tens of thousands. I ask her how things are with dad. She thinks the difference in years between them, which she saw as a strength when they first met, is now a problem and she worries that she now doesn't love him enough to want to nurse him through old age; she says she wants to be with me. I tell her I'm flattered but I only see us as great mates and I'd like her to go back to dad. At the moment that seems an eternity away.

I'm talking to dad on the phone lots. I explain that thanks to Project Jake there's no chance of being able to come up and see him but that doesn't mean I've forgotten about him. I ask how he's getting on. He says he's fine, watching plenty of cricket and also writing a history of his Yorkshire village; he's also taken up golf and he asks me if I'd ever considered trying it myself. It's so hard to get past the superficial with him. He does say he's missing Karen and hopes they can sort things out, as he puts it; he says that although whenever they talk it's amicable and they occasionally enjoy a laugh, the emotional gap between them doesn't seem to be narrowing as he'd hoped. Even that, he finds hard to put into words. I ask if he's angry with me and he says of course not. I know I'm never going to be sure of getting an honest answer to that one.

In other news, my decree nisi has gone through, a reminder that the unstoppable ran out of railway track. As for my fight against Ellman Rich, my ex-employers aren't budging and I've now got to decide if I want to take it to the next level. But after a day spent whacking through Chronicles, and Judges, and 1 Samuel and the rest, the next level seems way out of reach and I've not got the energy to hire a step ladder. I'm not sure when I'll ever find it.

*

It's in the middle of June that Maggie is due to make her promised visit. Lorrie's told me I don't have to be there, but I want to be there. If somehow Maggie has got, or gets, wind of Jake's recital I need to be able to provide Lorrie some backup. Lorrie's not the sort who'd allow herself to be intimidated, but I have no idea what Maggie is capable of and I can't risk Lorrie being browbeaten into pulling the whole shebang. Also, assuming she doesn't already know, we clearly can't trust Jake, on his own, to keep it a secret from her. I tell Lorrie, and she accepts, that one of us needs to stay with him throughout Maggie's visit, ready to divert the conversation away should we sense it moving towards the edge of the abyss.

Maggie's coming on a Sunday so not one of our working days. She's joining us for tea and, as might be expected, Lorrie has produced a spread which if relocated to the Ritz would justify their trebling the price of their afternoon teas and there wouldn't be a murmur from their patrons. Our honoured guest arrives at three. She's several inches taller than Jake; her dark hair is scraped back leaving a forehead so extensive that one might expect to see property developers banging in a planning application on it. Her lack of make-up to the cheeks is somewhat incongruously compensated for by her excessively rosy lips. She wears a plain light blue dress and flat black pumps. Her voice could cut through the Rock of Gibraltar. Her stare would make the Terminator think twice about coming back.

Lorrie goes off and brings Jake through. It's the first time I've ever seen Jake anywhere in her house outside his own room. I'm wondering if Maggie will have some special way with her brother that will draw out an altogether mellower and more agreeably human side to him that I've never had the privilege of witnessing outside of Bible-land. But no. Although she's obviously concerned about him, and cares deeply for him, everything she says to him is maternal, patronising, and superior. And I know Jake well enough now to realise that that is the very kind of approach that will antagonise him the most. She asks how often he's been out, whether he's enjoying the hot summer sunshine, whether he's been to the beach. He replies with shouts, respectively, of 'Not much' and 'No way' and 'No chance.' His evident dislike of her reverberates round and round the room. I'm praying that he won't let the B word slip. The real B word. Once or twice I can feel it might be on his lips and then I'm in there. But it's a near-run thing. She asks who I am and when I tell her I'm just a friend of Jake's she looks at me as though I've told her that in my previous life I was a flesh-eating keep-left bollard from Newport Pagnell. After ninety minutes of knife-edge stuff, I can't bear it any more, and I don't think Lorrie can either, judging by the look on her face. She and I have both excused ourselves for comfort breaks, and Lorrie's been out to top up the teapot with hot water, but now we've run out of acceptable excuses to quit the field of battle. I manage to catch Lorrie's eye and signal to her that I've had enough. Lorrie catches on, thank goodness, and announces that Jake needs his mid-afternoon nap. Jake has nothing to say on the matter. He just sits there, looking bored and apathetic, just as he has been ever since his sister's arrival. Maggie raises an objection, saying she's not aware of Jake ever having had, or needed, a mid-afternoon nap. But Lorrie overrules her and suggests that while she, Lorrie, is returning Jake to his room Maggie and I might like to help ourselves to another cup of tea.

Maggie decides she doesn't want one but leans forward and offers to top me up. Maybe she's not used to pouring from a pot or maybe she has similar difficulty to her brother at coping with inanimate objects but tea goes everywhere, soaking the papers and magazines that have been vying with the tea things for space on the table.

I hurry to the kitchen to collect a cloth and between us we mop up the affected area. One of the newspapers is ruined beyond repair and I take the liberty of consigning that to the bin. I then look round at Maggie who's sitting back in her chair and looking down at a typed sheet of paper which has emerged from the episode somewhat more favourably. It's at this point that Lorrie re-enters the living room.

'Little accident,' I explain, pointing to the sodden cloth.

'Oh, don't worry about that,' Lorrie says. 'As long as my Su Doku's safe.'

Maggie holds up the typed sheet. There are tea stains round

the corners but most of the content appears to be legible. 'Do you want this?' she asks.

'That? Oh…probably not,' says Lorrie. 'Choir newsletter, I think. Haven't got round to looking at it yet.'

Maggie screws up her face as she looks again at the sheet. 'Whitedean Methodist Choir.' There's an edge of incredulity in her voice.

'What's so wrong with that?' Lorrie demands.

'If you are going to leave Jake in the company of someone else for an evening, I'd have thought it would be for something worthwhile. Not caterwauling with a bunch of religious geriatrics. Is that worth compromising Jake's welfare for?'

'Are you suggesting I would neglect him? Endanger him?' Now Lorrie is bristling. She's shaking. She may have had well-chosen words to say to me on occasion, but I've never before seen her face as red as this. Nor have I seen her whole frame tremble as it's trembling now.

'Lorrie, you are in a position of trust,' Maggie says. 'I've trusted you. My mum and dad have trusted you. Jake trusts you. I'm getting worried. Seriously worried that you're abusing that trust. As far as I can make out, Jake's just sitting in that room of his pretty much the whole time. The odd trips out, but they seem to be the exception. No opportunities. No quality of life. You could at least let him sit in the garden sometimes. But no. Not even that it seems.'

'Of course I'd like to put him in the garden,' she says. 'But it's a mess. You can see it's a mess. And why is it a mess? Shall I give you three guesses?'

'Lorrie. He's sleepwalking through life. He's just had a nasty scare. I'm not having it. In fact, I'm thinking I might want to move him. Somewhere where he can be happy. Enjoy the outdoors. Enjoy proper Channel sea air. The views from the clifftops. The cry of the seagulls. And I think I know just the place.'

'You wouldn't,' says Lorrie.

'Oh, wouldn't I.' Maggie lets the newsletter drop into her lap. 'You, no blood ties, no contract, no court order, nothing that legally entitles you to have care of my brother for a single minute, telling me, his sister…I've been making enquiries. Do you know who I mean by Sue Masterson?'

'Doesn't immediately ring a bell,' says Lorrie. 'But I do know something. Jake's fine here. With me. And if I have to spend my life savings on getting a court order, I'll spend them.'

As she talks I happen to look round at Maggie and see she's studying the newsletter with a look of disgust on her face.

'What's wrong?' Lorrie asks.

'"Triumphant rendition of the Gospel According To St Luke in Whitedean Methodist Church,"' Maggie reads. '" Jake Terson, an autistic and severely disabled man from East Brighton, cared for by choir member Lorrie McEwan, stunned worshippers with his Mothering Sunday declamation of the entire Gospel of St Luke from memory." So. When were you going to tell me this.'

'Why would I tell you.' Lorrie's reply is devoid of any question mark.

'My brother is wasting precious hours, days, weeks, months, churning out this rubbish.' She waves the newsletter in Lorrie's direction.

'Maggie, that's offensive,' Lorrie retorts.

'That's good, coming from you. What was it you said when you were offered help by the local church after taking Jake in? Something about their knowing where they could stick it?'

'That is outrageous. I never said that and you know it.'

'I might have known. Might have guessed. My dear brother. Trotting out page after page of Bible.' She utters the last word as though she were referring to *Mein Kampf*. 'Is that why he's not doing what he should be doing with his time? I don't know how much time it took him, but as far as I am concerned it's time chucked away.' She shoves the newsletter down on the table. 'Do you know, Lorrie, this may come as a surprise, but I want my brother to have the chance to live a little. I just can't understand why you're so against that.'

'Maggie, I think you should go.'

'I'm going all right.' She gets to her feet. Then she points in the direction of Jake's room. 'I feel as though he's in prison. A condemned man, a sad, helpless, useless man. I know you love him, and he loves you, and I don't want to turn his world upside down unless I have to. But I want changes, Lorrie. I want them

now. And if I don't see them, and if things don't get better...'
She points to her phone which is poking out of the left-hand
pocket of her dress. 'One call and the party's over. Your party.'

Now Lorrie gets up and heads towards the door.

'And just one more thing,' says Maggie. 'If next time I come
I find that a Bible is so much as in Jake's possession I'll make
sure you never see him again. As long as you both shall live.'

*

Lorrie suggests I go off for a run and says why don't we
have a chat tomorrow lunchtime. So I go for my run and have a
quiet evening in my room at Di's, then next morning I'm back
at Jake's side listening to him ploughing through Exodus. The
first half of the book has its highlights, including the birth of
Moses and the Ten Commandments. But then it becomes more
turgid with chapter after chapter of instruction to Moses from
the Lord himself. Jake's struggling. He makes a complete dog's
breakfast of chapter 25 and as always when that happens he's
questioning his ability to complete the assignment, and I'm
telling him he'll be absolutely fine and he's still got a good few
weeks to go. I ask him if he enjoyed seeing his sister yesterday
and he barks at me that he wants to go back over chapter 25 and
will continue to go back over chapter 25 until he's got it right.
He rallies and completes Exodus. I tell him he's in the right
place in his cool room, as it's scorching outside. He doesn't
comment. 'Leviticus,' he snarls. We should be breaking for
lunch but he's having none of it. '"The Lord called to Moses
and spoke to him from the Tent of Meeting."' He shuts his eyes
and whips through the first five chapters. Then, and only then,
is it lunch. He thanks me. Just the two words. 'Thank you.' It's
never more than that and comes only at the end of the morning
and the end of the afternoon. I look at my watch and suggest
that as it's one twenty we reconvene at two twenty. He demands
to know why we can't start at two, as planned. So I agree we'll
start at two, as planned.

Lorrie's invited me to join her for a sandwich lunch. Usually
I bring my own or go out for something but we've agreed we
need to lunch together to address the M factor. Lorrie's been

shopping at Marks & Spencer and I've gone for the all-day breakfast on granary.

'I'll be honest with you, Matt,' she says. 'I'm scared. Scared of her.'

I don't need to ask who "her" might be. 'I thought you stood up to her pretty well.'

'I was like jelly inside,' she says. 'There's something about her…the whole package. Her grating voice. That ghastly lipstick. Those peering eyes. You'd never think she was just a civil servant. I've always thought she should have been a schoolteacher. Or a sergeant major.' She hands me my sandwich. 'And you know what really scares me. That what she's saying is…' She pauses.

'What?' I ask.

'That…well, she's right.'

'You mean, you think this Bible learning is a waste of time?'

'I don't mean that. I mean, yes. she's right that there are opportunities out there for him. Yes, she's right that it's not good for his health, being stuck in this place from dawn to dusk. Would I choose to live like that? Would you?'

I rip the side off the sandwich wrapping. I've never been any good at knowing which bit to pull at first. 'Maybe I would,' I say, 'if I knew that what I was doing made me different. Made me special. After all, isn't that what we all want, at heart? To be made to be special?'

'Trouble is, sweetie, Maggie's his sister. She loves him. Turn it round for a minute. I don't mean this disrespectfully. I know you're still hurting about Daisy and George and you always will. But if you had a brother or sister, and you were aware that there were changes that could be made, enhancing the quality of their lives, and there's this complete stranger who's dictating a different agenda, playing a different tune. Would you want that stranger's wishes to override yours?'

I don't need to answer. As closed questions go, they don't get much more closed than that.

'I mean, it would make it so much easier if Maggie supported it,' Lorrie continues. 'If she was happy to let us do what it took for him to achieve…I was going to say immortality…maybe I mean greatness. Something people will

260

remember him for. Something which really makes him a somebody. But we've not got that luxury. We've got an angry woman. An unpredictable woman. I can tell you, she may not share her brother's disability but I see some of Jake's worst traits replicated in her. Given the wrong circumstances I could see her becoming…well, dangerous, frankly. They're not empty threats, Matt. And if she saw what you and he were up to…' She runs her fingers round her throat.

Suddenly the bacon and egg in my sandwich has the attraction of deep-fried cockroach. 'What you're saying is, we can't carry on. Shouldn't carry on.'

'No, I'm not saying that,' says Lorrie. 'Yes, Maggie's right, of course she is. But at the centre of all this is Jake. The Bible is everything to him. I know how much he wants this. That's why I'm happy we take the risk. And if my risk failed, and I had to give him up, I'd give him up knowing that he'd done something special. That he was special. And he knew he was special.'

*

June turns to July and as the heat continues to intensify, so our sessions reflect that intensity. The dosage is upped. At Jake's insistence we're getting going at eight o'clock in the morning. Luncheon is cut to just thirty minutes, and we go on till six in the evening. By the end of the first week in July we've completed a third run-through of the entire Bible.

I know that come the day, everyone will be asking how he does it. I wish I knew. What I do know is that, given Jake's utter devotion to the task in hand, he's never going to want to take time out to tell me. Some of it is definitely ingrained from when he was a child. As for the stuff that wasn't ingrained, I do believe that having set out to memorise the Bible, all these years ago, he has got to know precisely where everything is on each page. Sometimes I see him doing it, moving his head from the invisible left-hand page to the invisible right-hand page. But I don't think that's everything. I do think, in fact I'm sure, from what Lorrie has said, that the quirks of his brain have given him some astonishing mental capabilities while leaving him hopelessly deficient in other areas. It's known as the savant

261

syndrome. Once or twice Lorrie and I have discussed whether given the choice it's better or worse to suffer these extremes. Lorrie uses an analogy from the game of bridge. It's a lot more entertaining to pick up your hand and find you've got nine spades and four hearts in it and voids in clubs and diamonds, than to have three or four of all of them. But as she ruefully adds, the consequences of an entertaining hand can, if a false move is made, lead to an awful lot of regret and an even greater amount of mess for others to clear up.

Jake may have determination in bucketloads but on top of the sweat on his brow, and the heaviness of his breathing, both of which have been there from the start, I can now see the stress in every line of his face, and it seems to be getting worse. A lot worse. Sometimes I can barely watch him. I don't want to see his pain, even though I'm feeling it. His stubbornness and doggedness and resolve seem to intensify with each passing day. I see a change in the colour of his cheeks and I notice more worry lines on his forehead, worry lines which always seem at their starkest when he fluffs a line and goes into one of his rages. When he's had an outburst, there's then a corresponding need to regroup. He'll get going again soon enough, like a train that's stopped at a red signal between stations, but it's almost as if he's now needing to regroup that bit more often, and he's then punishing himself for his stops by insisting that he goes on for the equivalent number of minutes at the end of the day's proceedings. I can almost feel the heat inside him. It's scaring me; no, it's freaking me. I'm fearful he'll work himself up into such a frenzy that he'll explode and, as Lorrie once suggested, millions of little letters will fly out of the inside of his head. I picture those little letters causing such an accumulation on the streets as to bring Brighton traffic to a standstill. I hate the thought that one day my phone might ring and it's Lorrie telling me that the explosion has taken place. I'm no medicine man but the thought crosses my mind that he may have a heart problem. And the thought having crossed my mind, I shoo it away and tell it not to come anywhere near my mind again. The last thing anyone with a heart problem needs is self-induced stressfulness. So I tell myself there is no heart problem. After all if Lorrie thought there was, she'd be saying something. Wouldn't she.

*

I'm seeing Karen pretty much every Sunday. She says she feels happier and more relaxed than she has done in years and she's relishing her independence. She still misses Daisy and George like mad but she's acquired so many coping techniques from her counselling that she can pull through the crap times rather than trying to sidestep them or pretend they're not there. She needs more time, lots more time, before deciding where her future lies and what she should do next. She makes no secret of the fact that she's still got strong feelings for me but she says she knows I'm in no position to reciprocate, certainly not at present. I tell her how pleased I am for her that her rehab's gone so well, and indeed part of me really is pleased, but then I think of dad, and I'm asking myself where he fits into all this, and I'm suddenly fearful for him, an ageing man who thought he was being given a second chance at life and it's now been whipped away from him and consigned to a shelf that's out of reach. So after one Sunday with Karen I ring him up and ask him what efforts he's making to bring his second chance back down to eye level and within arm's length again. And all he seems to want to talk to me about is England's woeful fielding at Edgbaston after the tea interval.

At least Maggie's not been back since that ghastly mid-June Sunday. Lorrie says that's partly luck, if luck's the right word, as her dad's been particularly poorly and Maggie's had to be around him virtually every day. But she, Lorrie, has also been "a bit naughty" in her words and told her about some of the changes she's been making, including frequent outings to the seaside, walks on the Downs and trips to Lewes Castle, Firle Place and Charleston Farmhouse. None of them have happened yet, only she conveniently forgets to add that bit. She says the way she's phrased it, she's not actually lied, but looking at the emails and texts I can see they're highly misleading. She's playing with fire and I'm sure she knows it.

*

Jake's performance is due to start on 12th August. We agree that during the weeks beginning 29th July and 5th August, Mondays to Saturdays, he'll do a final real-time run-through, and on the middle Sunday we'll go to the church around lunchtime for him to get the feel of the acoustic and meet the media. While we've left the press to Steve, providing him with an exhaustive press release, Karen and I have covered TV and radio. As far as TV is concerned we've got interest from a number of cable channels and we're also hoping the BBC and ITV will provide a presence at some stage. Three cable channels and several newspapers want interviews which we've fixed in the early afternoon of the middle Sunday at the venue, and a number of press photographers will be there at the same time. We've also arranged a good few radio interviews by phone on weekday mornings before we begin work for the day.

And so on the middle Sunday, 4th August, the four of us – Lorrie, Karen, Jake and myself – travel to the venue for the first time.

I've read up about the church where Jake is to perform, and have seen photos of it on my phone, but it's only when we get there that I appreciate its Betjeman-esque qualities. It's situated nearly a mile from the centre of the village it purports to serve, and is reached by way of a narrow no-through road that certainly wasn't built to accommodate four by fours and BMW's. The road comes to an end just by the church, at a small parking area which is wholly inadequate for the numbers we're expecting, so the owner of the farm immediately beyond has allowed the use of part of her farmyard for the purpose. Beyond the church and the farm, there are just acres of fields. For those who believe the church should be at the heart of the community it would be a disappointment. For those who seek and profess to find God in the space and the quietness and the timelessness, it is a gift from heaven. It's one of those places you think only now exist in a Sunday teatime serial on BBC1.

The church itself is of Norman origin; it boasts patched flint walls and a rather charming white-painted wooden bell turret. The nave walls are Norman and there are Early English features in the chancel. I'm no architectural historian: all this is told to me by the red-faced possibly-mid-thirties churchwarden who lets us in and invites us to enjoy a coffee before the press people arrive. The peace inside the church can almost be felt. It's honey to the soul. In purely practical terms I can't think of a better venue, devoid, as it is, of the distractions of modernity. I ask Jake what he thinks of it but he's never going to give me a positive response. I can see him going back over bits of Bible in his mind. He never switches off.

The media people we're seeing this afternoon are under strict instructions not to try to talk to Jake. His lack of social skills and his propensity to be rude and unco-operative to pretty much anybody mean that I'll in practice be doing most if not all of the talking on his behalf, with Lorrie chipping in from time to time. For a full two hours it's full on. The same questions again and again and again. How does he do it. What's the secret. Does he have a photographic memory. Are you going for a Guinness world record. Actually, in answer to that last one, we're not. We've made some enquiries and for it to be a record Jake would have to use a single translation and every word would have to be verified as correct. That simply cannot be achieved: not only are we using a number of translations, but from time to time Jake will transpose or use a synonym for the word actually printed in the translation of choice. What Jake is aiming for is to reproduce a faithful and complete rendition of the words on the pages, even if there is some paraphrasing. I emphasize that to our knowledge, nobody in the world has attempted even this before. The media people seem quite happy with that. They're interested in my role too. I tell them that I never thought I could care so much about a total stranger and that I'm desperate for him to complete the task, for my sake as much as his. They seem to like that too. At length they all disappear and the churchwarden makes us another coffee and we set off for home.

When we get home Lorrie does what she has to do for Jake then puts the kettle on for her and me. I've told her I'm in a Big Mac mood tonight and am not needing feeding, not by her anyway. She brings the teas through and we collapse onto our respective chairs.

'Happy?' she asks.

'We got through it,' I say. Then comes the question none of the reporters thought to ask but which has been on my mind all day. 'But be honest, Lorrie. Do you think he's up to doing it for real?'

'I can give you the response you're wanting to hear, if you like,' she says. 'Or I can tell you what I really think.'

'In other words, you think he isn't.'

She shakes her head and smiles. 'No,' she says. 'That's not what I think.'

'So what are you saying?'

She takes a slurp from her mug. 'You want me to tell you that he'll nail it, have his audience eating out of his hand, and invigorated by the magnitude of what he's done, will breeze his way through without breaking sweat.' Then she puts the mug down with a theatrical flourish. 'The truth. He'll get there because he's Jake. And because he'll find, from somewhere, enough to get him to the finishing post. But mark my words, it's not going to be a cakewalk. He may find strength he never knew he had, but my word he's going to have to scavenge for it.'

We sit in silence. Then Lorrie speaks again. 'Matt, I've got a confession.'

There's suddenly a blanket of gravity on her face.

'What's that, Lorrie?'

'It's been weighing on me for months. I need to tell you and I know you'll be angry with me.'

'Can't be any worse than some of the things I've done to you.'

She leans forward. 'That time he tried to strangle you. First time you met. Remember?'

I nod. I doubt I could ever forget it.

'Well, you asked me if I was on standby, if I was waiting, in case he did something like that.'

I nod again.

'Matt, I wasn't.'

I place an impulsive hand to my throat. 'I thought…'

'Yes. You thought. I didn't think he would ever do that. And there's more.'

'Mmm?'

'You asked me if he'd done it before. And I wanted to give you the impression he had, this was par for the course, but I could contain him, and I'd be there waiting to weigh in before he did too much damage. So I just said he'd been violent before. The truth is, he's never tried to strangle me. He's never tried to strangle anyone. Not to my knowledge. I trusted he wouldn't this time. I was wrong.'

'But you got to us in time.'

'Purely by luck,' she says. 'I needed something out of the airing cupboard. I just happened to be there when it kicked off. Right next to Jake's room. Normally I can tell from his shouting and screeching when he needs me and when he doesn't. I knew this one didn't sound like one of his normal hissy fits. No idea he was going to do that to you. And if I'd been in the kitchen I might not have got to you in time. I had nightmares about it afterwards. He could have killed you, make no mistake.'

'You do realise,' I say, 'that if I'd known you'd taken that risk I'd never have come back. And I'd probably have taken you to court.'

'I know, Matt,' she says.

'And Jake wouldn't be about to recite the Bible from memory.'

'He wouldn't, Matt.'

She's done this kind of thing to me often enough. Now it's my turn. I sit there in silence, poker-faced, for possibly three minutes. I can see her squirming in her chair, as if imploring me not to twist the knife any further.

Then I get up and come round to her side of the table and gather her in my arms. 'Thank you, Lorrie.'

*

Now with less than one week to go we're into the second half of the real-time run-through. The halfway point in the Bible comes towards the end of the Book of Psalms but we've agreed that by the end of week 1 we'll have completed that book. That means a very slightly shorter second half. I prefer the second half. The first half has its moments – the walls of Jericho tumbling down, David felling Goliath, Samson doing

267

his self-destruct act – but there's some desperately turgid stuff through Exodus, Leviticus and Numbers, and then we're onto Joshua, Samuel, Kings and Chronicles, lots of long names and lots of history lessons and an awful lot of opportunity for Jake to lose his way among the Hittites and the Jebusites and in the land flowing with milk and honey. In the second half we've got Proverbs to begin with, and its treasure-house of simple wisdom, and hard on its heels, the fragrant words of Song Of Songs, the Bible's love poem, and Ecclesiastes and its famous proclamation that there is a season for every activity under heaven. And although there are still the monster prophets Isaiah, Jeremiah, Ezekiel and Daniel to come, things get a great deal easier after that with a succession of minor prophets who don't really have a huge amount to say. Blink and you'd miss some of them. Amos, Hosea, Habakkuk, Zechariah, Zephaniah. Why them, I wonder. Why did they get the immortality which other probably equally deserving luminaries of the time did not. Then we're into the New Testament, and the Gospels, and the Acts of the Apostles, and a sprint through the epistles of St Paul and other letter writers. I often wonder irreverently if they were upset that they never seemed to get any replies, and whether nowadays they'd use social media to get their messages across. I'm sure they would. Then it's the grand finale, Revelation, and its extravagant imagery, from trumpet-blowing angels to multi-horned beasts. I reflect it might make a good Spielberg movie. Scarier than *Jurassic Park*, for sure.

On Sunday, the day before the performance is to start, I do a radio interview by phone on the BBC Radio 2 Sunday breakfast programme. I remind myself that it was my discovery of the producer Stewart Pimlott's email to Jake which started all this off. They're wanting to talk to me again next Sunday and are planning to record some of the final stages. The local radio station people are going even further and tell me after my interview with them that they'll be providing daily updates. It's probably because of the Radio 2 interview that the phone never stops after that. Everyone's wanting a piece of it: other local radio stations, a couple of overseas stations and three Christian broadcasting freeview channels. I'm getting quite good at fielding the questions although since they tend to be the same ones each time I jolly well should be getting good at them. The calls help occupy my time and when they stop, that time begins to drag. I want it now. I can't want it as much as Jake does but I still can't remember wanting anything as much before. Except possibly the model BMW in the window of The Tuck Shop in Maidstone at the age of six.

*

It's Monday. It's Day 1.

We've arranged to set off from Lorrie's at 7.30 on Monday, allowing an hour for the journey because of rush-hour traffic. I'm up at quarter past six and I'm just sitting down with a bowl of cereal when the phone rings. Lorrie.

'It's Jake. He's gone.'

'You mean he's died?'

'No. Maggie's taken him.'

16

I'm round at Lorrie's within ten minutes. I don't need to ring the bell. The door opens as I stride towards it and Lorrie's hustling me into her front room. Her eyes are bloodshot, her cheeks are pale and careless wisps of hair decorate her damp forehead. I can her the pant and wheeze of her breath. I ask her when and how and she shows me a text message from Maggie. It's timed at ten past six this morning. "I did warn you. So I've taken him."

'You mean she's only just done it?' I ask.

Lorrie shakes her head. 'I think she took him hours ago,' she says. 'Saw the papers, knew he was starting this morning, bang. Then thought she'd hold off telling me till she was well out of harm's way.'

'How did she get in?'

'You remember when she came down she had a go at me about the garden. Among other things. Well, as part of these supposed changes I told her I was making, I told her I was getting some estimates to have the garden spruced up. She mailed me on Wednesday evening to ask how I'd got on. I said I'd had no luck in getting an affordable quote. I mean, obviously I'd done nothing about it. I don't know if she saw through that but on Friday I got a call from someone who said he was local, offering to do an estimate for me. They said Maggie had asked them to contact me. I thought, great, Maggie's wanting to help me out. Thought she was being helpful and kind for a change. Anyway, we agreed for him to come on Saturday. To get through to the garden he'd have to come through the house. I keep a spare key to the front door on the key rack in the kitchen, always have done, in case I lose my main one or need someone to house-sit for me. I think I remember lending it to Maggie when she house-sat for me a year or two back. And she obviously remembered where I kept it. He must just have slipped it in his pocket as he passed. I never even realised it had gone. Last night, in she comes. I'm guessing, not alone. I suspect they gagged him or I'd have heard his screams.'

'Have you rung the police?'

'Of course. Given them her address, told them where her dad lives. But let's face it, he could be anywhere. Anywhere at all.'

'Anything, anyone else we can try?' I ask.

I've never seen such a look of defeat and despair on Lorrie's face. I've always believed her to be equal to any situation. But suddenly she appears to be five-nil down and the half-time whistle hasn't sounded yet. 'I don't know Maggie well enough,' she says. 'She's got no other siblings, I've no idea who her friends are…Matt, think. Think back to when you met her. Any clues at all. Anything.'

Then it hits me. 'Sue Masterson.'

'Come again?'

'When she came down she mentioned someone called Sue Masterson. When she was talking about where she might move him.'

Within seconds we're googling Sue Masterson but without any early success and it's clear that we're going to need to delve more fully into Facebook. This lists a selection of nine Sue Mastersons, six of whom are across the pond, one of whom is in Northern Ireland, one in Stornoway and the other…Seaford, East Sussex. Residential home proprietor.

'Channel sea air,' I say.

'Mmm?'

'Something else Maggie said. Wanted him to have some proper Channel sea air. Plenty of that in Seaford.'

Three minutes later we're in her car.

*

As we head towards the coast road, I get hold of Karen and ask her if she can let everyone at the church know there's a possible change of plan. She tells me to leave the communication to her and says she'll be with us as soon as she can. That's the good news. The bad news is that Sue Masterson's Facebook pages give no clue as to the name and address of the residential home of which she is the proprietor, and I know Seaford is full of residential homes. I've visions of spending the rest of my existence ringing the doorbells of all 389 of them.

But as we run into a queue of traffic waiting at the Longridge Avenue traffic lights at Saltdean, I find a possible lifeline on said Facebook pages. Tucked into an otherwise wholly unhelpful array of photographs of people I've never met and would have no wish to meet, and messages meaning less to me than the ingredients on a tin of budgerigar feed, there's a picture, dated 28th July, of "our gorgeous new recruit Tamara" – possibly helpful but probably not – and, of potentially far greater assistance, a photograph of two old ladies with a caption "Two of my babylicious beauties turn 102 on the same day." It doesn't give their names. But the photo is dated 16th July and because it's such an unusual event there'd be bound to be press interest. And if there were, it should be in the online issue of the local rag. I've no idea what rag that may be, but with almost every traffic light against us, and three sets of road works to negotiate, at least I can't say I've not got the time to find it. And after some hectic googling I've located Sue Masterson's establishment.

We crawl on through Peacehaven and Newhaven, stop at a petrol station on the far side of Newhaven for a necessary bite to eat, and fifteen minutes after that we're pulling up outside The Larches, on a wide tree-lined road running at right-angles to the promenade. We get out of the car and hurry across the forecourt to the main door. I can hear the splash of the waves from here and I guess we'd have to admit that there is a better chance of sampling some genuine Channel sea air at this place than in Lorrie's suburban pile. But its exterior walls are of unremitting dark grey and everything about it screams drabness and ordinariness. It's neither a characterful period piece nor a sleek modern edifice. Jake would hate it. Hate it.

We find the front door locked but Lorrie wastes no time in pressing the buzzer. 'Leave the talking to me,' she says.

A moment later, a female voice speaks through the intercom. 'Can I help?'

'Police. I'm here to see Tamara,' says Lorrie.

'Just a moment.'

We wait for perhaps ten minutes, maybe longer, and only then do I hear the sound of keys turning and hinges creaking and see the heavy wooden door swing open. On the threshold is the young woman depicted on the Facebook profile as Tamara. She wears a plain white top and plain black skirt and black sandals. She can't be more than eighteen. 'Er...yes?' she mumbles.

Lorrie whips out a small square leather purse inside which is a photograph of herself. She jerks it in Tamara's direction. 'DI McEwan. We've reason to believe that a brother and sister by the names of Jake and Margaret Terson have checked in here in the last few hours. We need to see them immediately.'

'They're...they're not here.'

'So they were here?'

'I...er...I don't...'

'Yes or no. Were they or weren't they?' I've never heard such stridency in Lorrie's voice.

Tamara's face has turned pale and she looks as though she's about to burst into tears. 'I'm...I'm...can I just phone my colleague.'

'Just tell us where they've gone and we'll leave you alone.' Lorrie's tone becomes kindlier but it's still assertive. It's as if she were speaking to Jake in one of his more malevolent moods.

'They've gone up to Beach...' she begins. Then she seems to check herself. 'I really think I should ring...'

'Beachy Head. That's right, isn't it, Tamara.'

'Er...I can't...can you just bear with me.' If the stakes weren't so high I'd feel sorry for the wretched youngster. The ill-prepared defence witness reduced to jelly by the merciless prosecution counsel. And though I'm far from an expert in the art, I can tell when a witness has no decent reply.

*

Beachy Head is some seven miles from Seaford but it feels like twice that. The main road plunges down to cross the Cuckmere River then crawls up the other side. In theory the rush hour should have peaked – it's now just coming up to nine

– but there are an awful lot of metal boxes in front of us still, as there have been pretty much the whole way. We were supposed to be starting the recital at nine thirty. A member of the local clergy was to open proceedings with a prayer of blessing for Jake and his recitation and all who would be attending it. Steve was confident there'd be at least four dozen press reporters to watch Jake start on his way. Karen may have told them there was to be a delay but we can't keep them waiting indefinitely. Lorrie points out that even if we found Jake at once, we've no idea what state he'll be in and because the venue is now so much further from where we are, we won't be able to get going till lunchtime at the earliest. I want to weep, not only for Jake, not only for me, but for everyone who's been getting behind this whole event. Lorrie does her best to try and lift the mood. In particular she's enjoying the reliving of her piece of amateur deception. She says it's very easy for anyone to erroneously mistake the word "please" for "police" and "Di" for "D.I." I hope the magistrates will see it that way when she's summoned to court for impersonating a police officer.

The skies have been virtually cloudless for most of the past week. But today the weather looks set to break. The forecast on Lorrie's car radio is for thundery showers. The sun is still shining but a wind has got up and I can see dark clouds lining up to the south. As we turn right off the coast road onto the Beachy Head road, the supremacy of sun is now being threatened by a sheet of dull white. I may have no faith to speak of, but I must have uttered two dozen silent prayers already and here comes another to add to my shopping list. Please God, let it stay dry so that Maggie's not getting Jake back under cover and driving him back to Colditz, as once he's back in there nobody and nothing will get him out. So there you are, God. That was prayer number twenty-five. Does that carry extra loyalty card reward points or will I get a better deal switching to another supplier. Sorry, Di. I don't mean that really.

We make it to the Beachy Head pub car park. There are two cars parked there; Lorrie thinks one of them is Maggie's but she can't be sure. Anyway there's no time to lose. A moment later we're crossing the road and running onto the grass that leads up to the redbrick shelter on the highest ground, well over 500 feet

274

above sea level and the loftiest coastal location in Sussex. I'm sprinting ahead of Lorrie, but she's had the prescience to put trainers on before she set out, and she's not far behind. Heaven help us if she'd gone for her flip-flops or her clogs.

There's no sign of Maggie or Jake by the shelter. But there is a white-haired woman walking a black Labrador and I ask her if she's seen a man in a wheelchair accompanied by a slightly older woman. She points westwards, down the hill towards the Belle Tout lighthouse.

And it's as I career down the hill across the grass, that I see Jake. He appears to be alone. I yell. I scream. I turn back to Lorrie and raise an exultant thumb in the air. She seems to find an extra sachet of energy inside her. I slow my pace to allow her to catch up and we join hands and reach the finishing line together. As we do so, a moan of thunder rolls across the ink-black horizon,

Please God, let him be all right. Please God, make sure you've not allowed this crazy woman to have damaged him. We turn to face him. His eyes are shut. He's breathing, and the breaths are deep and clean, not wheezy.

And it's as we're gazing at him, pausing before the next stage of operations, that I feel a pull on my arm. I wheel round and I'm staring right into Maggie's face.

The heavy lipstick's gone. Her lips, her cheeks and her nose are all hard and colourless. She wears a pink anorak and flowery knee-length skirt and white plimsolls. Her hair is covered by a light brown bobble hat. It's not the most gladiatorial outfit I've ever seen. But her eyes are molten lead and tongues of flame play all around her face.

'Get away from him,' she says. She doesn't shout. She doesn't need to. There's menace enough there without her needing to raise her voice.

I look round at Lorrie and she's turning the wheelchair round, back the way we've come. 'I'm taking him home,' she says. 'Maggie, you've had your fun and games.'

'Move that wheelchair one inch,' Maggie says, 'and I'm over that cliff.'

'Don't be ridiculous,' says Lorrie.

Another rumble of thunder, louder and closer.

275

Lorrie begins moving away, taking Jake with her. And as she does, Maggie, looking inland, begins walking backwards towards the cliff edge.

My first thought is, I've got to stop Maggie. So I walk with her, prepared to pull her back if necessary. I look down and I think I'm going to be sick. I've never had a problem with vertigo but that sea, an unappetising grey, looks an eternity distant. It's pummelling at the cliff edge, the white flecks of surf a pack of marauding crocodiles, waiting to pounce at the first sight of prospective quarry from above.

And Maggie's still moving backwards...

'Stop, Lorrie!' My voice now. 'Stop, for heaven's sake!'

Lorrie stops. And so does Maggie. No more than four steps from the edge.

'Move Jake back!' Maggie yells.

Lorrie, wheeling Jake, shuffles some twenty yards back towards Maggie. Maggie in turn retreats from the cliff edge. I walk with her.

'Maggie, let's talk about this sensibly,' says Lorrie.

'Don't call me ridiculous then,' says Maggie. 'Because I mean it. I will jump.'

'I don't think you would,' says Lorrie. 'I think you love Jake too much. Think about it, Maggie, sweetheart. If you go, how's that going to help him.'

'If I give him up without a fight, he'll go and do his Bible thing, and it will kill him.' I see a tear dropping down her cheek. 'You know, I've only had him back a few hours, but I've noticed a subtle change in him. From how he's been speaking to Sue and myself, I think he may have a heart problem. Not that you'd have noticed. Too absorbed in getting him to do this ridiculous task. If he goes through with it, I'm convinced it'll finish him. Murder him. And I couldn't bear to see it happen.'

'You don't know that, petal,' says Lorrie. 'None of us know.'

'When he saw the sea this morning, he smiled,' says Maggie. 'I told him to empty himself of all the anxiety and the tension that's got wrapped around him. And look at him now. Sleeping like a baby. This is his turning point. The start of his rehab. A human being again.'

'So his rehab's going to be stuck in a rest home with 102-

year-olds, is it? How's that going to make him more like a human being.' The flash of anger from Lorrie mirrors the flicker of lightning in the jet-black clouds above the sea.

'Sue Masterson is a brilliant woman,' says Maggie. 'She works with people who have a variety of needs. She's offered to have Jake for a month and at the end of that time we'll decide whether to make it permanent. And the bad news for you, Lorraine McEwan, is that there is absolutely nothing you can do about it.'

'I can go to court.' I know how Lorrie hates being called by her full name. She spits out every syllable.

'And how long will that take.' For the first time, Maggie's features soften. 'This is a fantastic opportunity for him, Lorrie. And I think he's benefiting already. So, okay, you may lose a bit of face with your Bible-bashers. May have to swallow a bit of pride when you tell them it's all off. But when in a few months' time Jake is thriving again, you'll realise it was the obvious thing to do.'

'No way.' Not Lorrie, but me.

'Oh, so let's see what Mr Mentor has to say about all this.' Maggie turns to me. The flames from her cheeks are aimed straight into my face and I'm flinching from their heat. 'Yes, of course. You're the coach, aren't you. The manager. The Brian Epstein of the Bible-learning world. Nice picture of you, by the way. And a lawyer, no less, from what I've been reading. Doubtless already licking your lips at the fat fees you can rake in when your friend here gives you her instructions. So, what part of all I've just said do you find it so very hard to understand.'

'Very simple,' I say. 'You could have stepped in and done this weeks, months, years ago.'

'In case Lorraine hasn't told you, I've had the little matter of a very sick father to deal with.'

'You still do,' I say. 'Nothing's really changed, has it. You've taken time off from him now, could have done it a while back. But now you've finally taken this step, you're saying it can't wait another second. Do you know what I think? This isn't about Jake's rehab. It's about jealousy. Jake's rediscovered his soul through his amazing memory and you hate the fact that he's not needed you to achieve it. Otherwise, why didn't you do all this back in June. I don't know why he's so peaceful now but I can't believe he'd have got to this state naturally. I don't believe you will jump.' I turn to Lorrie. 'Lorrie, this is my call. Get Jake back to your car. Now.'

'She won't do it.' Maggie's voice is petulant, almost childlike.

The next rumble of thunder is accompanied by a gust of wind which almost sweeps me off my feet.

'Lorrie, get him in. Before the storm starts.'

'Matt, are you sure about this,' says Lorrie.

'Just get him in. I'll deal with Maggie.'

Still Lorrie seems to hesitate.

'Now, for goodness' sake!'

A flash of lightning darts through the sky and as it does, thick, chunky raindrops begin cascading from above our heads. A moment later, as the sound of the thunder threatens to blow the cliffs to fragments, Lorrie is scurrying up the grassy hillside, wheeling Jake further and further from where Maggie stands.

Then Maggie turns to me, her back to the cliff edge.

'You don't know what you've done,' she says.

The darkness in her voice is still unmistakeable. But I can't be intimidated. I've no choice but to meet fire with fire.

'I think I've a pretty good idea,' I tell her. 'I've given Jake the chance to do something extraordinary. To be an extraordinary person.'

'To die. To die. To die!' The third time, the words screeched into my face, her nose and her lips so close that I see the beads of sweat and rain etched onto her cheeks.

'You don't know that, Maggie. You don't know that.' The rain is now intensifying and I have to make my move and make it now. 'I don't believe you will jump. I'm going with Lorrie and Jake. Okay.'

She stands there for a few seconds. Then suddenly, she steps backwards, and begins to repeat her backward movement towards the cliff edge. 'Do you still believe I won't jump?'

I find myself walking towards the cliff edge beside her. 'Maggie, don't do this.'

278

She takes a further three steps back. She's now once more just four steps from the edge. 'Do you still believe I won't jump?'

'Maggie, just wait. Stop. Think. Think what you'd be doing.' They're words plucked from the air. They're all that come to mind.

'What are you, a flaming Samaritan or something.' Another step back. 'Am I nearly there yet?'

'Of course you are. You're three steps away.'

And again. 'Two now,' I say.

I know that if I reach out to her she could lose her footing. There's another roll of thunder, less deafening than before, as the storm races inland. Still the rain falls, a mist envelops the swirling grey waters, and I'm looking out at a sea of nothingness.

More words arrive. 'Maggie. I know we don't really know each other. But I ask you please. Just as a fellow human being. Walk away. Let Jake do this. Then do for him whatever you wish. You and Lorrie together. Working out what's best for him.'

There's a silence of maybe thirty seconds. I look down at Maggie's feet and detect a very slight movement of them away from the edge. I've taken instructions from more than one client who's told me that if he loses his liberty he'll take his life. And it's been easy enough for me because all I've needed to say is that they should go and see the prison doctor or prison welfare and they'll help. Now I'm the prison doctor, prison welfare, all the things I've been happy not to be as I've left the cells and walked out of the court room.

'You're right,' she says. 'I'm not going to jump.'

A surge of relief and pride and elation courses through my body. 'Fantastic.'

'We're going to jump. We're both going to jump.' And instantly she's got her hands wrapped round my neck and she's manoeuvring me round so that I'm the one with my back to the cliff edge and I'm the one who's going over first...

17

For the third time in the past twelve months I'm being made to get ready to die and I'm not ready to die and I don't want to die.

I try to cry for help. I can't. I try to use my slightly greater weight to my advantage but as I press my hands against hers it's like leaning on a locked door. I try kicking but my feet begin to slither on the grass and I can't see how much grass there is to play with behind me. I can tell I've not got much left. This is the end. The precursor to the end. There's going to be that moment, that unspeakably hellish moment, when I'm hurled into space, knowing in that split second that there's nothing more to come.

And just as that unspeakably hellish moment is about to happen I'm aware the grip on my hands is loosened. Seizing the advantage I push like I've never pushed before and seconds later there's nothing to push because someone or something's yanked Maggie backwards. I'm left pushing fresh air, I'm flailing, and I go to the ground. I leap to my feet and I see Maggie, still writhing and squirming, while someone behind her is holding the collar of her pink anorak. I look to see who it is.

Karen.

I heave myself forward and somehow we pull the screaming, hysterical Maggie's protesting, shaking body up the grassy slope towards the redbrick shelter. And as we reach it, three police officers and two paramedics come to meet us.

*

On police advice Jake and I attend the nearest A & E to get checked out. Jake had been sedated, just as we thought, but the good news is that the effect of the sedative will wear off and shouldn't compromise his powers of recall. As for me, it's more the shock than any physical injuries. The only visible sign of the force Maggie used is redness around my neck which the police photograph for evidential purposes. I'm told Maggie's now in police custody. She may be charged, or she may be sectioned, or both, but I'm assured she's going nowhere.

By the time Jake and I are discharged from A & E in Eastbourne and I've been spoken to by the police it's late afternoon. Lorrie has liaised with Steve and undone all the arrangements for today. In many ways that's the easy part. The hard part is deciding when we can start. Or even if we can. Steve and Karen, the stars, have between them taken responsibility for doing all the liaising with the officials and the press people, and they'll advise them of our plans once we've made them.

But what plans.

Just now, the vision of standing on that cliff edge refuses to shift from the centre of my mind. It's like watching something on the iPlayer, pressing pause to put the kettle on, and then forgetting where the remote's gone. The picture's just stuck there. I keep thinking I should regard it as just one of the narrow escapes I've had in the past twelve months, on top of Jazz and his Smirnoff bottle, and Jake's own inroads into my neck area. I'm trying to think, well, maybe it's no worse than these. Did Maggie really have the strength. Would she have stepped back, in every sense, without Karen's intervention. It's the cold, lawyerlike analysis. But it's like with my suspension from work. When it's not me, when it's a client, I'm effectively just playing with it and I can let it go. But this *is* me: I'm the lawyer and the client. And no amount of legal logic can divert me from the instinctive belief that this latest reprieve was the biggest reprieve of all.

Lorrie can tell I don't want to talk, and she has the sense not to engage in conversation with me on the way home. But she does talk to Jake and asks him how he feels about continuing with his recital. And his response is unequivocal. 'I want to start tomorrow. Do you hear. I want to start tomorrow.' Lorrie responds that she's got the message and tells him that that's all very well, but what about Brian Epstein, as Maggie so charmlessly described me. I don't need to be told that if I refuse to play, the recital's off. Jake's made it clear, not just in the car but a hundred times previously, that he needs me there and nobody else will do.

281

When we get back I tell Lorrie I need to be on my own and I'll phone her to let her know what I've decided. She drops me at Di's and a moment later her car's disappeared round the corner. I go inside and shut the door behind me.

And having got inside the door I can't move.

I'm thinking back about the chain of events that's brought me to this point. Last October there's me, a not desperately unhappily married guy with a house and a job and happily-married dad. And because Lisa-Marie Williams walked out of Mountain Warehouse with a light green fleece top I'm no longer married, and I've no partner, and no house, and no job, and a dad who's separated, and I'm put within slippery grassy centimetres of a hideous death because despite having no real faith in the supposed Bible truths I want a man to recite the Bible off by heart. I'm just standing there in the hallway, immobile, and unable to think what I should do or where I should go next, fearful that whatever choice I make is going to create more incident, more drama, more stress, more fear...

As I stand there, a door opens and there's Di. She doesn't say anything. She gathers me in her arms. And I weep as I've never wept before. 'Just don't know what to do, Di,' I say between sobs. 'Just don't know what to do.'

'What you're doing is a wonderful thing, Matt,' she says. 'It is a wonderful thing to help someone else to achieve greatness without seeking any greatness for yourself.'

'I should be dead, Di. I should be dead.'

'God needs you to do this wonderful thing,' she says, 'To help Jake achieve greatness. That's why he's delivered you. He'll give you the strength to enable you to get through the next fortnight. I know you can. I know you will.'

I used to have a friend like this at school. Regardless of the company she was keeping at any given time, she'd invoke the Almighty at every opportunity. At the time I thought she had a screw loose although I didn't say anything. There were plenty of others who said a great deal. I wouldn't say I was any closer to God now than I was then. And I might be forgiven for wondering why, if God was seeking to preserve me for the sake of Jake's greatness, he'd allowed me to be alone with Maggie on that clifftop in the first place. But there's a time and place for everything and this isn't the time and place for entering into metaphysical or existential theory. It's the time and place for accepting that Jake and his needs have to come above my PTSD, that the months of working together and sweating together mustn't be wasted, and that there's a job there that's waiting to be done.

Then, once the job is done, I can perhaps permit myself the luxury of reassembling the broken pieces of my own existence.

'Thanks, Di,' I say. I extricate myself reach for my phone, and dial Lorrie's number. 'Lorrie, tell everyone we're starting at half nine tomorrow. I'll see you at seven twenty.'

*

It's the leading story on BBC Sussex next day. 'Jake Terson will start his attempt to recite the entire Bible from memory twenty-four hours late, after he was abducted from his home in Brighton in the early hours of yesterday by his sister Margaret. She remains in police custody on suspicion of kidnap and attempted murder.' Lorrie has been my spokeswoman, taking charge of my phone and fielding the calls that have come my way, referring them to Karen, Steve, Richard and Anne. And between them, they've not only dealt with referrals from Lorrie but a shedload of referrals to them direct, and conducted shedloads of interviews throughout the period. As a result the interest in Jake's venture is multiplying by the hour. And with the interest comes the interest in the causes for which the recital is being done and the financial pledges as well. This is not now just local news or even national news. It's gone worldwide. I'm now actually wondering if Maggie's done us a massive favour.

This time I'm able to enjoy my cereals before going round to Lorrie's. We set off for the venue at seven thirty and we're there by quarter to nine. The drive from the village along the narrow road to the church, just under a mile, takes twenty minutes by itself. We park in our specially reserved space just across the road from the church – the punters must make do with the farmyard beyond – and when we get to the church door the media people are already queuing to get in. I'm wondering how Jake will respond to this and whether it'll put him off. I'm sure Lorrie must be wondering the same but she doesn't say anything. I don't think Jake's switched off at all since the effects of the sedative wore away. He's been going back over bits of Genesis throughout the journey here from Brighton. Neither Lorrie nor I seek to dissuade him. It's something for him to do. I've asked him if he's feeling all right, and he's asked me why shouldn't he be, and that's the pleasantry for the day over and done with. What's worrying me far more than lack of pleasantries is whether Jake will be thrown by everything being put back a day. We've agreed that we will adjust the programme so he will do Tuesday to Sunday, take Monday off and then do another Tuesday to Sunday. Mid-morning services scheduled at the church on the Sunday have been cancelled. Because it's Tuesday now I'm wondering if that astonishing, awesome, incomprehensible machine inside his brain will think he needs to be churning out the material for the first Tuesday. I ask Jake if he realises that although today is Tuesday he's still starting at the very beginning. He asks me if I'm a total lamebrain.

At the church door we meet Karen, who's able to be with us all day today, then wheel Jake into the church, placing him as far from the press people as possible. We make it quite clear to them all that he's unavailable for questions. We're asked if we think he'll have been so affected by recent events that he won't get through it and all we can do is to say he'll do his damnedest and we must all pray that his damnedest will be good enough. I can't bear to think he won't get through it and I feel a tear in my eye every time the little voice pops up in my head warning me that maybe he won't.

At three minutes to nine, just as planned, Father Toby Bryant comes forward and welcomes the assembled hordes – every pew is filled – to this church where, as he says, Christians have worshipped for centuries. 'Yet what we are seeing today in this lovely building,' he continues, 'is something believed to be unique in the annals of Christian worship not only in this country but across the world. History is being made in this quiet corner of England.' He says a prayer, there are a few mumbled Amens, then Jake is wheeled forward.

'The book of Genesis,' he announces. '"In the beginning

284

God created the heavens and the earth. Now the earth was formless and empty, darkness was over the surface of the deep, and the Spirit of God was hovering over the waters.'''

Day 1 – Tuesday 13th August
Genesis, in full; Exodus, in full; Leviticus, chapters 1-4.
Genesis: the creation of the world and the early history of the human race with the accounts of Adam and Eve, Cain and Abel, and Noah and the flood, also an account of the history of the early ancestors of the Israelites including the stories of Abraham, his son Isaac, and grandson Jacob whose twelve sons were the founders of the twelve tribes of Israel.

Exodus: the account of the departure of the people of Israel from Egypt where they had been slaves, their journey to Mount Sinai where God made a covenant with his people and laid down the Ten Commandments, and the establishment of laws regarding the worship of God.

Leviticus: the regulations for worship and religious ceremonies in ancient Israel .

He sails through Genesis. I expected no less: as it's the opening book he's probably recited it more often than any of the other books. I see Lorrie chuckle from time to time. Of course she's heard all of this over and over again. He's fine throughout Genesis and most of Exodus but after chapter 20 of Exodus, when the Ten Commandments are handed out, the book of Exodus becomes a menu of instructions and I don't know if it's more painful to recite or to listen to. He's insisted that the whole Bible must be recited with nothing missed out, and when he does miss something out he's making himself go back and do the relevant bit properly. This happens three or four times in chapter 25 with the box and table of acacia wood. Why acacia, I'm thinking. What's so very special about acacia. And what is significant about all these measurements. Why does the atonement cover of pure gold have to be two and a half cubits long. What's wrong with rounding it up to three.

It's noticeable how as the afternoon wears on, more and more people are leaving. A good many had disappeared after Jake had done his first chapter and I heard a couple of them muttering that they'd be pushed to learn a single chapter let alone the 94 he's doing just today. Anyway, he rallies. He makes it to the 40th and final chapter of Exodus and gives us a tantalising taster of the joys of Leviticus before breaking at 6.15. As expected, he's gone over time, but as he completes chapter 4 – '"in this way the priest will make atonement for him for the sin he has committed, and he will be forgiven"' – he allows himself a smile. It's good news for the sinner and it's good news for us. The first day is done and we're not on again for nearly fifteen hours. He's paraphrased once or twice but he's not left anything out and he's got through it. He's insisted that I don't prompt him unless he calls for a prompt – which, let's face it, I'll never ever expect him to do.

Having kept my phone switched off while Jake is reciting, I've switched it on at lunchtime and there's a text from dad. He wants to come down and watch Jake in action next Thursday. Then he starts talking about Karen and asking after her. 'She was the best thing that happened to me,' dad says. For him that's quite an admission.

Day 2 – Wednesday 14th August
Leviticus, chapters 5-end; Numbers, in full; Deuteronomy, in full.

Numbers: The story of the Israelites during the time – almost 40 years – between their leaving Mount Sinai and reaching the eastern border of the Promised Land. The title of the book refers to a census of the Israelites taken by Moses prior to their departure from Mount Sinai.

Deuteronomy: A series of addresses given by Moses to the people of Israel as they were about to enter and occupy Canaan.

I always thought today would be a huge test for Jake. The excitement of day one is over and now he's the marathon runner out in the depths of the countryside. It doesn't surprise me in the least that between midday and three there are never more than six people in. One of those is Di. She couldn't make it yesterday and wouldn't have been able to make it on Monday but she's planning to come with us every day from now on. It may not please Jake to see only a handful of people but as he showed with St Luke's Gospel it doesn't stop him getting on with it. I like to see a full church. It lends validity to the event and it shows that people are listening to Jake just as he so wanted them to listen to him. During the morning Jake is assured and fluent, but after lunch it dips just as I feared it would and although he seems to improve later on in the day the slowness and hesitancy means that we get further and further behind. We're not done till gone ten past six.

When I get home there are two items of post waiting for me. One is my decree absolute, and the other is a card from Emma, presumably written when she received her copy, thanking me for our time together. Her postman is obviously lighter on his feet than mine. It's the first time I've heard from her since we resolved our financial affairs. She's never been a great card or letter writer – she's always preferred electronic – so this card is something of a collector's item. She says things didn't work out with Jumbo but she's met another guy, Rhys, through work, and they've been seeing each other for four months and are about to move in together. She says she's read all the press stuff and she's proud of me. She signs off with two kisses and then there's a PS. "I'm glad somebody stopped us."

Day 3 – Thursday 15th August
Deuteronomy, chapters 30-end; Joshua, in full; Judges, in full; Ruth, in full; 1 Samuel, in full; 2 Samuel, chapters 1-10.

Joshua: The story of the Israelite invasion of Canaan under the leadership of their eponymous hero, Moses' successor.

Judges: A collection of stories from the lawless period of Israel's history, centred round the exploits of national heroes, mostly military leaders, known as judges. One of these was Samson and this book includes the story of Samson and Delilah.

Ruth: Ruth, a Moabite woman, is married to an Israelite and after his death she marries one of his relatives and becomes great-grandmother of David, Israel's greatest king.

1 Samuel: This book records the transition in Israel to a monarchy, and the reign of Saul, the first king of Israel.

2 Samuel: This book is the history of the reign of David as Saul's successor to the throne of Israel.

Jake certainly seems to be more at ease now the very lengthy books at the start of the Bible are behind him and he's able to get a few more under his belt. In fact there's a smile on his face as he declaims the story of Samson and Delilah, certainly one of the great crowd-pleasers in this part of the Old Testament. The way he tells it, I'm on the edge of my seat, desperate to find out how it ends, even though I've heard the ending so many times before. We're done at just gone 5.45. An earlier tea beckons.

As we prepare to depart, a man dressed in a plain red T-shirt and jeans approaches me. Again Jake's audiences have been modest today, but red T-shirt man might as well have had superglue attached to his backside. He's not shifted at all. Anyway, he comes over, introduces himself to me as Will Hastings and informs me he's travelled all the way down from Manchester to see Jake in action. He's only able to be with us for a couple of days, today and next Tuesday, because of work commitments. He says he's seen from some of the publicity material that I'm a lawyer specialising in IP and crime, and asks if, while he is here, I can help him with a little legal query. He says someone of his acquaintance was commissioned by a publisher to write an academic textbook. It took him three years and involved considerable expense. The publisher proceeded to reject it ostensibly on the basis that the content wasn't what had been agreed. But the acquaintance has just discovered that the very same publisher has brought out another book by a different writer with large chunks of the acquaintance's material quoted almost word for word. Question, has the acquaintance got a case. It's a cracker. There are issues around contract law *and* intellectual property *and* copyright law; it's a lorryload of ifs and buts and maybes. I need something that evening to take my mind off Ruth and Saul and David and Samuel and the rest of them. At half past seven I sit down with a plate of scrambled eggs on toast and my laptop, and go to the Ellman Rich case-finder which I still find I'm able to access. By half past eleven I'm left with a plate of inedible mush but also my legal opinion which I'm emailing to Will. Di pops her head round the door and tells me I should be getting some sleep as I prepare to do the Lord's work again next day. I resist the temptation to tell her I've been spending the evening doing the Lord's work. Because Lord only knows who might be paying me for it.

Day 4 – Friday 16th August
2 Samuel, chapters 11-end; 1 Kings, in full; 2 Kings, in full; 1 Chronicles, chapters 1-10.
1 Kings: A continuation of the history of the Israelite monarchy including the succession of Solomon as king and an account of his reign, and the stories of the faithful prophet Elijah and the division of the nation into two kingdoms.
2 Kings: The continued history of the two kingdoms and in particular the destruction of Jerusalem in the southern kingdom of Judah by King Nebuchadnezzar.
1 Chronicles: Essentially, a retelling of events recorded in the books of Samuel and Kings but from a different point of view.

Jake sails through the rest of 2 Samuel and the books of Kings. But Chronicles is the definitive nightmare for the memory man or woman. It's one list of names after another. It's relentless. It would be bad enough if it was John and Mary and Christopher and William, or perhaps, given the current fad for turning surnames into first names, Harrison, Bradley, Riley and Tyler. But there's Togarmah. There's Raamah. There's Arvadites and Zemarites and Hamathatites. And this is just the first chapter. Jake clearly has his methods because he does it, and he does it without any apparent effort, and it's convincing me the text is all in front of him in his mind. Trouble is, it's not sexy. Certainly not sexy enough for any but the hardiest to warrant a retreat from the real world on a Friday afternoon. And in this case the hardiest comprises one of the churchwardens and a woman with a wire-haired dachshund which expresses its opinion on the subject matter more eloquently than any human could. As the churchwarden hurries forward with some disinfectant Jake just carries on. And on. And on. At least chapter thirteen brings relief from the name game, and I think this saves him. We limp into port at five to six.

There's an email from Will thanking me for my advice and telling me he'd like a longer chat next Tuesday. I wonder what he means.

Day 5 – Saturday 17th August

1 Chronicles, chapters 11-end; 2 Chronicles, in full; Ezra, in full; Nehemiah, in full; Esther, in full; Job, chapters 1-15.

2 Chronicles: An account of the rule of Solomon and a history of the southern kingdom until the fall of Jerusalem.

Ezra: A description of the return of some of the Jewish exiles from Babylon, the restoration of life and worship in Jerusalem and the rebuilding of the Temple.

Nehemiah: A story of the governorship of Judah under Nehemiah.

Esther: The story of the eponymous Jewish heroine who saved many of her people from extermination by her enemies.

Job: The story of a good man who suffers total disaster but retains his faith in his God.

The Bible was never written to be learnt by heart. That much is clear from today's relentless, remorseless onslaught of names, numbers, more names, and more numbers. Ezra is the killer. The author signals his intent to tax the memoriser in his very first chapter with an inventory of articles previously confiscated by Nebuchadnezzar from the Temple in Jerusalem. Then in chapter 2 he warms to his theme with a list of the people of Israel. It runs down a whole column. It is, in effect, a Biblical telephone directory. If they were alive now I'm quite sure Ezra would have wanted to add their email addresses, mobile phone numbers and where to find them on social media. Nehemiah is little better. I'm thinking if Jake can get through this he can get through anything. I can see Lorrie's not looking happy. She's been doing a lot of the meeting and greeting and also shaking the collecting tin but during the idler periods she's been sitting just watching and I can see the pain on her face as Jake struggles through the latest list of unlikely names from the inner recesses of Nehemiah's less than riveting prose. I don't understand why so many of them seem to have Z in them. There are hundreds of Z's, buzzing round the church. There must be enough to generate a shelf full of honey. Zerah, Zechariah, Zabdi, Zabdiel, Ziha, Zorah – and that's just page four hundred and ninety-seven. They didn't mean much to me when I first heard Jake go through it and they mean even less now. It doesn't help Jake's concentration that there's a lot of movement in and out of the church. It's the weekend and it's noticeably busier. Lorrie's worried that the increased movement and the larger numbers will put more pressure on Jake. I tell her that he'll be fine, absolutely fine. But I know I'm saying it not so much to reassure her as to try to convince myself.

It's a relief to reach the lunch break and I'm looking forward to half an hour's mindless You Tube when I hear what sounds like a troupe of performing elephants crashing through the south door. I look up and it's Danny. He never looked particularly smart even in his suit. Today, in his civvies, he looks as though he's been processed through one of the McDonald's burger makers. He wears a stained blue polo shirt which seems to have given up the struggle to find a way over his paunch. His jogging bottoms are plastered with white spots as though he's had an argument with a bottle of correction fluid. And to look at his feet which he's imprudently allowed to go on display courtesy of a pair of scuffed brown sandals, one would think he'd last cut his right toenail to celebrate Tony Blair becoming Prime Minister.

Before I can work out how I can or should react, he's come up and shaken my hand. He asks me to go and sit outside with him and I find myself sitting on a bench and watching him plonk his thirty-eight stone next to me.

'You might as well know,' he says. 'I've resigned from Ellman Rich.'

'You're kidding.'

'Wish I was,' he says. 'But no. And I deserved to go. Had to go.'

'What happened?'

'Wasn't just one thing. Three things. For starters I had a stand-up row with Geoff and basically lost it with him. Told him to go forth and multiply. That was a verbal warning. Then I made an application for bail and forgot to include some key information which resulted in the client being remanded and he

291

put in a formal complaint. That was strike two. Then I was trapped into divulging some privileged information to the police. Another complaint. I knew what was coming. I jumped before I was pushed.'

'You've always been so careful about things like that,' I tell him. 'What went wrong?'

'It was what I did to you. You knew anyway, didn't you. You knew I'd stitched you up. It's true the bosses were trying to slim down the criminal department. And I knew they didn't want to lose you. They liked you. I panicked. I thought I was out. So I did to you what I did. I hated myself. When they made you redundant I was thinking, that should have been me. And ever since then, I've been subconsciously thinking, I don't deserve to be running that department. So maybe it's my subconscious that's wanted me to fail. Put me out of my misery.'

'What will you do?'

'Goodness knows. I mean, look at me. Who'd have me. No firm with any sense, that's for sure. Never mind. Rumour has it they're opening a new Lidl at the end of my street. Bound to be wanting staff. It's you I'm worried about, Matt. I deserve every sleepless night you've given me.' He signals behind him. 'I knew I'd find you here and I know you hate me for what happened. So go on. You can do to me what you've been dying to do ever since.'

'Eh?'

'You can take me round the back of the church out of sight and beat the living daylights out of me. Kick me, punch me, do whatever you want to me. It's fine, I'm agreeing to it. I'll sign something if you like. Just…do your worst.'

I don't think I've ever felt so much pity for another human being, not even when I was eight years old and my mum made me sit through Michael Buerk's reports of the Ethiopian famine.

'What would that solve?' I say. 'Do you honestly think that's going to make anyone, anything better? Anyway, Danny, I've moved on. And I like where I am now. So I should be thanking you. You've done me a favour.'

Minutes later, I find I'm shaking his hand. And it's no pleasanter now than it was the office.

Day 6 – Sunday 18th August

Job, chapters 16-end; Psalms, in full.

Psalms: the 150 psalms make up the longest book of the Bible. Composed by different authors over a long duration, but many attributed to David, they were collected and used by the people of Israel in their worship. Extensively quoted in the New Testament and in various modern-day Jewish and Christian liturgies, anthems and hymns, they embrace every human emotion, from praise and exultation to despair and desperation. Psalm 119 contains 176 verses, making it the longest "chapter" in the Bible.

It's Jake's best day so far and it's my best day. Karen's had to work every day since Tuesday but she's got today off and she's with me throughout. We're past the worst – the names, the inventories, the tribal telephone directories – and today we're reaching the Psalms, my favourite book of the Bible. It's Sunday, when it feels right to be in church and it seems others think the same. The clergy have not only vacated the mid-morning service but have cancelled all mid-morning worship in the parish so that the congregation can come and hear Jake. First he has to get through the rest of Job, but with that out of the way by coffee time, everyone can sit back and enjoy the psalms and they are flawless. Jake has gone for the Prayer Book version which Lorrie tells me as a child he became very familiar with; she says he went to a prep school and his school choir shadowed the choir of the nearby cathedral and deputised for them on frequent occasions. So he'd got to know huge chunks of the psalms before most boys of his age could spell the word psalm, let alone recognise one when they heard one. I don't just love the old favourite psalms, 23 (The Lord's my shepherd) or 100 (O be joyful in the Lord, all ye lands). Close to the top of my own psalm hit parade is Psalm 104. Jake declaims it as though it were gift-wrapped especially for me. "'Thou deckest thyself with light as it were with a garment; and spreadest out the heavens like a curtain. Who layeth the beams of his chambers in the waters; and maketh the clouds his chariot, and walketh upon the wings of the wind.'" When he reaches the end of that psalm I want to kiss him. I want to tell him how much I love him. It's hard to explain what it is about him that is lovable. Love wasn't the first word which sprang to mind when I first saw him. And at times over the past three months I've wondered whether he actually wanted me to hate him. But I love his determination to do his very best with what he's got. I love the pleasure and pride he takes in delivering his performance. I love his total dedication. I love the fact that he wants to do this and see it through. Most of all, I love the fact that I know he loves me. He'll never tell me but he doesn't need to.

This is perfect. It's turned into a clear, fresh, sunny Sunday afternoon. Karen is sitting beside me, Di is in the pew across the aisle, and there are just the right number of people in the pews behind us. The half-full church means there's plenty of support but there's still a sense of peace and intimacy. The words flow from Jake's mouth like runny warm raspberry jam and on his face I see a serenity and a contentment that I've never seen in anybody before. I'm looking at a man who's at peace in this space and in this time and, could it possibly be, with his God. Whilst every day this week so far I've been willing Jake to reach the finishing line, today I don't want him to. I wish the rest of the task could be like this. But the bruisers are starting to queue up and I can see them on the horizon. Isaac, Daniel, Ezekiel and Jeremiah all stand in his way. I tell myself to put them back in their boxes till they're ready. Enjoy these last few psalms, from the sheer immensity of Psalm 119, all 176 verses of same, to the tear-jerking Psalm 139, "'If I climb up into heaven, thou art there; if I go down into hell, thou art there also,'" and beyond that to the grand finale, Psalm 150, "'O praise God in his holiness…Let everything that hath breath, praise the Lord.'"

The end of the psalms means not only have we completed today's work but Jake is more than halfway. Jake duly finishes Psalm 150 and I leap to my feet, announcing he has indeed passed the halfway mark. There's a burst of applause. As the clapping dies away, Lorrie gets up to wheel Jake off, but Jake holds up a restraining hand. 'I've decided I'm not taking tomorrow off,' he says. 'I'm carrying on. I want to finish on Saturday.'

294

There's another round of clapping. We're hailing Jake the indefatigable, and Jake the indestructible. Days off are for wimps. Which is all fine. But it means that before we can be released to celebrate Jake passing the halfway mark, Karen and I have to confer with Richard and Anne and the churchwardens to make the necessary adjustments. We've agreed right from the start that what Jake wants, Jake gets. I look at Lorrie, wondering if she'll try and talk him out of it, but she just shrugs. It's Jake all over. He was down to finish on Saturday, he's been expecting ever since the end of April to finish on Saturday, so on Saturday he finishes.

As the psalmist might put it, a rich plenteousness of telephone calls later and the job's done. Lorrie's keen to get away and get Jake rested before he starts again in the morning, so I have to decline Karen's suggestion of a drink at the pub at the top of the road leading down to the church. She asks if I can spare her a couple of minutes in private and I find myself taking her to the bench where Danny poured out his woes yesterday. She puts her arm round me and kisses me on the lips. 'I meant what I said in Brighton at Easter,' she says. 'I mean it now more than ever.' Then she draws back and it's time to go home.

Day 7 – Monday 19th August
Proverbs, in full; Ecclesiastes, in full; Song Of Songs, in full; Isaiah, chapters 1-60.

Proverbs: A collection of moral and religious teachings in the form of sayings and proverbs.

Ecclesiastes: The writings of a philosopher unable to understand the ways of God or the meaning of life but encouraging readers to enjoy God's gifts as much and as long as possible.

Song Of Songs: A collection of love poems interpreted by Jews as a picture of the relationship between God and his people.

Isaiah: The writings of a great prophet whose work has been interpreted as foretelling the birth and suffering of Christ.

When we're driving to or from the venue it's very rare that Jake ever speaks other than to himself, lost as he is in last-minute revision for whatever particular biblical challenges await that day. But this morning as we wait at traffic lights at Worthing with what seems like the rest of the civilised world, he suddenly says out loud, 'I want to be Memory Guy.'

It's just Lorrie and me with Jake this morning, as Di's unwell. 'What do you mean, darling?' Lorrie responds.

'Well, Guy's my middle name, right?'

'Yes,' says Lorrie.

'Not rocket science is it. Can't call me Memory Jake. That sounds silly. So, Memory Guy. That works. Doesn't it?'

'What's wrong with Memory Man?' I ask.

'That's what all the papers call me,' he says. 'I want something different.'

'Rebranding, then,' says Lorrie. 'Right you are, sweetie. Consider it done. We can get our marketing gurus on to it right away.'

'No!' He bellows the word so it bounces around the inside of the car. 'Don't you dare make fun of me. I don't want it yet. I never wanted to be called Memory Man yet. Only when I'd done it. I want to be Memory Guy when I've done it. When I've finished. And not a minute before.'

We arrive at church and it's on with the dance. Karen's back at work and can't be with us again till Saturday, so, like Di, she's having to sit this one out. I miss them both, and I also miss the psalms. But the Book Of Proverbs undeniably has its moments, and there's a mischievous glint in Jake's eye as he wades through the pages of advice contained therein. I think I even see him winking at me when he declares "If anyone turns a deaf ear to the law, even his prayers are detestable." I treasure the moments where Jake in the course of his task is able to communicate with me. He's done that a few times when he's reached a passage that he knows has amused me or tickled my fancy. I treasure them because outside of the task Jake isn't interested in anything around him, myself included. I may be the crutch on which he leans to carry out his task but when the crutch isn't needed it's left lying abandoned on the floor and if it gets in the way it can expect to get thrown aside. It's actually an easy day for Jake. Ecclesiastes with its oft-quoted "time to weep and a time to laugh" presents no real difficulty and the

Song Of Songs, with its worldly and often explicit images – I overheard Richard today describing it as the page 3 bit of the Bible – is a refreshing contrast to the menu of Z-listers amongst the tribes of Israel. Then comes Isaiah. Jake's grown to love Isaiah, as he tells me each time we get to it, and he sails through its sixty chapters scheduled for today in a masterful and relaxed style. He's done by five fifteen and we're back in Brighton soon after six.

There's not been a cloud in the sky all day, I'm in need of a run, and I ask Lorrie to drop me off some way short of home so that I can get straight on with it. I've not planned a route but will just keep running wherever the mood takes me and if necessary I'll get a bus back. As I run, I pass a street with a familiar name, Alciston Rise. It's where I first met Lorrie. Or rather, the place where Lorrie first found me. I decide not to linger on or around the exact spot where that happened, but rather I keep running, and find myself passing a line of shops and cafes that I certainly don't recall from my previous visit. One of the cafés has tables and chairs outside and at one of the tables I see…the one who walked out of Mountain Warehouse with a light green fleece top. I see Lisa-Marie.

She catches my eye and does a double take, as though she's not sure it's really me. Then she springs up and leans forward and puts her arms round me and kisses me on my cheek. She introduces me to her mum Jackie who's sitting with her, and invites me to join them. Lisa-Marie looks well. She wears a smart light-coloured jacket, a dark blue top underneath, blue jeans and high-heeled sandals. Her hair has that same frizziness that first wowed me at the custody centre nearly ten months ago. Her eyes sparkle and there's a freshness and vigour streaming across her face.

'So,' I say. 'How have the last few months been?'

'Interesting,' says Jackie. 'I think that sums it up, doesn't it, Li.'

'In what way?' I ask.

'I've been in prison,' Lisa-Marie answers.

'No way.' In an instant I'm recalling her protestations of innocence. Knowing Crown Court scheduling as I do, I wouldn't expect her to be going to trial till way later in the year.

Unless there's something else...

'Got twelve months early April,' says Lisa-Marie. 'Came out on a tag. Back living with mum now.' Only now does she lift up her left foot and pull back the end of her jeans to reveal the chunky electronic device jostling for ankle space with the strap of her sandal. She looks down at the phone in front of her. 'Tag kicks in in fifteen minutes. We'll need to get cracking, mum.'

'Was this...for the drugs?' I ask.

She nods. 'They did a plea bargain. I admitted possession of cannabis with intent to supply, they reduced the cocaine and heroin to just possession. No supply. My barrister tried to argue I should get a suspended but the judge said it was too serious.'

'I'm so sorry,' I say.

'Don't be. It was what I needed. Had to get away from Jazz and his mates. Best thing that could have happened. Yeah, prison sucks. It's horrible. But it did for me what nothing else could.'

'She's come off the booze and the heroin,' Jackie says. 'She attended courses on addiction when she was in prison. Li, tell this gentleman the best news.'

'I'm now going to get to see Nelson twice a week,' Lisa-Marie says. 'And social say that if I don't go back to how I was he can start staying over with mum and me. You know what, I'm glad I got done. Sounds a crazy thing to say, right, but I'm glad. If that makes sense.'

Day 8 – Tuesday 20th August
Isaiah, chapters 61-end; Jeremiah, in full; Lamentations, in full; Ezekiel, chapters 1-27.

Jeremiah: The writings of a 6th century BC prophet who correctly forewarned God's people of the destruction of Jerusalem because of their idolatory and sin.

Lamentations: A collection of five poems lamenting the destruction of Jerusalem.

Ezekiel: The writings of a prophet who lived in exile in Babylon both before and after the destruction of Jerusalem, prophesying that destruction but also offering comfort and the promise of a brighter future.

Di calls us early to say she's feeling very poorly and won't be able to join us possibly till Friday or Saturday. And that sets the tone for what's to come. It's the worst day so far. The subject matter is turgid and for the most part downbeat and gloomy. It's pouring with rain outside and as Jake labours through chapter 20 of Jeremiah and its cheerful exclamation "'Cursed be the day I was born, may the day my mother bore me not be blessed,'" there is actually only Lorrie and myself in the church. The churchwardens have had to go to work, and the duty welcomer – the church has kindly organised welcomers on a rota basis – has been called away leaving Lorrie to hasten to the south door should we be invaded by a posse of seekers after the wise words of Jeremiah or a brisk dollop of Lamentations. It's been Jake's custom to leave a short gap between each chapter. Those gaps are getting longer and as he starts a new chapter I'm noticing a movement of his body akin to that one might expect to see before lifting a heavy object, as though instead of the Bible being his plaything it's become an unwieldy bag of turnips.

I just don't know what or who is propelling him along. If the question's been asked once in the last eight days it's been asked a hundred times. What keeps him going. And, not far behind that, the next question is how's he stored it all. Could anybody do it. Could anybody, say, pick up the Bible one day and say, I can do that; a few verses each day, build it up, and when you're ready, off you go. No, I reply. I don't think so. As a lawyer I've had to commit a great deal to memory, but I find as one lot of material comes on board, another lot has to be shoved aside. Goodbye, it's been nice knowing you. Bit like a London bus. It relies on passengers getting off so that there's room on the bus for more as the journey progresses. If the bus is full, wait for one that's not so crowded. With Jake, it's come one, come all. Don't worry if the two decks are crammed to bursting, we'll hang them from the roof of the bus if we have to. Yes, a lot's been retained from childhood. Yes, he's had the luxury of more prepping time than most of us would be likely to get right across our three score years and ten. But there's something in that savant syndrome brain of his that makes his gift unique and impossible to replicate…except, perhaps, inside a son of Jake or a daughter of Jake. A being we may be fated never to see.

The pauses in between chapters assuredly contribute to a finish that's a terrifying hour and a quarter late. But Will Hastings has returned as promised and has stuck it out into Ezekiel-land. He comes over and extends his hand and asks me how I am. I tell him I'd be a lot happier if it was five o'clock rather than nearly seven but other than that, I'm bursting with rude vigour. He tells me he's delighted because if I accept his offer I'm going to need to be positively erupting with aforementioned rude vigour.

'How do you mean?' I ask.

'Your analysis of my little legal problem was impressive to put it mildly,' he says. 'You found all sorts of aspects I'd not even considered when I was looking at it.'

'You mean you're a lawyer yourself?' I ask.

'I'm senior partner at Dashwoods in Manchester. IP is what we do. I think your firm and my firm locked horns a few years ago. Phillips v Struther, does that ring any bells?'

'You got lucky there,' I tell him. 'Awful decision.'

'Quite possibly.' He smiles. It's not a smug generous-in-victory smile. I see compassion in every centimetre of it.

'But I liked your guy. Mike Peacock,' I say. 'He was very easy to work with.'

'Well, it was actually Mike who saw your name when Jake's exploits got in the paper,' Will says. 'Asks to be remembered to you. And you'll have plenty of time to remember together if you say yes.'

'To what?'

'Our IP department is expanding. There's a vacancy and I've interviewed five candidates. None suitable. If you're interested then the job's yours.'

Day 9 – Wednesday 21st August
Ezekiel, chapters 28-end; Daniel, in full; then Hosea, Joel, Amos, Obadiah, Jonah, Micah, Nahum, Habakkuk, Zephaniah, Haggai, Zechariah and Malachi, all in full.
Daniel: At a time when the Jews were suffering under the

persecution of a pagan king, the writer, through a series of visions, encourages them with the hope that God will dethrone him and restore sovereignty to God's people.

Hosea-Malachi: known as the Minor Prophets in the context of the Old Testament, these authors all speak to the people of God, with prophecies of revenge on their enemies and the triumph of the righteous. Highlights include the words of Joel, quoted by Peter in the New Testament, "Your young men shall see visions and your old men shall dream dreams;" Micah's prophecy of the significance of Bethlehem, to be the birthplace of Jesus Christ; and the story of Jonah being consumed by a whale.

I've spent much of yesterday evening reading up on Dashwoods and chatting to Mike Peacock and then Will Hastings again and I like everything I've read and heard. It's the sort of work I love doing and comes with a salary I'd love to have. As I tell Lorrie on the way to the church this morning, I can't see any catch. She tells me to go for it.

But there's the small matter of getting Jake through the rest of the Bible first. And that's all I feel I can properly focus on just now.

Today we reach the end of the Old Testament but at a worrying cost. Jake has insisted he wants to stay and get through it tonight, and the result has been the latest finish yet. We stagger out of the church at twenty past seven. Again, thanks to some parish meeting, it's just Lorrie and myself who've been there to witness Jake reaching this massive milestone. The scary bit's on the way home. All our journeys, out and back, have seen Lorrie and me sit in silence while Jake's gone over bits out loud. It's fine, except of course when he wants me to check the correctness of something and I'm supposed to know, in response to his bark, whether he's in the middle of Ezekiel or Paul's seventeenth letter to the Thessalonians. But this evening we're all sitting in the car in silence, Jake included.

We get back to the house and Lorrie goes and attends to Jake. It's usually at this time that I'd return to Di's on foot, glad of a bit of exercise. But tonight I need to talk to Lorrie. She has her routine and I know roughly how long it should take her to get back to the kitchen to put on some dinner for herself. It seems to take a lot longer than usual this evening and there's this nagging fear in my mind that starts as breadcrumb-sized but as the minutes pass is outgrowing Westminster Abbey. It's only when I'm about to give up and head back to Di's that I'm hearing her cheery cry of 'Nightie night, sweetheart' and now I'm doubling back to the kitchen to meet her.

'Still here, Matt, darling? Thought you'd gone ages ago.'

I put my arms round her. 'Lorrie, you do think he's going to make it, don't you.'

'What do you want me to say, dear.'

'How was he just now? When you were putting him down?'

'Matt, it's been a long day. Go and get some food inside you. And let the man know you want the job.'

Day 10 – Thursday 22nd August
Matthew, in full, Mark, in full, Luke, chapters 1-21.
Matthew – the first of the four Gospels chronicling the birth, ministry, death and resurrection of Jesus Christ, the central figure in the Bible, portrayed as God in human form on earth. St Matthew's Gospel points to Jesus Christ as the fulfilment of Old Testament prophecy with many quotes from the Old Testament. Stories unique to Matthew's Gospel include the slaughter of the innocent, the flight into Egypt, and Pilate "washing his hands" of responsibility for Christ's crucifixion.

Mark – the second Gospel and the shortest, being a whistle-stop journey through the life of Christ with virtually no material that isn't found in the other Gospels.

Luke – the third and arguably best-loved Gospel with the emphasis on Christ as minister to the poor and least advantaged in society. Stories unique to Luke's Gospel include the visit of the angels to the shepherds, the parables of the Good Samaritan and the Prodigal Son, and Zaccheus climbing a tree to get a better view of Christ.

I've not had much sleep. I keep thinking back to how Lorrie answered, or more accurately did not answer, my last question last night. I'm thinking back to what Maggie said about his possible heart problem. It all fits so terrifyingly with the symptoms he was showing during the latter part of rehearsals, symptoms I could barely bring myself to believe might be those of a heart problem. The more I think about it, the more I'm sure Lorrie suspects and has suspected for a long time that there's a heart problem but she's not wanted to say anything to me. I can imagine her thought process. If her suspicions are right, any doctor is going to tell him to pack the recital in, to relax himself, to get more sea air…all the things Maggie herself was advocating and attempting to force through. Yet what else does that mean but take away from Jake all that really matters to him in the world. I don't just think Lorrie knows that now. I know she knows it. Better to say nothing, she'll be saying to herself; better to hope, against the odds, that the suspicion is all wrong. Better, she'll add to herself, not to ask for fear of what the answer might be, and the almost impossibly hard choices that flow from that answer.

After the struggles of yesterday Jake actually seems fine again this morning. The fact of his having reached the New Testament is a huge psychological boost to him, and the words and deeds of Christ roll off the tongue, flowing with the ease and effortlessness of a mountain stream in sunlight after a winter storm. Of course, he's recited St Luke's Gospel in public before, and I'm almost wondering if today he's doing that on autopilot, saving his brain for when it's most needed, in the more testing Epistles.

Brian from Whitedean Methodist Church is here today. He apologises to me that because of pressure of work today is the only day he can make it. He's there from the start and he's still there at the end. I tell him, as he tucks into his lunchtime sandwich while still sitting in his pew, that he is allowed a comfort break. But he tells me he's hooked.

I'd had a text from dad late last night saying he'd be getting to us at half two today and would spend the afternoon listening to Jake. He was then planning on treating Karen to a surprise evening dinner and he'd asked me to make sure she kept the evening free. He's not said anything about what's to come after that but I wonder if he's actually got a hotel booked for them both as well. I'd rung Karen and having told her about my job offer, said I needed her at the church at the end of today to meet a couple of her Twitter followers who've lost children to the same illness that befell Daisy and George. Even though she wasn't planning on joining us again till Saturday afternoon for the grand finale I knew in the circumstances she'd agree to get off work early and come down today, and she'd done so without demur. Then this morning she's texted me to say that owing to a cancellation she's free all day and will be down late morning.

She's actually with us by eleven thirty and sits through an hour and a half before Jake stops for lunch. He's ahead of schedule and on course to finish possibly as early as quarter to five, so I persuade him to take a slightly longer lunch break. That then enables me to suggest to Karen that we go and have a decent fresh coffee and some hot food at the café in the centre of the village. She doesn't need much persuading and ten minutes later we're sitting at one of the outside tables with coffees and baguettes crammed with tuna, cheese and cucumber.

'So,' she says. 'Seems all to be going very well.'

'Touch wood,' I reply.

'You think he'll do it? Finish it?'

I shrug. 'Worth a flutter at William Hill.'

'And then what?'

'How do you mean?'

'After Saturday. What do you do then. I mean, obviously, what you're doing, what you've done, it's brilliant. But then on Saturday it's over. He gets there, or he doesn't. And then you're starting again. But where. Doing what. And most important, who with.'

She's dressed to impress today. Of course she believes that she's meeting some Twitter followers who've undergone similar trauma to dad and herself. So no skimpy vest top or short denim shorts. She's in a deep blue dress today, as cool and as exuberant as a Lakeland mountain stream. Its short length shows off her long tanned legs running down to meet black shoes with stiletto heels. She's got the best dress sense of any woman I've ever met. And she always seems to know what I like to see her in.

'Who knows,' I tell her. It's a pathetic response. But it's as if the effort of the past four months, the wonderful thing as Di describes it, has drained me of the ability to think for myself, about myself, at all.

'Matt, you're not twenty-one any more,' she says. There's no hint of admonishment in her voice. It's all caring, caring and more caring. 'Playing the field, going on the pull…those days are gone. You're a middle-aged man. I hate the idea of you being lonely. Of you going out trying to find love and getting hurt.' She moves forward so her face is barely twelve inches from mine. 'Look, Matt, I don't know if this helps. But I've made up my mind. I can't go back to your dad. Not today, not tomorrow, never.' She kisses me on my lips. 'You get what I'm saying. Don't you, honey.'

I've made it clear to her, couldn't have made it much clearer, that she and I are just mates. And yet there's that part of me. That part of me which I've managed to quell since the small hours of New Year's Day but which keeps on struggling to find a way through my defences and doesn't seem to want to give up. Maybe it's the weeks and weeks I've given myself to serve Jake in his quest for greatness. Maybe it's the full realisation of what she did for me on those stormy cliffs ten days ago. But as I sit gazing at her across the café table, that part of me seems excitingly, dangerously real.

'Of course,' I say.

'I love you so much, Matt,' she says. Then she kisses me on my lips again.

And I'm consumed by the moment. I move the food and drink aside and lean across and put my arms round her. She puts her arms round me and our lips meet and play and then it's our tongues and it's so wrong but at the same time so totally right and real and exciting and…

Then out of the corner of my eye I see dad.

He's standing there, on the pavement no more than eight feet from where we're sitting. He's looking directly at us.

Someone has to do something. And I'm the one who's getting up and walking up to him, the naughty son who's just smashed a cricket ball through the living room window and broken a priceless collection of vases. I'm going up for my punishment and am holding out my quivering hand in anticipation of six of the best.

He takes my hand and shakes it. 'Good to see you, Matt. How far away's this church, then?'

*

It's no surprise that Karen flees the scene immediately. It's even less of a surprise to receive a text message from her minutes after I return to the church, telling me that she's been called away on urgent business, she can't be around tonight, her Twitter followers will have to come again another time, and she'll see me on Saturday. I tell dad the dinner date's off and all he says is 'What a shame.' This I know is what Karen can't hack. He's just too nice about the whole thing and in its way it's more infuriating and harder to deal with than if he were to fight. If I were in his position I'd be wanting to fight because he's never going to be with a woman this beautiful again in his life. But no. He simply changes his plans, saying that when Jake gets to the end of his day's work he'll take me out to dinner instead and will drive me back to Brighton afterwards.

It's not been an easy afternoon. Jake's stumbling and spluttering and although he keeps it together, just, I can see just from his eyes how tired he is now. Even if, contrary to Maggie's assertions, his heart was in mint condition, the pressure he's putting on himself is off the scale. I've spent much of the afternoon comparing how much he's done and how much, or rather how proportionately little, he's got left. I'm sure that's what most marathon runners do when they see the wall and realise they're about to hit it and there's nothing they can do to avoid a head-on collision. From very early on into this afternoon's session it's been obvious he's not going to make the projected five fifteen finish and he limps home at five fifty. I permit myself a glance at Lorrie once or twice during the afternoon and I can sense her unease. The only morsel of comfort I've got is that Di's texted us to say that she's getting better and will definitely be joining us on Saturday. Perhaps her certainty that God has it all under control will transmit to Jake and he'll find some new strength from her presence and her spirit of prayerful and worshipful positivity. But he's got to get through Friday first.

Dad and I go for our dinner. We choose a riverside pub just outside Arundel which Richard has strongly recommended. The air is warm enough for us to sit outside by the river Arun. The air is heavy with late summer scents and the drone of insects. The wine fizzes with cool, fresh vitality. It is, or would be, the perfect place to start a romance, and, more potently, the perfect place to rekindle one. Dad tells me I'd be an idiot not to take the Manchester job. He's right. Of course he's right. I give Will a ring from our riverside table and he asks how 30th September sounds to start work. It's actually the day after my birthday. I tell him I'm fine with that.

It's only at the rhubarb crumble and custard stage that the K word comes up. And I'm the one uttering it first. I tell dad that if I'd be an idiot not to take the job, he'd be an idiot to let his wife go without a fight. I explain that it was her who came on to me at lunchtime, and I was caught up in the moment. I see a strange look cross his face and I know it's because he wants to say something important and un-matter-of-fact when he doesn't generally do important and un-matter-of-fact. I find myself rooting for him. Please, dad, if you've something significant to say to me now, do a good job of it. Say what you really feel.

'I've been with her fourteen years,' he says. 'We've shared so many profoundly romantic times. But I've never seen her looking at me the way I saw her looking at you this afternoon. Matt, it's you she wants. Not me. Not your old man. Not this old man.'

Day 11 – Friday 23rd August
Luke, chapters 22-end; John, in full; Acts, in full; Romans, in full; 1 Corinthians, in full.

John: the fourth Gospel, quite different from the other three, focusing not so much on Jesus Christ did but rather who he was: the Good Shepherd, the Bread of Life, the Way, the Truth and the Life, and the Resurrection and the Life. Unique to this Gospel is his turning water into wine, his first miracle.

Acts: the story of the founding and rapid growth of the Christian church across the Middle East and beyond, including the conversion and ministry of St Paul.

Romans and 1 Corinthians: epistles of St Paul to the fledgling Christian churches in Rome and Corinth, providing encouragement to their adherents in the face of persecution and opposition and urging them to lead more godly lives.

Jake starts hesitatingly and once we get to Peter's first address to the assembly of believers in Jerusalem at the beginning of Acts, he's in big trouble.

And what makes it worse is the fact that so many more people than in previous days have gathered in the pews and are witnessing this big trouble. If a marathon is the right analogy for this task, minus the unflattering running shorts and sweaty armpits, he's now entering The Mall and can hear the roar of the crowds urging him on to the end. This was what he wanted. He wanted people to listen to him like they once used to. And now they are listening to him, but they're hearing disjointed sentences, transposed sentences, ums, ers, pauses, hesitations, deviations, and repetitions. It's just as well Kenneth Williams and Clement Freud aren't sitting beside him with their fingers on their buzzers. I continue to be under strict instructions not to give a prompt unless he asks for one, and so far the church walls have yet to echo to my not-so-dulcet tones, but more than once I've detected Lorrie throwing a warning glance in my direction as if to say I should intervene to keep him on track.

He knows it. I know he knows it. When rehearsing all this, he was sailing through the hard factual accounts in the Gospels and Acts. St Paul's arduous and tortuous journeys through the various states and provinces, proclaiming, encouraging, and doing intellectual and philosophical battle, would normally be made to feel as simple and effortless as a ride on a number 14 bus. But today's service has arrived late, it's taking unscheduled detours along side streets, it's bashing against parked cars and it's worrying its passengers into a belief that the driver's making for a different destination altogether.

I blame Nehemiah. If Jake does enter through the Pearly Gates and meets Nehemiah I hope he flings all those Z's, Zerah,

Zechariah, Zabdi, Zabdiel, Ziha, Zorah et zal, straight zback into his zstupid zfat zface. Because right now it seems as though all those verbose Old Testament writers with no smartphones and no streaming services, and with nothing else to do than commit overlong chunks of their supposed brilliance to paper, are the ones who may just have done for my lovely, sad, gifted, flawed, infuriating, exceptional man.

By lunch we're four pages further behind than we should be and the afternoon's work, while nothing like as demanding as what Jake had to battle through a week ago, is considerably more taxing than the more prosaic factual material that's occupied the morning. I decide to pop out for a walk and a sandwich at the café Karen and I went to yesterday – we've agreed Jake needs at least 45 minutes' break so there's no time difficulty – but as I head out, I'm being asked by some of the press people if I think he'll make it. It's clear from the way a couple of the reporters speak to me and frame their questions that they don't want him to make it; I suspect they'll regard it as a bigger story, capable of selling more papers, if he literally drops dead while in mid-sentence. I feel like asking them what they've done in their own miserable lives to take a shot at greatness.

It gets worse. After we reach the end of Acts, round about 3.15 this afternoon, Jake announces he wants to stop for fifteen minutes. He doesn't start again for twenty-five. The same thing happens at the end of Paul's epistle to the Romans. This is, and has always in rehearsal come over to me as, a bold and robust statement of Christian truth with possibly one of the most inspiring passages in the whole of the Bible: "'I am convinced that neither death nor life, neither angels nor demons, neither the present nor the future, nor any powers, neither height nor depth, nor anything else in all creation, will be able to separate us from the love of God that is in Christ Jesus our Lord.'" But the way Jake declaims it one might have thought he was reading verbatim an EU directive on the import and export of dicarboxylic acid. He battles to the end of Romans, wading through ten acres of mud punctuated by shell holes and flattened barbed wire, and announces another fifteen-minute break which this time turns out to be half an hour in length. The result is that as he embarks on Paul's first letter to the Corinthians, all sixteen chapters of which he is scheduled to read before the school bell rings for the end of today's classes, he is an hour behind schedule and even if he completes this book in regulation time we will still not be done till ten past six.

He slips and slides through chapter one. He tiptoes his way through chapter two. He screws up his face as though trying to find some additional focus to guide him through chapter three. But after a marginal improvement, chapter four sees him sink into a quicksand from which there appears to be no escape. I open my mouth to give him my first prompt. But before I can do that, Lorrie gets up and walks over to him.

'Enough Jake. Enough for today.' She looks out at the now impressively large assembly in the pews. 'Ladies and gentlemen, thank you for coming. We will resume, all being well, at nine tomorrow morning.'

'I want to carry on!' The volume of sound which now thunders from Jake's lips creates an involuntary gasp from one end of the church to the other.

'You can't Jake. You're too tired.' Lorrie's voice, firm but measured.

'Chapter five!' Jake bellows. '"It is actually reported that there is sexual immorality among you, and of a kind that does not occur even among pagans…"'

'Shush, Jake.' Lorrie now starts pushing his wheelchair down the aisle.

'"…A man has his father's wife. And you are proud! Should you…shouldn't you have been….should you rather have filled with….have been filled with…."'

'Jake, stop it.'

'I hate you!' Lorrie may now have reached the south door, but the words are clear enough. The words would be clear enough in the mud huts of Zanzibar. 'I hate you so much!'

Day 12 – Saturday 24th August
Epistles in full, as follows: 2 Corinthians, Galatians, Ephesians, Philippians, Colossians, 1 Thessalonians, 2 Thessalonians, 1 Timothy, 2 Timothy, Titus, Philemon, Hebrews, James, 1 Peter, 2 Peter, 1 John, 2 John, 3 John, Jude;

Revelation, in full.

Epistles: More of St Paul's letters to other Christian communities culminating in his 2nd epistle to Timothy, written by Paul when in prison and condemned to death. There then follow epistles written by other apostles and followers of Christ.

Revelation: The final, climactic book of the Bible, consisting of an account of a vision experienced by St John on the island of Patmos, concerning the Last Days. Much of it based on Old Testament prophecy, it foretells a new heaven and new earth where there shall be "no more death or mourning or crying or pain, for the old order of things has passed away."

Di's joining us today, and Lorrie promises she'll come and pick us both up for what will be the final journey to the venue. As we wait for her, I'm dreading That phone call: the one that says Jake can't come out to play. Di's confident there won't be one. She tells me she's prayed about it last night and again this morning. I tell her I have as well. I ask Di if maybe I'm being hypocritical given my lack of faith. She's unequivocal in her response. 'Everyone has faith,' she says. 'God created us and he put faith into each one of us. Those who say they don't have it only deceive themselves.' She takes my hand and holds it in her hands. 'And when Jake finishes the task, as he will, I want you to thank God because he heard your prayer.'

There's no phone call. They're with us on time and as we're getting into the car, Lorrie has a surreptitious word. 'He's determined to get there,' she says. 'I've asked him a dozen times if he's quite sure. And I've had half his breakfast thrown back at me in reply.'

As we drive, Karen phones to say something's come up with work and she may not be able to get to us till near the end of the afternoon. It's a shame but she's already done more than enough for us so I can't complain. I tell her we'll expect her when we see her. Otherwise we travel to the church this morning in absolute silence. As far as Jake's concerned I don't know if that's good or bad. Calmness is easier to deal with than agitation but there's no way of telling if it's the calmness of a focused, peaceful mind that has girded itself for the challenges of the day ahead, or the calmness of the machine that's burnt itself out and has no more to give. Di's normally a chatterbox but she's a sensitive chatterbox and she knows that there's a time and place for quiet and this is such a time. Only at the end of the journey does she turn to me and announce 'That was the best prayer time I've had. God is going to get you there, Jake.' I always thought places of prayer were surrounded by stone walls and stained glass, and there would be fewer places where one was less likely to find and hear God than in the fast lane of the A27 round Worthing. Mum wouldn't be comfortable with Di's remark. Mum's faith was deep and seemed to acquire more depth notwithstanding the faith-challenging kicks to the face her illness bestowed upon her, but she would never openly express it as Di just has done. Perhaps if the stakes were not so high today I would say that Mum's approach was more rational. But today rational is taking a day off and I just have this feeling that today I'll be hearing all the things I as a human being want to hear and will be choosing to dismiss the things I don't.

The prospect of Jake actually completing his monumental task today has been the lead story on local radio this morning and it's had a mention on the Radio 2 news. And even at ten to nine, as we make our way into church, the number of people in the pews is far greater than we've seen since day one. I'm not the one who's reciting but in some ways mine is the greater burden: I've no idea how Jake is going to perform in front of this crowd and if it disintegrates after the first five syllables I've got to take responsibility for dealing with the mess. I try to think of other key moments in my life. I recall opening the notification of my Legal Practice Course examinations; awaiting the verdict on my first contested IP action; and asking Rosie Ballantyne if she wanted to go blackberrying with me on our last day before we started our third year at big school. But none of these seem to come close to what's happening today. Exams, court hearings, dates…well, they're everyday, commonplace, who cares. What we've got in this church today, and have had for the last fortnight, is a man reaching out to something beyond the everyday and commonplace. Something which means more to him than everything or everyone else in the world and because it means so much to him it means so much to me as well. But while I feel I've one hand on the prize

I can feel a pull that's preventing me gripping it with the other. Please, Jake, I've been saying to myself since the moment I got up this morning.. Please find something inside you that will pull you through this last day. You've left the name-crunching behind in the world of Chronicles and Nehemiah, and the epistles in front of you, though dry in places, aren't really that hard. That just leaves Revelation, and that should be a breeze; the imagery is so ludicrous and so far-fetched that you couldn't go wrong…

We should be starting with 2 Corinthians today but we've unfinished business from yesterday to get through first. At one minute to nine Lorrie manoeuvres Jake into position, as she's been doing each day. At nine o'clock precisely I ask for hush, as I've been doing each day. And at six seconds past nine Jake draws breath and begins. "'It is actually reported that there is sexual immorality among you, and of a kind that does not occur even among pagans. A man has his father's wife. And you are proud! Shouldn't you rather have been filled with grief and have put out of your fellowship the man who did this?'"

And so he goes on through chapter 5, and 6, and 7, and 8. He's word-perfect and moving at a speed that threatens to be captured on police cameras.

Tears fill my eyes. He's found what he'd lost yesterday. I look across at Lorrie and I can feel her relief. I look across at Di and I don't need to ask what's going through her mind. It's there, all over her face: God has filled that empty tank with petrol just as I asked him to.

He marches on. "'If I speak in the tongues of men and of angels but have not love, I am only a resounding gong or a clanging cymbal…Love never fails. But where there are prophecies, they shall cease; where there are tongues, they will be stilled; where there is knowledge, it will pass away…For he must reign until he has put all his enemies under his feet….the last enemy to be destroyed is death.'" He reaches the end of 1 Corinthians and Di is on her feet, leading the applause and crying 'Praise the Lord.' He marches straight on into 2 Corinthians; it's not so memorable, this, with none of the crowd-pleasing poetry of the first letter to have reached the Corinthians' in-box. Once that one's done there's a whole succession of short, punchy books, each with their own highlights. '"But the fruit of the spirit is love, joy, peace, patience, kindness, goodness, faithfulness, gentleness, self-control...Speak to one another with psalms and hymns and spiritual songs...therefore God exalted him to the highest place and gave him the name that is above every name..."' I can see Di mouthing the words as he says them. She's united with him in intimate knowledge of the sacred text.

He elects to break for just five minutes instead of the usual fifteen. The break's long enough for the press people to be talking into their phones and I hear it again and again, 'He's going to do it. He's smashing it.' Is it a bird. Is it a plane. Off he goes once more. '"Clothe yourselves with compassion, kindness, humility, gentleness and patience...the day of the Lord will come like a thief in the night...While people are saying Peace and Safety, destruction will come on them suddenly, as labour pains upon a pregnant woman..."' I keep glancing at Lorrie and I wonder if she's thinking what I'm thinking, that it's going almost too well. '"Here is a trustworthy saying that deserves full acceptance...Christ Jesus came into the world to save sinners...I have fought the good fight, I have finished the race..."' Not quite yet, Jake, you haven't, and please don't think it's over till it really is over because I don't think I could bear it if it all went tits up now. The start of the letter to the Hebrews takes him to the halfway point of the day's work and it's just gone twelve thirty. He's clawed back pretty much all the time he's lost yesterday. He really ought to be having a proper break but he announces he'll take fifteen minutes and then start again.

He resumes on the dot of twelve forty-five with Hebrews, chunkier than the last few books but full of Old Testament quotes so he's actually repeating a lot of stuff he's done. '"Today if you hear his voice, do not harden your hearts, as you did in the rebellion...This is the covenant I will make with the house of Israel after that time, declares the Lord..."' Then come a whole load more short books. James first: '"Do you want evidence that faith without deeds is worthless?"' Peter, two epistles. John, three epistles, but the man was clearly running out of steam, his first letter five chapters long, the other two not

314

even covering a page each. '"Dear friends, let us love one another, for love comes from God. Everyone who loves has been born of God and knows God..."' After John comes Jude; just two pages and that's done. It's now three o'clock. Jake is just one hour and fifteen minutes from completing the task. He's done sixty-five books and has just one more to go – one more beast standing in his way. The 22 chapters of the book of Revelation.

Off he goes. '"And when I turned I saw seven golden lampstands and among the lampstands was someone like a son of man...His feet were like bronze glowing in a furnace, and his voice was like the sound of rushing waters..."' He's on his way, and nothing, surely nothing, can stop him. '"And the one who sat there had the appearance of jasper and carnelian. A rainbow, resembling an emerald, encircled the throne."' How distant seem Adam and Eve, Noah and the flood, Joseph and his coat of many colours, Samson and Delilah, and David and Goliath. '"Worthy is the Lamb, who was slain, to receive power and wealth and wisdom and strength and honour and glory and praise."' I look at Di and her eyes are shut but she's smiling as if part of her is in that world that St John the Divine is describing for us. '"After this I saw four angels standing at the four corners of the earth, holding back the four winds of the earth..."' Just keep it going, Jake. You've fifteen chapters left, that's all. Fifteen. In chapter 8, there are just thirteen verses; in chapter 10, just eleven verses. I look round and every pew is filled and it's standing room only and I think I'm hearing the churchwardens ask people to pass further down the car. He breezes past the halfway mark and there are just ten pages to go – ten out of 1250. '"If anyone has insight, let him calculate the number of the beast, for it is man's number. His number is 666."' The anorak in me is dancing with joy as I find a milestone for each chapter completed. That was chapter 13, so the number of chapters left is in single figures. He powers on to chapter 14. '"Fear God and give him glory, because the hour of his judgment has come...so he who was seated on the cloud swung his sickle over the earth, and the earth was harvested..."' Chapter 15 has eight verses. Just eight. A tiddler. '"And the temple was filled with smoke from the glory of God and his power...and no-one could enter the temple until the seven plagues of the seven angels were completed..."' How appropriate, those sevens, as there are just seven chapters left. He enters chapter 16. '"Then I heard a LOUD VOICE..."'

It is a loud voice. It's unnaturally, abnormally loud. I've heard Jake shout out often enough but he's never shouted any of the Bible verses, not even when we were rehearsing them together.

'"The first angel went and POURED OUT his bowl upon the land..."' There it is again. A few lines down. '"The sun was given power to SCORCH PEOPLE WITH FIRE..."'

Why. What's he doing this for. I glance over at Lorrie and I see a look on her face that spells panic. Could this machine be starting to malfunction. Or, to see it from Di's perspective, is Jake now drawing on the very last reserves of fuel that her prayers to God have generated. I flick over the pages and see there just six pages. That's all. Just six. '"The sixth angel poured out his bowl on the GREAT RIVER EUPHRATES, and its water was DRIED UP to prepare the way for the KINGS FROM THE EAST."' At least I think he said kings. It's one of the easiest in the English language to pronounce but from his mouth it comes out as "kerrings." He needs a break and he needs one now. I can see Lorrie pointing at her watch as if to say he's bags of time. Just half an hour maybe, a bit of fresh air, and he can come back and get the job done. Those in the pews and those straphanging further back can wait. We'll tell them there's been a signal fault at Bermondsey but normal service should be resumed shortly. I know Jake would hate to stop in mid-chapter and he's just over halfway through this one, so I decide to wait till he gets to the end of it.

'"Behold, I COME LIKE A THIEF! Blessed is...is...is he who stays awake..."'

He stops. Just like that, he stops. He slumps back in his wheelchair and shuts his eyes.

I leap to my feet and run forward but Lorrie's beaten me to it. 'Jake. Jake.' Solicitous, controlled, *mezzo forte*.

Nothing.

'Jake!' Her voice louder this time.

Nothing.

316

'Jake!!!' Now shrill, urgent, desperate.

She grabs his arm and puts it to her ear. Then she turns to the crowd. 'There's no pulse.'

18

There's uproar. A T-shirted man rushes forward, pronounces himself to be a doctor and starts administering CPR. Lorrie's grabbed her phone from her pocket and screams for an ambulance. Reporters are reaching for their phones in order to relay the news to their respective HQ's. Di's on her knees, I guess pleading with her God to revive Jake before it's too late.

I just stand there. And as I stand, I'm gazing at the slumped body, seeing within it the ruination of everything that mattered to him, of everything he was living for, and everything that he really loved.

Then people start coming up to me. They're people I've never seen before and people I've no wish to see now. What's happening, they ask. What's going on. Is he going to be all right. There's a lot I could say to them but given that for all I know I might be talking live on a radio station that's being beamed to millions I just confine myself to four inoffensive words. Too early to say. Too early to say. Too early to say. Perhaps I should be varying it but I can't be bothered to consult the thesaurus on my phone. The only sound I really want to hear is the siren. I push my way past the hordes that are infesting each pew, each aisle, each last square inch of space, and hurl myself out into the porch. A moment later I hear the siren's wail. It's probably no more than ten minutes from the time Lorrie calls. It feels like ten hours. I brief the paramedics, they dive in, and moments later, they're wheeling him out and loading him into the ambulance for the journey to A & E in Chichester eight miles away. Lorrie and I agree that we'll follow as soon as I've dispersed the vultures. Everyone's still in the church, evidently unsure what's meant to happen next. I make my way to the very spot where Jake was reciting just minutes before. It's my show now but I've got no script. I pull myself together. This is what you do, Matt; it is, or rather was, your day job, to represent others who can't speak for themselves. Make this your best speech ever.

'Ladies and gentlemen,' I say. 'You've witnessed something

amazing over the past twelve days. A man who gave everything so that he might achieve greatness through accomplishing a feat unequalled by anyone who's ever touched a Bible: the commitment of these sacred texts to memory and their declamation in public. The task appears to have proved six and a half chapters too much. It's still a momentous achievement. We pray he will revive. Failing that, we pray that he will rest in peace and rise in the knowledge of what he has done. That's all I want to say. Please can I ask you now to vacate the church while I join him and Lorrie, his carer, at hospital. And please give generously to the retiring collection.'

I've no intention of staying a moment longer. Steve's there, Richard and Anne are there, and the churchwardens are there. They can do whatever they need to do. My place is with Jake. I turn to Lorrie and Di and tell them we've got to go. And for the second time I'm pushing my way through to the door, shouting for a gangway to enable Lorrie and Di to follow me, shouting three words, 'Can't talk now,' at those clustering round the porch. And I'm trying all the while to hold back the tears as I think of the man who so very nearly was Memory Guy.

*

We don't speak a word as we head towards the hospital. I think we're all stunned. What's stunned me is the cruelty. Had Jake tailed off into terminal disintegration yesterday afternoon and decided he couldn't come back for more it would have been hateful, yes, but not cruel. It's almost as if there is a malign spirit, one that has evaded the attentions of the guardian angels mustered by Di, and who has intervened by first gulling us into thinking Jake was sailing through to the end of the task and then throwing a heap of twisted metal into his inner workings. Lorrie may not have invested as much into this emotionally as I have, and she certainly doesn't share Di's faith, but when I glance at Lorrie's face I can see the pain and anguish of defeat: in football parlance, it's the pain and anguish of a side leading by two goals to one and conceding two goals in stoppage time. I just know that at the end she was wanting it almost as much as me. I wonder if, like me, her thoughts have turned to Maggie.

319

This is exactly what Maggie feared: that we were gambling with Jake's future. We gambled on the thought he could make it. We've probably made things worse by losing that precious rest day. I've gambled, Lorrie's gone along with the gamble, and the roulette ball has popped out of its winning hole at the last moment and bounced into an oblivion of heartbreak.

As we're arriving at the hospital my phone goes and it's Karen. In the ghastly frenzy of the last hour I've not given her a thought. I tell her what's happened and ask where she is. She says she's running late but she'll get to the hospital within the hour. Then Steve rings. He says he, Richard and Anne are just turning the last stragglers out of the church and they'll be joining us as soon as they can.

We bundle inside and having found the right floor and the right department and the right people we find Jake's still alive. If it hadn't been for the CPR we'd have lost him. But he's unconscious, his breathing is laboured, and in my heart I'm fearing the worst and from the expression on Lorrie's face I know she is as well.

In due course we're allowed to go and see him and we just stand there, impotently, stupidly, nobody quite knowing what to say. Perhaps we could say to him how well he'd done but we all know that if he had his consciousness he wouldn't say he'd done well. He would say he'd failed and he might as well have recited the first verse of Genesis, fluffed it and given it up as a bad job. It's the same difference. The only success he would recognise is getting to the end of Revelation chapter 22. After twenty minutes of silence we adjourn to a waiting area with a vending machine and an assortment of magazines. We agree we're going nowhere.

I sit with Lorrie on one side and Karen on the other. It's not as warm today and Karen's sporting a leather jacket over her T-shirt. The leather is soft and supple and soothing and as the mental and physical exhaustion begin to catch up with me as the evening goes on, I'm resting my head on her shoulder and I can smell her Christian Dior perfume. I know it's Dior as dad loves it and she's told me he always buys it for her. I wish dad were here now. I've tried calling him but I can't get hold of him. I recall him on Thursday saying he was spending a couple of days with friends in Kent before travelling back to Yorkshire this evening. I know that when this is all over I've got to talk to him and Karen and try and sort out the mess we've got ourselves in. But all I can properly think about is the fact that Jake Guy Terson was only six pages and six and a half chapters from being Memory Guy.

Karen and I must sit like that for three, maybe four hours. I know if I didn't move she would just let me stay there as long as I wanted; maybe for ever. I know that she'd do anything for me because she said it again within minutes of her arrival here. I know I should be grateful to be so wanted and so loved. But it doesn't seem important now, just as nothing else seems important except Jake. The doctors and nurses pass by from time to time with updates but there's never anything new. He's stable. There's no deterioration, but there's no improvement. I glance up at the clock and it's now ten past ten. Steve says he needs to get going and departs. Richard and Anne say they're wanting to get home too as Richard's got to be up early for sidesman's duties at the 8am service next morning. So off they go as well.

Service to what. Service of what. What's the point. Why, when most right-thinking people are still buried under their duvets, drag yourself out of bed on a Sunday morning, all for an act of worship to a God who's thrown back Jake's endeavour into his face. Not just his face. All our faces. Was this not the ultimate piece of service. Was not Jake's unaided retelling of the entire truths of the Jewish and Christian faiths the ultimate sacrifice to the Lord. And what's the Lord done with it. I feel like saying this to Di and watching her squirm in her attempt to mount a defence of her faith. I wonder how she'd respond. I expect she'd answer that God moves in a mysterious way. That's the usual one, the trump card when the tricks against declarer are mounting up. Ours is not to reason why: ours is but to do our best, to do our utmost, and then to taste the acrid taste of failure when even our best still falls short.

At eleven a middle-aged man with a stubbly chin and dog collar wanders up to us. 'Matt Chalmers?' he says.

I get up. 'Yes.'

He extends his hand. 'Chris Vincent. I'm the hospital chaplain.'

As I take his hand, my heart dives downwards. His advent can surely only mean one thing.

Or maybe not.

'Obviously I've been following Jake's remarkable journey,' he says. 'Along with millions, maybe tens of millions, of others. It's massive.'

'Would be even more massive if he'd got to the end,' I say. I realise I'm wallowing. I've not permitted myself a wallow since the implosion. 'Just seems so monstrously unfair.'

'Matt, none of us know how this is going to play out,' he says. 'You wouldn't thank me for giving easy and glib answers and you won't get them. You wouldn't expect me to raise false hopes and I won't raise them. But you're entitled to expect me to be here for you, and I will be. I'll gladly stay with you or I'll be around somewhere and the nurses will find me if you need me.'

I decide to cut the wallowing short. 'It's very late,' I say, 'and it could be hours.'

He smiles and places his hand on my arm. 'You and Jake together have given so much,' he says. 'You deserve to have something given back to you.'

*

He sits with us in silence for a while. It all feels a bit awkward. I guess he doesn't want to make us chat if we don't want to chat. And I have no idea what I should be or could be saying to him. It's Lorrie who breaks the spell by thanking Chris for his time with us and suggesting he leave us while we think about getting something to eat. Off Chris goes, then Lorrie turns to me.

'I'm going to try and find a café or a cafeteria,' she says. 'If it's just takeaway, what do you want?'

What do I want. What a question. Of course I want Jake to come round. To live. But if he does come round, he'll know. Know that he hadn't quite made it and realistically even if he lives he may never get this close to making it ever again. Maybe then it is best for him to slip away now, with no knowledge, not this side of eternity anyway, of what he so

322

nearly achieved but didn't.

So I've no idea what I want.

As for food, I've not eaten anything since the Mars Bar I had at lunchtime. I'm not hungry now but Lorrie tells me I need to eat something as there's no knowing how long we might have to wait here and I wouldn't be popular if I found myself occupying another hospital bed as a result of chronic undernourishment. I tell her a sandwich would do fine. Di and Karen say they just want white coffees.

Lorrie returns at half past midnight, just after an update from a nurse that Jake is stable and there's no change. She, Lorrie, announces she's had to shop out of town, and produces a Big Mac meal for me, Filet-of-Fish meal for her and regular white coffees for Di and Karen as requested. At uni we once had a competition to see who could make a single McDonald's meal last the longest and I think the most anyone managed was two hours and a quarter. And even then it wasn't the sight of the tempting food that did for him but the thought of having to listen to another Spice Girls single over their sound system. I'm on course to smash his record. Two hours and twelve minutes after the meal was handed to me, there are still six French fries sitting at the bottom of the box. Four o'clock comes and goes, and it's down to three French fries. Karen's been asleep since ten past two and Lorrie and Di have followed soon after…

At ten past four I hear quick, purposeful footsteps coming in our direction. They sound like the quick, purposeful footsteps of someone with important news. I look up. I see a male nurse accompanied by Chris, the chaplain. They're both looking directly at me.

I shout to the other three to wake up then leap to my feet. 'What?'

'Jake Terson,' says the nurse. 'He's speaking. But what he's saying…it's nonsense. Can't make head or tail of it. Doctors can't either. He says he wants you urgently.'

We hurtle along the corridor and into Jake's ward. He's sitting up in bed and his eyes are open. He looks straight into my eye.

'You weren't there when I started again,' he says. 'Only a nurse and that doesn't count.'

*

I turn to the nurse who brought us the news. 'What's he been talking about?'

'Weird stuff,' the nurse replies. 'Great cities splitting into three parts, hailstones weighing a hundred pounds. It was like…like already he was in another world.'

'Hailstones weighing a hundred pounds,' I say. 'That's Revelation, isn't it.'

'Revelation, yes,' says Chris. 'Near the end.' He whips a small Gideon Bible from the inside top pocket of his jacket. He rifles through the pages.

'Chapter 16!' Jake yells. 'From where I left off before!'

I snatch the Bible from Chris and find the page. Every second is crucial. Next I turn to Karen. 'Get onto the press. Get onto anybody you can.'

'Are you sure?'

'Just do it!'

What am I doing. What am I saying. These could be the final delirious murmurings of a man who has already gone into shutdown. We may have a car crash of a non-story. Or Jake may finish before anyone gets here. But maybe it's forces from another world that are directing my actions as well as Jake's. Something or someone's dumped me onto this carousel, I don't know who or why, but now that I'm on the carousel nothing's going to make me fall off.

Karen disappears and I look towards Jake. 'Can you go back to the start of chapter 16?'

'I don't need to!' he barks. '"Blessed is he who stays awake and keeps his clothes with him!" That's when I stopped. Remember?'

'Of course I remember, Jake. From there. Go!'

'"Blessed is he who stays awake and keeps his clothes with him, so that he may not go naked and be shamefully exposed. Then they gathered the kings together to the place that in Hebrew is called Armageddon."' He's doing it. He's only doing it. That weird thing he was doing, emphasizing words, he's not doing it any more. '"Then the angel carried me away in the

Spirit into a desert. There I saw a woman sitting on a scarlet beast that was covered with blasphemous names..."'

I see the nurse looking uneasy. I'm worried Jake's outpourings might just be perceived as the final confused mutterings of a soul that's fastened its seatbelt for takeoff, and might in turn prompt the nurse to some action which might fatally interrupt the proceedings. But then I see Chris whispering to the nurse and whatever he whispers it seems to have done the trick. The nurse's face relaxes and now he just stands there by Jake's bedside, with Lorrie, Di and myself, transfixed by his words and by the clarity of delivery.

"'The ten horns you saw are ten kings who have not yet received a kingdom, but who for one hour will receive authority as kings along with the beast.'" What does it mean. Who can ever explain it. To me it means one thing and one only, that Jake Terson is getting closer and closer, line by line, to the finish. That was chapter 17 that was. Next up is chapter 18: a chunky 24 verses but much of it is in the form of quotes, with plenty of repetition, a gift for the memory man. "'Woe! Woe, O great city, O Babylon, city of power...Woe! Woe, O great city, dressed in fine purple...Woe! Woe, O great city, where all who had ships on the sea became rich through her wealth...'"

I can't take my eyes or my concentration off Jake for more than a second but Karen comes and shoves a note under my nose. She's managed to get hold of a freelance who does stuff for *The Times* and lives locally and will be here in fifteen minutes. Technically we don't need him. We have witnesses. We have Karen, Di and Lorrie, and also the nurse and Chris who can provide the verification from outside Jake's circle of supporters. So we have the validity and credibility as well.

Now he just has to finish it...

"'Hallelujah! For our Lord God Almighty reigns. Let us rejoice and be glad and give him glory!'" He's got stuck into chapter 19 now. As Jake quotes this hymn of praise I look across at Di and there's a smile on her face and I know it's not the smile that asks how I could ever have the audacity to have doubted her but it's the smile that confirms she never had any doubts. "'I saw heaven standing open and there before me was a white horse, whose rider is called faithful and true.'" I look round and see people coming in. There are nurses in uniforms and doctors in white coats, there's a woman who by her protective clothing would appear to have come straight from an operating theatre, there's an elderly man with a long apron, mop and bucket, there are two uniformed police officers, and there are three or four others who might just have wandered in off the street. Word's obviously spread that a real-life miracle is taking place on a hospital ward in a Sussex town at four thirty on a Sunday morning. '"Then I saw the beast and the kings of the earth and their armies gathered together to make war against the rider on the horse and his army."' Less than a minute later, chapter 19 is done. Three chapters are left. Five columns of text are left. Just over two full pages are left. Chapter 20 is just fifteen verses. '"The sea gave up the dead that were in it, and death and Hades gave up the dead that were in them, and each person was judged according to what they had done."'

He reaches the end of chapter 20. And stops.

No, no, surely no. Two chapters left. How much more unspeakably vicious would that be.

He remains sitting up in bed. His eyes remain open. The nurse moves towards him just as Lorrie had done over twelve hours ago. But Jake shakes his head.

'I'm stopping,' he says.

'Jake, no!' My agonised cry echoes round the ward and seems to shake the hospital walls.

'I want everyone to get out except Matt,' he says.

I turn to the audience. 'Go. Please,' I say. What am I saying. What am I doing. This isn't my hospital. There are doctors and nurses present. They're the professionals and I'm ordering them out. And yet they go, as if stunned into submission by the momentousness of what's unfolding before them.

I wait till they've gone then walk closer to Jake. He reaches out and puts his right hand in mine.

'You don't need to worry,' he says. 'I'll get to the end. I promise.'

The relief causes me to burst out into a mixture of laughing and weeping. 'You had me going there, you swine,' I tell him.

He tightens his grip. 'But when I get to the end that's me done.'

'Sorry?'

'I can feel it,' he says. 'I just know. It's fine. I'll have done what I wanted to do.'

'I love you, Jake.' Where did that come from. I've never told my mum or dad I loved them and here I am saying it to a man who eight months ago I'd never met and who for so many days I wished I'd never had the misfortune to meet.

'I know you do, Matt. I know you do. You've done more for me than anyone could ever have done. I'm sorry if I've shouted at you. I'm sorry for being a bully. Thank you for not being frightened of me.'

'Well done,' I tell him. 'Well done, Jake Terson.'

'I'm not done,' he says. 'I've a bit to do yet. Wouldn't do to tempt the fates. I'll take the "I love you." That's all I want from you. Need from you.'

I put my arms round him.

'One last thing,' he says. 'Before the grand finale. In every sense.'

'Mmm?'

'Tell my wife I love her.'

'Your...your wife?'

'That's what I said.' The tenderness evaporates. It's back-to-work time. 'Now get them all back in and let's finish it.'

Wife. Wife. What wife. Who. Why. When, How.

Maybe though that's all part of the package. The world he's now living in is his twilight world. And, as he prepares to pass through the portal of death, his brain has begun to work, like God, in a mysterious way. If the surreal is the only price to be paid for his calm and relaxed acceptance of what's happening to him, who am I to raise an objection.

I withdraw my arms from Jake, go and gather in the spectators, and off he goes.

'"And I saw a new heaven and a new earth, for the first heaven and the first earth had passed away, and there was no more sea...He will wipe every tear from their eyes. There will be no more death or mourning or crying or pain, for the old order of things has passed away."'

I've heard these words before, at least twice, outside Jake's constant rehearsal. They were said at mum's funeral and I last

327

heard them in *Titanic*. But I've never wanted them to be true more than for Jake. I remember a conversation I had with the vicar who'd presided over mum's funeral. I asked him what heaven was supposed to be like. He played another get-out-of-jail-free card. We don't know. It's not given to us to know. If we knew, we would be no more than the people we are now. All we do know is it will be as Revelation said it would – free of death, mourning, crying and so on. Yet I've heard other vicars being quite specific on certain aspects, saying for instance that we'll recognise each other in heaven. Who knows. Who really knows. All I know now is that I want this heaven for Jake more than he himself could possibly realise. Only please not for another chapter and a half.

'"The city was laid out like a square, as long as it was wide. He measured the city with the rod and found it to be 12,000 stadia in length."' And it's back to those exact statistics one might have thought had been left behind in Leviticus-land. Leviticus. Was that just ten and a half days ago. It feels like a railway station in the suburbs of a city we've left six hundred miles away. '"The first foundation was jasper, the second sapphire, the third chalcedony, the fourth emerald."' That was a page turn, ladies and gentlemen, and that was the last page turn. I know Jake knows it. I notice the slight tilt of the head as he reaches for what will be on page 1250 of 1251. On the opposite page, there's a bit of print but then lots and lots of white. Our destination is unquestionably, unequivocally in sight.

'"Nothing impure will ever enter it, nor will anyone who does what is shameful or deceitful, but only those whose names are written in the Lamb's book of life."' The irreverent streak in me has always likened that bit to one of those glitzy award ceremonies. And the winner is…long, far too long, pause. Then the winner is announced and steps forward, trying to act surprised, and is soon thanking all the people who made it possible. Their agent, their mother, their plastic surgeon, their milkman, their milkman's plastic surgeon. If Jake's in that Lamb's book I wonder if he'll put in a good word for Matt Chalmers. Matt Chalmers who now, more than ever before, wants all that he, Jake, has been reciting, to be the truth.

'"Then the angel showed me the river of the water of life."'

This is it; chapter 22 of 22 in book 66 of 66. Now I'm counting the lines in chapter 22 that he's done and the lines that are left. A dream passage for the memory man comes and goes. '"Let him who does wrong continue to do wrong. Let him who is vile continue to be vile."' Again I'm being a bit naughty, thinking that bit must have been put in by criminal law solicitors struggling on pitiful legal aid rates and desperate for more work. I think I can afford to be naughty. There's just 36 lines to do.

'"Blessed are those who wash their robes, that they may have the right to the tree of life and may go through the gates into the city. Outside are the dogs, those who practise magic arts, the sexually immoral, the murderers, the idolaters and everyone who loves and practises falsehood."' Poor old dogs. What about guide dogs, what about life-saving dogs. Perhaps the celestial Supreme Court will find an exemption when someone takes it on appeal.

'"I warn everyone who hears the word of the prophecy of this book: if anyone adds anything to them, God will add to him the plagues described in this book. And if anyone....'

We've reached the last page. The very last page. 1251 of 1251.

'"...takes words away from this book of prophecy, GOD WILL TAKE AWAY FROM HIM HIS SHARE IN THE TREE OF LIFE..."'

He can't have over-emphasized those words. Must be my ears. It's fine. He's said he'll do it and he'll do it.

'"...AND IN THE HOLY CITY, WHICH ARE DESCRIBED IN THIS BOOK."'

Book sounded like berk. I see glances. Lorrie to me. Karen to Lorrie. Di to me. Di to Karen. You can't do this to us, Jake, you can't do this to yourself...

I can see lines appearing on Jake's face where I couldn't see them before. There's a rigidity about even the parts of his body he could move previously. I know, just know he's in pain.

A machine by his bedside which has been bleeping constantly is now bleeping more urgently. I see a look of alarm exchanged between two of the nurses.

There are just six lines left. Twenty-seven words. '"HE

WHO…'

He stops. He shuts his eyes.

Di runs forward. She grabs his arm. 'Lord Jesus, give him the strength to finish. Lord Jesus, give him the strength to finish…'

I hear the buzz of apprehension from the others surrounding his bed. It may be barely perceptible to the ear but I can feel it as though it were the jabs of a thousand needles.

'Hear us, Lord Jesus, give our brother Jake the strength to finish…hear us, Lord Jesus….'

'"TESTIFIES TO THESE THINGS SAYS YES, I AM COMING SOON."'

Di's still holding his arm and she's still praying. '"Hear us, Lord Jesus, sweet Jesus, hear us…'

'"AMEN. COME LORD JESUS."' His eyes are still tight shut and I can see the sweat of agony on his face. Then he closes his mouth.

Now the bleeping is getting faster. One of the nurses rushes forward. She grabs his hand. 'Get Martin! Get Martin now!' she yells. Then she looks towards me. 'I'm sorry. This stops now.'

'No!' I bellow. 'He's got eleven words to go. That's all. Eleven.'

'Hear us, Lord, the provider and giver of all good gifts…' Di's not giving up.

There's a sickening pause. It's followed by the sound of a door crashing open, and then rushing footsteps.

Then, not one, not two, but three medics hurtle to Jake's bedside. I can see they're about to engulf him when his mouth opens once more.

'"THE GRACE OF THE LORD JESUS BE WITH GOD'S PEOPLE. AMEN."'

He's done it. He's Memory Guy.

*

Memory Guy's mouth shuts. He clutches his chest and he slumps back. And as he does so one of the doctors is shouting at us to get out.

We get out and I don't know what to do. I want to celebrate

because he's Memory Guy and I want to weep because I don't think Memory Guy will live long enough to know what he's done. I'm hugging Karen then I'm hugging Lorrie and I'm hugging Di, and now our tears are flowing with joy and flowing with sadness. Di's telling me not to give up hope but something's telling me that the seconds lost after the bleeping changed may have cost Jake his life. Other people are querying if Jake actually made it or not. I'm telling them that those final words that he said signified his successful completion of the task, but I can tell they too don't know whether they should be rejoicing or mourning. I just want them to leave so that Lorrie, Karen, Di and I can be left alone.

One by one they melt away leaving just one who's still hovering around. Karen introduces him to me as the reporter from *The Times;* he's probably about the only press person I don't recognise from the last fortnight so I have to fill him in on all the details. It's the last thing I feel in the mood for doing but he's taken the trouble to turn up and I know Jake would have wanted me to do it. Then off he toddles, and it's just us four. We go back to the seats we were on before and we're all huddled there, united in our total joy and our total trepidation, our total relief and our total fear.

Twenty minutes or so after we've sat back down, I see one of the nurses approach, not the one who alerted us to Jake's imminent curtain call, but an older, female nurse. I've only ever seen that look on a nurse's face once before. That was when mum lost her battle. I grip Karen's hand.

'I'm very sorry to say that Jake has just passed away,' she says. 'He suffered a very severe heart attack just as he approached the end of his recital. The doctors did everything they could. Please accept my deepest sympathy.'

*

Lorrie bursts into tears and falls into Di's arms. Karen echoes Di's words, 'sweet Jesus,' and falls into my arms. There's no sense of shock. The signs had been there but we'd chosen to continue on the path leading to this moment. Maggie

331

had been right about his heart. Of course she'd been right. Yet I think we all saw that this was Jake's life's work. And this being so, he needed to be at his desk to get the work done, and couldn't leave his desk until it was done. Now it is done, there's nowhere else he would need or wish to go.

But there's still pain. So much pain.

It hurts more, so much more, because nobody was there at the end to congratulate him. Maybe one of the nurses or the doctors said something but I can't help thinking his soul had left our world the moment the last Amen had been declaimed.

Then I remember I told him I loved him and he said that was enough.

The four of us, Di, Lorrie, Karen and myself, are allowed back to his bedside. Chris is already there. He tells me he's formally commended his soul to the Lord. But of course Jake had, in a sense, administered his own last rites through the words of those two final chapters. I trust Di not to overegg it. I trust her not to observe that he's gone to be with the Lord, or, worse, he's gone to be with "your mum, Matt, dear." No. She knows better. She knows when it's best to say nothing at all.

I put my hand on Jake's arm and tell him he's Memory Guy.

*

There are so many formalities, and Lorrie, as his primary carer, is stuck with them. I ask if she needs me to stay to help her, not that there's a lot I personally can do, but she suggests Karen should run Di and me back to Brighton so that Di can catch up on some sleep, while Karen and I, working from my lodgings, deal with the media in conjunction with Steve and put out appropriate press releases.

I'd decided to make the priority phone calls as we drove, but Di's fallen asleep almost the moment we've pulled out of the car park. I don't want to disturb her so I text people instead, telling them I'll have more information and be available for interviews from 7am. We get back to Brighton and while Di goes straight to bed, I make coffee for Karen and myself. We sit at my table, nursing our hot drinks, not saying much. I'm still not sure if we should be celebrating or mourning, and it's clear that Karen isn't sure either. In one respect of course we should be celebrating: celebrating a life, and celebrating an unparalleled achievement. But we wouldn't be human if we didn't ask ourselves if that achievement was worth the price.

Before we start the calls to the media there's time for me to try dad again and, thank heavens, this time I do get through. He tells me he's back home and was probably on the road when we were calling. I'm wondering if in fact he hadn't been wanting to talk to us. I couldn't blame him if that were true. He says he's just heard Jake completed the task. He says he's proud of me. Then he asks after Karen, almost as though he knows I'll be with her. It's clear he thinks he's lost her for good.

As for the media, even though Steve is more than happy to do his share, the list of people who need calling seems to expand with each call we make: not just local and national organisations, but people from abroad as well. There are at least three freeview Christian broadcasting channels in the States that want to Skype us, and during the morning we link up with radio and TV stations in New Zealand, in Canada, and in Italy. Karen's holiday-gleaned Italian comes in particularly handy on that last one, given that the guy who's trying to talk to us can't speak a word of English. And when Karen doesn't know the Italian word for whatever she's trying to say, she resorts to the expedient of saying the English word and adding 'io' to it, employing a cod-Italian accent in the process. I know dad thought she should go into acting but maybe she'd be well advised not to give up the day job.

Just before lunch I get a call from Stewart Pimlott, the sender of the email that proved to be the catalyst for Memory Guy's heroics. He tells me he'd actually looked in on Jake earlier in the week although he hadn't had time to see me or talk to me. He says he's been in touch with a publisher who wants to meet me with a view to my writing a book about how Jake conquered his condition to learn the Bible. I have to correct Stewart: it's because of his condition that Jake has learnt the Bible. Stewart's not the first person to have made that mistake. I tell him I'm flattered to be asked but I'll want time to think about it.

And then, early on the Sunday afternoon, it all stops dead.

The abruptness of it is brutal. I've been in regular touch with Steve during the morning and I call him again early in the afternoon to say how quiet it's gone. He tells me that that is the joy of the mass media. They move on. They treat you and your story as a holdall you take on a flight. Once you've reached your destination and the holdall has been unpacked that's it; it's not wanted any more and you're not wanted any more. There's been talk of some other media events aside from the book deal but Steve warns me that's what they all say. Oh, they'll gush, we'll definitely want to do a big feature, let's pencil in a couple of dates fairly soon and we'll get back to you as soon as it's been run past the boss. Yes, it's a great story. Yes, we'll want to package up the achievement for the delectation of a worldwide audience. But a day after they call, something bigger happens. That was your fifteen minutes of fame, that was, and now it's someone else's turn. Not that you'll ever be told that your fifteen minutes are up. The silences in response to the texts and emails say it more eloquently than words ever could or would.

It's the worst time because now I have the chance to think. We've been occupied almost every minute of every hour since the moment Jake uttered those glorious final syllables. Having felt all the time with Jake that I mattered to him, and to what he was doing, I can't see myself ever mattering to anyone in quite the same way again. The future, even with the new job, is suddenly a tundra bordered by uniform clusters of saggy pine. And Karen's making it worse. Everything she's saying is we and us. In her eyes we're now an item. We could meet up in Cranleigh for a weekend, and maybe you could stay over, she says. Alison won't mind, she says. Wouldn't it be great for us go abroad for a few days before the move, she says. We deserve it, she says. I'm fearful that next thing I'm going to catch her on her phone or laptop looking at properties for us to rent together in Manchester.

I'm prepared to tolerate it for now. It's not the time to slap her down. But as far as I'm concerned, it's as if that part of me that bubbled over outside the café last Thursday lunchtime has been safely locked back away in its box and the key's gone and got mislaid. Just now I can't share her enthusiasm for we and us, nor can I get past the fact that all the time there's we and us, my own father is being left to contemplate the collapse of his existence.

*

Karen leaves at four. I'm suddenly hungry. I've eaten nothing except a couple of biscuits all the time she's been with me so I make myself some beans on toast, then, as it's now a clear sunny afternoon, I go for a run. It's while I'm on my way back that I get a call from Lorrie saying she's now home and asking if I'd like to join her for a cuppa. I say yes and having gone back to Di's to shower and change I'm at her front door within the hour.

She opens the door and without exchanging any words we're in each other's arms. We must stay like that, in silent embrace, for five minutes or more.

She's the one who breaks the silence. 'I'm so sorry, Matt,' she says.

'There's nothing for you to be sorry for,' I say.

'Oh, there is,' she says. 'I've not made a cake.'

'That's it. I'm off.' It comes out just like that and I hope Lorrie's not still so traumatised by the events of the last couple of days that she thinks I'm serious. But no. She laughs.

She may not have made a cake but the iced fruit bar she picked up from M & S on the way back from Chichester is very nearly half as good as one of hers. I also manage to eat my slice without bits going in my nose, on the floor or halfway to Penzance. As I eat the cake, and drink tea, I tell her about my day then she tells me about hers, and the mass of things she's had to sort out with still more to sort out when the new working week begins tomorrow. She tells me she's flaked out and I can see it in her eyes. She explains the funeral arrangements are up in the air to a degree because there are still some outstanding issues, and she needs to see her solicitors in the next day or two to sort out the will, as Jake had one or two specific requests. Then she sits back in her chair as though talking about the day has been as exhausting for her as living it. And then she looks at her watch.

'Half past six,' she says. 'He should have had his tea and

buttered scone by now.' She smiles and cups her ear. 'I'm waiting,' she says. 'Waiting for him to yell I'm late.'

Together we sit and listen to the silence. A moment later she bursts into tears.

I realise I've never, not once, seen her cry before. Even in the short time I've known her she's had so much thrown at her but never, not once, has she failed to smile or laugh her way through it. Her crying now is making me want to cry in sympathy. I get up and come round and kneel at her feet and put my arms round her.

'I'm sorry, Matt,' she says through her sobs. 'It's ridiculous, isn't it. When you think about it. He wasn't a child of mine. Wasn't a relative of mine. Can't really say he was a friend of mine. He could be impossible. Rude, surly, moody, shouting, yelling, screaming, violent – well you saw that. We may have laughed together and joked together but the next day he'd be shouting for England again. He told me he hated me a hundred times a day. I don't think he ever told me loved me. But I loved him, Matt. When his yelling was at its worst I wanted to put a gag over his mouth. But now I hate the thought of him not being there yelling. Tell me I'm being ridiculous.'

'And it's all my fault,' I mutter.

'Excuse me?'

'I came into this guy's life and I didn't mean to turn it upside down but I did. Without me there'd have been no Memory Guy. He'd have carried on, free from the stresses of it all, maybe you and Maggie between you could have worked something out, given him a few more years maybe. But I pushed him and now you've lost him.' And by this time I'm blubbing.

'Now you're the ridiculous one,' she says. She produces a hankie and wipes my face. 'It was his choice. He could have chosen more life. Instead he chose greatness. And you gave him the ability to choose greatness. You brought out the greatness in him. Whatever else you do in life, Matt, you'll be doing very well to top that.' She pushes me gently backwards. 'Now go and sit down. I'll make us a fresh brew in a minute.'

I go back and sit down. 'Talking of Jake's wishes,' I say, 'he did say something really strange to me when he asked to speak to me in private at the hospital. You know, in the middle of those last few chapters.'

'Oh yes?'

'He told me he wanted me to tell his wife he loves her. I mean, the guy was clearly hallucinating, but all the same…'

'He wasn't.'

'You mean, he's married? He's got a wife?'

'She and I barely speak, we try to keep out of each other's way, but…yes, Matt. He has.' She reaches for her phone and allows her thumb to dance round it. Then she gets up, comes round, thrusts the phone into my hand and points to an image on the screen. 'That's her.'

It's Fiona.

19

I let the phone slip through my fingers and it drops down onto my empty plate with a bang.

'What's wrong, sweetie?' Lorrie's face is a sudden study in maternal anxiety.

'It's Fiona.'

'You know her?'

'We dated. Two or three times. She told me her husband's name was Pete.' My legs have turned to aspens and I find myself slumping back into my chair. 'I loved her, Lorrie. And she broke my heart. No. She trashed it. Jumped on it. Stamped on it. Beat it to pieces.'

Lorrie shakes her head and sighs. 'It's what she does, Matt, my dear. Take it from me. She's not a nice person, I'm afraid.'

'Is that why you never mentioned her to me? Because she's not nice?'

'Call it my defence mechanism.' She picks up her phone from the thankfully undamaged plate and puts it on the arm of her chair. Then she sits back down. 'I knew that once I started telling you about her I'd end up bitching about her. And life's too short to bitch. I learnt that when Colin and I broke up. I spent ages bitching about him to my friends, the choir I was in, anyone who'd listen basically, and all it did was make me feel vindictive, spiteful, and actually hating him more than he deserved to be hated. Bitching doesn't move the world forward. So with Fiona I decided to put myself out of temptation's way. Decided not to talk about her. At all. So I haven't. Not with you. Not with anyone. Not unless I had to.'

'And Jake? Who also never mentioned her? Never wore a wedding ring?'

'Jake loved her to pieces.' She puts her palms together as though in prayer, and holds them against her chest. 'He worshipped her. And I know he'd have died still loving her to pieces. He hated being apart from her. His Bible was *his* defence mechanism. That was what kept him going when she wasn't there for him. He told me once that if he started talking

338

about her, even thinking about her, it would just send him over the edge. Whatever he meant by that. As for the ring, he had a hissy fit once on Brighton pier. Frustration I think. The realisation that his marriage was – well, not over, but not the same. Never going to be the same again. He pulled the ring off in a rage, threw it into the sea. Regretted it ten seconds later but too late.'

'So where was she when he was dying? When he died?'

Lorrie strokes her chin. 'That's a very good question, Mr Paxman,' she says. 'Last time she condescended to speak to me was a day or two before Jake started his recital. She said she was having to go away. Wouldn't tell me where, wouldn't tell me why, wouldn't tell me for how long. I've left a million voicemail messages. Another million texts. Not a sausage in response. Still nothing even today when half the world knows he's dead. There's me, having to get his affairs in order for him, having to arrange his funeral, trying to respect his dying wishes. And there's her, his next-of-kin, impersonating the Invisible Woman. While his sister's locked away in a secure unit and unlikely to see the light of day till after England next win the World Cup. There, she's set me off again. I'm bitching. So when did you last get anything out of her?'

'Months ago,' I tell her. 'I've been there too. Ringing, texting, trying her workplace...never got to find where she lived.'

'Oh, she wouldn't have let you know that.' Suddenly Lorrie's playing not at mother of an adult lawyer but at mother of a lovesick teenager. 'I've heard from Jake what she was like when she was younger. Hurt some boys so much they were screaming.' She folds her arms and leans back in her chair. 'You were well clear of her, my dear. Well, well clear.'

I shake my head. 'I loved her, Lorrie.'

Her face hardens. 'You're better than that, Matt,' she says.

*

Having been up all last night, spent hours today conversing with every radio station from BBC Sussex to Shanghai FM, and provided copy for every journal from the *Lincolnshire Evening*

Star to *South West Montenegro Farmers' Monthly*, I need my bed. I've had my shower earlier so it's just a case of getting off my trousers and Converses, then peeling off my shirt and scrambling on a T-shirt, and I can plonk myself down and with luck I can get some much-needed...

My phone goes. I glance at the name of the caller.

Just the sight of it sends my heart leaping over Brighton Pavilion.

For a moment I wonder if I can possibly pick up and speak to her. Then I think of Lorrie's million voicemail messages and million texts. For her sake if nobody else's, certainly not mine...

So I pick up. 'Fiona?'

'Matt!'

'What...wh...who...why...wh...where the hell are you?'

'Matt, I need you now. Need you so much.'

'Where the hell are you?'

'Prague.'

'Sorry?'

'I said Prague.'

'Fiona, you need to be back here.'

'I can't come back. Not till I've seen you.'

'I'm not coming to Prague and that's that.'

'There's stuff I need to talk to you about,' she says. 'Big stuff. I need your advice. Professional advice.'

'Can't we just talk now? Or Skype? Facetime?'

'No, Matt,' she says. 'I mean, for a start I don't know who could be listening. Who could end up listening.'

'People Skype all the time, Fiona. Unless you're about to divulge state secrets I really wouldn't worry about that.'

'It's not just that,' she says. 'I want you with me. Around me. Want someone I can speak to properly. You're the only one I think I can trust. I'll pay back your air fare if you need...'

'Why can't you just come home? Then we can talk.'

'I can't. I'm not coming home till I've seen you. I'll say it again. I want you here with me. Need you here with me. Matt, I'm desperate. I know I hurt you and I'll explain everything, but I'm desperate.'

'You'll have to give me time to think about it.'

I tell her I'll call back and hang up.

For the second time this evening I let my phone slither from my trembling grasp. Then I lie back on my bed and start to think. The rational in me is telling me not to be intimidated by someone who waltzed from my life all those months ago, put up a wall of silence thick enough to withstand a demolition squad, and brought forth more tears than the EU onion mountain.

But then I remember Jake and the fact that even though I know nothing of the nature of their marriage at all, she was a wife and she's now, as of less than twenty-four hours ago, a widow. And I'm seeing a frightened, vulnerable widow who needs love and warmth and tenderness more than maybe any time in her life and she's asking me to give it. I'm also seeing Jake's primary carer, herself mourning the man she grew to love, lonely and isolated and fearful, now charged with sorting out the consequences of his death, a death which happened because I persuaded him he could be Memory Guy...

*

Fiona may think it's easy for me just to hop on the next flight, but it's far from easy. Tomorrow's Bank Holiday Monday, when it's obvious a lot of people will be travelling home from long weekends or holidays, and the next flight with free seats from Gatwick isn't till 6pm tomorrow evening. There's nothing available out of Heathrow tomorrow at all. However there is an empty seat on a flight from Stansted at ten tomorrow morning. That will have to do.

I complete the booking then ring Lorrie and tell her what's happened. Her immediate reaction is, how nice of Her Ladyship to condescend to get in touch, but hey, sounds like she's up to her old tricks again, you should have called her bluff, told her there was no way you were going out there, told her she should be the one getting on the next flight home, and chances are she would have done. But I tell Lorrie I'm the one who's spoken to Fiona, and I can sense not only her, Fiona's, desperation but her loneliness, and I genuinely believe the only way to get her home is to dance to her tune. Lorrie says she hopes I know what

341

I'm doing and wishes me bon voyage and that's that.

I try to get some kip but perhaps it's no surprise that despite extensive enquiries of Amazon and eBay there's none to be had. At times like these I wish I were a sports statistician, able to get off to sleep by trying to recall Wimbledon singles title winners or Football League champions since 18-whatever. I try going back over some of my wins in IP actions prior to being ensnared in Daniel's lion's den. It's as my mind goes back to Barton v Baines, involving the pinching of some lyrics from a third-rate pop song for use in an advert for a fourth-rate carpet cleaning fluid, that I feel slumber coming over me, and then, what seems like only moments after that, my phone's ringing the 4.30 alarm.

At least the trains are kind to me, I'm at Stansted in excellent time, and it's with an air of optimism that I enter the check-in area. It's only then that I find that, owing to a combination of computer malfunction and baggage handlers being in a bank holiday mood, we're delayed by eight hours and the best guess is we won't reach Prague until 9pm tonight – just five minutes ahead of the 6pm flight from Gatwick.

I wonder whether to cancel the whole venture and go home. I know Lorrie wouldn't blame me if I did. But the forecast is for temperatures so high you could fry breakfasts for the entire England cricket team on the Stansted station down platform and I decide it's actually less effort to stay put. For a while I just sit there. Then I go back to last Friday's *Metro* quick crossword which has been stalking me ever since it came into my life on Brighton station five hours previously. Having given up on an African antelope, I get out my phone to look at what there is to see in Prague and to try to book somewhere to stay in the city. But there's nothing, absolutely nothing, that's suitable. Nothing with a roof on it, anyway. Unless Fiona herself can suggest something, the only feasible address in the Czech capital now leaping out at me is Long Wooden Bench, Near Church Doorway, Low Knife Crime Area, Somewhere Out In The Suburbs. It's had 63 positive reviews on Trip Advisor.

Then I call Fiona to discuss the practicalities of where to meet and when. Previously we'd agreed four o'clock this afternoon but now we've put it back to ten thirty this evening.

She says the venue, Charles Bridge over the Vltava river, may as well stay the same. I remember that this is the bridge with the lines of sculpted figures down each side where she'd told me she'd supposedly met Pete. I've been wondering if Charles Bridge was as much an invention of Fiona's as Pete was, but now I know it certainly does exist and is indeed one of Prague's top tourist attractions. If I want to get there by public transport from the air terminal I'll apparently need to catch a bus and then an underground train and then walk. Or there's a taxi which Fiona says could cost at least ten times as much. But my outlay for this whole escapade has long since skyrocketed through the ceiling and is on course for Mars. The *Dragons' Den* moguls would be having a field day. Your expenditure is way out of control. Your operation is haemorrhaging money. You've wildly overvalued your business. You're uninvestable and I'm out. Another bit of haemorrhaging won't make any difference. A taxi it shall be. I've also asked Fiona about somewhere to stay. She says I can go back to where she's staying. I thought she might.

The day drags on. At some point I permit myself two exercise yard breaks, one for some lunch and one to visit the shops, but my mind is really only focused on how long my actual full term of custody is likely to be. The good news is that the message on the departures board, "delayed until 1800," hasn't changed since ten this morning and is still saying it at four this afternoon. At five we're invited to go to our gate, and at six twenty we're airborne.

*

I've never visited Prague. I've heard and now read good things about it and my taxi driver, who speaks good English, reels off at least three hundred and thirty-five places I must not leave the city without seeing: the castle, the palace, the cathedral, churches, museums, towers, viewpoints, and much more besides. If his taxi firm folds he has a great future as a tour guide. But it's now dark and all I'm seeing around me are industrial estates and car headlights and drive-thru fast-food restaurants. Frankly I might as well be in Crawley which looks just the same, only I wouldn't have needed to sit in Stansted for most of the past decade in order to get to Crawley. As we progress, though, the buildings begun to look smarter and grander and I get my first view of the castle, its towers silhouetted against the moonlit sky.

And at ten thirty, eighteen hours after rising from my beauty non-sleep, I'm standing on Charles Bridge looking out over the Vltava.

There are hundreds of people. Although it may have been a stiflingly hot day – well, it has been in Stansted – it's now night and a stiff breeze is blowing and I'm wondering why all these folk haven't got homes or Airbnb's to go to. But through the crowds I have eyes for only the one woman, and sure enough I see her standing as she promised she would, by the statue that a helpful man has confirmed to me is that of St John of Nepomuk. It's the one you touch for luck. That's no invention either.

She wears a light blue T-shirt and black shorts and flat-heeled sandals with straps winding up and round her legs like spaghetti round a fork. She has no jewellery apart from a thin silver-coloured neck chain. Her eyes are large and damp and red. Her hair looks as though it's suffered the amorous intentions of an autumn leaf blower. She stands very still, her legs tight together as if they've been glued to each other. There's a fearfulness and vulnerability etched into every part of her body. Her face is the face of an extra in a dinosaur movie who's about to be crunched into small pieces by the velociraptor.

I come up to her and put my arms round her. I don't kiss her. I feel no passion nor excitement, and certainly no arousal. It's not just what she's done, or rather not done, for me or for those who in the past weeks have come to mean more to me than my own flesh and blood. It's not just the grief at losing Jake. It's the train smell, and the plane smell, and the people smell, and the heat, and the sleep deprivation, and the distance from home. It's the practical, boring stuff that's called trying to get on with living.

'You came,' she whispers. She's now got her arms round me and her head rests on my shoulder. 'You came all this way for me.' Then I hear the sobs. I can feel the desperation, the collapse, the defeat, and the brokenness, and I'm not even looking into her face. 'Matt, you have to help me. Please.'

We come apart and I look around me. There are still too many blasted people. They're clearly enjoying their summer getaway or their bargain weekend break. It may be paradise to them but it's no place for a disintegrating woman to be pouring out her soul to someone whose intimate knowledge of an Essex airport has threatened to become a medical condition.

'Let's get out of here,' I say. 'Let's find a place to be alone.'

She dries her eyes and points to the statue. 'You need to touch him for luck first.'

I force a smile. 'And you so obviously have.'

'I guess it can't hurt,' she says. She looks as if she's about to start crying again so I let her take my right hand and allow her to slam it down on the stone. I certainly get no tingle, nor any sense of imminent good fortune from my close encounter with it. It feels cold, freezing cold, and it feels lifeless.

She releases my hand and I plunge it into my pocket to warm it up. 'So where shall we go?' I ask.

'I know a café bar a couple of streets away. It's got lots of little nooks and crannies. Should find some privacy there.'

She takes my left hand. I wonder whether to free it but decide it's easier and less upsetting to play along. She leads me to the end of the bridge on the castle side of the city, and we walk down some stone steps along a narrow alley into a street where almost every establishment seems to be a bar. A few moments later, still holding my hand, she's leading me through the door of Olivetto's and soon we're sitting opposite each other at a candlelit table sharing a jug of a fruity red. There's dull inoffensive music in the background and I can hear others talking and laughing but apart from people passing there's nobody in sight and we can hear each other speak. We share a smattering of small talk. But then the work has to start.

'So, just to get this right,' she says, 'you've been in the papers. Helping Jake to recite the Bible by heart.'

'I have.'

'When did you find out I was his wife?'

'Last night.'

'Lorrie never told you before that?'

'What do you think.'

'How long have you known him?'

'I first met him properly in early January,' I say. 'Just after the second time I saw you. Met him through Lorrie after I visited her to thank her for helping me when I had an accident. I loved him, Fiona. He could be impossible at times, he was selfish, he was demanding, he was in many ways unlovable...but he was exceptional. I couldn't not love him for what he was. What he did.'

She screws up her face and tears again begin to fall from her eyes. 'I could tell from looking at the two of you,' she says. 'I need to tell you something. Something important. You're the only person I think I can say it to. This is why I need your help.'

I lean forward. 'Go on.'

'I killed him, Matt.'

*

I sit forward in my chair. 'You what?'

She repeats what she just said. The tears are a deluge now. 'There. I've said it. I've owned up. And I don't know what to do next.'

Her announcement is too important for me to want to reply straight away. I allow the words to waft across the candle-scented air above us and wait for the sobbing to burn itself out.

She takes out a tissue and dries her eyes.

'You'd better tell me everything,' I say. 'And I mean everything.'

She nods. 'The truth, the whole truth and nothing but the truth. That's what you say, isn't it.' Now she smiles.

I don't smile back. 'Yes,' I say. 'I want it all. From the beginning. Can you do that.'

'Of course, Matt.'

'Go ahead.'

I take the jug and top up our glasses.

'I met Jake thirteen and a half years ago,' she says. 'I was just twenty-three, he was nearly twenty-seven. I don't know if he told you this, but he was a writer. Not a novelist. An

346

academic writer. Psychoanalysis. He was a very very clever man. I was in my final year at uni and got myself an Easter holiday placement with an academic publisher in Oxford. And while I was there he was writing a book for them. I was asked to help copy-edit. In other words, suggest how things might be better expressed, query choices of words or phrases, that kind of thing. So he and I found ourselves in correspondence, exchanging emails, having phone calls. Then we agreed to meet for lunch to discuss some changes I was suggesting. I think I was expecting some balding professor, some ageing boffin. So I was kind of amazed when this young guy, only late twenties, comes into the restaurant. And it was clear from the moment we started talking that he was such a clever man. Brain the size of St Paul's Cathedral. IQ off the scale. And it wasn't, like, cleverness in a boring way. He knew a lot about interesting stuff as well. He'd done a fair bit of travelling, he was a wine connoisseur, and he loved reading. We started dating. I'd been with the IP lawyer, everything I told you about that was true, but then I finished with him, and Jake caught me at just the right time. And while we were dating he explained that he was autistic. He admitted to me he was brilliant at certain things, but hopeless at others. And he was. And by hopeless I mean, hopeless. Very underdeveloped social, people skills. Incredibly rude, intolerant, impatient. And a complete routine obsessive. Routine was everything to him. Getting up at precisely the same time, expecting people he was meeting to be on time for everything. I was always terrified of being late for a date with him. He was often really rude to me, was uncomplimentary about my clothes and make-up. Even my choice of mouthwash one time. But I was prepared to cope with the downside because the upside was so fantastic. I loved him despite everything. We travelled round Europe together. We'd sit and talk psychology for hours and hours. And yes, believe it or not, he would recite chunks of the Bible to me. Pages sometimes. May sound dull, but believe me, he was good, Matt. Really good. I couldn't stop listening. Sometimes I told him to carry on when he would have gladly stopped. Captivating.

'About a year after we met, we went to Spain on holiday. He proposed to me in the cathedral of Santiago de Compostela.

Maybe you've heard of the pilgrimage route. We went on holiday to Spain, walked a few bits of the route, then on our last afternoon we went inside the cathedral and...well, I never thought I was a very religious person but it was just so so beautiful and you could sense a kind of divine presence inside it. He wasn't a Catholic but he was High Anglican which is pretty much the same in my eyes and I could see this was like a home from home for him. I think they'd just had a service and you could smell the incense and see the slight fog above the main altar. And there was this stunning chapel which was roped off, but he had a word with one of the staff – he was fluent in Spanish so that was easy – and they unroped it and he took me inside and five minutes later when we came out I was his fiancée.

'We married about a year later. You remember I told you I went to touch the St John statue for luck and met Pete. Well, there was some truth in all that. Because we did honeymoon in Prague and we found ourselves together at the statue and I did touch it then. But he said he didn't need to touch it because he'd already had all the luck he could ever want and didn't think he deserved any more and someone else should have some. Quite sweet, really, in a way. Only I could tell he wasn't joking. He was quite serious, almost intense. But that was the way he was.

'I'd got myself a job in London and he was a lecturer at UCL and we rented in Kilburn. Then a year after we married we decided to get out of London and moved down to Sussex. Matt, we had everything. Nice house in Falmer, doing lots together, both of us with interesting jobs – he'd relocated to the University of Sussex and I commuted into London – and yes he could be difficult at times but so could I. His mum and dad were getting quite frail by now but they'd come down and see us and I got on really well with them. Problem was, there was Maggie.'

'Sister Maggie. The one who tried to kill me. The one they've put away.'

'That's the one. She and I never got on from the start. There was something about her. To be honest, I found her quite frightening. She had some of his characteristics, I think. The

348

negative ones. She loved him but he loathed her. I think she resented me because she saw me as pulling him apart from her. She was always finding fault, making snide remarks about my clothes, make-up, anything. I wanted to like her but she made it impossible.

'Anyway, when we came to Brighton, Jake's autism seemed to get a lot worse. No obvious reason. He was often really rude and abusive to me but I tried to rationalise it. Tried to tell myself it was nothing personal, it was his condition that was talking, not him. It was never controlling or coercive. He was actually out of control. And it wasn't just me. He would yell at people or burst into tears without warning. He'd fly off into a rage at the smallest thing. But even with all that, we still loved each other. We still had good times. I was coping. It was hard but we just took one day at a time. I still loved him. I knew he still loved me.'

'Was there nothing the doctors could do?'

'No. Obviously he was referred to specialists but they were as clueless as we were. Not just NHS specialists, private ones as well. We spent thousands on trying to find treatment for him. But none of them, not the doctors, nor the psychologists, nor the psychotherapists, could do anything. All they could do was give him medication which stabilised, calmed him. It treated the symptoms but never ever the causes. And it became like a vicious circle because the more we sought help and the more we failed to get it, the worse it made him. He hated being examined. He would always try and cut to the chase, telling the doctors what he thought was wrong. The psychoanalyst in him, you see. I was still commuting but actually got the job with the Wilbury Press in Brighton so I could be nearer to him.

'Then after we'd been married two years, not long after I'd got the new job, he had his accident. That arose from his autism. I expect Lorrie said. It was a double whammy. It put him in a wheelchair and he was told he'd never walk again. To begin with the uni kept him on but it soon became clear that it wasn't working out and they retired him on medical grounds. And all of this just made him angrier and more aggressive. He still had the use of his hands. He'd never struck me before but now he was lashing out at me. He made me cry then he'd yell at me that I was a cry baby and not fit to care for him. And talking of babies, no, we never had children.

'I stuck it for a few months but I knew I couldn't live with this any more. It wasn't fair on me, wasn't fair on him. He needed someone who could care for him pretty much 24/7, and had the experience to know how to respond to his extreme behaviour. I couldn't. None of his family could help. His mum was terminally ill by this time and his dad had a degenerative illness and was completely out of it. They lived in Buckinghamshire and Maggie was wanted up there for them. She couldn't have been expected to take on Jake as well and to be honest she didn't have the know-how either, never mind the right temperament. I couldn't put him in a home. Just couldn't. So we were stuck.

'That's where Lorrie McEwan came in. She was friendly with his mum and dad and was very experienced at dealing with people who had mental health issues. I didn't really know her but Maggie put her in touch with me. She, Lorrie I mean, had just come out of a messy divorce and was out of work and I think she saw Jake as a project. If you asked her, she'd tell you that I was only too happy to wash my hands of him. But, Matt, that's not how it was, I promise. You've got to believe me. I know I've lied to you about my marriage but this is God's truth. She said she'd be really happy to have Jake live with her and to be his full-time carer for as long as was needed. She was always going to be way better at caring for him than me. She had a suitable room for him, and she had experience of mental health patients before. We were able to sort out state benefits, disability living allowance, that kind of thing. We all three of us, her, Maggie, me, signed an agreement that she would have Jake to live with her but that I should be able to see him and have him home whenever I wanted providing I gave her enough notice.'

'And how did Jake feel about all this?'

'He hated it. Of course he hated it. Hated the fact that he didn't have a normal married life any more. He gave Lorrie such a hard time. I guess you saw him angry but it was nothing to what it was in the early months with Lorrie. How she stuck with it I still don't know.'

'And you and Lorrie? How did you get on?'

'To begin with, really well. But then things started to go wrong. She thought I should be taking him out more, getting more involved. Kept on quoting from the marriage service, "for better for worse, in sickness and in health." As though it had never crossed my mind. I kept telling her I had commitments, a very demanding job, a house to look after. Like water off a duck's back. Then a couple of years back it really kicked off. We put out a crowdfunding appeal to get Jake across to the States for some ground-breaking treatment. Some people did actually give us money up front. Very generous amounts. But when it was clear we were never going to get anything like the funds we needed we fell out on what to do with the money that had been donated. Lorrie screamed at me. You've probably never seen her really angry, have you, Matt.'

'I have,' I say. 'But it usually blows over in minutes.'

'There you go. With me it was more like months. I said I didn't think it was honest or right to keep people's money when they knew it wasn't going to where it was intended. She said it was still useful, could give him a bit more quality of life. We ended up not speaking to each other. We'd do everything by text. We were like divorced parents squabbling about child contact. Then we started arguing about other stuff. She kept on accusing me of not being a good wife. In truth I think she was jealous of me. She wanted Jake as her project, her toy, and didn't like me suggesting she might do things differently or saying I thought something she had in mind for him may not be right. And she ended up refusing to speak to me unless she had to, and refusing to acknowledge my existence in front of others. That's why she never told you about me. Pretended I never existed. Maggie was the same. She would never acknowledge my existence either. She never even consulted me before shipping Jake off to that place in Seaford. Although by then I think she'd lost the plot anyway. It got back to me quickly enough. In their eyes I was just "a woman" or "this woman" or "that woman" who maybe saw him or took him out sometimes. Lorrie could be devious as well, believe it or not. I knew she tried to coax out of Jake stuff I'd told him, like about when I'd dumped blokes as a teenager. Telling herself I was always the one to blame. Just wanting more ammunition to use against me. I tell you, Matt, there's an awful lot of things she said and did that she'd never want to admit to. Least of all to you.

'She'd probably tell you I cared nothing for Jake. Not true. After Jake's accident I started working compressed hours, taking Wednesdays off, and having him at my...well, our house, on those Wednesdays. I don't drive so she'd bring him round and we'd spend days together. If I'd let you into my house on the day we went cycling you'd have seen the equipment I've got for him. The stairlift. The special bathroom. Then I'd go and see him at weekends. He always asked me to make an effort with what I wore. I couldn't cycle in my smart clothes, and I wasn't going to spend silly money on taxis, so I took the bus. I bet Lorrie would say I just came over first thing Saturdays and Sundays to get it all over with for the day. Not true. The fact was, she liked going out then to get her hair done and meet one of her cronies for a coffee. I was often prepared to stay longer, only she would bounce me out if she thought he had a better offer. Sometimes she'd ring to say don't bother to come over because she'd planned to do something with him instead, taking him to the zoo or feeding the ducks, boring him senseless. Do you know something, I think he found her really patronising at times. The point is though, that that was time I would have been willing to spend with him. Okay, I didn't enjoy coming to see him. But there's a difference between doing something for someone and not enjoying it, and doing nothing for someone. And I was doing something and I'm not having Lorrie suggest I was shirking my responsibility. Of course I didn't enjoy it. Most normal people have their lie-in at the weekend then shove on their T-shirt, jeans and trainers, off to town, the gym, whatever. Then there's me at half eight on a Saturday morning. Layering on the make-up, ironing a long skirt, hobbling up the road in high-heeled shoes or boots that are murdering me before I've even got to the bus stop. And this has been going on years. Not just those couple of occasions you saw me. But I knew I had to do it. This guy's life's been completely screwed, through no fault of his own, what callous wife is going to walk away. And I've not walked away. Lorrie probably wanted you to think I was walking away. And she

352

probably wanted to make out that she was all that mattered to Jake. Not true. He often said he treasured the times we were together, him and me. He'd insist on taking selfies of us both to remind him he was married to a beautiful woman. He used to hate it when I had to leave him.'

'You didn't hate leaving him though. Did you.'

'I'm not going to lie, Matt. No. I didn't hate leaving. I was relieved to be away. But I was also sad because I kept thinking of how it was. It made me cry. I'd go into that godforsaken café because I needed a coffee to calm myself before getting the bus home. So, I guess, those times I saw you, you were on your way to see him?'

'Well, him or Lorrie.'

'No other earthly reason why you'd want to be in that part of town. Certainly not in that café. Drinking that awful coffee.'

I wonder if I'm the one being thick here. 'Okay. I get all that,' I say. 'But why couldn't you just have told me straight about why you were there? Why did you make up this Pete person? Why make up about the aromatherapist? Why didn't you tell the truth?'

'I couldn't, Matt. It would just have made me more miserable. I didn't know you, you didn't know me. It was easier to pretend. And nicer too. To think what my life could have been like. And once I started pretending, I felt I had to carry on. I mean, it wasn't all lies. There was some truth in the aromatherapist thing. After Christmas the Jake business was getting to me so much that I really did go and see someone near the café. I'd go there sometimes after seeing Jake. But I wouldn't call her a professional. Just a friend really. Dabbled in it.'

'Did you stay faithful to him?' I'm hoping she won't be offended by the question but I've got to take that risk.

'Completely,' she says. 'I did wonder, would it be such a terrible thing if I did have an affair. About four years ago I began spending quite a bit of time with a guy from work. I said nothing to Jake, obviously. But then somehow Maggie found out. Goodness knows how, as she lives so far away. I started getting these vile texts and emails from her. She was convinced I was sleeping with him. Which I wasn't. But she said if she ever found out I was cheating on her brother she would rip my eyes out. I think she must have told Jake she had suspicions. Because from that time on, he would quiz me, every single time we met. Have you got another man. Are you sleeping with another man. On and on. It was like some Soviet interrogation routine. The same questions every time. Probably six times each visit. And then Lorrie wonders why I'm walking out of her house with my nerves shot to bits. I mean, I made sure he couldn't hurt me. Physically. But Maggie certainly could. I know she would have done.'

'You don't need to tell me that.'

'Thing is, and I don't mean to boast, I've had a lot of admirers. Friends and strangers. I've always liked to dress up, look good. Maybe I would flirt a bit as well. I'm only human, Matt. And even though I was wearing my ring, guys would ask me out. They saw me on my own, perhaps thought I was available. With people who knew me, knew my situation, I'd tell them the truth, that I couldn't cheat on Jake. Which was fine if I didn't fancy them back. Not so fine if I did. And then there were strangers. Like you were. If it was a stranger, someone who didn't know, someone who was never likely to, I used Pete. Lot easier all round. Pete the pretend perfect husband. All the manly qualities a woman is supposed to love. So perfect that any potential rival was easily scared off. I thought that Pete was all I'd need to scare you off. Never failed before. Cheered me up as well. The idea of being with someone so perfect. So you got the perfect Peter treatment, complete with pictures of someone who wasn't perfect Peter at all. Of course I had to close down my social media accounts. Didn't want you finding the truth. And in case you're wondering, the surname on my business card was my maiden name. I wasn't ashamed of the name Terson. I just liked my maiden name better.

'You remember me showing you those photos in the café. I was thinking that'd scare you off. But even as I was showing them to you and looking at you I realised I was falling in love with you. I wanted to be with you. Wanted to find a way for us to be together. Then I thought, your travel book. You can bring that to the office and we can have coffee. I loved you more than you could ever know. I still do, Matt.

354

'It all came to a head that day we cycled to Alfriston. You know I was late. It was because I was in two minds. Wondering if I could go through with it all. I was so much in love with you and I wanted to be with you but I didn't see how it could end well. I was scared. I was scared of what would happen if Jake found I'd cheated on him. But I loved you so much I decided I was prepared to risk it. Then I was afraid that you'd be put off by this Pete I was supposed to be married to. So I thought I'd make you think I had issues with Pete. And that was another problem. I thought, if I said straight out Pete was seeing another woman, you wouldn't have believed me, especially after I'd been singing his praises only a couple of weeks back and hadn't mentioned about an affair before. I didn't want you to think I was lying. So I made up that story about Pete going up to Yorkshire, and me only just now thinking he was going back to his ex. Was rehearsing it till I was blue in the face. I left it a bit vague, bit speculative, threw it into the conversation and hoped you'd swallow it.

'Then of course I came off my bike and we got stuck at Falmer and I knew if we went back to my place you'd see something that told you it all didn't add up. The stairlift, the disabled loo, wedding photos of me with this guy who looked nothing like the picture of Pete I'd shown you. And that brought it home to me that it was hopeless. As we sat watching *Titanic* that night I knew I was never going to be able to keep up the pretence. But I also knew I was deeply in love with you and I knew what was coming. I lost my nerve. Thought I'd be able to go through with it but I couldn't. Couldn't cheat. That's why I had to call time on the whole business. Put a stop on our dating. The only way to do that was just to block you. Block your messages, keep you away from my work. Seems so heartless now but at the time I didn't know what else to do. I realised I couldn't have anything more to do with you while Jake was still alive. Was dreading seeing you around somewhere in town. I did once. Just after Easter. Jake's birthday. I ended up hiding under a van. So you wouldn't see me.'

'Wouldn't it have been easier just to talk with me? Be straight with me?'

She starts sobbing. 'I wanted to, Matt, I so, so wanted to.

Tell you everything. But I couldn't bear to. Because then you'd know I'd been lying to you all along and I remember you said you hated liars. I didn't know what to do. If I owned up I knew you'd dump me and hate me forever. And in my eyes that would have felt worse than simply leaving you. If I didn't own up, and I'd slept with you, I'd have been taking such a risk. And looking back now, I know, I just know, if we'd slept together after that bike ride, Jake would have got it out of me in five minutes. He had this incredible knack of getting the truth out of people. Seeing through their lies. Then he'd have told Maggie. And once Maggie had finished with me, she'd have started on you. I had to put the brakes on it, Matt. I hated having to do it but I could see that every time we met up after that it was going to end in tears. But at the same time I couldn't bear to lose you.

'Anyway, it was by this time that Jake had made up his mind he wanted to die. He'd hinted at it a few times in early to mid December. But then when I was round there on Christmas morning he came straight out with it. He told me he was determined to die. He wanted to do it that day. And of course I said no, you can't do that. I suppose there was a part of me thinking, would it be such a bad thing if he did, but there was a bigger part of me that still wanted to love him and try and make life a little bit better for him. I mentioned it to Lorrie, of course I did, and she said she'd be extra careful not to put him in harm's way. But then each time I saw him after that, he said he wanted me to help him. Assisted suicide. I kept on saying no, I wasn't going to, I couldn't do it. He wouldn't let it go, and we were just going round in circles. Then, early March time, he stopped mentioning it. He told me he was going to do St Luke's Gospel on Mother's Day. In that ghastly Methodist church.'

'You should have come.'

'I did,' she says. 'Sneaked in at the back just after it started. Was mesmerised. Never saw who else was there watching. They all had their backs to me anyway. I only had eyes for him. My husband. I couldn't stay long as I was meeting a friend and left before half-time. Would love to have stayed longer.

'I saw him three days later and he told me that was it. No more recitals for him. And he now said he didn't just want to die. He needed to die. Quickly. He actually threatened to find a way to hurt me if I didn't help him to die. I was scared. So scared. And...I gave in. I rationalised it. I said to myself that he's so miserable, so empty inside, with no chance whatsoever of any improvement, he'd actually be better off dead. I thought I was being kind.'

'Were you aware of him ever self-harming?'

She shakes her head. 'I think Lorrie tried to make sure he couldn't.'

'But there was something in it for you if he did. If he was dead. Wasn't there.'

I see her face reddening. 'Matt, I can't lie. I mean, of course part of me liked the thought of getting my life back, being free to date who I wanted, but I promise that wasn't my main concern. I got him to sign a statement that he was wanting to die. I still have it. The next problem. How to do it. I didn't want to hurt him or make him suffer. I didn't want to come in one Saturday with him alive and walk out again with him dead. I was never going to finish him off, just like that. And I didn't want Lorrie to know. I knew she'd think I was the driving force. And I know she didn't want him dead. She loved him. He was her thing. So anyway, we decided, Jake and I, the best thing was put stuff in his food and drink. Just small amounts. Not enough at a time to kill him outright but would do the job slowly. A gradual, very peaceful death. That's what I wanted. He was ok with that. I researched, went online, found what I needed and got it. To be honest I wasn't sure it would work but I didn't dare speak to anyone. Then I started. Two or three times a week, starting from about the 10th of April. I told him what food and drink I was lacing and told him he didn't have to touch it. He was fine with it.'

'But what if he'd told Lorrie.'

'He knew better than to do that. She'd have most likely thought I was behind it and got me arrested. He was the world's most undiplomatic person but he wasn't stupid. It was our secret. And I could see it working. Working very quickly. Lorrie could see it as well. She couldn't understand it. His existing conditions weren't terminal. Anyhow, it was all going to plan. He was going to die relatively peacefully. Not that it stopped him creating. I think in fact he was getting frustrated I wasn't letting it happen more quickly and the effect of the stuff I was giving him was to make him even more frustrated, more suicidal. I remember his fortieth birthday. The 25th. I think that's when you saw me. I'd been round there and had a card and a present. He said the only present he wanted was to go to sleep and never wake up. Well, he didn't say it. He screamed it. He said how appropriate it would be if I could knock it on the head that day. Those were his very words. Happy birthday, happy death day. I did speak to Lorrie and she told me she'd heard him saying he wanted to die and he'd find a way of ensuring he did. I tell you, if I'd laced his food again I probably would have given him enough to finish him off at once.

'Two days later, Saturday, I went round as usual. And the weirdest thing happens. He says he wants me to stop lacing the food and drink. And he wants me to stop because he's got a chance to learn the Bible off by heart. He said there was this guy who was going to help him and Lorrie had agreed because she could see he was so unwell.' She forces a laugh. 'It's crazy isn't it. Lorrie told me she wouldn't have been letting him do it if he'd not been deteriorating like he was. And that was all down to me. Anyway, I was really relieved. Really relieved. I'd not been completely comfortable about the assisted suicide thing from the start. I felt like I was off the hook. Once Jake started rehearsing, we chatted about it, of course we did. And yes, he told me the guy who was helping him was called Matt, and he said he was nice, but I never made the connection. Lorrie never really spoke to me about you, well, she never spoke to me about anything if she didn't have to. Matt's quite a common name. I know a few Matts or Matthews. And when you and I dated you'd never ever mentioned Jake's name to me. So no, I made no connection at all. But then I saw the newspaper coverage and I realised it was you, that you knew my husband, and you were helping him do this amazing thing. I was so proud of you, so proud.

'But there was a problem. Well, kind of. Lorrie took him to the doctor who obviously had no idea what I'd been doing and so wasn't sure what it was that had made him so ill. His normal doctor was away and the one who saw him didn't know much about him. About his condition, his history. He put him on a course of medication and yes, it worked in one sense. Got rid of the symptoms. But maybe it was the wrong thing to give him because then he's complaining to me of different symptoms, and I do some research on the quiet and it's clear the combination of what I've given him and this new medication's messing with his heart. He's never had heart problems before. And I'm certain that his stressing with the need to get his Bible learnt is making them a whole lot worse. I don't know what he was like with you near the end, but with me he was hell. Hell on earth. Shouting, yelling all the time. It got to the stage where I wouldn't have him on Wednesdays because I was scared of him. I've always tried not to shout back but on one occasion I did and we had this row and I wondered then if he might have a heart attack.'

'And Lorrie knew there was a heart problem?'

'I think she may have suspected it, put it like that. But I reckon she was terrified of disrupting Jake's schedule, Jake's routine. She knew this Bible learning was all that mattered to him. Any doctor would have said, stop, and Jake would have ignored it anyway. So what was the point. I mean, clearly if he'd survived, she'd have taken him back to the doctor and I think Jake's view would have been, they can do what they like, I don't care what happens to me.

'Anyway, during July I meet this guy called Kieran, on the train. We get chatting. And it's like with you all over again because I'm giving him the Pete stuff but at the same time I'm really attracted to him. And it plays out just like it did with you. Like an idiot I keep up the Pete pretence, but hint he might be having an affair. And just like with you it works. He invites me back to his. We're sitting chatting with our coffee and we get talking about my mum and dad's place in the New Forest. He says he loves the New Forest too and I go and show him some pictures of it on my phone. And then this one of Jake and me pops up. And he says, isn't that the guy who's learning the Bible, the guy with the autism in the wheelchair. And stupidly I deny it. I try and lie my way out. Tell him I'm so full of admiration for what Jake's doing that I've downloaded a picture of him for my album. He doesn't buy it. He snatches the phone off me and brings up these other photos of us together. So he knows I've been lying. Not just about Jake but about Pete. And maybe I've had a bit too much to drink but it's loosened my tongue and I tell him everything about Jake and lacing his food and drink. I trusted him. Thought he'd understand. But he got nasty. He threw me out. Called me a self-centred liar. Told me he never wanted to see me again. Thank heaven he didn't keep the phone. He might have seen screenshots of the stuff I was lacing his food with. But I really thought he might go to the police. I panicked.'

The air is colder now, and the buzz of voices around me is melting away. 'So you decided to come out here?'

'In a word, yes. Somewhere I couldn't be found. Somewhere I knew. I love Prague. It's where Jake and I honeymooned, I feel happy here. I've been staying in this crap hostel but it's a roof over my head and I can stay as long as I need. I actually came here the day before Jake started his recital. I rang in sick at work but didn't dare tell anyone else. I kept checking for updates on him. Wanting him to finish the recital. Willing him to make it. But at the same time I'm thinking, I've tried to help to kill him, and someone with a grudge against me knows about it. Then I checked the news update on my phone yesterday morning and there it was. Died. My husband. Heart failure.'

She scrapes another cubic metre of tears from her cheeks.

'So what have you been doing?'

'Just wandering the streets. Thinking. My mind just going round in circles. If I go to the police, tell them what I did, I risk being done for assisted suicide, maybe even attempted murder, you tell me. If I say nothing, Kieran doesn't report it, it'll still be nagging away at me for ever. And I'm not sure how long I could live like that. I just don't know what to do. You're the lawyer. I need your help. Tell me what I should do, Matt. Please.'

I don't know if it's the effect of the waiting at Stansted Open Prison or the travelling or both, but all the time she's been talking my hydration levels seem to have suddenly plunged through the floor. I also need time to consider the legal implications of what she's told me. 'You could go and get me a large iced orange juice,' I tell her. I dig into my wallet, find a Czech banknote and press it into her hand. 'And get something for yourself.'

'Don't be silly,' she says. She drops the banknote on the table, rises to her feet and totters off towards the bar with the jug, while I get working on my phone in order to confirm the correctness of my understanding of her legal position. In a few minutes she comes back with a vessel containing what looks like enough juice to have decimated the entire orange crop of southern Spain. And there's so much ice sitting on the surface that I expect it to start exciting interest from climatologists fearful for what's left of the Polar regions.

I drink perhaps half of its contents at once. Then I move it aside and place my folded arms on the table in front of me

'Okay,' I say. 'You asked for my advice. As a lawyer. This is how it is. And remember, I'm being the lawyer, not your friend. It's an offence to do any act capable of encouraging or assisting someone to take their life or to attempt to take their life. But you knew that. By preparing Jake food and drink that's been laced, you're doing just that. Even if what you've done hasn't actually had the effect of killing him it's an offence. Okay. Let's assume this Kieran doesn't report you. In that case you could choose to say nothing, do nothing. So assuming nobody else knew about it, whatever it was you did might never come to light. You could just go on as though nothing had happened. But let's say you were interviewed by the police, either because Kieran or someone else reported you or because you went off your own bat. Again you can stay silent and as long as you've deleted the images from your phone, even if someone had shopped you it's going to be very hard to prove anything against you. But let's say you talked. Told the police everything. You may be unburdening yourself, but you'd actually be creating evidence against you which might otherwise never have got out there. And if there was enough evidence to charge you, the next question is whether they would charge you, that is, take you to court. There are guidelines on whether it's in the public interest to charge in cases like this. If the police accepted Jake was determined to take his life and you felt under pressure to do as he asked, they might decide it wasn't in the public interest for you to go to court. But they'd be bound to ask if there was evidence of his self-harming which you say there wasn't. And if they thought you might have something to gain by helping him to die, maybe his money, maybe that you'd be free to have a life of your own, that it wasn't just compassion, that maybe they didn't believe you when you said his wishes were your chief concern…well, then, it's more likely you could be charged.'

'And if I did go to court and admitted it?'

'You could expect to go to prison.'

She starts weeping again. 'This is awful. Hateful. I own up, I risk being banged up. So you're basically saying, don't own up, don't talk. That's right, isn't it.'

'I'm not saying that. I'm just advising.'

'I don't know if I can live with myself if I don't own up. I really don't, Matt.'

'I can only advise,' I say. 'That's what I've tried to do. Nobody can decide but you. But there's one thing you do need to do.'

'What's that?'

'You need to come home and you need to come home now. All the time you stay here, particularly if you've not told people where you've gone, it's not helping. It only takes a bit of vile Twitter gossip from people who know you and Jake, and then everyone will be asking questions. Why have you disappeared at just this time. That in itself could be seen as suspicious. And it's not just that. There's a funeral to arrange. All Jake's personal effects. His wishes. The legal side. All sorts of things Lorrie needs your help with. I know you dislike her but she needs you now.'

'I can't come home. Not yet.' She's slumping down on the table in front of her, her elbows plonked on the surface and her head resting in her cupped hands.

'Why not.'

'If I decide to take your advice and say nothing I might never want to come home. Never dare to.'

'Why don't you just come back and help Lorrie out. Do what you have to. Then decide. And disappear if you like.'

'Would never work. For all I know Lorrie's somehow got to find out. Maybe something in Jake's papers. She might be waiting to tip the police off the moment she set eyes on me.

She'd love that. Love to see me behind bars.'

'Don't be stupid. Come on. Come now.' I push the still half-full glass away and get up from the table.

She makes no move from her chair. 'Matt, you've only just got here. You can't just get up and go.'

'Just watch me.'

She bursts into tears again. 'Matt, please. Not yet. I need time to think. Give me a chance.'

'There's nothing to think about. Come on.' I'm no longer the lawyer but the parent threatening his stroppy daughter with being left alone on the beach when she refuses to pack away her bucket and spade. Maybe there's no way of getting home tonight. Maybe I'd be better off staying the night with her, then trying to get her to come home with her in the morning. But I need her to see the urgency and to test her resolve. The morning may bring fresh reasons to procrastinate.

She shakes her head. 'Stay. Please.'

I walk off towards the door. I'm convinced she's going to be following me but as I turn round at the door I see she isn't. I walk out down the street. I look back expecting to see her coming after me but she doesn't. I think about going back. But if I do go back, then she'll have won – well, won this battle anyway. And having lost one battle I know I'll be in danger of losing the war.

In less than ten minutes I'm in a taxi bound for the airport. Alone.

20

I might have guessed there'd be no more flights back to England tonight. The next flight to Gatwick which isn't fully booked doesn't leave for another thirty-six hours, but there's an empty seat on a flight at 9.30 in the morning to…Luton. I can't face getting to know Prague's airport as well as I've got to know Stansted, so Luton it is. Having made the booking I stay the night at the airport, and thank goodness the flight departs on time and I'm home by two o'clock on the Tuesday afternoon.

I've already rung Lorrie and given her a summary of my late-night rendezvous and its outcome. 'How unsurprising,' is all she says. I go round to her late afternoon and spend a couple of hours with her. Together we make a start on sorting out Jake's possessions, and between us we liaise with the undertakers, and arrange to see the solicitors who hold his will. Lorrie has a copy, and it names her, Fiona and Maggie as executors. It's confirmed Maggie remains incarcerated indefinitely, and we have to assume Fiona is out of the picture possibly for the duration. Of course I've tried calling her again and normal service, or should that be normal non-service, has been resumed. And Jake's only other surviving relative, his dad, doesn't know what day it is. It's ages since I last touched any probate law and I've not the first idea how one's supposed to manage the affairs of a dead person when their only surviving relatives, and two out of the three executors, aren't coming to the party. The solicitors say they can meet us at ten on Friday morning to try and sort things out. We then make some provisional arrangements for the funeral: we agree there should be a church service and then a private cremation. Already I'm getting calls from some of the national as well as local press wanting to know what the funeral details are. I don't begrudge a second of the time I'm spending on all of this, but each second seems to bring a new layer of anger that Fiona has just walked away from it.

Meanwhile, my draft contract of employment with Dashwoods has arrived and I've a confirmed start date of 30th

September. I've a month to pack Brighton away and to unpack a new city, and a new sort of life. I should feel excited. But just now I feel as if I'm on a windswept railway junction in the middle of nowhere on a November afternoon, where the view behind is submerged in smog and the prospect ahead stinks of nothingness.

I decide that I need a run to lift my spirits. As I'm scrambling into my running vest my phone goes, and it's Karen. We've not spoken since Sunday evening. She says she needs to see me as soon as possible. Given that there's so much to do I'm not sure I want to but I'm still conscious I owe her more than I could possibly repay. She suggests we meet on Thursday at the café in the village where Jake did his recital; she's got work in Portsmouth that day so it's actually a good halfway point for us both. We agree we'll meet at one o'clock.

I'm with Lorrie pretty much all day Wednesday, and by the end of the day, to almost quote from *Oklahoma!*, we've gone about as far as we can go. So I treat myself to another run on Thursday morning then get the train over for my date with Karen. Soon after one o'clock we're sitting in exactly the same seats in which we sat exactly a week ago, with tuna mayo doorstep sandwiches and Americanos in front of us.

She clearly likes her all-in-one's; she sports a denim one today, combining it with white trainers. As we eat we do the bland easy stuff. She tells me how much the recital has raised so far, and how much more money's still to come. In just the few days since the recital was completed there's been a huge upsurge in numbers of visitors to the church; a lot of people have just wanted to stand on the spot where Jake sat, as though, like the statue on Charles Bridge in Prague, it will bring them luck. Conspicuous notices at strategic points round the church have encouraged these visitors to give generously in Jake's memory, and in fact they've been more than generous. By anyone's reckoning the total sums raised so far have been astonishing. Karen's been in conversation with not only Richard and Anne but the clergy and churchwardens, and there's every chance of a special church window painted by a reputable local artist, funded partially by visitors' donations and partially by the church itself, in memory of Jake and what he has done. The church are hoping that that itself will serve as a tourist attraction generating money for them as well as the charities. Everyone's a winner – or will be.

That's the feel-good bit. We finish our doorsteps, wipe the traces of tomato sauce from around our mouths and drain the last of our coffees, and at Karen's suggestion we walk back down to the church. It's a warm sunny afternoon, but the warmth is tempered by a cool breeze. One can tell the countryside is gearing up for autumn. Blackberries have congregated in the hedgerows, leaves are starting to fade and flutter from the trees, and the tree by the lychgate groans with horse chestnuts. I think back on the crowds of people and the cars and the TV and radio units that were here less than a week ago, and tell myself that civilisation has returned and sanity has been restored. The silence becomes audible again. It's as it should be; it's as God intended.

We go into the church which is empty and yes, I can't resist standing on That spot. I somehow knew it'd be too much to expect a ray of sun to beam down on it as I stood there. But that doesn't stop me knowing that Jake will, in a sense, always occupy the spot. He was at peace when he died and I know that he is safe where he is now, and he's contented, and he's going to be fine. I feel his presence and his peace and his love and as I stand there I'm praying that I always will.

Karen's sat herself down in the front pew and I come and join her. We embrace and kiss. It's not the first time we've done that today and I'm sure it won't be the last. Then we stay seated and listen to more of the silence.

'Your dad's suggested he and I make a new start,' she says. 'He wants to sell the house. Downsize and in the meantime go off travelling. Like we were going to do.'

'I thought he loved your house.'

'He does. But he says he'll do whatever it takes. Whatever's going to make me happy. ' She runs her hand up and down her denim-covered thigh. 'He came all the way down to see me on Monday. We had lunch. He seemed different. More determined, if you like. None of that "I quite get it if you think I'm past it" stuff I've heard before.'

'I thought he'd given up on you.'

'So did I,' she says. 'But he's been talking to Bev.'

'The village pub Bev?'

She nods. 'He confided in her a bit when he and I were dating. He wondered if the age gap was too much and she told him to go for it. I know he talked to her a lot when George died and I was in denial. He's not said so, but I think he spoke to her at the weekend and she told him to fight for me. Told him not to give me up so easily. I can just hear her. Asking him if he wanted to die a sad lonely old man. And then I can imagine him. Telling himself of course she's right. The new confident Alan Chalmers. So. Yes. He's not given up after all. He now thinks we've a future.'

'And what did you say to him?'

'I was a bit lost for words,' she says. 'I couldn't just reject him there and then. I'm not that cruel. I told him I needed to think about it, and I'd talk to him again later in the week.'

'So what are you going to do?'

Now she places her arm round me and holds me against her. 'It's you I want, Matt. I'm not just a hundred per cent certain. I'm a thousand per cent certain.'

'Karen, this isn't the *X Factor*,' I remind her. 'You realise what's at stake here. It's dad's life, dad's happiness, you're playing with.'

'I know,' she says. 'But see it from my position. The last thing he'd want was for me to go back to him just to keep him happy. He'd only want me back if he knew I was happy as well. And I know I wouldn't be. There's only one person I want in my life. I want you, Matt. Not just a friend. Not just a stepson. Someone to love. All the time I'm with Alan, I can't be certain I can keep up my progress in getting over George. I'm worried I may slip back and I don't think I could bear that. It's not like that with you. It'll be a new beginning. Great new start for me. For us.'

'I don't know, Karen.'

'You do know, Matt.' She plants a kiss on my lips. 'If you were in any doubt you'd be out of this church by now. You'd be scurrying back down the path for the next train back to Brighton. I know you think you'd be betraying your dad. I don't see it like that. I don't think he sees it like that. I know he's making an effort now. But I know he'd never want me back just to please him. I know if I said no to him he'd be a good loser. I know he'd still love you whatever.'

'I'm sure he would.' I picture him now as a guest at our wedding. I see him standing there in his morning coat, throwing confetti with the confidence and accuracy of Freddie Flintoff. I see him sidling up to me just after we'd cut the cake to ask if I fancied England's chances in the second one-day international against Pakistan. I see him handing me an envelope with a cheque for us to treat ourselves to something nice on the honeymoon. And as we set off in the car, tin cans clanking on the road below, I see him looking on, calm, dignified and proud, never for one moment prepared to admit that his heart had been as much as bruised, let alone mutilated, by what his only surviving son and his ex-wife had done to him.

The vision fades and more practical considerations take hold.

'Look,' I say. 'Let's imagine it happened. Let's say dad's fine with it. But in the next month I'll be going. Moving away. Adjusting to a new place. I don't know Manchester, I've nowhere to live, I've no idea how the job will work out, whether I'll be happy there….'

'You will,' she says. 'It's a great place. I love it. And I want to be there with you. We could have a great future. An amazing future.'

'You make it sound so easy,' I say. 'What about you. You'd need to find work as well. No guarantee of that.'

'I've got contacts. I'll make a few calls this afternoon. I'll find out about places to live as well. Give me a call tonight, I'll tell you how I get on. Won't be a problem.'

'You say that but you can't be sure. I'd hate things to go wrong.'

'Why should they go wrong.' Her voice now barely a whisper. 'We'll be together and we'll work through whatever does go wrong and we'll come out stronger.' She kisses me again. 'We could be great, Matt. We will be great.'

*

I'm not back in Brighton till nearly six in the end. I'm just about to step inside Di's house when my phone goes. It's Fiona.

'I thought about what you said,' she says. 'You're right.'

'What do you mean?'

'You were right I should be back in England. Sorting things out. But I need to see you. Again.'

If she thinks I'm going to be on the next plane to Prague, whether it's out of Stansted Airport, Luton Airport or George Best Airport, Belfast, she can rethink, and rethink fast. 'Give me a call when you get home and we'll fix something up,' I tell her.

'I am home,' she says. 'Can you come round in an hour?'

*

It can't be more than five minutes' walk from Falmer Station. I think back to the Sunday evening in January and how anxious she was to avoid our making that short, simple journey. It's a modern semi, with nothing on the outside to distinguish it from the other hundred or so semis on the same street. I never thought she and Jake would have owned a luxury mansion and I'm not expecting luxury inside. I am sort of expecting the same smell, that smell of beeswax mingled with stale sweat, that I experienced each time I came into Jake's presence. And although I've no idea what time Fiona got back I'm expecting to find her face suffused with travel-weariness and her choice of clothes reflecting that weariness.

I ring the bell and a moment later Fiona opens the door. There's no sign of fatigue on her face and she seems in dress-up rather than dress-down mode. I realise she's wearing exactly what she wore when I first saw her in the café last November and knew I wanted to love her. She takes me in her arms. She wants to kiss me on the lips but I turn my cheek to stop her. It's the first awkward grope at the teenage party. She ushers me into her front room. As I enter the front room I detect no smell of beeswax or stale sweat but rather an aroma of sandalwood. There's a settee and two armchairs round a low-level coffee table and on the table is a lighted candle and two glasses and a bottle of Beaujolais. She's the one who sits first and she sits on

369

the settee. She indicates the vacant part of the settee next to her. I opt for one of the armchairs, placed at right-angles to the settee. She pours wine into both glasses and having done so she raises her glass.

'Cheers,' she says. 'To a lovely evening.' And she takes a mouthful.

'Sorry?'

'I've lined up a little surprise for us.'

'Mmm?'

'I've booked us a table at Stimpsons-by-the-Sea. My treat.'

'You've what?'

'I know it may seem indecent. Jake still warm in his grave. But it's what he'd want. Life goes on.'

I've passed Stimpsons umpteen times during my time in the city. It stands on the coast road near the junction with East Street and close to the pier and I've often thought I'd love to go there...if I secured a significant Lottery win. Now I come to think of it I remember telling Fiona as much at our meal in the Horse Guards back in January. It has enough Michelin stars to fill a galaxy and is particularly recommended for its seafood dishes and the million and one things the chef can do with a piece of salmon. Everything about it screams luxury and elegance and extravagance.

But she might as well be offering me a bacon sarnie at the Fatty Spoon on Whitehawk Road.

I sit and say nothing.

'I want to thank you, Matt. Properly. For all you've done for Jake. And for Lorrie, of course. For coming all the way out to Prague. Giving me that advice. And...and...' She wipes a tear from her cheek. 'I want to say I still love you.'

'You've just said it all, haven't you. You don't need to spend three weeks' salary to say it any more clearly.'

'I do.' She takes another sip. 'I want to say sorry as well. I know I've messed up. Messed up everyone. Lorrie. Jake. You. Who else.'

She looks up at me and then at the vacant seat next to her. It would be easy, so easy to move to that seat and put my arms round her and let her weep into them until the tears threatened to flood the entire neighbourhood.

But I stay put.

'I've rung Lorrie,' she says. She gulps down another mouthful. 'I'm seeing her tomorrow. Going through all the arrangements. Sorting out Jake's belongings. Seeing his wishes are respected. Organising the funeral. All of that.'

'Right.'

'Then I'm being interviewed under caution by DC Richards at the police station on Saturday.'

'Okay.'

'I'm going to tell him everything. Clean breast. I really hope you can be there with me, but don't worry if you can't. I'll manage. Somehow I'll manage. If I get put away for it, I can bear it. It'll be hard, course it will, but I can't live with knowing I may have done something terribly wrong and not pay back.'

'Okay.'

'Just okay?'

I see the glistening in her eyes and I know the next cascade can't be far off.

'What else do you want me to say.'

'Things. Nice things. Kind things. Positive things.'

'I had them waiting for you once.' I still haven't touched my drink. 'Waiting for when you'd pick up the phone. Waiting for when we next met and did stuff together. My battery was charged ready for all the nice and kind and positive things I was going to say. But the battery's run down. And I've lost the charger.'

'I get it. I do get it, Matt.' She sits forward in her chair and stretches out her boots towards me. It's Lisa-Marie in the Half Moon all over again.

But this time there's no need to apply the brakes because I can't even start the engine.

I sit back in my chair and manoeuvre it backwards with my backside. 'You're not getting it, though,' I say. 'Are you. Really.'

The smile fades. 'What do you mean?'

'You really think you can make up for what you did to me so quickly, so easily.'

'Not easily, Matt.'

'I don't think you've any idea what you did to me when you

371

walked out of my house in January,' I say. 'Treated me as though I never existed. It destroyed me. I was losing my house, I was about to lose my job, and I so wanted you to pick up just once so I could share stuff with you and feel loved and needed. But no. Not once. Do you know, I thought we were soulmates. I did think we'd been drawn together. I was that much in love with you. I was crazy about you, crazy for you, and you knew that. I don't judge you for what you did to Jake. Maybe I'd have done the same. I don't know. But I do judge you for what you did to me. You dumped me out of your life, and now here you are thinking you can get me back into it with a bit of make-up and some sexy clothing and a fish dinner.'

'Matt, that's not fair.' She gets up from the settee and comes and kneels on the ground in front of me. 'I've told you why I blocked you. I hated doing it but it seemed like the only thing I could do. This really isn't easy. Isn't easy at all. I've lost my husband and I'm having to face all the stuff around that, horrible stuff, and face it with someone who's been horrible, really horrible to me. I know you think Lorrie's God's gift but I've had her call me everything under the sun, effing and blinding at me, constantly accusing me. I know you think how non-judgmental she is but, I tell you, she's judged me. Judged me, sentenced me, condemned me to rot in hell forever. And now all I am in her eyes is "the woman." I don't even get the luxury of a name. And because I love you and want your love back, I'm prepared to face it and I'm going to face it tomorrow. Do you think that's easy?' There's not a trace of aggression in the question. It's desperation: desperation for the answer she desires.

But I say nothing.

'And then after her, I've got the law. I've got a hard-faced CID man, total stranger, unpicking the whole of my marriage, unpicking the hell of seeing the man I loved disintegrate in front of my eyes, a man who gave me so much, had so much to give his fellow men, turn into an object of pity. Just another job to the police. To me, reliving stuff I'd never want my worst enemy to go through. Half the time running round after him, just being rewarded by getting screamed and yelled at and, yes, having plates, saucepans, you name it, chucked at me. Do you think I want to talk about it? But because I love you and want your love back and when all this is over I want us to start again without stuff in the way, I'm prepared to do it and to risk the consequences. Do you think that's easy?'

But I say nothing.

'Matt, please. Say something.'

'All right.' I push the chair back further and rise to my feet. 'Listen. Thanks for telling me what you're doing. I'm pleased. Of course I am. I know Lorrie will be. And if you can both start behaving towards each other like grown adults, great. You want to speak to the police, unburden yourself, fine. As long as you know what you're doing. You know you don't have to but I respect you for doing it. And of course I'll be with you at the police station. But this isn't a passport back into a relationship with me. Doesn't change a thing. You hurt me once. You've hurt others. And I'm not letting you hurt me again. Ever.'

'I love you, Matt.' She rises to her feet. 'I love you so much.' Now she's got her arms round me and she's sobbing and pressing her head against and around my neck and I feel the heat and the wetness and the salt of the tears on my face and my lips.

'I need to go.' I tear her arms away and head for the door.

'Where are you going? Where are you going?' Her voice is suddenly shrill, hysterical, and crazed.

I daren't look back.

'I'll call you. All right.' I walk through to the hallway and fling open the front door. Seconds later I'm striding down Boothby Road. A phone call later and I'm on my way to Lorrie's.

*

Lorrie pours me a cup of tea but there's no cake in sight. I don't want cake anyway. I want comfort and I want reassurance. And, after I've told her what's just happened, Lorrie doesn't disappoint.

'Just like I said. It's what she does best,' she says. 'She's a clever girl. She knows what she's doing.'

'So you don't think I was too hard on her.'

'My dear, I suspect she'd have been disappointed if you'd been anything else. She loves putting in a shift as the Wronged Woman.'

'Guess she has had a lot to put up with.'

'I think the expression's "Don't get me started,"' she says. 'She's been very fortunate in many ways. Very good-looking. Comfortable upbringing, good education, walked into a great job. And then another great job. She's had it easier than most despite what's happened. She's never been short of admirers. You disappear from the picture, plenty of guys she can call on to take your place. Guys who'll lap it all up just like you did. Get hurt just like you were. You've come out the other side. Just be glad of that.'

'Lorrie,' I say. 'You will…will accept her help, won't you. Sorting out Jake's estate, I mean. You will work with her. Won't make it harder for her than it needs to be.'

She smiles. 'I'm bitching, aren't I,' she says. 'Stop it, Lorrie.' She gives her wrist a light slap. 'Sorry, Matt. I don't like doing it. I shouldn't do it. Life's too short. There, you see. I'm a human being. I don't always get it right.' She gets up from her chair and makes her way to a table in the corner of the room. It's covered in bits of paper. She produces an envelope. 'This came for you in the post today. I was going to pop it round to Di's later. Just haven't had time.'

She hands it to me. Whatever it is, it's addressed to me, care of Lorrie. It's not handwriting I recognise. The postmark gives no clue either. As it's care of Lorrie I'm inferring it's someone who knows us both. So I decide to open it straightaway.

Dear Matt,

I'm writing to ask your forgiveness. At the time I was in an awful place and I took Jake away because it seemed best for him and I was prepared to literally do anything to protect him. I'll have nightmares till my dying day about what I nearly did to you. I'm locked up where I deserve to be and will probably stay locked up for years. After which I guess dad will be dead so I'll be making a fresh start. Probably abroad. You were right all along. Jake died happy because he'd fulfilled his life ambition and if I'd taken that away from him he would have hated it and

374

hated me. At the time I was still angry with Lorrie about Jake and the knife on Christmas Day and I wasn't thinking straight about what was best for my brother. I was selfish. I know how tough these last few months were for Lorrie and Fiona and I'm sure you saw that too. I know some might say Fiona could have done more. But I don't think she could. She stood by him and never strayed. Well done again and take care of yourself. Yours Maggie

I read it to Lorrie. And as I read it, I see the colour draining from her cheeks. Her face seems to turn to stone.

'What's the matter?' I ask. 'It's a really nice letter. I'll probably think I've dreamt it, I'll wake up in a minute, but still…'

'It's the Christmas Day thing,' she says. 'She promised we'd never speak of it again. That neither of us would ever refer to it again.'

'It's all right,' I say. 'Forget it. Whatever it was.' I put the letter back in the envelope and stand up ready to leave.

'No. You need to know,' she says. 'Otherwise you'll be wondering. I owe it to you to tell you.'

I sit down again. 'Tell me what?'

'Christmas Day last year,' she says.

I remember Jake's words. His reference to "this last Christmas" when he realised he couldn't learn the Bible on his own any more and was having to give up. It makes sense now. It makes good, perfect, horrible, ghastly, putrid sense.

'Maggie had come down to see us,' she says. 'We had a nice afternoon, well, as nice as could be expected, then Jake said he felt tired and I wheeled him back to his room. After a bit he yelled for me and said could I bring him some Christmas cake and a mug of tea. I didn't know what size slice he wanted, he'd get funny about things like that, so I brought the whole cake in to him, intending to cut him a slice in front of him. I was just about to cut it then realised I'd forgotten his tea. I went back and fetched it and then to my horror realised I'd left the knife, my sharpest kitchen knife, on the cake plate with him in his room. I rushed back and there he was, with the knife in his hand, poised to slash his wrists. I screamed to Maggie and somehow the two of us managed to pull the knife from him and he's now in floods of tears, saying he'd wanted to kill himself and he was mad with us for stopping him.' I notice that she's shaking. 'It was the worst day of my life. All my stupid fault.'

'Wasn't Fiona with you?'

'She'd gone. She'd spent the morning with him then she'd gone.'

'She never told me about this.'

'That's because she never knew,' says Lorrie. 'Still doesn't.'

I let the letter drop to the ground. 'You never told his wife?'

'I know I should have, Matt,' she says. There's a look of intense vulnerability on her face that I've never seen before. 'But I knew that if I did she'd find some way of using it against me. Every time I said she wasn't doing enough, she'd have been able to remind me that I nearly allowed him to die. Perhaps I just hoped it would go away, that we could pretend it never happened.'

'And Maggie never told her either?'

Lorrie shakes her head. 'I begged her not to. Not that I think she would have done anyway. Fiona might have found a way of pinning some of the blame on her as she was in the house at the time. She wouldn't want to risk Fiona scoring points off her, believe me. After that I was so careful. Anything I gave him, I was wondering could he use it to kill himself. If he was in a particularly stormy mood, I might sit with him while he had his coffee. In case he smashed his mug and used the broken bits...' She sighs. 'It was horrible, Matt. Nightmare.'

We stay in silence for a minute or two. Lorrie looks as though she might be about to cry again. I don't want to see her cry again. Suddenly I feel tired.

'I'd better go,' I say. 'Promised Karen I'd call her.' I get up and head for the door.

Lorrie rises to her feet. 'Before you go,' she says, 'yet more fan mail for you. Found in Jake's room today.' She disappears for a moment and returns with an envelope. It's got my name on it and it's marked Private. 'Read it when you get home,' she says. 'I'm obviously not supposed to know what he's written. See you tomorrow. I'll be round to pick you up at half nine.'

I walk back to Di's and open the envelope.

EPILOGUE

The woman in the light green fleece top seems to sense my weak knees. 'Are you all right?' she asks.

For a few moments I can't reply. I'm wondering if I should tell her that it was a light green fleece top, hung on a display rack in Brighton's Mountain Warehouse one October Monday afternoon, that changed my life. It was that light green fleece top that meant, via Lisa-Marie Williams and her friend Jazz and a Good Samaritan named Lorrie McEwan, that I met and coached Memory Guy.

Of course, if I did now tell Green Fleece Woman, she might react with a smile of recognition of his amazing feat, and offer a word of congratulation for me and a word of sympathy for his no longer being with us. But it's equally possible that, perhaps oblivious to the media coverage of the scale of Jake's achievement, Green Fleece Woman would favour me with a blank stare, then turn away, continue her walk and reflect that it takes all sorts. I don't want that. Indeed I don't want anything or anyone to mar the beauty and solemnity of this walk and what I'm planning to do at journey's end.

So I play it safe.

'I'm fine,' I tell her. 'It's gorgeous up here, isn't it.' It does its job: an uncontroversial, irrefutable statement that evidently satisfies her that I'm not a risk either to her or to myself. She nods and smiles and tells me to enjoy the rest of my walk, and on she goes in the opposite direction.

Jake had always said he wanted to be scattered on Firle Beacon. It was there in his will and he'd told Lorrie so a number of times. She said he used to go up there a lot when he had his mobility, and on a few occasions in the past few years she'd actually taken him there, driving to the Firle Bostal car park and then wheeling him all the way from there to the summit. She said it was always a handy way for her to shed a few excess pounds. I'd asked her if she wanted to accompany me today but she told me her back was playing up. She'd never complained of a bad back before. I've a suspicion she'd just get too upset and doesn't want me to see it. I think she misses Jake more than she'd ever admit. On the surface she's always philosophical. He's in a better place now, she'll say: one less mouth to feed, more time for her to complete the Giant Su Doku without the risk of her eardrums being shattered for the tenth time that morning. But it all sounds a bit too forced and a bit too unnatural. She loved him so much.

I never expected the urn to be so bulky and to weigh such a lot. My biggest fear is that somehow the top will get detached from the rest of it and I'll end up with fragments of Jake all over the inside of my backpack. Then again I suppose it's theoretically possible that one of the bits of Jake that did end up amongst the miscellaneous sweet wrappers and supermarket receipts was the bit of his brain that caused him to become Memory Guy and that made a human a superhuman. In which case having identified the fragment in question I'd keep it locked up in a glass case and never let it go.

I want it to be just the two of us at the summit. Of course there's nothing that can be done if there are others lurking, but it's not the sunniest or warmest afternoon and somehow I think I may be in luck. As I approach the summit I see nobody except the one I was expecting and wanting to see. She stands there with an embarrassed smile, the stiff breeze playing with her bright red cagoule and twisting and weaving the locks of her hair, the exertions of the climb evident in the droplets of damp on her reddish-brown cheeks.

'I was sure you'd said to meet up here,' she says.

'Doesn't matter, sweetheart. It's fine.' I put my arms round her and place a kiss on her lips, then another, then another, and I tell her I love her and she tells me she loves me as well. For a few moments we stand in silent embrace. And I kiss her once more.

I remove myself from her arms, slip the backpack off my shoulder and lower it to the ground. It hits the floor with a clunk. I unzip the backpack and remove the urn and sigh with relief that the top hasn't detached itself from the rest. Then we take up our positions, the wind blowing into our backs, and look out across the acres of unspoilt Sussex countryside.

We say together: 'Jake, the Memory Guy, may you always

find peace here.'

The next moment his ashes are flying into the air and we watch as the wind plays with them and teases them and toys with them before allowing them to come to rest in the lush downland grass. After they've all reached the ground we continue to stand together in silence.

And I find myself reaching in my pocket and unfolding the letter from Jake that Lorrie found and gave to me and for what seems like the hundredth time since I've received it we look at it together.

'Thanks Jake,' I say.

'Thanks Jake,' says Fiona.

*

It's getting on for two years since Jake passed away and we're in the church where his recital – well, all of it save the final six and a half chapters – took place. And today, the memorial window's being unveiled. Thanks to the generosity of the many people who attended the recital or who've since come to see where it all happened and where it all unravelled, there's been more than enough money, on top of that set aside for the chosen charities, to enable the parish to commission one of the country's foremost artists to do the work. Because of his existing schedule of commissions it took a while for him to get to our project but it is well worth every second of the wait. I've already had a sneak preview: he's managed to incorporate into the mix an astonishing likeness of Jake, together with a representation of both the little church we're sitting in, and the Bible – which naturally enough is depicted as a closed book. It's a pageant of a hundred different shades of colour and there's exuberance and celebration in each stroke of the paintbrush.

The church is full and indeed I'm told it's not been this full since Jake's funeral.

I'm sitting in the same place that I sat while Jake was in full flow, and next to me is Mrs Fiona Chalmers.

I knew Lorrie had her doubts. I suspect she still does. Di is quite certain that Jake is watching over us and loving the fact that he, Memory Guy, has brought Fiona and me together in the way he has. The story, she says, albeit half-jokingly, will be complete when we produce a child and bring him back to this church and christen him Guy. And Fiona and I cherish the thought that it might happen. But I suspect Lorrie sees Di's narrative as a bit like that of the Christmas Nativity story. In other words, it's something you want to believe and something that it's good to believe but which the cynic will always seek to pick holes in.

If Lorrie's said it to me once she's said it fifty times: don't want to see you getting hurt, Matt, would hate you to be hurt. But more than once I've shown her Jake's letter. The one that said MATT LOOK AFTER FIONA, SHE'S LOVELY, SHE'LL BE JUST RIGHT FOR YOU WHATEVER LORRIE SAYS. I've also reminded her of Maggie's letter and the bit which said Fiona couldn't have done any more for him. I think Lorrie still struggles with that: the thought that after all she did for Jake, it was Fiona getting the kudos. But it has made her more accepting, or should I say less non-accepting, of our togetherness and our relationship. I know Fiona regrets so much what she did to me and I've lost count of the number of times she's said sorry. In fact it's got to the stage where I think she's getting too hard on herself and I find I'm the one reminding her that I can have no real idea of the pain she went through when Jake's illness took hold and how tough it must have been to stay faithful to him as she did. She misses him and I like that she misses him. I'd hate her to think, thank heaven he's gone, that awful burden's been lifted from her neck. It's not easy, though. None of it's easy.

It certainly helped when after extensive interviews and investigation the police decided to take no further action in relation to what Fiona did to Jake. Crucial to that outcome was the document Jake had signed for her indicating he was wanting to take his own life. Equally important was Lorrie's statement of what happened that Christmas afternoon, corroborated by the letter from Maggie who was under no pressure to write it and had nothing to gain by what she wrote. Of course to get Lorrie to make a statement we had to tell her why we needed it, namely that Fiona had tried to help Jake to die. But I guessed, correctly, that Lorrie wouldn't judge Fiona too harshly for doing so, not only because of what she, Lorrie, had so nearly allowed to happen but also because Jake had put Fiona under almost intolerable pressure to assist his suicide. In fact I think the whole business may have brought them closer. The fact that they'd worked together to sort out Jake's affairs, and had done so without it ending in World War 3, was an important first step, and Lorrie's concession that she'd been less than gracious to Fiona during Jake's final years was also significant in rebuilding some cordiality between the pair of them. Although they'll never be bosom buddies, they do at least talk to each other now.

We've grown to love Manchester. Of course there's much that we miss about Brighton. We miss the sea air, the Lanes, and the rich smooth green of the Downs. But I love my work, we love the vibrancy of Manchester city life, we love the fact that the Peak District is on our doorstep, and it's great that dad, who's still in the same house, isn't all that far away.

He's sitting just behind me today and next to him is the love of his life. They've not long come back from a European adventure, an adventure I suspect involving rather fewer nights spent in the camper van, and rather more nights in hotels, than he might care to admit. I'm thrilled it's worked out for him after everything he went through. He's like a man reborn. I'm not blessed with the greatest intuition but I can see how much happier he looks even though he'd never admit to being anything less than happy during his period of singleness. As for her, she's in deep red: red dress, red hat, red heels. One might almost call it elegant except she'd hate to be called elegant because it implies mature, not sexy, not sassy. I love that dad, even in his mid-seventies, has something about him that evidently appeals to the sexy and the sassy. First it was Karen. And now it's Joanna. I've never seen him look so relaxed and content as he did at her sixtieth birthday bash last week.

I was dreading having to tell Karen about Fiona and me, and I resolved to let her down over chicken supreme at the Roebuck in Hove. But she was the one who got in first and we hadn't even bought the first round of drinks. She told me she realised at the bottom of her heart that we were never destined to be any more than mates. Not long afterwards she got the offer of a job in the States, met a guy there, and is now settled in Florida with him and his two daughters. We still Skype each other lots and she's assured us she's with us today in spirit.

Also with us in spirit only is Di. She's been in hospital and hasn't felt up to joining us today. She tells me that before she went into hospital she was suffering with pain that was bordering on the unbearable at times and she still has bad days. We often speak on the phone and I ask her if she ever gets angry with God for putting her through all this. "He's not putting me through all this," she will say. "He's helping me through all this." To not quite quote from the world of Meg Ryan, I'd love to have what she's having. Her faith, I mean. I do believe that there was something God-made about Jake's ability and achievement which in faith terms perhaps qualifies me for a provisional licence and L-plates. But I still feel a million miles from passing my test; meanwhile Di, a member of the advanced school of faith motorists, continues to glide along in the fast lane, her foot hardly touching the accelerator.

As for Maggie, she was eventually charged with kidnap and attempt murder. There was a suggestion that through her lawyers she was going to argue that she was mentally unfit to plead, but in the end she did in fact plead guilty. She was ordered to remain in a secure hospital and I've no idea when she'll get out; presumably it'll be when she satisfies a tribunal that she's cured. I ought to hate her for what she did to me. But it may just be that her letter is what has allowed Fiona and me to be together in this church rather than together through my weekly visit to her as a guest of Her Majesty.

Lorrie's got a new man. Not that kind of man; I think Colin's antics put a stop to all that. Once the novelty of having a bit more time for her Su Doku-ing and her word searching had worn off she decided she was lonely and wanted someone else to care for. His name's Edward, or Ed as she calls him. I'd asked her if he'd got any special gifts or skills that might be put to good use with my help. I'd expected her to laugh and say no thank you. But she'd put on a serious face and asked how I felt about helping him to build scale models of every capital city across the globe. He's done one and a quarter so there are only 193 and three quarters to go. Only after watching me go snow-white – well, that's how she described the look on my face – did she tell me she was joking.

And yet. And yet. Maybe, as we sit in church on this Sunday morning, the tranquillity of this precious place of worship disturbed only by the gentle hiss of the morning breeze through the branches of the chestnut tree just outside the south wall, there is, somewhere out there, a man or woman like I was. A man or woman who is destined to tap the potential in this Edward, whatever that potential might be, to change lives as Jake did, and shape futures as Jake did, and enrich the world around him more than anyone could believe possible – as Jake did.

The official unveiling of the window comes after Toby Bryant's sermon. We rise to our feet and Toby says a short prayer then turns to the window and pulls a curtain revealing the artistry in all its colourful splendour. Then we all say the words chosen by Fiona, Lorrie and me. We'd tried to find a Bible verse but there was nothing which quite fitted, so we'd decided on something simple but also something that was succinct – and, most important of all, something that was Jake.

'In loving memory of the man who never forgot – Jake Guy Terson, The Memory Guy. May you rest in peace and rise in glory.'

THE END

383

Printed in Great Britain
by Amazon